SPIDER'S WEB

BEN CHEETHAM is an award-winning writer and Pushcart Prize nominee. His writing spans the genres, from horror and sci-fi to literary fiction, but he has a passion for dark, gritty crime fiction. His short stories have been widely published in magazines in the UK, US and Australia.

If you want to learn more about him, or get in touch, you can look him up at: www.bencheetham.com

BEN CHEETHAM

SPIDER'S WEB

HEAD of ZEUS

First published in the UK in 2015 by Head of Zeus Ltd

9 7 5 3 1 2 4 6 8

A catalogue record for this book is available from the British Library.

ISBN (HB): 9781784970444
ISBN (XTPB): 9781784972448
ISBN (E): 9781784970437

Typeset by Ben Cracknell Studios, Norwich

Printed and bound in Germany by GGP
Media GmbH, Pössneck

Head of Zeus Ltd
Clerkenwell House
45-47 Clerkenwell Green
London EC1R 0HT

WWW.HEADOFZEUS.COM

To Clare

SPIDER'S WEB

14 FEBRUARY 1993

The whistles and chants swelled to a crescendo as Anna and Jessica entered the living-room. Rick Young was leaning forward on the sofa, hands clasped as if making a silent plea for help, eyes fixed tensely on the television. The stud-chewed turf of a football field filled the screen, punctuated by players wearing the familiar red and white stripes of Sheffield United's home kit and the unfamiliar yellow and green halves of Manchester United's away kit. The camera swung back and forth, chasing the ball with the same breathless urgency as the players. 'Touched on by Giggs,' came the commentator's over-excited voice.

'Just get hold of the bloody ball!' yelled Rick, half rising to his feet as Manchester United drove forwards en masse.

'Dad,' said Anna. 'Can we—'

She broke off as Rick gesticulated angrily at the television. 'Come on, ref. Where's the whistle?'

As if in response, the referee raised his whistle to blow for full time. 'Sheffield United have won a famous victory,' exclaimed the commentator, his voice half drowned out by the cheers that simultaneously tore from twenty-odd thousand throats.

Laughing, Rick flung up his hands and danced a little victory jig, then sprang forward to embrace his daughters and rain kisses on their blonde heads.

'Urgh! You stink of beer,' said Anna, squirming out of his grasp. Her younger sister snuggled in closer, giggling with delight – Jessica had always been a daddy's girl.

'Can we have some money for the cinema, please, Daddy?' Jessica asked in the wheedling voice she used when she wanted something.

'Of course you can, love.' Rick took two tenners out of his wallet and divided them between his daughters.

'Ten quid! Thanks, Dad.'

'Anything for my two favourite girls. Now give me a kiss.'

As the girls leant in to kiss their dad on opposite cheeks, he scooped them off their feet and twirled them around, singing, 'Two–one, two–one.'

'Hey, put me down,' protested Anna, but with laughter in her voice.

Rick released his daughters, his gaze returning to the television. Home supporters were on the pitch, triumphantly mobbing their team. Anna and Jessica exchanged a victorious smile of their own. They'd hung around the house all afternoon, listening to the muffled sounds of the match, waiting for the right moment to pounce. Anna had made her move a fraction early, fearing a last-gasp equaliser would put a damper on their dad's generosity. Jessica's timing had been perfect. She knew how to play Dad like a finely tuned instrument. And he was happy to let her do so.

'See you later, Dad,' the sisters chirped together.

'Take a key with you. I've got to pick your mother up from work in a couple of hours. We might not be in when you get back.' As the girls turned to leave, Rick added as an afterthought,

'Anna, promise me you'll look after your sister. Don't let her wander off anywhere alone. There's going to be some seriously pis—' he checked himself and continued, 'seriously angry Red Devils supporters out there.'

'I can look after myself,' said Jessica, thrusting her bottom lip out petulantly. 'I'm thirteen, not five.'

I promise, Anna mouthed over her sister's shoulder. There was only a couple of years between the girls, but it had always seemed like more. Jessica was small for her age and built like a doll. Straight blonde hair fell halfway down her back, framing big blue eyes, lightly freckled cheeks and lips that constantly seemed to be on the verge of pouting. She was what their mum called a girly girl. She liked nothing more than playing around with makeup and clothes. And she had a tendency to be kind of ditzy. Although Anna knew that was more of an act to get people to do things for her than a reality. Anna had the same colour hair as her sister, but hers was wavy and tomboyishly short. Silver-rimmed glasses, whose thick short-sighted lenses magnified her pale-grey eyes, lent her a serious air beyond her years. Ever since she could remember, she'd been labelled as the level-headed one. She didn't resent the role – it had always come naturally to her to protect her little sister when they were out of their parents' sight.

Pulling on coats and scarves, the girls headed out of the front door. The afternoon was as grey as the pebbledash of their small semi-detached house. Shoulders hunched against a bitter breeze, they descended a steeply sloping street. The sound of cheering carried on the air, like waves pounding a distant cliff. Half a mile or so beyond the foot of the hill, the red and white walls of Bramall Lane stadium loomed over a tangle of terraced streets. About the same distance again further on, a cluster of brutally angular concrete, steel and glass buildings rose like exclamation points marking out the city centre.

They crossed a bridge spanning a railway line and the River Sheaf, and turned right onto Queens Road, which was clogged with car- and bus-loads of supporters heading back to Manchester. At the end of Bramall Lane, police were directing traffic and keeping a close eye on the stream of away team supporters flowing along the pavements.

'They look proper pissed off, don't they?' said Jessica, giggling at the supporters' unhappy faces.

'Shh,' cautioned Anna. 'You'll get us in trouble.'

Jessica laughed carelessly. She'd never got into any trouble that she hadn't been able to wriggle out of with a smile or some tears. As they neared the city centre, the stream thinned to a trickle. The sisters argued about what film they were going to see. Anna knew it was pointless – Jessica always got her own way – but the argument was like a ritual they had to go through every time they went to the cinema. And anyway, as much as she hated to admit it to herself, Anna took a guilty pleasure in watching the Hollywood fluff Jessica loved.

Jessica wrinkled her nose at Anna's suggested film. 'That sounds sooo boring. Who wants to see a film about someone killing people?'

Anna smiled. Jessica had a point. 'OK, you win, we'll—'

She fell silent as a dirty white van slowed alongside them. A chubby-faced man with crew-cut dark-brown hair was peering through its passenger window. Jessica followed her sister's line of sight. 'Who's he?'

'How should I know?' Anna replied, frowning. She didn't like the way the man was looking at her sister. There was a strange intensity in his eyes. 'Don't look at him.'

'I think he fancies you.'

He's not looking at me, thought Anna, as her sister went

on, 'How old do you reckon he is?'

'I dunno. Twenty-five or something like that.'

'Urgh, imagine snogging someone as old as him.'

To Jessica, anyone over nineteen was old. The idea wouldn't have seemed so bad to Anna, if the man hadn't been so ugly. Not that he was particularly bad-looking or anything. Rather, there was a deeper kind of ugliness that shone through his close-set dark eyes. 'Just ignore him and maybe he'll go away.'

Catching the unease in Anna's voice, Jessica said, 'OK, Big Sis.'

The sisters quickened their pace, both staring straight ahead. The van continued to crawl alongside them. Anna walked as tall as she could, her expression calm although her thoughts were sliding towards fear. *What did this guy want? Did he or whoever the driver was think they knew them? Or were they deliberately trying to shit them up?* A car behind the van sounded its horn. To Anna's relief, the van accelerated.

'Yeah go on, sod off, weirdo!' shouted Jessica.

The van's brake lights flared and it screeched to a standstill, forcing the car behind to swerve sharply into the outer lane. The sisters stopped dead too. Ten, then twenty seconds passed. And still the van didn't move. Nothing moved. To Anna, the world seemed to have been placed on pause. Thirty seconds. 'Anna,' began Jessica. Her voice was no longer cocky, it was small and held a slight tremor. Anna slid her arm protectively through her sister's.

The van suddenly accelerated again. This time it didn't stop until it reached the junction at the end of Queens Road. As it turned from view, Jessica's cheeks puffed with relief. 'My heart's beating really fast.'

'Mine too.' Anna lanced a look at her sister. 'One of these days you're really going to get us in trouble.'

Jessica's eyes widened apologetically. 'I didn't think they'd hear me.'

Anna sighed. She could never stay angry with Jessica for long – how could anyone when they looked into those big eyes? A thought came to her. 'Did you see the registration number?'

'No, did you?'

Anna shook her head. 'Come on. We'll miss the beginning of the film.'

During the remainder of the walk Anna kept an eye out for the van. It didn't reappear. By the time they reached the cinema, Jessica was back to her usual giggling, teasing self. Despite – or maybe because of – Anna's protests, she bought enough popcorn, chocolate and sweets to make herself feel sick. Anna struggled to follow the film. Her thoughts kept returning to the man in the van. It gave her a crawling feeling to think of how he'd looked at Jessica as if he was sizing up a piece of meat. When they left the cinema, it was dark outside. Anna hesitated at the entrance, faint lines forming between her eyes as she scanned the quiet Sunday evening city streets. 'I'm going to phone Dad and see if he'll pick us up.'

'Why?' asked Jessica. 'Are you still worried about that stupid van?'

A defensive note came into Anna's voice. 'No. I just don't feel like walking.'

Jessica cocked an eyebrow knowingly. Ignoring her, Anna slotted a coin into a payphone and dialled home. She let the phone ring five, six, seven times. 'No one's answering.'

'Dad said they might not be in, remember. They've probably gone for a drink or something. We could catch the bus.'

Anna briefly considered the suggestion, then nodded. They crossed a road lined by tall unlit office buildings, heading for a bus stop. Anna squinted at a timetable dimly illuminated by a streetlamp. 'The next bus isn't for half an hour.'

'We could walk it in less than that.'

Anna glanced back towards the pyramidal roof of the Odeon cinema, wondering whether they should wait for the bus within the safety of its confines.

'Come on, Anna, let's just walk it,' persisted Jessica, tugging at her sister's sleeve. 'I need to get home. My tummy's hurting.'

'Well you shouldn't have been so greedy,' snapped Anna. Seeing the scolded puppy look in her sister's eyes, she sighed. 'OK. Come on then.'

They started walking, Jessica with her arms hugged across her stomach, Anna peering uneasily into the headlights of passing traffic. The streets were pretty much deserted, except for occasional groups of Sheffield United supporters, crawling from pup to pub, rowdily celebrating their team's victory. Anna's pace quickened as they passed along the lonely lower end of Queens Road. To their right, beyond a stone wall about the same height as them, a thin curtain of bushes and trees lined the near bank of the faintly murmuring River Sheaf. To their left, an identical wall ran alongside the opposite pavement, terminating after some eighty or a hundred metres at the local ice rink – an almost windowless rectangular concrete and brick building.

'Slow down, will you,' complained Jessica. 'My tummy—'

'Hurts. Yeah, I know, you already told me,' cut in Anna, her voice quick with nervousness. They were nearing the place where the van had slammed on its brakes. 'And I told you that you shouldn't have—'

Anna broke off as Jessica suddenly doubled over, retching. Rolling her eyes, Anna rested her hand on Jessica's back while she vomited. Jessica straightened, wiping a hand across her mouth. 'Please don't tell Mum and Dad about this, Anna.'

'Do I ever tell them anything?'

Genuine gratitude and affection gleamed in Jessica's eyes. 'Thanks, Big Sis. You're the b—' Her voice died and her eyes sprang wide at the sight of something over Anna's shoulder.

Her heart giving a quick thump, Anna started to turn. An arm snaked around her midriff from behind, pinning her right wrist and lifting her roughly off her feet. She started to scream, but the sound was muffled by a gloved hand pressing over her mouth. A man ran past Anna. The man from the van! He wasn't much taller than her, but he was far more heavily built. He was wearing a black jacket and matching jeans that, along with his dark hair, gave him the look of a living shadow. He was moving fast, but not fast enough to reach Jessica before she could scream. The quivering high-pitched sound split the night air for a second, before being suddenly silenced by the man's fist slamming into Jessica's chin. Her slender frame crumpled like a broken flower under the blow. The man caught her as she fell back against the wall. He scooped her off her feet and started back the way he'd come.

The sight of her sister's rolling eyes and lolling head sent Anna into a frenzy. As her own assailant whirled her towards the road, she kicked and writhed like a trapped wild animal. 'Bitch,' grunted a distinctly male voice at the repeated impact of Anna's sturdy Doc Martens. He loosened his grip, but only to hammer a fist into her stomach. Her eyes bulging, all her breath rushing from her, she stiffened then sagged forward. The other man was swiftly approaching the van, which was parked with its engine running, its lights off and its back doors wide open. The van's interior was as dark as the inside of a mouth. *Once we're in there, that's it, we're as good as dead.* The thought hit Anna harder than her assailant's fist had, pummelling fresh desperate strength into her. She bit down on the gloved hand. Her assailant yanked it away with a loud 'Ow!'. His hold on her midriff loosened again. She thrust herself away from him and suddenly she was free.

'Help!' she screamed breathlessly, lurching towards Jessica. She made a grab for her sister, but caught hold of the dark-haired man's jacket instead. There was a tearing sound and a bunch of keys fell out of his pocket. 'Hel—' she started to cry out again. Her voice was cut off by a gasping outrush of breath as something slammed between her shoulder blades, snapping her head back. She pitched forward and her chin smashed into the pavement, sending her glasses skittering away. A jarring pain lanced down her spine. White lights burst in front of her eyes. Through them she saw the keys half a metre or so away. They were attached to what looked like a red devil's head keyring. She groggily reached for the keys, thinking that maybe she could use them as a weapon. A gloved hand descended to snatch them up. She groaned as what felt like a knee pressed hard into the small of her back.

The dark-haired man threw Jessica into the back of the van as though she was a sack of coal, before wheeling towards his accomplice. 'Help.' Anna's voice came more weakly now. The street was swimming in and out of focus like a bad television reception. Her unseen assailant hooked his hands under her armpits and started to haul her upright. The dark-haired man hurried to grab her feet.

'Hey! What are you doing to that girl?' The shout came from off to Anna's right. She twisted her head and, through a blur of tears, saw several figures running across the road outside the ice rink. Her would-be abductors instantly released her. The dark-haired man dived into the back of the van and yanked the doors shut. His accomplice, who was wearing a green parka coat with the hood up, jumped into the driver's seat. The van screeched away in the direction of the city centre.

Her head reeling, Anna scrambled to her feet and sprinted after the van. 'Jessica!' she screamed. 'Jessica!' Her gaze dropped to the registration number, but without her glasses she couldn't make it out. The van ran a red light at the end of Queens Road and turned sharply from view. Anna tripped and fell hard. The uprushing pavement split open her palms. She barely noticed the pain. As she struggled to rise, hands took hold of her shoulders, not roughly, but tentatively. She shrugged them off, gasping, 'They've got my sister!'

'My mate's phoning the police,' came the concerned reply.

Without bothering to look at the speaker, Anna started running again. She knew it was hopeless – the van was gone, Jessica was gone – but she couldn't stop herself. She ran until her lungs burnt like acid and her legs gave way beneath her. Then she lay on her back with tears streaming from her eyes and blood from her chin, sobbing over and over to the night sky, 'I promised I'd look after her. I promised I'd look after her...'

CHAPTER ONE

2013

Like a kestrel hovering over its prey, Jim Monahan studied the man on the other side of the interview room's one-way window. He took in the salt-and-pepper hair neatly combed across a bald spot, the brown eyes peering through puffy pouches of skin, the slightly baggy cheeks, the lips set in an impassive line. Thomas Villiers was leaning back in his chair, hands folded together in his lap. He was meticulously dressed in what appeared to be the same solemn navy blue suit and matching tie as on the previous two occasions he'd attended the station. The bastard wore his clothes in the same way he wore his respectability – like a suit of armour. He looked relaxed and confident. But appearances could be deceptive. Those bags under Villiers' eyes were new. He hadn't been sleeping. Or he'd been drinking too much. Or perhaps a bit of both. Whatever the cause, they hinted at an inner tension.

'He looks tired,' noted Reece Geary.

Jim glanced at his colleague. There were dark smudges under Reece's eyes too. His broad angular face had a washed-out look. 'So do you.'

'I'm fine. Come on, let's do it. I've got a good feeling about this one. I reckon he could be our ticket in.'

Jim's gaze returned doubtfully to Thomas Villiers. Maybe he was their ticket in. But not today. Today they had the same on Villiers as they'd had when they first interviewed him almost a year ago – the same being fuck all. This interview wasn't about trying to lever or trick information out of Villiers, its purpose was more simple – it was a reminder, a message that said loud and clear, *We haven't forgotten you, we're not going away, we're going to keep after you for as long as it takes.* Villiers turned with an impatient frown to the pudgy, bespectacled man sitting at his side. Miles Burnham made a calming motion and whispered something to his client. Burnham was one of the most experienced solicitors in the game. He was fully aware of every police tactic in the book. Jim didn't need to hear his words to have a good idea of what he was saying. *Relax, Thomas, they're just making you wait, it's what they do when they've got nothing to come at you with.* The lines faded from Villiers' forehead. He even managed a smile.

'I can't stand that fucking bloke,' said Reece, eyeballing the solicitor.

'Don't ever let him know that,' warned Jim. 'He'll use it against you every chance he gets.' He glanced at his watch. Villiers had been waiting almost an hour. Normally he would have given him a while longer to stew, but with Burnham in there that could do more harm than good.

Jim entered the interview room and seated himself at the opposite side of a table from Villiers and the solicitor. He pointedly opened the file he'd compiled on Villiers, while Reece turned on the recording equipment. Reece inserted three blank tapes into the machine – a working copy for themselves, a master copy, and a copy for Burnham if his client was charged. Jim glanced at his watch again and began in a slow, deliberate voice,

'The time is four fifteen p.m., on Friday the fourteenth of June, 2013. This interview is taking place at South Yorkshire Police Headquarters. Those present are Detective Chief Inspector Jim Monahan, Detective Inspector Reece Geary, Mr Thomas Villiers and his solicitor, Mr Miles Burnham.' Jim looked at Villiers for the first time, keeping his expression studiedly impersonal. 'OK, Mr Villiers, I now need to caution you.' He read him the standard caution and asked if he understood.

'Yes,' replied Villiers, his voice well-spoken with the barest hint of a Lancashire accent.

'I must also inform you, Mr Villiers, that you're not under arrest. Nor are you obliged to remain at the police station. You're entitled to leave at will unless you're placed under arrest.'

Again, Jim asked Villiers if he understood. And again, Villiers replied in the affirmative. Jim settled back in his chair and stared at Villiers a moment, before asking blandly, 'Would you like some kind of refreshment before we begin? Tea? Coffee?'

'No thank you.' Villiers' voice was as flat as Jim's.

'In that case, Mr Villiers, I'd like to start by asking you why you think we asked you to come here today?'

'I assume it's the same reason as on the previous two occasions.'

'Which is?'

'You want to know why my name is in Herbert Winstanley's book.'

'Herbert Winstanley's alleged book,' corrected Burnham.

'Two handwriting experts have matched the writing in the book to Mr Winstanley,' said Jim.

'Handwriting can be faked.'

'Mr Winstanley's fingerprints are all over the book.'

'That still doesn't mean he wrote it. Unless you have a witness who can directly connect Herbert Winstanley to the book, then it cannot be stated with certainty that he was its author. Are we agreed?'

'No we are not agreed, Mr Burnham. But the book is only part of the reason your client is here today. We'd also like to get a fuller understanding of Mr Villiers' relationship to Edward Forester.'

'My client has already explained his relationship with that person to you.'

'I realise that, but it would be a great help to us if he could explain it again. Just in case we missed anything last time.'

'I'm employed by the Craig Thorpe Youth Trust,' said Villiers. 'As you know, the Trust is a charity set up to help disadvantaged children. And as you also know, it's a charity which Edward Forester was deeply involved in. He—'

'Involved how?' broke in Jim.

A slight rise came into Villiers' voice, barely discernible but there. 'If you'll allow me, I'll tell you.'

Jim took a small measure of satisfaction at his response – he'd noted during their previous interviews how much Villiers disliked being interrupted. 'Please do.'

'The Trust recently opened a home for runaway and homeless youths, of which I'm the manager. Edward Forester organised several fundraising events to help finance the home, as well as donating many thousands of pounds of his own money. I—'

'According to our notes,' Jim interjected, casually leafing through Villiers' file, 'you first met Edward Forester in April 2011 at one of the aforementioned fundraising events.'

Villiers' lips compressed in silence. Jim leant further back in his chair. The two men stared at each other for a long moment. Then Jim said, 'Could you confirm yes or no whether our notes are correct.'

'Oh sorry,' Villiers said with obvious feigned surprise. 'I didn't realise you were waiting for me to speak. I assumed you were merely stating a fact. Yes, I can confirm your notes are correct.'

'And on how many other occasions did you meet with Mr Forester?'

Villiers blew out his cheeks. 'It's difficult to say exactly. I met him at many social functions. I also met with him numerous times on a one-to-one basis to discuss business.'

'What kind of business?'

'Mr Forester liked to be kept up to date on how things were going with the setting up of the children's home. And considering what a good friend he was to the Trust, I was happy to oblige him.'

'So you'd say you and Mr Forester were good friends.'

'You're putting words in my client's mouth,' said Burnham. 'What he said was Edward Forester was a good friend to the Trust. Mr Villiers and Mr Forester were business acquaintances. Nothing more.'

Keeping his gaze focused on Villiers, Jim continued as though he hadn't heard the solicitor, 'Where exactly did you and your friend Mr Forester meet on a one-to-one basis?'

'Chief Inspector Monahan, I really must object. As I said, my client and Mr Forester were—'

'Acquaintances, yes I heard you,' cut in Jim. 'Now, could you please answer the question, Mr Villiers?'

'Of course, Chief Inspector. We met at my office or at his house in Woodhouse.'

'Did you ever meet at Herbert and Marisa Winstanley's house?'

Again, Burnham answered for his client. 'Mr Villiers has never been to the Winstanleys' house.'

'But he did know them.'

'I was acquainted with them,' said Villiers, adopting the language of his solicitor. 'Herbert Winstanley offered his accounting services to the Trust. For free, I might add.'

No, not for free, thought Jim. *He was going to get paid. Just not in money.* 'And what about Marisa?'

'I met her at the same social functions where I met Mr Forester.'

'What about Mr Forester's half-brother, F—' Jim's voice caught on the name of Margaret's murderer – only for a heartbeat – then he forced it out of his throat, 'Freddie Harding? Are you acquainted with him too?'

'No.'

'And how about the other names listed in Herbert Winstanley's book—'

'Alleged book,' Burnham corrected again.

Ignoring him, Jim continued, 'Are you acquainted with any of them?'

'Yes, some of them,' said Villiers.

Jim withdrew a sheet of paper from Villiers' file. There were forty-two names printed in alphabetical order on the sheet. He placed it in front of Villiers. 'Point out which ones and tell us exactly how you know them.'

'Once again, my client has already been through all this with you,' said Burnham. 'Mr Villiers is a busy man with other pressing commitments. So unless you have any new questions to ask or information to verify, I—'

'No, no, Miles,' interjected Villiers, holding up a hand. 'It's fine. I want to do whatever I can to help the Chief Inspector.' He scanned the list of names: Stephen Baxley, Laurie Boyce... Sebastian Dawson-Cromer, Alvaro Gabriel Gaspar... Rupert Hartwell, Charles Knight... Henry Reeve, Thomas Villiers...

Corinne Waterman, Donald Woods... 'Rupert Hartwell worked for Mabel Forester. He attended one of the fundraisers with Mr Forester. I think I spoke to him briefly.'

'About what?'

'Erm, I honestly can't remember. It was well over a year ago.'

'What about the other names?'

'Charles Knight, well, you know who he is.' Villiers paused as if for effect. Jim winced behind the mask of his face. Yes, he knew who that corrupt, murdering piece of shit was. As did probably most people in the country and a lot beyond. Charles Knight was a stain South Yorkshire Police might never wash off. 'I used to bump into him occasionally at social functions. We spoke a couple of times, just general chit-chat. The only other person on the list I know – or rather, knew – is Dr Henry Reeve. We met regularly on a professional basis in early 2012 when he treated a number of children under our care who had mental health problems.'

Fourteen – eight girls and six boys, aged eleven to seventeen – that was the number of Craig Thorpe Youth Trust children Henry Reeve had treated. Jim and his team had spoken to all of them. None had reported anything that could be overtly construed as abuse, although several said Dr Reeve had asked for graphic details of their sex lives, two girls remembered the doctor 'accidentally' brushing up against them, and one boy had been shown a homosexual pornographic film then asked how it made him feel. The boy had answered that it made him feel sick and that anyone who tried that on him would wind up in hospital. He'd subsequently been told he was unsuitable for therapy. As had another boy who'd strongly objected to answering questions about his sex life. Jim had got the impression that these therapy sessions had doubled up as a kind of screening process. Fortunately, Dr Reeve's death and everything surrounding it seemed to have saved the children from whatever it was they were being screened for.

That was only a suspicion, of course. No direct evidence of criminal intent had been uncovered. But it wasn't Henry Reeve that Jim had really wanted to talk to the children about. It was Thomas Villiers. Only he hadn't been permitted to talk to them about him – at least, not in any way that implied Villiers was anything other than the upstanding member of society he appeared to be. As Miles Burnham never tired of pointing out, his client had been working with children for over thirty years, during which time not one accusation had been made against him. To publicly associate him with the crimes of Edward Forester, Henry Reeve and the Winstanleys simply because he appeared on an anonymously authored list of names would amount to criminal slander. A few misplaced words or indiscreet questions were all it would take to ruin Villiers' career. And Burnham had made it clear that if that happened he wouldn't hesitate to bring a civil case against South Yorkshire Police. So, much to Jim's frustration, he'd been forced to bite his tongue and tread lightly around Villiers' name.

'And did you and Dr Reeve discuss what took place during his therapy sessions?' asked Jim.

'We discussed the well-being of the children, but not the actual conversations that took place between themselves and Dr Reeve. Those were confidential, of course.'

'Of course.' Despite himself, there was a sardonic turn to Jim's mouth. 'So you don't recognise any of the other names on the list?'

'Mr Villiers has already stated that to be the case,' said Burnham.

'And what about Edward Forester and Freddie Harding's victims?' Jim and Reece had gone through what would happen during the interview beforehand. At this point, Reece was supposed to produce the photos of the victims – not the standard mugshots that had been provided for the press, but copies of the photos that had wallpapered Forester's bunker. Jim wanted to see how Villiers reacted to those horrific images. But Reece made no movement. Jim glanced at him. Reece was staring at Villiers, but his tired brown eyes had a faraway look in them. 'Inspector Geary,' Jim said insistently, 'the photos.'

Reece blinked back to the room. He withdrew the photos from an envelope and began setting them out on the table. Each was marked with a name and a date in Edward Forester's or Freddie Harding's handwriting – 'Roxanne Cole (20/2/1980)', 'Carole Stewart (1/5/1982)', 'Jennifer Barns (12/7/1983)'... There were thirty-seven photos in all. Singly they were sickening enough. But together they formed a tableau of torture and abuse that even now Jim found difficult to look at. Their subjects' eyes stared out of bodies that had been beaten, bitten, burnt, twisted, torn, sliced and starved until they looked more like grotesquely mutilated waxworks than human beings.

'Chief Inspector Monahan, I must protest,' exclaimed Burnham, a grimace of revulsion pulling at his face. 'You already know full well that Mr Villiers has no knowledge of any of these people.'

'Like I said, we want to make certain Mr Villiers is one hundred per cent sure about his previous statements.'

'This isn't about making certain, it's about using cheap shock tactics to try and provoke some sort of response from my client. It's not acceptable, Chief Inspector. And I shall be making my feelings known to Chief Superintendent Garrett.'

For the first time, an angry rise came into Jim's voice. 'Thirty-seven young women and girls are dead, Mr Burnham. And your client's name was found in a book concealed in their murderer's attic. A book we believe belonged to a man who was part of a suspected paedophile ring responsible for several further murders. So don't you tell me what's acceptable.' As he spoke, he kept one eye on Villiers, watching every movement of his face. Villiers watched him right back, his lips pressed into that familiar impassive line.

'I would remind you, Chief Inspector, that my client has never been arrested for any offence,' retorted the solicitor. 'I would also remind you that he's provided a DNA sample, which you've failed to match to thousands of hair, blood and semen samples recovered from the scenes of the crimes you're investigating.'

Jim turned his full attention on Villiers. 'Look at the photos please, Mr Villiers.'

Villiers lowered his gaze. The line of his lips quivered. He put the back of his hand to his mouth as if nauseated, his eyes sweeping slowly over the photos. 'I don't recognise any of them,' he said at last.

'I suppose that's not surprising. I doubt whether their own mothers would recognise them.' Jim folded his arms, staring at Villiers as though waiting for him to elaborate on some unasked question. After fifteen or twenty seconds, Villiers blinked away from his steady gaze.

'Are there any further questions?' asked Burnham.

'I think that's about it.' Jim paused a breath before adding, 'For now. Is there anything you'd like to add or clarify, Mr Villiers?'

'No.'

'In that case, I'm now handing you the notice that explains what happens to the interview recordings.' He passed Villiers a sheet of paper, then glanced at his watch. 'The time is now five ten p.m., the interview is concluded and Detective Inspector Geary is switching off the recording equipment.'

Reece removed the tapes from the recorder. 'Which would you like to be the master recording?' he asked.

Villiers pointed at one of the tapes, which Reece slid into a plastic sheath. The sheath was sealed, before being signed by everyone in the room.

Villiers extended his hand to Jim. 'I hope I was of some help. If you need anything else from me, please don't hesitate to get in contact.'

Smiling thinly, Jim took Villiers' hand. It was dry and cool, he noted. 'Oh, don't worry. We won't.'

'My client's a generous man, Chief Inspector,' said Burnham. 'I'm not. In my opinion your behaviour is bordering on harassment and I assure you I'll be—'

'I know, you'll be taking it up with my superiors,' broke in Jim. 'You do what you have to do, Mr Burnham, and I'll do what I have to do. Now if you could just wait in the corridor, Inspector Geary will be along in a moment to walk you out of the building.'

Once Burnham and Villiers were out of the room, Jim turned to Reece. 'So what do you think?'

'About what?' Reece replied absently, gathering up the photos.

'Villiers' reaction to the photos. He was faking it.'

'Maybe.'

A note of exasperation came into Jim's voice. 'What do you mean "maybe"? Of course he fucking was.'

'I'm sorry, Jim. My head's all over the place.' Reece squeezed his eyes shut suddenly, clenching his fists in a kind of helpless rage. 'Oh Christ, first I lose Dad to cancer. Now it's happening all over again with Staci.'

Jim's forehead creased. 'Cancer? I thought it was hepatitis?'

'So did we, but—' Reece broke off, shaking his head as if in disbelief. He heaved a breath and continued, 'It seems all the

shit Staci stuck in her veins over the years fucked up her liver worse than they thought.'

'But they can treat it, right?'

Reece gave a small shrug of his big shoulders. 'She's been having chemo for the past few weeks. You should see her, Jim. All her hair, her beautiful red hair, it's falling out in clumps.' Tears came into Reece's eyes. Blinking them back, he turned away from his colleague and reached for the interview tapes. Jim gently laid a hand on his arm.

'Get yourself off home. Staci needs you more than I do.'

Reece motioned towards the corridor. 'What about them?'

'I'll deal with those pricks.'

Reece approached the door and hesitated. 'I'm sorry, Jim, I've been meaning to tell you since we found out, but I couldn't bring myself to talk about it. I just keep thinking about Dad, about how much he suffered...' His voice trailed away with a little choke.

'You don't need to explain, Reece. I'll see you after the weekend. You know where I am if you need me. Give Staci my love.'

'I will. Thanks, Jim.'

Jim's gaze followed Reece from the room. Beyond the big detective's shoulder he glimpsed Villiers. Anger replaced the concern in his eyes. Why did it always seem to be people like Reece and Staci who suffered, whilst scumbags like Villiers flourished? The guy was as dirty as used toilet paper. Jim knew it. Could almost smell it. And he felt sure he could prove it too, if only Garrett would allow him to delve deeper into Villiers' life. Somewhere there was someone – a former or even a current resident of the children's homes he'd worked at – who could expose that dirt. And if they could snag Villiers, maybe they could use him as bait to hook the other big fish in Herbert Winstanley's

book. But that wasn't going to happen unless Garrett— Jim broke off his line of thought with a sharp shake of his head. He'd been thinking in circles for months now, wasting his time on ifs and maybes, dancing to Garrett's tune. And where had it got him? Fucking nowhere. He frowned at the list of names. Maybe it was time to start dancing to his own music.

There was a knock on the door. Miles Burnham shoved his head back into the room. 'Can we hurry things up, Chief Inspector? My client's a busy man.'

Jim grimaced inwardly. Yes, Villiers was a busy man – busy running the home Edward Forester had helped him set up. The thought of it was like a kick in the gut. With deliberate slowness, Jim led Burnham and Villiers to a yard enclosed by the severe concrete façade of Police HQ, tall walls topped with spiked railings, and a three-metre steel gate. The yard was full of police vehicles, except for a Mercedes with tinted windows. As Burnham and Villiers approached the Mercedes, a camera was thrust through the gate's vertical bars. Its flash went off and Villiers ducked down behind the car as though a sniper had taken a potshot at him.

'Chief Inspector,' exclaimed Burnham. 'Did you see that?'

Jim had seen it alright. He'd seen the face behind the camera too. It was one he'd known for years – twenty years, to be precise – but it had become especially familiar to him once again in the past few months. Under different circumstances, in a different life, it could have been a pretty face. But *this* life had made its eyes penetratingly direct, its lips thin and taut, its cheeks pale and sharp-boned. The woman it belonged to was in her mid-thirties, maybe five five or so, wearing heavy-duty Doc Martens, skinny black jeans and a black leather jacket. Her hair was blonde, short and as styleless as the black-framed glasses she always wore.

Permitting himself a ghost of a smile at Villiers' startled face, Jim called for the gate to be opened. 'Stay there,' he shouted at the woman. 'I want a word with you.'

A motor whirred into life and the gate slid sideways. As Jim crossed the yard, the woman spread her arms as if to say, *What have I done wrong?* Jim pointed to her camera. 'Hand it over.'

'Why should I?' she responded. 'This is public property.'

Jim thumbed over his shoulder. 'Yes, but that isn't. And I've warned you before about what would happen if I caught you taking photos here.'

The woman still hesitated to hand over her camera.

'Do you really want to do this the hard way, Anna?' Jim's voice was authoritative, but there was an underlying tenderness in it.

Reluctantly, Anna gave her camera to him. 'You'll get it back once the appropriate photos have been deleted,' he assured her.

'I'll delete them for you right now.'

'Sorry, but I have to make certain that deleted means gone for good.'

Anna glanced past Jim at the Mercedes, behind which Villiers was still squatting. 'He must really be someone important. Especially if he can afford a scumbag like Burnham.'

'Go home. You're wasting your time here.'

'I disagree.' An edge of frustration sharpened Anna's voice. 'I don't understand why you refuse to see the connection between your case and my sister's abduction.'

'I don't refuse to see it. I don't see it because right now it doesn't exist.'

Anna began counting off points on her fingers. 'Freddie Harding was abducting young girls in the early nineties. He used to drive a white van. Manchester United football shirts and match-day programmes were found at his house.'

'Harding wasn't opportunistically snatching kids off the street. He was taking prostitutes who he knew wouldn't be easily missed. Granted, he drove a white van at the time of his 2005 arrest. But no such vehicle was registered to him in 1993. As for him being a Man U supporter, well, there are about half a billion of them out there. And anyway, you don't know for certain that Jessica's abductors were Man U supporters.'

'What about the red devil keyring? And why else would they have been driving around so close to Bramall Lane that afternoon? Correct me if I'm wrong, but isn't it an accepted fact that in most abductions the perpetrator had a legitimate reason for being at the scene of the crime? They might work or live nearby. Or they might have been involved in a social activity, such as attending a sporting event.'

'You know you're not wrong. As I'm sure you also know that the majority of abductions are crimes of opportunity. And as I said, Harding wasn't an opportunist.'

'What about the girl he raped on Pitsmoor Road in 2005?'

'Ellen Peterson was the exception.'

'How do you know there weren't other exceptions?'

'I don't,' conceded Jim. 'What I do know is that Harding has a thing for prostitutes who remind him of his mother. And your sister doesn't fall into that category.'

'But she was the type Edward Forester would've gone for.'

'What's taking so long, Chief Inspector?' called Miles Burnham. 'Can you please hurry up and get rid of that bloody woman?'

Jim ignored the solicitor. Every opportunity to inconvenience Villiers was an opportunity not to be missed. 'OK, look, let's assume for a moment that you're right. The man you saw grab Jessica was neither Harding nor Forester. Which means a third man was working with them. And that's where the theory starts to fall apart. We've found no evidence to suggest an unidentified third man ever visited Forester's bunker. Nor have we found a DNA match for your sister from the recovered remains of the victims.' *Recovered remains* – the words seemed to echo in Jim's head with added sardonic bitterness. *What a fucking joke.* Apart from two semi-gelatinous bodies in barrels, the only remains they'd recovered were from a jar containing thirty-eight torn and shrivelled nipples – one for each of the half-brothers' dead victims, plus Melissa Doyle, the only girl known to have escaped the bunker.

'Maybe Freddie Harding had an accomplice his brother didn't know about.'

Jim pushed his lower lip out thoughtfully. 'It's possible. But it's pure speculation. And right now I don't have much use for that.' He raised a hand as Anna made to say something else. 'I realise you're perfectly within you're rights to stand out here all day, Anna, but as a favour to me I'm asking you to move along.'

'Alright, but it won't make any difference.' Anna jerked her chin – which bore a thin pearly white scar – towards the Mercedes. 'Camera or no camera, I'll find out who he is. And when I do I'll put his face out there for the world to see.'

Jim took hold of Anna's arm and firmly guided her out of sight of the yard. 'I'd think long and hard before doing that if I were you.' His voice was low with concern. 'Trust me, that man's not someone you want to antagonise.'

Anna's lips curled into a contemptuous smile. 'Oh yeah, what's he going to do, sue me? You'd better tell him to get in line.'

'Look, I know I can't stop you from doing what you feel needs to be done. But just be careful how you go about it. Please. I'd hate to see you get hurt.'

'Is that how you brought down Forester and Harding? By being careful?' Anna held Jim's hangdog brown eyes for a moment, letting the words sink in. She wrote her mobile number on a notepad and tore out the page for him. 'You'd better not damage my camera, Chief Inspector, or you'll be the one in trouble.'

Jim waited for her to get into a beaten-up old VW camper van across the street and accelerate away, before heading back to the yard. 'Is she gone?' asked Burnham.

'Yes.'

With a nervous glance to make sure Jim was right, Villiers rose from behind the Mercedes. 'Did she recognise me?'

'No.'

'Who was she?'

'Nobody you need worry about.'

'For once I agree with the Chief Inspector,' said Burnham. 'She's just some wannabe journalist. Her name's Anna Young. She runs a blog called The Truth.'

'The truth about what?'

'About whatever gets her goat. She fancies herself as some kind of crusader exposing injustice. Personally I think she's got a screw loose. What about you, Chief Inspector?'

I think I'd like to slap the smugness off your face, thought Jim. He kept his voice neutral. 'Thank you for your time, Mr Villiers. I'm sure we'll be seeing each other again.'

'Don't bank on it,' countered Burnham. 'Not unless you've actually got something worth talking to him about.'

Villiers and Burnham ducked into the Mercedes. As Jim watched them drive away, Anna's words stalked around his mind like a caged tiger. *Is that how you brought down Forester and Harding? By being careful?*

CHAPTER TWO

On the way home, Anna stopped to pick up some flowers. She bought two bunches – lilies for her mum and yellow roses for her dad. As she neared Queens Road, a familiar tightness rose into her throat. Her hands twitched with the urge to make a sharp left into the warren of back roads and rat runs she usually took. She resisted it. *Not today*, she told herself. Today she felt the need to see where *it* had happened. She pulled across two lanes of oncoming traffic and parked up in the same spot that the white van had done. A car beeped her. She didn't notice. She was back in that terrible moment again, fighting for breath as the gloved hand covered her mouth, eyes bulging at the short, stocky figure of Jessica's abductor. With the vividness of a lucid dream, she saw his chubby cheeks, his short-cropped hair, his dark, ugly eyes. She felt the fist driving into her stomach, felt herself lurching towards Jessica, grabbing for her. So close. So agonisingly close. Then the pain between her shoulder blades and she was falling. The keyring... distant shouts... the van speeding away... Jessica gone...

Anna snapped into the present with a trembling intake of breath. She shoved the camper van into gear and accelerated away in the opposite direction to that which the white van had taken. There was one more stop she needed to make on the way home. She turned off Queens Road and, after a short distance, pulled over by some iron railings that enclosed a green space of lawns, trees and paths. She got out of the van and headed through a gate. She stopped by a bench shadowed by an oak tree. A small brass plaque on the bench read 'IN LOVING MEMORY OF RICK YOUNG. DIED 13TH JUNE 2003, AGED 50'. This had been her father's favourite spot to sit and think. After Jessica's abduction, he would come here day after day and spend hours staring out across the River Sheaf and the terraced roofs towards his beloved Bramall Lane. And one day, when all hope had finally deserted him, when he could no longer endure the endless grief, he'd come here to die. He'd tied one end of a rope around a branch and the other end around his neck. And then he'd stepped off the bench. A dog-walker had found his lifeless body.

The council had wanted to cut down the tree, almost as if it was guilty of some crime. Anna had convinced them not to. Removing the tree would solve nothing. Just as leaving Sheffield behind to start fresh somewhere else would solve nothing. You couldn't outrun memories. And besides, she didn't want to. She wanted to hold onto each and every tormenting memory and use them like batteries to power her search for Jessica.

Anna laid the roses at the base of the tree. She closed her eyes briefly, then headed back to the VW. When she got home, she found her mum sitting in the living room, staring at a framed photo of her late husband. Anna put the lilies in a vase and placed them on a table at the side of her mum's armchair.

Fiona Young looked up at her daughter. Deep creases spread from the corners of her sad blue eyes as she smiled.

'Hello, love.'

'Have you been to the cemetery?'

Fiona nodded. 'I waited for you until four.'

'I'm sorry, Mum. I was busy. I've left flowers in the park.'

Fiona's gaze returned to the photo in which Rick and she were sitting with their faces pressed together on a balcony overlooking the sea. It was an old photo, taken on a rare family holiday to Spain. Fiona looked tanned and healthy, her blonde hair shone in the sun, her eyes twinkled with the same cheeky spark that Jessica's had done. That spark was gone now. Nor did her hair shine or her skin glow. There was a sallowness to her complexion and a greyness to her hair that she'd long since ceased to conceal with makeup and dye. 'Ten years,' she said. 'It's difficult to believe it's been so long.'

Anna stooped to kiss her mum's head, then made her way upstairs to a bedroom that obviously doubled as an office. A desk with a PC on it was squeezed in between a wardrobe and an unmade single bed. Filing cabinets lined one wall. Cardboard boxes were stacked under the window. A set of shelves sagged under the weight of books on criminal psychology, law and investigative procedures. More books lay open on the carpet, their pages marked with post-it notes. There were no pictures or photos, no ornaments, no makeup. Next to a lamp on the desk was an ashtray brimful of cigarette butts. Shrugging off her jacket, Anna picked her way through the clutter. The room had long been difficult to move around. Her mum had suggested many times that she use the spare bedroom as her office. The very thought of it made Anna shudder. After her dad's death, her mum had finally stripped the room of Jessica's belongings. But it would always be Jessica's bedroom to Anna. A sacred place. A haunted place.

As she dropped onto a chair, her elbow knocked over a tower

of boxes. One burst open, scattering dozens of Red Devils keyrings across the carpet. 'Shit,' she muttered, gathering them up. Her conviction that Jessica's abductors were Manchester United supporters had compelled her to visit sporting goods and memorabilia shops all over the country and scour the internet in search of the same keyring that had fallen from the man's pocket. She'd never found an exact match. But if they even vaguely resembled a devil, she bought them anyway. Occasionally she would lay them all out in front of herself. It had become as much of a ritual as the yearly laying of roses at the tree. Yet another reminder, if one were needed, of what had happened and what needed to be done. She'd also spent many – too many – Saturdays and Sundays watching Man U supporters file in and out of Old Trafford and opponents' grounds. All to no avail.

Anna lit a cigarette and scanned through her emails. Over a hundred more had landed in her inbox during the afternoon. They came from all over the UK. All over the world. Many of their senders were people like herself. People whose loved ones had been abducted or gone missing. People stuck in a psychological limbo of endless suffering. People who spent their lives in pursuit of the truth about what had happened to their child, brother, sister, boyfriend, girlfriend, wife, husband or whoever. Most approached her for the same reason that she'd started up her blog – they wanted to raise awareness about a case, keep it from fading out of the public consciousness, as even the most shocking inevitably did. Others were seeking advice. And others still simply wanted to confide in someone who understood what they were going through. Not all the emails concerned abductions and missing persons. Over the years, her blog had grown to encompass almost every kind of crime and miscarriage of justice. In particular, she'd highlighted the cases of rape, abuse and domestic violence victims who'd been failed by the legal system, naming and shaming perpetrators who thought they could hide behind the law, encouraging her thousands of loyal readers to spread the word to every corner of the internet. And in doing so, she'd come into conflict with Miles Burnham and his ilk. They'd brought dozens of civil and criminal cases against her. The fines had piled up until she was forced to declare herself bankrupt. She'd even served a couple of short prison sentences. She didn't care. All she really cared about was finding Jessica – or rather, finding her abductors, for Jessica herself was surely long since dead.

Who were they? That question had possessed Anna for twenty years, and would continue to do so until she answered it.

She opened a filing cabinet drawer. Inside were dozens of folders containing newspaper clippings, dossiers she'd compiled on potential suspects, transcripts of police interviews, and anything and everything else she'd managed to get her hands on relating to Jessica's case. She withdrew two time-faded composite sketches. One was of the chubby-faced man. It was a good likeness, except for the eyes. She'd had the man's face sketched many times over the years by different artists. But none of them had ever truly managed to capture the ugliness that had shone through his eyes. The second sketch was of a more slimly built figure in a parka with the hood up. She navigated to her blog, clicked on 'new post' and typed 'Ten years ago today these men killed my dad' into the title box. She scanned the sketches into the main body of the post, before continuing typing, 'They didn't put the rope around his neck, but they killed him nonetheless...'

When Anna was done writing, she took out her iPhone and touched the photo icon, bringing up the photos from outside Police HQ – photos which had been wirelessly transferred to her phone the instant she took them. 'Now,' she said, studying Villiers' sharp, hawkish face, 'let's find out who you are.'

****

Jim rested back in his chair, staring at the names pinned to the board. There were forty-four – all those from Herbert's book, plus the author and his wife's. Beneath each name there was a photograph and a few particulars. An interlacing web of lines had been drawn between some of the names, accompanied by a few words indicating how they were connected. More lines radiated from one name than any other – 'Thomas Villiers. DOB 1955. Manager of Craig Thorpe Youth Trust Children's Home.' Jim's gaze dropped to Anna's camera. He scrolled through the photos of Villiers. There were three of them. In the first two, Villiers was focused on the Mercedes, his face as composed and smooth as usual. In the third, he was staring into the camera, his eyes wide with surprise. No, not just surprise. Fear. The bastard was terrified of public exposure. Of course, given the sensitive nature of his work, some would say he had good reason to be. But Jim had spent most of his life staring into the eyes of innocence and guilt. And he'd rarely seen that kind of fear in the eyes of the innocent.

Jim deleted the first two photos. He hesitated over the third, his forehead knotting. Again, Anna's words reverberated in his mind. *Is that how you brought down Forester and Harding? By being careful?* His finger was still hovering above the delete icon when Garrett knocked and entered the office. The Chief Superintendent showed no surprise at finding Jim at his desk several hours after he'd been due to knock off. Since being cleared to return to duty, Jim had been first in the office and last out. His cardiologist had warned him against working long hours. Those who knew him better knew such warnings were a waste of breath. The job was all he had left.

'Evening, Jim.'

Jim nodded in return. The greeting wasn't exactly friendly – their approach to the job and life was too different for them to ever be friends – but there was a grudging respect in both men's eyes. 'Let me guess, Miles Burnham's been on the phone.'

'He's not happy. What were you hoping to achieve by showing Mr Villiers those photos?'

'I just wanted to see his reaction.'

'Well you certainly got a reaction. Mr Villiers is threatening to file a harassment complaint against you.'

Jim grunted with amused contempt. 'The last thing Villiers wants to do is draw attention to himself by kicking up that kind of stink.'

'You're probably right, but...' An uneasy frown pulling at his forehead, Garrett indicated the board of names. 'These aren't people to be toyed with, Jim. They have the power to hurt us just as badly as we can hurt them. That's why we need to be—'

'Especially careful how we deal with them,' Jim interrupted, finishing Garrett's sentence for him. He'd heard this speech too many times over the past year. 'Well I'm sorry, but being careful doesn't always get results. I know you don't want to hear this, but if we're going to move this investigation forward we need to start taking more risks.' He jerked his thumb at the board. 'And that means stopping giving these pricks such an easy ride.'

'We've interviewed every living person on there more than once. Taken DNA samples. Run detailed background checks. I fail to see how that equates to an easy ride.'

Jim made a sharp dismissive motion. 'We need to pull their lives apart. Talk to their families, friends, colleagues, anyone who might have information.'

His frown deepening, Garrett shook his head. 'We have no evidence of criminal activity by these people.'

'We have Herbert Winstanley's book.'

'That's not enough. If we were to do as you suggest, it would amount to publicly linking them to murder, rape, paedophilia and corruption.'

'Would that be such a bad thing?'

'Yes. Yes it bloody would. As things stand, it would mean the end of this investigation. And most probably the end of our careers too.'

Jim gave a sneer that he didn't allow to reach his lips. Since inheriting Charles Knight's uniform, Garrett had made a lot of noises about changing departmental culture, adopting a zero-tolerance approach to crime and the conduct of his officers. But when it really came down to it, nothing had changed. The same principle still reigned supreme – look out for number one.

'There are a lot of people watching us, waiting for us to slip up,' continued Garrett. 'So we have to do this right.'

'I don't understand. Why give me this job, why even set up this unit if you're just going to box us into a corner?'

'You're not boxed into a corner. Get back out there on the streets, start interviewing prostitutes again. All we need is one witness who's willing to talk about what went on at the Winstanleys' house.'

'We've already spoken to every prostitute and pimp in South Yorkshire. Nobody's talking.' Jim jabbed his finger at Thomas Villiers' photo. 'Villiers is the weak link. No one else can be directly connected to both Edward Forester and the Winstanleys – at least, no one who's alive. If you'd just give us permission to talk to the former residents of homes he's worked at, I'm sure we could dig up some dirt on him.'

Before Jim had finished, Garrett was shaking his head again. Jim threw up his hands in exasperation. 'Then you might as well shut us down.'

'Actually, that brings me to another thing I have to tell you.' Garrett's voice took on a faintly apologetic tone. 'It's been decided that from today your unit will be stripped back to yourself and Detectives Geary and Greenwood.'

No flicker of surprise showed on Jim's face. He'd been expecting something like this for the past couple of months. Nor was it a surprise who'd been chosen to remain on the unit. Scott Greenwood was Garrett's man through and through, his earpiece. As for Reece, Garrett was clearly uncomfortable with his continued presence on the Major Incident Team. The Chief Superintendent didn't need to be much of a detective to realise Reece's past was less than pristine. And that posed a threat to his future vision for both the team and himself. It was obvious to Jim that Reece's days were numbered. Sooner or later, Garrett would find some excuse to shunt the big detective out of Major Incidents, quite possibly even out of his job. He would probably have already done so if Jim hadn't taken Reece under his wing. 'Decided by who?'

'The decision's been made. That's all you need to know.'

Garrett's reply confirmed what Jim already knew. The decision had come from higher up. And when enough time for the sake of appearances had passed, no doubt another decision would be made to shut down the unit altogether. Jim could just imagine the ripple of relief that would pass through the force's upper echelons when that day came. This case was simply too much of a hot potato for the top brass to handle.

Garrett glanced at his watch. 'Anyway, I'd better be going. My wife will be wondering where—' He broke off, realising the insensitivity of his words. 'I'll see you Monday.' He started to turn away, then added as an afterthought, 'Oh, and Burnham told me about what happened outside the station. Have you deleted the photos?'

Jim was silent a beat, before replying, 'Yes.'

When Garrett was gone, Jim opened a desk drawer and took out a key. It was flat with notches on both edges. He ran his thumb thoughtfully over the notches. With a sudden decisive movement, he picked up the phone and punched in a number. After several rings, Anna Young's ever-intense voice came down the line. 'Who is this?'

'Jim Monahan.'

'Chief Inspector Monahan, I didn't expect to be hearing from you so soon.'

'Call me Jim. We need to meet.'

'Where and when?'

'Do you know the White Lion?'

'On London Road?'

'That's the one. I'll see you there in about twenty minutes.'

'This is about more than just my camera, isn't it?'

Jim's eyebrows lifted slightly at Anna's perceptiveness. 'Yes,' he said and hung up.

****

The White Lion hummed with the conversation and laughter of Friday-night drinkers. The softly lit bar with its dark-stained beams, worn varnished floorboards, old round tables and stools, brought a little rush of memories back to Anna. The pub was a popular match-day haunt for Sheffield United supporters. Her dad had taken her there many times for a pre-match drink. She hadn't been back since his death. Spotting Jim at the bar, she threaded her way through the drinkers to him. He was sipping whisky and staring at a key, turning it over in his hand. 'You look like a man with a lot on his mind,' she observed.

Jim's rugged face creased into a smile. 'Thanks for coming, Anna. What are you drinking?'

'I'll have a pint of cider, thanks.'

Jim caught the barman's attention and ordered Anna's drink and another whisky for himself. They took them to a vacant table. 'I've never been able to get used to seeing women drinking pints,' said Jim as Anna knocked back a good portion of her drink. 'My ex-wife, Margaret, used to say I was a sexist.'

'She was right.'

Jim glanced into his own glass. 'She would have given me hell for drinking this too. I had a heart attack last year.'

'Sounds like your ex-wife was an intelligent woman.' The 'was' indicated Anna knew what had happened to Margaret.

'She was the best woman I ever knew. Far too good for me, really.' Jim was silent a moment, his face tense with scarcely subdued pain. Then he took out Anna's camera and handed it to her. She switched it on. Her eyebrows lifted.

'You haven't deleted all the photos.'

'His name's Thomas Villiers. I have reason to believe he's part of the Winstanley house paedophile ring.'

Anna's eyes widened some more. 'What reason?'

'Herbert Winstanley had a book. It contained a list of clients or members.' Jim placed a sheet of paper on the table. Anna's forehead contracted as her gaze ran down the names printed on it.

'Why hasn't this been made public?'

Jim pointed at a name. 'Laurie Boyce is an aide to a cabinet minister.' His finger moved down the list. 'Maurice Chaput is a French diplomat. Sebastian Dawson-Cromer is a High Court judge. Alvaro Gabriel Gaspar is a high-ranking EU official.

Andrew Templeton is also a judge. As for the rest of them, they're CEOs of big companies, financial managers, stockbrokers, doctors. There's even a fucking celebrity on there.'

Anna met Jim's gaze, her eyes hard. 'Let me get this straight. You're protecting these people.'

'No. Not any more.'

'So you want me to publish this?'

'I want every single person in this fucking country to know who and what these people are.'

'I get the feeling you don't exactly have permission to do this.'

Jim's smile returned, crookedly. 'Not exactly.'

'Why me? Why not go to the newspapers?'

'The newspapers wouldn't touch this with a ten-foot pole. They'd be sued for everything they've got.' Jim heaved a sigh. 'The fact is, we don't have anything concrete on these people.'

'But you're certain they're guilty.'

'As certain as that heart attack I had.'

Anna's eyes returned to the list. An edge of uncertainty entered her voice. 'If I do this, what happens to me?'

'I won't lie to you, Anna. They'll try to destroy you, financially, emotionally, any way they can.'

A moment passed. So did Anna's uncertainty. Her lips thinned into a smile as uncompromising as her eyes. 'Is that all?' She took another big mouthful of her pint and banged her glass down like an exclamation point. 'So what else can you tell me about these wankers?'

Jim laid it all out for her – where Villiers worked; how he was connected to Forester; the work Dr Reeves had done at the children's home. She shook her head incredulously. 'How is it possible that the newspapers haven't got hold of any of this?'

'There are a lot of powerful people working hard to keep it quiet.'

Anna scowled. 'It makes me want to puke. Bastards like these think they can fuck us with impunity. Well it's time they learnt differently. I'm going to make their lives a living hell.'

'And they yours.'

Anna let out a disdainful laugh. 'They're about twenty years too late for that.'

Jim looked at her with concern. He tapped the list. 'Is there any way you could publish that anonymously?'

'Yeah sure, but why would I do that?'

'I know you don't think so, Anna, but it seems to me you've got a lot to lose. Your blog's almost certain to get shut down.'

Anna shrugged. 'So I'll start another. And if they put me in prison, I'll write it from there. That's the beauty of the internet. They can't silence us, no matter how hard they try.'

'And what about your mum? Will she be able to handle it if you end up in prison?'

Anna eyed Jim narrowly. 'I'm a little confused. You brought this thing to me. Now you're trying to talk me out of it.'

'I just want to make sure you're going into it with your eyes open.'

'My eyes have been fully open for a long time now. Look, we both know that if I'm going to do this it's got to have my name attached to it. Otherwise it's just another bit of worthless internet shit-flinging.' Anna smiled again, and this time there was a trace of softness in it. 'Your concern's touching and all, but believe me I can take care of myself.'

So could Margaret, thought Jim. His expression troubled, he unconsciously took out the key again and thumbed its edge. He hadn't wanted to involve Anna in this, but her blog was the perfect platform to get the word out. Her integrity was untainted by any allegiances other than to the victims of crime themselves. Moreover, her readers didn't simply trust her, they loved her. That much was obvious from the comments beneath her blog posts. And that combination of factors gave her a kind of power no mainstream media possessed.

'What's with the key?' asked Anna.

'It's a copy of one found in Edward Forester's bunker that had Freddie Harding's fingerprints on it. I've spent months trying to work out where it's for. To be honest, I'd almost given up on it until you mentioned the red devil keyring. Not that I have any reason to believe the two things are connected, but... well it got me thinking about it again.'

'Can I have a look at it?'

Jim gave Anna the key.

She turned it over in her hand as he'd done. 'It looks like a garage door key.'

'That's exactly what it is. It's a Gliderol key. They manufacture residential and industrial roller garage doors.'

'There are no markings on it.'

'There aren't any on the original either.'

'So this is most likely a copy of a copy.'

Jim nodded. 'You've got a good eye for detail.'

'So where have you tried it?'

'Harding's work place, Forester and his mother's garages and work places, the Winstanleys' garages, various storage units near Harding's house in Wath upon Dearne. Problem is, Gliderol doors are so common it's an almost impossible task. Bar trying it in every roller door in South Yorkshire, I'm not sure what else to do.'

'Do you mind if I have a go at finding where it fits?'

Jim's eyebrows drew together. Noting his concern, Anna continued, 'I'm about to put myself directly in the line of fire. I hardly think it'll make much difference if I make some enquiries about a garage door.'

'OK, but don't broadcast it over the internet or anywhere else. I'm the only one with a copy of that key. If my superiors find out you've got it, it'll be pretty obvious where it's come from.'

'Don't worry. I know I've got a big gob, but I can do things on the quiet too.'

Jim didn't doubt that. Anna clearly had a talent for this kind of work – a talent that had been sucked into one long fruitless search for her missing sister. He felt a familiar surge of impotent anger at the thought of it. He handed her his card. 'If you happen to find anything out, call me straight away.'

'I will.'

'I mean it, Anna. Straight away,' stressed Jim. 'The same goes if anyone contacts you about the list. Don't try to deal with it on your own. These are extremely dangerous people.'

Something about Jim's tone reminded Anna of her dad. After Jessica's abduction, Rick Young had become so smotheringly protective he'd barely been able to let Anna out of his sight. Even when she was at school, he'd phoned to check up on her dozens of times a day. In the end, she'd had to threaten to leave home unless he gave her some space. She held in a sigh. 'You've read my blog, right? So you know about the type of people I've gone up against – rapists, abusers, murderers.'

'I'm sorry. I don't mean to patronise you, it's just that...' Jim trailed off, his eyes growing distant. In his mind, he saw Margaret – the torn tights, the knife in her chest, the bloody voids where her eyes had been. After her death, he'd sworn to himself he wouldn't risk any lives other than his own. And yet here he was, doing just the opposite. 'I don't want to be responsible for you getting hurt.'

'You're not going to be, no matter what happens. If it makes you feel any better, I've got other copies of the photos of Villiers.'

Anna took out her phone and showed Jim the photos. 'I'd have put them online as soon as I worked out who the fucker was. And then I would've drawn fire just the same, but without you backing me up.'

Jim's expression relaxed a little. Anna wasn't Margaret. She knew exactly what she was getting into. He held out his hand. She shook it, sank the remainder of her pint and stood up. 'I'll be in touch.'

During the walk home, Anna spotted a roller door. On impulse, she tried the key in it. The lock didn't turn. She stared at the key as if it was taunting her. Was it possible? Might this key have once been attached to the red devil keyring? The link was tenuous, if not existent only in her mind. She knew that, and yet for the first time in years she felt a fresh swell of motivation. 'I'm going to find out where you fit, you little bastard,' she told the key. Then she continued on her way, eyeballing every garage she passed.

****

The graveyard was locked up for the night. Jim squeezed through a gap in the railings and traversed the ranks of graves, until he came to a grey marble headstone inscribed with simply 'MARGARET HARRIS. 1957–2012. ALWAYS MISSED'. *Harris.* Jim had never got used to seeing her called by her maiden name. She'd always be Margaret Monahan to him.

'Hello, love,' he said, stooping to clear away the few leaves and weeds that had gathered on the grave since his previous visit. He was silent a long moment, head bowed as if in thought, before continuing, 'I've done something. I don't know if it's the right thing. You'd know. You always knew...' He faded off into another extended silence.

He kissed his fingers and touched them to the headstone. 'I'll see you again soon, love.' Slowly, he stood. Slowly, he walked away.

CHAPTER THREE

Jim was woken by a knock at the door. It was a familiar kind of knock – one that demanded to be answered. The thought came to him at once: *Anna's done it, she's published the list!* Pulling on his dressing-gown, he hurried through to the spare bedroom of the flat he'd moved into several months after Margaret's death – he'd tried to remain in the house, but the place was haunted by too many memories, too many nightmares. The knock came again as he booted up his PC. 'Alright, hold your horses. I'll be there in a minute,' he shouted, navigating to Anna's blog. He wanted to know what he was about to open the door to – if the list had been published, it was most likely Garrett come to give him the hairdryer treatment.

'*The high-society paedophile ring the authorities don't want us to know about*' ran the blog headline. Jim avidly scanned down the page. Anna had been a busy girl.

'*We've all heard the rumours,*' continued the post. '*They've been doing the rounds for years. High-society orgies where for the right money boys and girls of any age can be bought, used and abused. The revenge killings of Herbert and Marisa*

Winstanley and Dr Henry Reeve gave us a glimpse into the truth behind the rumours. The uncovery of Labour MP Edward Forester and his half-brother Freddie Harding's terrible crimes, and Chief Superintendent Charles Knight's corruption, shed further light on this sickening little world. We waited for more revelations, more names. But they never came – until now...'

There was a vague reference to a 'source with police connections'. Followed by several paragraphs recapping the events that had been set into motion by Stephen Baxley's fateful decision to attempt to murder his family, and culminating in the discovery of Herbert's little black book. Then came the list itself. Anna hadn't simply published the names. She'd put together bios with details of their owners' nationalities, ages, professions and any connections they had to each other. She'd even managed to dig up photos of most of them. Beneath the post, there were already hundreds of comments, many from other bloggers promising to spread the word. The blog had clearly been getting a lot of traffic.

The insistent hammering forced its way back into Jim's consciousness. He headed to the door and squinted through the spyhole. As expected, Garrett was on the other side of it. He was dressed in an old grey tracksuit. His usually neat hair was dishevelled, his chin was dark with stubble, as though he'd jumped out of bed, grabbed the first clothes to hand and left the house in a rush. He looked angry – angrier than Jim had ever seen him.

Jim took a breath and opened the door. 'Sorry, I was in b—'

'Have you seen it?' broke in Garrett, pushing past him into the hallway.

'Seen what?'

Garrett's eyes flashed behind their spectacles. 'Don't play the innocent with me. You know exactly what I'm talking about.'

'Do I? I don't think I do.'

'You must think I'm a bloody fool! Maybe I am for putting my trust in you.'

Garrett thrust out several sheets of paper. A glance told Jim it was a printout of the blog post. He kept his face expressionless – to a cop, false surprise was as transparent as a freshly cleaned window.

'What have you got to say about that?' demanded Garrett.

'What do you want me to say?'

'I want you to own up to what you've done.'

'You think this came from me?'

Garrett made a dismissive slash with his hand. 'Let's cut the bullshit, Jim. I know you. I know what you're capable of when you can't get your own way.'

'You make me sound like a spoilt child.'

'Maybe because that's what you remind me of sometimes. Do you realise what you've done? You've torn down everything you worked so hard for.'

'There was nothing to tear down,' Jim stated matter-of-factly, 'because you never gave me the proper tools to build anything in the first place.'

'How can you say that? I allowed you to handpick a team to work this case.'

'Yes, but you didn't allow us to work it the way it should be worked.'

Garrett stabbed at the printout. 'Those people have a right to anonymity until their guilt's been proven.'

'And we have a right to warn the public that their children are in danger.'

'So you admit you gave Anna Young the names.'

'No. But I admit I'm glad that someone did.'

'And what about the investigation being suspended, are you glad about that too?'

'Suspended on whose authority?'

'On Chief Constable Hunt's. And if that's not enough for you, on the authority of the Home Office, who woke the Chief Constable with a none-too-pleasant phone call this morning.'

Jim exhaled a sharp breath through his nose, nodding as if to say, *That sounds about right.* 'And what about me? Am I suspended too?'

'No. But believe me, I'm going to find out who leaked this information. And when I do, I'll have no choice but to hit them with the full weight of disciplinary proceedings.'

'Well, good luck.'

Garrett's face twitched with conflicting emotions. 'I realise I owe you a lot, Jim, but I'm not going to let you ruin my career for the sake of some futile crusade. I mean, for Christ's sake, if any harm should come to anyone on that list because of this...' He cringed visibly at the thought of the repercussions of such a thing.

'Yeah, God forbid that should happen.' There was more than a hint of sarcasm in Jim's voice.

Garrett grimaced angrily. He whirled away from Jim as though he couldn't stand to look at him any more and headed out the door, throwing over his shoulder, 'Make sure your mobile's switched on. I'll be calling you very soon.'

Jim went in search of his mobile and dialled Anna Young. 'Who's this?' she asked upon picking up, her tone abrupt and suspicious.

'It's Jim Monahan.'

'Oh, sorry, Jim, I didn't recognise your number. My phone's been going crazy all morning. I can't believe this is happening so fast. I only put the list out there a few hours ago and already I'm getting calls from lawyers, journalists and your lot. I've even had some Home Office dickhead on the phone trying to pressure me into giving up my source. They're threatening to close down my blog, just like you said they would.'

'How long do you think it'll take them to do it?'

'I'm not sure. Considering how much heat this thing's generating, I'll be amazed if it's still up by the end of today. But that's the least of my worries. The word's already out and spreading like a fucking virus, nothing they do can stop it now.'

'What else did they threaten you with?'

Anna's breath whistled between her teeth. 'It's more like what didn't they threaten me with. Legal action, suspension of my benefits. They're even threatening to take away my mum's house. It's a three-bedroomed council house. There are only two of us living here now, so apparently they can force us to move somewhere smaller. I told them straight out, they can do anything they want to me, but if they go near my mum I'll dedicate the rest of my life to exposing each and every one of them for the heartless, paedophile-protecting bastards they are. That shut them up.'

Jim smiled sourly. 'I'll bet it did. What about the journalists?'

Another hiss of breath filled the line. 'You called that right too. No way will they dare publish the list. There's a lot of scepticism out there. I suppose it's understandable. They've been burnt by this kind of thing before. But I get the sense there's a good chance they'll write about what we're doing without mentioning names. How about you? Any trouble?'

'Nothing I can't handle. It's obvious where the leak came from, but they'll struggle to prove anything so long as we're careful who we tell what.'

'Don't worry, I'd never reveal a source.'

'I know you wouldn't. Call me if there are any developments, especially if anyone tries to intimidate you.'

Jim hung up and returned to the computer. The blog's

hit counter was ticking over fast – there'd been more than a thousand visitors since he'd last looked. He Googled Anna's name along with some of the names from the list. Pages of links came up to other blogs that had republished the post. For months he'd felt as inert and lifeless as the investigation. But scanning through the links, he had a sense of things moving, both inside and outside himself. Were they moving in the right direction, though? Right then he didn't really care about the answer to that question. All that mattered was that the status quo was broken.

****

All day Jim remained in front of his computer. By the afternoon brief articles had appeared in the online editions of several newspapers, carrying headlines such as 'Blogger Reveals Alleged High-Profile Paedophile List' and 'Suspected Paedophile List Leaked'. As expected, the fear of libel was too great for the mainstream press to name names. There were also references to past witch-hunts of suspected 'establishment paedophiles', where names had emerged online, only for the accused to later be fully vindicated. There was mention too of Anna's bankruptcy and prison sentences, and one newspaper insidiously marked her out as a scrounger by quoting her as saying that she 'chose to be unemployed so that she could concentrate on her blog'. The first hints perhaps of a smear campaign to come.

At half past four, Jim tried to access the blog again and got an 'Error 404 Page Not Found' message. His phone rang. It was Anna. 'It's down,' she said.

'I know.'

'That was even faster than I expected. There are some people with serious influence throwing their weight around here.'

'What will you do now?'

'Nothing. They're doing far more for me than I could ever do for myself. Their eagerness to silence me only makes my words all the more credible. It's a lesson these idiots never seem to learn. Oh, by the way, I had a visit from Chief Superintendent Garrett earlier.'

'What did he have to say?'

'Only that I'd completely scuppered your investigation.'

Jim blew out a derisive breath. 'The investigation was scuppered before it even got started.'

'He also said he knew where the leak came from.'

'Of course he did. I'll bet he didn't accuse me directly though, did he?'

'Nope.'

Jim's mouth spread into a thin smile. Garrett was far too cautious and calculated to make public accusations he couldn't back up with hard evidence. That was one of the reasons they were in this position. 'Anyone else been in contact?'

'Yeah, I've had a few more threats of libel and injunctions. A silent phone call too.'

A little rise of interest came into Jim's voice. 'What happened?'

'Nothing much. The phone rang. The home phone, not my mobile. I answered and it went dead.'

'What time was this?'

'Just after one.'

'That was three and a half hours ago! I thought we agreed you'd phone me if anyone tried to intimidate you.'

'It was only a silent call. I've had plenty of them over the years. They're par for the course.'

'It could be a lead. You should have let me know straight away.'

'Alright, keep your pants on. If it happens again, I will do.'

Sighing, Jim wondered if Anna's head was screwed on as tight as he'd thought. 'I don't suppose you got a number?'

'Actually, I did. I think it's a phone box number. I tried to find out its location, but BT gave me the usual data protection bollocks.'

Jim reined in his irritation, reminding himself that Anna was a lone wolf with an inbuilt cynicism of authority. He was going to have to win her trust. 'That's where it helps to have a friend in the police. Remember, Anna, we're a team now.' He took the number, hung up and rang someone he knew at BT. They confirmed what Anna suspected – the call had come from a public phone box. What's more, a phone box on Prospect Road, Sheffield. He frowned. That was about five minutes' walk from her house. He phoned her and repeated what he'd been told. 'My guess is this was a warning shot across your bow.'

'I hope so because that'd mean we've really got the fuckers rattled.'

'If you want, I can put a car on your house tonight.'

'No. It would upset Mum. Besides, they wouldn't dare actually hurt me. That'd be as good as an admission of guilt.'

'I'm going to head over your way, find out if anyone saw anything.'

'Are you sure it's wise, you getting involved like this? Won't it make it obvious that the two of us are in contact?'

'It's obvious anyway. This makes it legitimate.'

'So in a way, the caller's done us a favour.'

Jim smiled despite himself. You had to admire Anna's way of looking at things, if not her apparent lack of a self-preservation instinct. 'I'll talk to you soon.'

As Jim drove to Reece's house – a modest semi eerily reminiscent of the house he'd shared with Margaret – he contacted forensics and asked them to check out the phone box. Reece's car was in the driveway with a couple of holdalls in its open boot. The house's front door was open too. As Jim approached it, Reece emerged with another bag and stopped abruptly at the sight of him. 'Jim, what are you doing here?'

'Have you heard what's happened?'

'Yeah, the Chief Superintendent phoned me. He's not a happy bunny.'

'What about you? What do you think?'

Reece puffed his cheeks. 'To be honest, Jim, right now I've got other things on my mind.'

Jim glanced at the bag. 'You going somewhere?'

'London. Only for the night. Staci's got an appointment with an oncologist down there tomorrow morning.'

'A private consultant?'

Reece nodded. 'He's supposed to be the best around.'

'Sounds expensive.'

'It's not cheap. But I've got some money left over from the sale of my dad's house.' Reece turned at the sound of footsteps. Staci and her young daughter, Amelia, appeared at the door. Amelia looked up at Jim, but she didn't have her usual cheeky smile for him. There was a kind of bewildered incomprehension in her eyes, as though she didn't know exactly what was going on, but she sensed it wasn't anything good.

'Hi there, gorgeous,' said Jim, smiling at her.

'Hi,' Amelia replied quietly, her gaze dropping away.

Jim turned his attention to Staci. She was wearing a heavy coat, but even so it was immediately apparent how much weight she'd lost in the month or so since he'd last seen her. Her face looked sucked in and there were shadows of pain around her eyes. Her once-thick strawberry-blonde hair was scraped back into a ponytail, through which showed pale glimpses of scalp. Self-consciously reaching up to check her hair, Staci asked the same question Reece had done, 'What are you doing here, Jim?'

He gave her a small, gentle smile. 'I came to see Reece about something.'

'Do you two need a minute to talk?'

'No. It's nothing that can't wait.' Jim's gaze returned Reece. 'Go on, I don't want to hold you up.'

Reece hurried to put the bag in the boot, before returning to help Staci to the car. With a tenderness that belied his burly frame, he supported her by the hand and elbow. 'Good luck,' Jim said as they passed him.

Staci smiled wanly. 'Thanks.'

Jim flicked them a wave as Reece reversed the car out of the drive. Reece lowered his window. 'About what you asked me before,' he said to Jim. 'It was high fucking time someone did something.'

Jim acknowledged his colleague's support with a nod of thanks. He drove to the phone box and spent the next hour knocking on the doors of nearby houses, asking their occupants if they'd seen anyone using the pay phone around one o'clock. Unsurprisingly, no one had. Equally unsurprisingly, forensics pulled numerous prints off the phone box. The handset, however, was clean. Too clean. Almost as if someone had wiped it over to make extra sure they left no trace of themselves on it. Jim knew then that his guess was right – the call *was* a warning.

By the time he was done, his body was heavy with fatigue. Since his heart attack, he'd lived clean – except for the odd lapse – eaten well and adhered to the prescribed exercise, but even so his energy levels had never really returned to what they'd been. He stopped at a shop on the way home to buy some water to swallow his medication with. His gaze strayed to the alcohol behind the till. How he would have loved a drink, and a cigarette too.

His phone rang. Garrett's name flashed up. He reluctantly put the receiver to his ear. Garrett was the last person he felt like talking to, but he knew he had to answer the call. 'Guess who I've been on the phone to,' snapped the Chief Superintendent.

'Forensics.'

'Got it in one.'

'Anna Young contacted me concerned about a silent phone call.'

Garrett huffed out an incredulous laugh. 'You're a brazen bastard, Jim.'

'I'm just doing my job.'

'Yes, well, how much longer you'll be doing your job for remains to be seen.'

The line went dead. Jim's gaze returned to the alcohol. 'Can I get you something else?' asked the woman behind the till. With a quick shake of his head, he paid and left.

CHAPTER FOUR

For the second morning in a row Jim was woken by that certain kind of knock at his front door. *Christ, what does Garrett want now?* he wondered. 'If he's just going to give me another earful, he can fuck off,' he muttered to himself, heading to the door. He glanced through the spyhole to make sure he was right about who was knocking. He wasn't. On the other side of the door was a broad-shouldered old man wearing a grubby, frayed suit. A thick white beard covered much of his nut-brown, leathery face. Dour brown eyes peered out from beneath equally bushy eyebrows. In contrast, his hair was short and wispy. He had the appearance of someone who'd long since ceased caring what he looked like. Jim guessed him to be somewhere in his mid-seventies. Under one of his arms was tucked a cardboard folder of a type Jim recognised. The sight of the folder sparked Jim's curiosity as much, if not more so, than the presence of its bearer. He opened the door and waited for the man to speak.

'Jim Monahan?' The voice had a gravelly Mancunian accent.

'Who's asking?'

'Lance Brennan.' The man pulled out a battered leather wallet and flipped it open, displaying the silver star logo of the Greater Manchester Police and a detective inspector's ID, which Jim noted had expired over twenty years ago. 'I want to talk to you about Thomas Villiers and *that* list of names he's on.'

His eyes pinching at the corners, Jim glanced over the ex-detective's shoulder at the quiet Sunday morning street. 'I'm alone,' said Lance, and something about the way he said it suggested he was talking in the broader as well as the narrower context.

Jim's gaze returned to Lance's grizzled face. He looked genuine. Still, you never knew. Villiers and his scumbag pals would no doubt be looking for ways to discredit or disgrace their accusers. And there were plenty of hacks around who would stoop to dirty tricks to get a story. 'Lift your arms.'

Lance did so. 'I'm not wearing a wire.'

Jim patted him down and checked his pockets for recording devices. He was telling the truth. There was a lock-blade knife in one of his pockets. Jim eyed him narrowly. 'What's this for?'

'Protection.'

'From who?'

'You know who.'

The two men stared at each other a moment. Jim got the feeling that Lance was checking him out as much as he was checking the ex-policeman out. 'You'd better come in.'

'What about my knife?'

'I'll hold onto it for now.'

Jim led Lance to the spartanly furnished living room. He gestured to the older man to sit on a faded floral patterned sofa – one of the few pieces of furniture he'd brought with him from the house. 'Do you want a cup of tea?'

'That'd be good, thanks. I'm parched. I've been travelling since six this morning.'

'From Manchester?'

'Uh-huh.'

'Who gave you my address?'

Lance gave him a look as if to say, *C'mon, you know I can't tell you that.* It was the response Jim had been looking for. No good cop – and as the cliché went, once a cop always a cop – ever revealed their sources. Somewhat reassured, he went into the kitchen, picked up a notebook from beside a phone and flipped through it until he came to the name 'Don Hunter'. Don was a Manchester DI he'd worked in conjunction with on several cases over the years. He dialled the number next to the name. 'It's Jim Monahan,' he said, when Don picked up. 'Sorry to bother you on a Sunday, Don, but I need a favour. What can you tell me about an ex-DI from your neck of the woods named Lance Brennan?'

'The name doesn't ring any bells. I'll see what I can find out.'

Jim thanked Don and turned his attention to the kettle. He made two mugs of tea and took them to the living room. Lance pulled out a hip flask and poured a generous slug of something into his mug. He proffered the flask to Jim.

Shaking his head, Jim sank onto an armchair. Lance took a swig of tea, then raised his wily old detective's eyes to Jim. 'You hate Villiers, don't you?'

Jim made no reply. Yes, he hated Villiers. He hated everyone in Herbert's book, savagely, uncompromisingly. But he wasn't ready to admit that to a stranger.

Lance nodded as though he'd read all he needed to know in Jim's eyes. 'I do too.' His voice was thick with bitterness. 'I hate that bastard worse than anything, and I don't care who knows it. That's one of the benefits of growing old – not having to lie about how you feel any more. And I'll tell you something else, I've been thinking a lot lately about using that knife of mine on Villiers.'

Jim frowned. 'You should be careful what you say to me, Mr Brennan. Regardless of my personal feelings, I'm still a copper.'

Lance dismissed his words with a disdainful grunt. 'It's not a crime to think about something. Not yet. And anyway, what you've done is almost as good as sticking a knife in Villiers.'

'If you're implying what I think you are, Mr Brennan—'

'Please, let's dispense with the Mr Brennan crap. And all the rest of the horseshit too. I'm not here to put one over on you. I'm here to shake your hand. You've done what I didn't have the balls to do twenty-odd years ago.'

Jim's voice quickened as curiosity overcame his caginess. 'Are you saying you knew about the names on the list back then?'

'No. But I knew about Villiers and...' Lance's voice faltered. A spasm of self-disgust passed over his face. 'And I did nothing. Well, not quite nothing, but that's what it amounted to.' He looked at Jim with a kind of haunted appeal in his eyes. 'You see, they gave me a choice: keep my gob shut or lose my pension. I couldn't lose my pension. It was all I had left. They'd already taken the job away from me. I had a wife and kids to support. And I couldn't even get work as a security guard because of all the lies they spouted to cover their arses. I tell you, for years I used to wake up every day thinking about suicide. Only one thing stopped me from doing it. Do you know what that thing was? It wasn't my wife, God rest her soul, or even my kids. It was my allotment. That was my escape. The one place I could get away from thinking about how I let Villiers off the hook. There's something about planting and growing that—'

'So what exactly do you know about Villiers?' interrupted Jim, eager to keep Lance on topic, but also uncomfortable with the talk of suicide – he'd entertained many dark thoughts of his own since Margaret's death.

Slowly, as though arranging his thoughts, the ex-detective began, 'Back in 1989 we arrested a sixteen-year-old boy named Dave Ward for—'

Lance broke off as a phone rang. Jim went into the kitchen to answer it. Don Hunter came on the line. 'Lance Brennan served with the Greater Manchester Police from '71 to '90. He spent ten years in CID before taking release on health grounds. Is that enough for you, Jim? Or do you need me to do some more digging?'

'No, that's great, Don. I owe you one.'

When Jim returned to the living room, Lance eyed him knowingly. 'Well, are you satisfied that I am what I say I am?'

Jim nodded. He'd already made up his mind that Lance was for real; the phone call just confirmed it. He motioned for him to continue his story.

'Now, where was I?' Lance took a swallow of his alcohol-laced tea. 'Ah yes, Dave Ward. We arrested him for soliciting sex in a men's toilet. Whilst in custody Ward started on about how he was the way he was because he'd been sexually abused. So I was called in to assist from the Sexual Crimes Unit. Ward came from a bad background. He'd spent most of his life in care. From the age of thirteen to sixteen he'd lived at the Hopeland children's home in Manchester. It was there he claimed the abuse had taken place. I'll bet you can guess who ran the place?'

'Thomas Villiers.'

'Got it in one. According to Ward, the abuse began with small acts that might have simply been interpreted as friendliness. And it wasn't initiated by Villiers. There was a live-in caretaker at the home. A man who by all accounts was only a year or three older than the eldest children there.'

Lance withdrew a sheet of paper from the cardboard file and passed it to Jim. On it was a composite police picture of a man's face. The man was white with short brown hair, brown eyes and black-rimmed glasses. He had a broad blunt nose and thick lips. His face too was broad, the cheeks smooth and round with puppy fat. He looked little more than a boy himself. But that didn't mean he wasn't dangerous. Older paedophiles often used younger accomplices – who many times had been victims of abuse themselves – to entice and ensnare children.

'Supposedly his name was William Keyes,' said Lance.

'What do you mean "supposedly"?'

'I'll get to that in a bit. And besides, the children at Hopeland didn't call Keyes by his name. They called him Spider because he had a spider's web tattoo on his chest. So that's what I call him too. Spider started working at Hopeland in October '87. He had a mixed relationship with the children. Some couldn't stand him. Others got on well with him. Ward fell into the latter group. He used to go to Spider with his problems. And when they were talking, Spider would put a hand on Ward's knee or an arm around his shoulder. The touching gradually became more inappropriate, until one day Spider groped Ward's genitals through his trousers. When Ward pushed him away, Spider claimed it was an accident. Ward didn't want to get him in trouble, so he didn't tell anyone what had happened. Spider bought him some clothes as a thank you. A few weeks went by. Then there was another incident. And this wasn't an accident by any definition of the word. One evening Spider invited Ward to his room to smoke cannabis and watch what turned out to be a pornographic movie. During the movie, he began to fondle Ward. When Ward asked him to stop, Spider pinned him down and forcibly masturbated him. Once again, Ward told no one what had happened. Do you know why?'

'Because Spider threatened him.'

Lance shook his head. 'He didn't need to. Ward was ashamed because he'd ejaculated. He thought the other kids would call him a puff if they found out. Can you believe that?'

Jim could believe it only too well. He'd encountered similar stories across the whole spectrum of abuse – victims who kept silent through fear of ridicule or not being believed; victims who'd been manipulated into blaming themselves; victims whose shame irrationally led them to believe silence was their best defence against a world that had betrayed them.

'So anyway,' continued Lance, 'the next day Spider bought Ward some trainers he wanted. And that was the pattern from then on. The incidents continued and grew more serious, and after each one Spider would buy Ward a present. After a couple of months it must've been deemed that Ward was ready for the next step in the...' His broken-veined nose wrinkled as he sought a suitable word. 'Process. One night, after plying Ward with alcohol, Spider took him for a drive in his van.'

'What type of van?'

'It was a blue Peugeot that was provided by the home for Spider's use. Ward was made to sit in the back so he couldn't see where they were going. After what he reckoned to be an hour or so, they pulled up at a house. A big place. It was dark and Spider parked in a garage connected to the house, so Ward didn't get a proper look at its exterior. There was a party going on, with lots of what Ward called "important-looking people in suits". He was fed alcohol and drugs until he barely knew up from down. Then the poor sod was subjected to a series of sexual assaults, including multiple anal penetrations. Basically, they used him like a piece of meat. And when they were done he was given a couple of hundred quid and returned to the home. He was warned too that if he told anyone about what had happened, he would find himself facing prostitution charges. And he believed it. Over the next two years, Ward was taken to the house on eight or nine occasions. Sometimes there were only one or two people besides himself and Spider there. Other times parties were taking place, where he and other children, males and females, were – as he described it – passed around like joints.'

Jim felt a fist of anger pushing up his throat. The description was horribly apt. To their abusers, Ward and his fellow victims weren't human beings. They were objects, things to be enjoyed and disposed of. He swallowed the feeling. Now wasn't the time for anger. Now was the time for calm, rational thought. One thing Lance had said struck him as particularly relevant: the house Dave Ward had been taken to had a garage connected to it. Whereas the Winstanleys' house had a detached garage. 'Did you try to find the house?'

'Of course. I took Ward out several times in search of it. But we never found it.'

'What about the other children? Did you find out who they were?'

'No. But I interviewed dozens of current and former residents of the Hopeland home, and I did manage to find others who were willing to talk about how they'd been groomed and abused by Spider.'

Lance withdrew three mugshot-type Polaroids from the folder and handed them to Jim. One was of a black boy of about fifteen or sixteen. 'Jamal Jackson' was written on the Polaroid's margin. The others were of white girls. Both had blonde hair. Both also looked to be in their mid-teens. Their names were Heather Shanks and Debbie Tompkins. All three had the blank-eyed thousand-yard stare that Jim had seen so many times in abuse survivors. Again, the fist pushed up his throat. Again, he swallowed it back down.

'I took those at the time I interviewed them,' explained Lance. 'Shanks was thirteen when the abuse began. Tompkins fourteen. They'd both been taken on separate occasions to parties at different houses to Ward. Jamal was twelve. Things hadn't got that far along with him. He'd engaged in masturbatory and oral sex with Spider, but not penetrative sex. That seems to have been the final test, as it were. If they were willing to take part in penetrative sex, they were ready for the next step.'

'I don't suppose you found the houses the girls were taken to either?'

'No. Not for want of looking.'

'What about names? Did they give you any?' When Lance replied in the negative again, Jim said, 'So they didn't implicate Villiers.'

'Not directly. But he was well aware of what was going on. You see, not all the kids were willing to put up with Spider's *accidental* touching. Some complained about it to Villiers. But their complaints fell on deaf ears.'

'Did you speak to Villiers about the complaints?'

'Yes. He claimed he'd investigated them and found them to be unjustified.'

Jim tapped the composite sketch. 'And what about Mr Keyes? Did you speak to him too?'

'That would have been difficult, unless I could talk to ghosts – which I can't.'

'He died?'

'In '83 in a car accident. Four years before Dave Ward was first abused.'

Confusion momentarily creased Jim's face, then realisation gleamed in his eyes. 'Spider was using a dead man's identity.'

Lance nodded. 'I first visited Hopeland three days after

my initial interview of Ward, by which time Spider and all his belongings were gone.'

'Did anyone there know you were coming?'

Lance shook his head, tilting his eyebrows into a crooked arch, as if to say, *Make of that what you will.* 'His room had been cleaned top to bottom too. I can still remember it now. Every surface sparkled. We didn't manage to recover a single usable fingerprint. What's more, all of the caretaker's equipment had been replaced. The mops, the brushes, the cleaning fluids, the tools... everything was brand spanking new. Someone had gone to a lot of trouble to make sure no trace of Spider was left behind. And no one at the home knew anything about where Spider came from or where he'd gone. I spent months searching for the bastard without success. To all intents and purposes, he might as well have been a real ghost. So I decided to focus on building a case against Villiers. I didn't do a bad job of it either. Spider had a reputation amongst the kids as a "toucher". Three complaints had been made against him during the two years he worked at the home. All three complainants had subsequently been moved to other homes. There were no records of Villiers formally investigating their accusations. At best, Villiers' actions amounted to criminal negligence. At worst, they implicated him as an accomplice to the abuse. I was ready to prosecute, but then...' Lance's voice and eyes trailed away. Lines gathered on the lines of his craggy face.

'Then what?' pressed Jim.

Lance heaved a sigh. 'Ward was found dead with a needle hanging out of his arm. There was a coroner's inquest. Verdict: overdose. Death by misadventure.'

'But you thought otherwise.'

'You bet I bloody did. Traces of heroin were found in his bedroom. It was ninety per cent pure. Potent enough to kill him before he could even remove the syringe from his vein.'

'Someone sold him a hot-shot.'

'Exactly. Of course, it was impossible to prove.' Lance sighed again. He pulled out his hip flask and drank directly from it, before going on, 'A few days after Ward's death, Jamal Jackson withdrew his statement. Then Debbie Tompkins and Heather Shanks followed suit. It was as clear as day that they were being pressurised. They were all of them scared half to death. You could see it in their eyes. The final nail came when I was informed that the case was being dropped.' Contempt drew his lips back from his yellowed teeth. 'The powers that be had decided it wasn't in the public interest to proceed with a prosecution. Insufficient evidence. So the file was marked "No Further Action" and shelved. But I wasn't willing to take no further action. I kept on talking to former residents of Hopeland and following Villiers in my spare time. One day I went to consult the case-file on some detail or other and found it was gone. My superiors would only tell me it had been taken elsewhere for safe keeping. After a lot of asking around, I learnt a couple of Special Branch officers had shown up at the office and left with it. I called Special Branch and got stonewalled. They refused to even admit they'd been to the office.'

'You're saying they buried the file.'

Lance nodded. 'That's when I realised how big this thing was. The next thing I knew I was summoned to my Super's office. He had photos of Villiers looking like he'd been ten rounds with a gorilla. The bastard claimed I'd done it to him. And he had a witness who'd seen me following him the night he said it happened. I was suspended from duty while an investigation was carried out. I was sure I was going to be cleared. After all, it came down to my word against Villiers'. And I was a copper with almost twenty years' service. I thought that counted for something. I was wrong. It was decided there was enough evidence to charge me. But Villiers was willing not to press charges as long as I bowed out quietly. So that's what I did.'

Lance's gaze dropped, taking his head with it. Jim could almost feel the weight of shame pressing on the ex-detective. After a minute or so, Lance went on in a subdued tone, 'That's the one thing I can't forgive myself. When I think about Villiers and those children and all the other children who must have come under his care since then, it's like all the good things I did – the thieves, rapists and murderers I locked up – it's like all that counts for nothing.'

Jim wondered if Lance was fishing for sympathy. If so, he was casting a hook in the wrong place. Jim understood why Lance had compromised in the way he did, but he had no respect for it. His own unwillingness to compromise had cost him a higher price than he could ever have imagined. He briefly wondered what he would do if he could go back in time, knowing what he knew now. Would he let Edward Forester off the hook if it saved Margaret? The question was arbitrary. There was no going back. 'What else is in that file of yours?'

Lance pulled himself upright with a visible effort. 'A few years after getting sacked, I decided to put together a file of my own on Hopeland. I already had copies of some of the victims' statements. I rewrote the others and my own notes as best I could from memory. I hoped the file might one day be of help to someone. Although, to be honest, I stopped believing a long time ago that my hope would ever be fulfilled. Then, yesterday, my son rang me to tell me about the list.' A spectre of guilt flickered in his expression again. 'After cancer took his mother four years ago, I told him about the Hopeland case. I wanted to try and make him understand why things had gone so wrong for our family. Turns out he set up an alert on his computer to let him know if Villiers was mentioned on the internet. So here I am.'

Slowly, carefully, as if he was handing over a flaming torch, Lance proffered the file.

Jim accepted it. 'Why bring this to me?'

'I considered coming to you when it first came out about what went on at the Winstanleys' house. But I had to be sure you weren't just another puppet of the same bastards who did for me. Now I know you'll do what I couldn't and nail Villiers.'

Not just Villiers, thought Jim. *All of them.* He rose to his feet. 'I'd better phone my Super. He needs to hear your story.'

Lance stood up too. 'You'll have to tell him it for me. I've never had much liking for the brass.' He indicated the case-file. 'My number's in there if you need me.'

They made their way to the front door. Lance held out his thick, dirty-nailed hand. His eyes were watery, pained. 'If you do speak to the children, let them know how sorry I am.'

Jim wondered whether Lance was referring to Debbie, Heather and Jamal, who would be in their late thirties by now, or whether he meant all the children who'd ever come under Thomas Villiers' care? He shook the ex-inspector's hand. Lance shuffled away, stooped with regret. Still, no flicker of pity came into Jim's heart. If anything, he felt a touch of envy. Lance had been given a choice, and as perhaps any right-minded person would, he'd chosen his family. That didn't mean he'd made the right choice, if such a thing even existed. But whatever the rights or wrongs, his regret was a small price to pay for the knowledge that he wouldn't live and die a lonely man. For many years Jim had thought of the police force as a kind of extended family. By the time he realised his mistake, Margaret had already walked out on him. He felt close to no one in the job now, apart from Reece. In some perverse way, the names from Herbert Winstanley's book were more akin to family. They were bonded to him by blood. Margaret's blood. There were no more choices. Only two things could part him from them – imprisonment or death.

He returned to the case-file. As Lance had said, there were photocopies of statements mixed in with seventy or so pages of handwritten notes. There was also a map of Manchester and the surrounding region with red lines drawn on it to indicate Lance's fruitless search for the houses the children had been taken to. *Is this it?* he wondered. *Is this the break that will finally bring it all down?* As he skimmed through the pages, he reached for the phone and dialled Garrett. 'What do you want?' the DCS asked coldly upon picking up.

'I need to speak to you.'

'So speak.'

'Face to face. Some new information's come to light.'

A hesitant note entered Garrett's voice. 'What new information?'

Jim's gaze moved back and forth over the notes, lingering on words and phrases like 'inappropriate sexual contact', 'touching', 'oral sex', 'vaginal and anal penetration'. 'I don't want to say over the phone.'

'OK, I'll meet you at headquarters. But this had better be good.'

Good. The inappropriateness of the word struck Jim. There was nothing *good* about any of this. He quickly showered and shaved. He considered putting on a work suit, but decided against it. Garrett was never more at ease than when they were wearing their respective uniforms. And he didn't want him to be at ease. He wanted him to know – as if he didn't already – that this was about more than simply doing the job.

When Jim arrived at Police HQ, he didn't go directly to

Garrett's office. He stopped off first at the photocopy room and made a copy of the case-file. Then he locked the original in his desk drawer. He didn't bother to knock on Garrett's door. He stepped straight into the office – a dour room with the usual desk, computer, chairs, telephone and shelves of folders and manuals, and a window looking out on an equally soulless concrete building. Garrett was sitting behind the desk in full uniform. Unlike the previous day, he was shaved and composed. Only the faintest ripple of annoyance passed over his face at Jim's unannounced entrance. Jim slapped the folder down on the desk. The DCS looked at it, but didn't reach to pick it up. Again his voice came hesitantly, almost as if he feared he was being led into some kind of trap. 'What's this?'

'Read it,' came the abrupt reply.

Garrett motioned for Jim to sit. But Jim remained standing, looming over the desk like a lion ready to pounce. Shifting a little uncomfortably in his chair, Garrett opened the folder. After flipping through several pages, he looked up at Jim, his forehead marked by deep furrows. 'Where did you get this?'

'From the man who wrote it.'

'And how is it possible we don't already know about this?'

'Because it was buried beyond our sight.'

Jim repeated what Lance had told him about Special Branch appropriating the case-file. Garrett's expression became dubious. 'Are you seriously suggesting Special Branch suppressed evidence about a paedophile ring?'

'Why is that so implausible? In fact, why is it so different to what's been happening around here these past months?'

Garrett's thin veneer of composure faltered. His voice rose. 'There's no comparison. This file contains direct evidence of abuse. If I'd known about its existence previously, I'd have—'

'What would you have done?' broke in Jim, his voice harsh

with challenge. 'Would you have let me interview the children at the Craig Thorpe home about Villiers?' He slapped the file with the back of his hand. 'Would you have even let me talk to the names in there?'

'I would have let you do whatever the evidence warranted.' Garrett slammed a palm against the desktop. 'We do not protect criminals around here, Chief Inspector Monahan, no matter who they bloody well are.'

Prove it, retorted Jim's eyes.

'I—' Garrett started to say, but he bit down on his words and continued in a controlled tone, 'I need to make some enquiries. I'll let you know when I'm done.'

'I'll be in my office.'

Whilst Jim waited, he gave the file a more thorough read through. Lance's hatred of Villiers shone through in his writing. Usually such files consisted, for the most part, of a dry recounting of facts. But Lance had included his personal impressions of Villiers as being, amongst other things, manipulative, arrogant, devious and egocentric. What had really raised Lance's hackles, though, was Villiers' refusal to admit any kind of responsibility for the abuse that had taken place right under his nose. At that point in the notes, Lance's writing took on an unbalanced, ranting quality that left Jim wondering whether he had been truthful about not assaulting Villiers.

He set the file aside. The background information it contained on Villiers added nothing to what he already knew. Far more important were the victims' statements. He logged onto the PNC database and searched to see if any of them had a record. Heather Shanks had convictions for drugs offences and prostitution. Jamal Jackson had a long history of assaults, petty theft and burglary. As recently as 2012, he'd served time in HMP Leeds for handling stolen goods. Jim wasn't surprised.

In the race of life, the poor sods had started so far behind they'd never stood a chance. According to the computer, Heather still lived in Manchester and Jamal lived in Liverpool. Jim found Debbie Tompkins on the DVLA database. She lived in Tideswell – a pretty Peak District village located between Sheffield and Manchester. Jim felt a glimmer of hope that maybe she'd found some way to overcome the handicaps of her past.

The office phone rang. It was an internal call. Jim didn't bother answering it, he simply stood and returned to Garrett's office. Garrett's mouth was set in a tense line, as though he was prepared for a confrontation. He cleared his throat and began. 'I've been on the phone for the past hour and I've learnt some interesting things about this,' he tapped the case-file, 'and its author. Firstly, the original file wasn't taken by Special Branch. It was simply removed by Lance Brennan's superiors to a place beyond his reach.'

'Why?'

'Because Brennan was obsessed with Thomas Villiers. He publicly accused him of murdering Dave Ward. And when the Hopeland case was dropped, he made all sorts of threats against him. Several of his colleagues expressed their concerns that he would carry them through, and it seems they were proved right.'

'Brennan claims he never touched Villiers. But even if he did, it doesn't change the basic facts of the case.'

'And what are those facts? Four children were abused at Hopeland by a man who called himself William Keyes. There was no evidence that Villiers, or any staff at Hopeland besides Keyes, were involved in the abuse.'

'What about the three children who made complaints against Keyes? Complaints which Villiers didn't investigate.'

'He may have failed to properly carry out his duties, but that doesn't prove he was an accomplice to the abuse.'

Jim gave a dismissive swipe of his hand. 'Villiers was in on it then, and he's in on it now. Have you read the victims' statements? How they were *accidentally touched*, asked questions about their sexual experiences, shown pornographic films. Sound familiar, does it? Well it should do, because Henry Reeve was pulling the same tricks at the Craig Thorpe home. And what about the country house orgies? I suppose it's all just coincidence, is it?'

'Of course not, but the fact is this case-file changes nothing. We still don't have the evidence to charge Villiers.'

'No, but we might be able to get it now.'

'How? By talking to the children at the Craig Thorpe home? If anything, this just proves that would be a waste of time.'

'What about talking to the Hopeland victims?'

Garrett shook his head. 'That case was dead in '89. What good would resurrecting it do?'

Jim threw up his hands. 'I knew it! I fucking knew it. They're going to bury my investigation the same way they buried Brennan's. In fact, they already have done.'

'No one's burying anything. There's no conspiracy here.'

'Isn't there?' Jim fixed Garrett with a penetrating stare. 'You know me as well as anyone around here. And I know you. I know exactly what you're about. Now look me in the eyes and tell me I'm wrong.'

Garrett held Jim's gaze and repeated, 'We don't protect criminals.'

'Then let me talk to the Hopeland victims.'

'For what purpose? What could that possibly achieve besides opening up old wounds?'

'Probably nothing with Jamal Jackson. But Debbie Tompkins and Heather Shanks might recognise their abusers from amongst the names in Herbert's book.'

'And what if they did? Where would that get us?' Garrett gestured at the victims' statements. 'These people have zero credibility. They retracted their statements. And they've kept quiet for over twenty years. Nothing they say will stand up in court.'

'Not necessarily. If I can prove they were intimidated into dropping their accusations—'

'How are you going to do that after so much time has passed?'

'I don't know. And if I don't try, I won't find out. That's all I ask, just let me try.'

Garrett was silent a moment, his forehead wrinkled as though he was pained by what he had to say next. He gave a little shake of his head. 'I'm sorry, Jim. I can't.'

The apology as good as confirmed to Jim that his suspicions were true. He could almost hear the thud of the 'No Further Action' stamp being brought down on the files he'd compiled against Villiers and the rest of them. He made a cutting movement with his hand, as though severing an invisible cord. There was no point arguing further. Garrett was nothing more than a mouthpiece for higher forces. 'Do you know something? There was a moment back when you gave me this job that I thought I saw something else in you. Something more than just a badge on a uniform. Clearly I was wrong.' He made to pick up the case-file, but Garrett laid a firm hand on it.

'Listen to me carefully, Chief Inspector Monahan,' he said. 'If I find out you've talked to the Hopeland victims, you will be suspended from duty with immediate effect. Do I make myself clear?'

'Yes.'

Garrett's voice jumped. 'Yes what?'

A sardonic edge came into Jim's tone. 'Yes, sir. May I be dismissed?'

'Go on, get out of my sight.'

Pausing at the door, Jim glanced back at Garrett and said sadly, 'There are some wounds that never heal.'

The Chief Superintendent blinked and looked away from him.

On his way out of the building, Jim collected the case-file from his office, along with printouts of the Hopeland victims' up-to-date particulars and photos of everyone in Herbert's book. A reckless anger was surging in him – anger at Garrett's cowardly careerism; anger at himself for being foolish enough to expect any different; but mostly, anger at the invisible fingers of power that were pulling him back at every step. He punched Anna Young's number into his mobile phone and when she picked up, he said, 'We need to meet.'

CHAPTER FIVE

The camper van grumbled its way up the hill. Ahead loomed a broad sweep of purple-flowering moorland. Behind, Sheffield stretched away into the haze of the summer day. Anna pulled into a layby thinly screened from the road by bushes. Jim was already there. He got out of his car and approached the camper van, glancing around warily. He was holding a cardboard folder. Anna leant across to unlock the door and he climbed into the passenger seat. 'Did you do as I said?' he asked.

Anna nodded. 'I drove all the way to Manor Top before doubling back on myself. I'm positive no one followed me. You sounded properly pissed off on the phone. What's happened?'

'Before I say, you have to promise you'll keep what I tell you to yourself until I give you the go-ahead to put it out there.'

'Sure, I promise.'

'An ex-inspector named Lance Brennan came to me today with information about Villiers.' Jim gave Anna a quick rundown of the Hopeland case details.

She listened with an increasing expression of disgust. 'The filthy fucking bastards,' she growled when Jim finished. He couldn't tell whether she was referring to the abusers, the officials who'd buried the case or both. 'No one can say now that you haven't got good reason to come down on Villiers with everything you've got.'

'You'd think so, wouldn't you?'

'What does that mean?'

'I've been ordered not to talk to the victims.' Jim's voice was low, as though he was ashamed of what he was saying. 'The Hopeland case is closed, and as far as my superiors are concerned, it's going to stay that way.'

Anna let out a scathing laugh. 'It really is true what they say, isn't it? It's one fucking law for the rich and another for the rest of us.'

Jim made no reply. Like most coppers, he'd joined the force believing in one law for all. And like most coppers, he'd quickly come to realise that money, connections and lawyers made a mockery of such ideals.

'So let me guess,' continued Anna, 'you want me to talk to the victims, find out if their abusers are on the list.'

'Yes.'

'Have you got their addresses?'

Jim patted the folder. 'Everything you need's in here.'

'You'd better hand it over then.'

Jim started to do so, but a familiar hesitation stayed his hand.

'You're not going to try talking me out of doing what you need doing again, are you?' Anna said, reading his troubled expression. 'Because if you are, don't waste your breath. I'm in this now. All the way. With or without you.' Her voice was as inflexible as Jim's obsession with bringing down Villiers.

With a small sigh, he passed her the folder. 'If anyone asks where you got it from, tell them Lance Brennan gave it to you. He'll back you up if necessary.'

Anna flicked through the case-notes. She stopped suddenly, her face rigid, white. 'It's him.' The words came like she was dragging them from some place deep within. 'It's one of the fuckers who took Jessica.'

Jim's eyebrows pinched together. Anna was looking at the composite picture of Spider. 'Are you sure?'

Her eyes snapped up to his, blazing at his doubt. 'Of course I'm fucking sure!' She snatched out her phone and brought up a photo of the sketch the police artist had drawn from her description twenty years earlier. The chubby cheeks, the cropped brown hair, the snub nose and thick lips. It would have been an exact match, if Spider had been wearing black-rimmed glasses.

Jim couldn't deny the truth of his eyes. 'You're right. It's him.'

Anna's gaze moved like a dreamer's between the two sketches. 'And I was right about something else too – the other one of Jessica's abductors *was* Freddie Harding.'

'We still can't know that for sure.'

'Bollocks we can't!' Anna flipped the file shut and started the engine. She cast Jim an impatient look, as if to say, *What are you still here for?*

'Where are you going?'

'Where do you think? Tideswell's nearest to here, so I'll go there first.'

'Maybe you should take a few hours, clear your head and think about what you need to ask.'

'Fuck that. I've been thinking for twenty long years about what I'd ask if I had a chance like this. And the only thing that'll ever clear my head is finding out what that bastard,' she stabbed a finger trembling with eagerness at the sketch, 'and Harding did to Jessica.'

Jim took on a tone of concerned warning. 'Don't let your need to know the truth get the better of you, Anna.' As her mouth fell open incredulously, he continued, 'I realise I'm hardly the one to be handing out such advice. But take it from someone who's been there, it's not worth it. Do you hear?'

Sucking in a steadying breath, Anna nodded. Jim looked at her a moment as though trying to gauge the genuineness of her response. Then he got out of the van.

Without even a glance of goodbye, she accelerated away from the layby. Following signs for Chapel-en-le-Frith, she crossed the moor and descended its far side into a deep wooded valley. Her speed crept up, until she was careering around bends. Then she was climbing out of the valley onto a plateau of drystone-walled fields and limestone outcrops. Familiar gut-wrenching images looped through her brain. Jessica's abductor – Spider – carrying her limp body towards the van; herself lurching after them; the tearing sound; the keyring; the van speeding away; then... What then? Was this it? Was she finally about to find out what then? A vague sense of panic wrapped itself around her. Did she really want to know what then? Jessica had to be long dead – surely. She knew that, and yet until that moment, she realised, she'd never accepted it. Not truly. She thrust the panic away. She had to find Jessica, dead or alive. She had to know the truth. Jim was wrong. No matter how painful the consequences, the truth was always worth it.

She eased off the accelerator as she reached the outskirts of Tideswell. The road wound through a narrow high street of stone cottages, small shops, cafés and pubs overlooked by the pinnacled tower of the parish church. She pulled over, took out her phone and typed Debbie Tompkins' address into Google maps. Debbie's house was on a side road not far beyond the church. Before making her way there, she forced herself to take a moment to read through Debbie's background history and statement. In 1988 social services had removed Debbie from the house on Moss Side she shared with her crack-addicted parents and placed her at Hopeland. Debbie herself had been heavily experimenting with drugs since the age of eleven. She was an easy target for Spider. He supplied her with a steady flow of alcohol and softer drugs such as cannabis and LSD, cultivating her dependence on him until she was willing to provide sexual favours. Over a period of nine or ten months, he'd taken her to five parties at what she thought were two different houses – she'd been too out of it on booze and drugs to be certain of that last detail. Her experiences had been pretty much identical to Dave Ward's. She'd travelled to the parties in the back of Spider's van. She didn't know the location of the houses or the names of any of the people she'd been abused by at them. She'd been paid two hundred quid – more money than she'd ever seen in her life – and warned to keep her gob shut.

A tormented rage gleamed in Anna's eyes. Is that what had happened to Jessica? Had she been taken to some country pile to be the plaything of rich perverts? She screwed up her face uncertainly. It didn't seem to fit the pattern. These people carefully groomed their victims. They didn't snatch them randomly off the streets. More likely Jessica had suffered the same fate as Freddie Harding's and Edward Forester's victims. Again, threads of doubt pulled at Anna. If that was the case, why hadn't Jessica's DNA been found at Forester's bunker? And why had Harding and Forester deviated from their own pattern? For over thirty years the half-brothers had successfully abducted and murdered prostitutes. Girls they knew were unlikely to be missed. Not girls from loving families. The only known time Harding had strayed from that formula he'd ended up serving a four-year prison sentence. No, Jessica's abduction was something else. Her gaze returned to the sketch of Spider. She remembered the ugliness she'd seen in his eyes. The desire.

He'd looked at Jessica as though no one else existed, a look that said, *You're mine and mine alone.*

Debbie Tompkins' house was a pretty cottage with a small, well-kept garden. She appeared to have done well for herself, especially considering what she'd been through. Anna knew only too well how difficult it was to break free of past trauma and build a new life. She felt uneasy about raking up that trauma. But there was no hesitation in her movements as she approached the door and knocked on it. The truth – that was what mattered most.

A slimly built woman of around forty – bobbed auburn hair and a tanned, makeupless face – answered the door. She looked at Anna with direct, clear blue eyes that betrayed no hint of her past. 'Hello, Debbie,' said Anna, recognising her from her driving licence photo.

'Hello. Do I know you?'

'No. My name's Anna Young. I was wondering if we could speak for a moment.'

'About what?'

Anna could detect no trace of a Manchester accent. Debbie had obviously worked hard to reinvent herself. 'Do you mind if I come in? It would be better if we talked inside.'

A faint wrinkle formed on Debbie's forehead. The first indicator, perhaps, of some well-concealed inner anxiety. 'Is this some kind of sales pitch, because if—'

Anna cut Debbie off with a shake of her head. 'I just want to talk. It won't take long.'

'What did you say your name was again?' Debbie's voice was tinged with caution now. 'And how did you get my address?'

'Anna Young. I got your address off someone who I suppose you could say was a mutual friend of sorts. I'm searching for my sister. I was hoping you might be able to help me find her.'

'Why would I know where your sister is?'

Anna showed Debbie the dog-eared photo of Jessica that she carried everywhere with her. It had been taken at Jessica's thirteenth birthday party and it captured her dollish eyes and pouting lips perfectly. Debbie's gaze flicked doubtfully between the photo and Anna. 'You're thinking that she's too young to be my sister, aren't you?' said Anna.

'Well… yes, actually I am.'

'That photo was taken twenty years ago. Less than a month before my sister was abducted by this man.' Watching closely for Debbie's reaction, Anna showed her the sketch of Spider. In an instant, Debbie's face became as blank as ice. Her lack of expression was more telling than any amount of histrionics. 'You recognise him, don't you?'

Debbie mutely shook her head.

'He was the caretaker at Hopeland children's home at the time you were there,' persisted Anna. 'You knew him as William Keyes or Spider.'

With another shake of her head, Debbie started to close the door. Anna jammed her foot between it and the frame. 'Please, Debbie, I know what you went through. I know how hard this must be for you.' She pointed at the sketch. 'But him and Thomas Villiers and all the others like them can't be allowed to get away with what they've done and what they're still—'

'Move your foot,' cut in Debbie, her voice as deadpan as her face.

'We have a chance to stop them. It might be the only one we get.'

Debbie jerked the door back then slammed it forwards, forcing Anna to withdraw her foot. Anna hammered her palm against the door, shouting, 'Look Villiers up on the internet.

82

You'll see what I'm talking about. We can get the bastards, Debbie.'

Anna bit down on any more words she might have said. The last thing she wanted was to arouse Debbie's neighbours' curiosity. Tideswell was a small, isolated village, the kind of place where once word of anything got out it spread fast.

She retreated to her camper van, lit a cigarette and waited to see if her parting words had any effect. Fifteen minutes passed. Debbie's door showed no sign of opening. Anna reached for the case-file again. Heather Shanks was only twelve when she was placed at Hopeland. She'd been there several months when Spider came onto the scene. Like Debbie Tompkins, Heather was the product of a loveless, abusive home. Unlike Debbie, Spider hadn't groomed her with drugs, he'd used something even more insidious. For months he'd bombarded her with affection, carefully nurturing her emotional dependency on him. He'd made her believe he was the only person in the world who truly cared for her. Then he'd betrayed that belief in the worst way imaginable.

Her nose puckering as though she'd touched something slimy, Anna set the folder aside. She glanced at the dashboard clock. It had been half an hour. Debbie clearly wasn't about to change her mind any time soon. Anna wasn't surprised. Nor did she feel any anger towards Debbie. It took a special kind of person to escape a past like hers. Most never truly managed it, no matter how hard they tried. And those that did would have to be extraordinarily brave – or perhaps foolish – to revisit it.

Anna looked up Heather's address before starting the van and heading back to the main road. An hour or so later, she hit the suburbs of Manchester. She followed the signs for Levenshulme, passing through a heavily built up area of terraced houses, council estates, bustling open-air markets and local shops.

She pulled over outside a flat-roofed block of maisonettes facing a rectangle of scruffy grass and a boarded-up, graffiti-tagged building. Heather only lived four or five miles from the Hopeland home. She apparently hadn't needed, or perhaps been able, to get away from Manchester. Maybe, reasoned Anna, she would be more willing to talk about the abuse. She climbed a flight of stairs to an external landing and knocked on a battered and flaking door. There was no answer. She tried again. Still no answer. She returned to the van and settled down with a cigarette to watch and wait.

The daylight was just beginning to fade when Anna spotted Heather teetering along in high-heels, a miniskirt and a tight vest that showed off her cleavage. Her face was artificially orange and pasted with makeup. Her hair was jet black at the ends and blonde at the roots. She was arguing with a scag-faced, heavily tattooed man. A girl of eleven or twelve trailed along behind them, staring vacantly at the pavement. Her hair was the same colour as Heather's roots. She had Heather's broad, sullen face too.

Anna waited until they were inside the maisonette, then climbed the stairs and knocked again. The young girl opened the door on the security chain and eyed Anna suspiciously. 'Who are you?' she asked in a thick Mancunian accent.

'My name's Anna. I'd like to talk to your mum, please.'

The girl's face disappeared from the gap. 'Mum,' she shouted, 'it's for you. Someone called Anna.'

'Anna?' came the mystified retort. 'I don't know any fucking Annas.' Heather's frowning face appeared at the door. 'Who are you and what do you want?'

Anna had already decided to try a slightly less direct tack than with Debbie. 'I'm Anna Young and I was hoping we could help each other.'

Heather rolled her eyes. 'Fucking hell, I should've guessed.'

A man's smoke-roughened voice came from further within the maisonette. 'Who is it?'

'It's another one of them God-botherers.'

'Well tell 'em to piss off.'

'I'm not a God-botherer,' said Anna. 'And I'm not here to sell you anything. I've lost something. And I know you've lost something too. It's not anything we can ever get back. But maybe between us we can get to the truth of it.'

Heather's frown deepened with uncertainty. She stared at Anna as if trying to work out whether she knew her from somewhere. Then she closed the door. A second passed. Two, three... ten seconds. *She's not going to let me in*, thought Anna. But then there was the rattle of a chain and the door swung open. 'Come in,' said Heather.

Anna nodded thanks and followed her along a dingy hallway that stank of dog and cigarettes to a small living room. The scag-faced man was stretched out on a scuffed white leather sofa. The girl was slouched across a mismatched armchair. Both were staring at a blaring television. A thickly muscled bulldog curled up on the threadbare carpet lazily eyed Anna. Smoke spiralled from an ashtray on a smeared glass coffee table.

'What the fuck did you let her in for?' the man demanded to know.

Ignoring him, Heather said to the girl, 'Go to your room, Leah.'

'I'm watching the telly,' protested Leah.

'Fucking do as your mum tells you,' snapped the man.

With an irritated huff, Leah left the room. Heather gestured for Anna to sit in the armchair. She shoved the man's legs off the sofa and dropped down next to him. Muttering to himself, he lit a cigarette with the end of his old one and offered the packet to Heather. She shook her head, staring at Anna as if to say, *So come on then, let's hear it.*

'It might be better if we talk alone,' said Anna.

'Me and Kyle have got no secrets from each other.'

Kyle scowled at Anna and spoke through his cigarette. 'What are you, a copper or something?'

Anna shook her head. She told them the story of Jessica's abduction, taking particular care this time to describe her sister as fully as possible. She wanted to make Jessica a real person in Heather's mind, not merely a photo to be cursorily glanced at. Kyle made some impatient noises, but Heather shushed him sharply. A trace of softness came into her hard-pinched face when Anna showed her Jessica's photo.

'She's beautiful,' said Heather. She didn't ask the question that subsequently came to many people's lips – how could anyone ever hurt her? Something in her eyes – some glimmer of sadness – said she was only too aware of the answer to that question.

'That's a shitty thing to happen,' said Kyle. 'But what's it got to do with us?'

'I have to find my sister,' answered Anna, keeping her gaze fixed on Heather. 'I have to know what happened to her.'

'I'd be the same if anyone took Leah,' said Heather.

Bracing herself for Heather's reaction, Anna showed her the sketch of Spider. 'This is one of the men who abducted Jessica.'

Heather stared at it for a long moment. Her eyes glistened as though she might cry, but she blinked away any tears. 'Give me one of them ciggies.'

Kyle did so and she snatched up a lighter and lit it. There was a tremor in her hand.

'Who is he?' asked Kyle.

'He's the one I told you about when we first got together. Remember?'

'The one you used to have nightmares about? The paedo?'

'Yes.'

Kyle's gaze jerked to Anna. 'Do you know where this motherfucker is?' The bulldog lifted its head, growling at the anger in its master's voice.

'That's what she's here to try and find out,' snapped Heather. To Anna, she added, 'I take it you know what that man did to me.'

Anna nodded. 'I've read the case-file Lance Brennan put together on Hopeland.'

'Lance Brennan.' Heather said the name with a slight wince. 'They fucked him over good and proper, you know. And I helped them. I helped the bastards who raped me. Do you know what I got in return? Five hundred quid.'

'That was a lot of money in them days,' said Kyle.

Heather scowled. 'I was a stupid little bitch.'

'You were scared,' said Anna.

'Yeah, that as well.'

'Who gave you the money?'

Heather was silent a moment, her gaze returning to the sketch. She stubbed out her cigarette as though she was grinding it into Spider's face. Anna listened with barely contained excitement as, with an expression that suggested something nasty was crawling up her back, Heather began, 'I got a phone call off some bloke. I've never forgotten what he said. He said, "You need to buy something black." I asked, "What for?" And he said, "Because that's what people wear at funerals." Then he said my parents' names and where they lived. And he said my little brother's name and the name of the children's home he was in. I was only fifteen, but I wasn't stupid. I knew what he was getting at. He told me if I told the police I was lying, there'd be a lot of money in it for me. I didn't give a toss about my mum and dad, but I loved my brother. So I said I'd do it. The next day an envelope of money arrived for me at the house of the foster family I was living with.'

'Tell me about Spider.'

Heather sucked on her cigarette, her eyes growing distant as she reached back into her memory. 'He was a young bloke when I met him. Maybe nineteen or twenty, and he had this baby face. Like butter wouldn't melt. He was nice to me. Made me feel like... well, y'know, like I was worth something. No one else had ever made me feel like that. I used to sneak up to his room at night. They always locked our dorm after lights out, but Spider gave me a key.'

Anna thought about the key Jim had given her. She took it out. 'Was it a key like this?' She knew the answer the answer would be no. After all, it was a garage door key. But she had to be certain.

'No. It was a big old door key.'

'Was Spider a Man U supporter?'

'I dunno. Why do you ask?'

Anna told her about the keyring that had fallen out of Spider's pocket. Heather nodded recognition. 'Yeah, I remember that. Only it wasn't a Red Devils keyring. It was a...' Her forehead creased in thought. 'Now what did he fucking call it? The horned something or other.' She wagged a long, painted fingernail. 'Yeah that was it, the Horned God.'

'The Horned God,' repeated Anna, stunned. All these years she'd been wrong. All those days spent outside football stadiums had been for nothing. The realisation was like a blow to her solar plexus. The feeling quickly passed, overridden by the knowledge that a whole new avenue of investigation had opened up, and there was no doubt this time that it was the right one. 'What's the Horned God?' She struggled to keep her voice calm. With almost every word she could feel herself getting closer to the truth. Closer to Jessica.

Heather shrugged. 'Spider was into all sorts of weird shit. Witchcraft. Paganism. He had loads of books on that kind of thing. He kept them locked in a suitcase. He said I was the only one at the home he trusted enough to show them to. He used to do these... What do you call them? Rituals. He'd light candles. Burn ribbons and stuff and scatter the ashes. Read aloud from his books. Pray to all different gods. He reckoned they gave him magic powers. That he could control people, even make them fall in love with him. He was off his fucking rocker. I realise that now. But back then I was... well, I was thirteen. You know how thirteen-year-olds are. Easily impressed. Spider was different to anyone I'd ever known. I thought he was special. But he wasn't. He was evil. And I mean pure evil. He used to talk about...' Heather trailed off, glancing at Anna as if uncertain whether she should say any more.

'Go on,' urged Anna.

'He used to talk about human sacrifice. He said the best kind of sacrifice was a virgin. I don't think it mattered whether it was a boy or a girl. He said that if you killed a virgin you'd become so powerful no one would be able to hurt you. But you had to do it right or it wouldn't work. He used to look at me sometimes and I swear his eyes would be black. It scared the shit out of me. Luckily for me, by that time a virgin was the last thing I was.'

A queasy feeling rose in Anna as she listened. She swallowed it in a hard lump. 'How come you never told Lance Brennan about this?'

Heather shrugged. 'I was just a girl. I was in love, or thought I was in love with a bloke who drugged and pimped me out. My head was a fucking mess. Besides, all Brennan was interested in hearing about was the sex.'

'I'd like to hear about that too.' Anna immediately realised *like* was the wrong word. She despised hearing about this stuff. The right word was *need*.

'What for? You've read my statement, haven't you?'

'Yes, but I want to make sure we haven't missed anything else.'

Heather sighed wearily. 'Alright, but there's nothing much to tell. It started with the odd grope and ended with fucking. Then one night Spider said he was taking me to a party. He put me in the back of his van with some cider and drove out to the countryside. He must have spiked the cider with something cos by the time we got to the big house I was totally wrecked. I couldn't even walk. Spider carried me to this massive room where there were loads of people. Mostly men, but some women too.' Heather's mouth twisted upwards in the mockery of a smile. 'And that's when the fun began. Some of them started having sex with me. I'm not sure how many. Others watched and filled in when their pals were done.'

'Do you think you'd recognise their faces if you saw them now?'

'I dunno. Spider always made me drink the spiked cider before we got to the house, so everything was kind of a blur.'

Anna began laying out the photos of the people from Herbert's book on the coffee table. With their self-assured expressions and conservative, tasteful appearances, the photos' subjects reeked of everything Heather and Kyle lacked.

'Who are they?' asked Heather.

Anna explained about the list, omitting, of course, where she'd got it from.

'They look rich,' Kyle said, with a thoughtful twist to his mouth.

'That's because they are.' Anna watched Heather's gaze travel over the photos. She noted how Heather's eyes lingered on several of them. 'Anyone look familiar?'

Anna opened her mouth to reply, but Kyle jumped in. 'She's not saying another fucking word.'

Heather turned to him. 'What do you mean?'

'I mean you're not giving her any more information. Not unless we get something in return.'

Frowning hard, Heather shook her head. 'The only thing I want is to see those bastards locked up for what they did.'

'Use your noggin.' Kyle jabbed at the photos. 'These people could fuck up our lives big-style.' He made a sweeping gesture. 'We might have to leave this place. How we gonna do that if we've got no cash? And if we've got nowhere to live, the social might take our Leah off us. She could end up in care like you did.'

Heather's frown turned into fear at the thought of that happening. 'No fucking way. Not over my dead body are they taking my baby.'

'I have a contact in the police,' said Anna. 'Maybe he could put you into some sort of witness protection.'

'Bollocks to that,' scowled Kyle. 'Two thousand quid. That's what it's gonna cost you for the information.'

'But Heather's already said the only thing she wants is to do what's right.'

'Yeah, and that's what she's gonna do. But you do right by your family first. Have you got kids of your own?'

Anna shook her head. After what happened to Jessica, she'd sworn never to have children. How could it be fair to bring a child into a world so full of cruelty and evil? In recent years, as she'd become increasingly aware of her biological clock ticking, she'd found herself wondering more and more what it would be like to be a mother. She knew that in all likelihood she would never find out. She didn't even have enough of herself to give to hold down a relationship. Never mind bring up a child.

'So you don't know how you worry all the time about where they are, what they're doing, if they're safe. Isn't that right, Heather?'

Heather nodded. Anna gave her a look of appeal. 'I'm sorry,' said Heather, her eyes dropping. 'I want to help, really I do, but I've got to think of Leah.'

Anna sought her gaze. 'Don't you see? That's exactly why we need to stop these people.'

As though she'd been accused of being a bad mother, anger flared in Heather's voice. 'Are you saying I'd let them hurt my Leah?'

'No, of course not. I only meant—'

'Yeah, I know what you meant,' broke in Heather, folding her arms. 'Well, it's three thousand quid now. Keep on talking and I'll add another thousand.'

A triumphant gleam in his eyes, Kyle put his arm around Heather. Resisting an urge to swing for him, Anna gathered up the photos. She gave Heather a thin smile of thanks and made her way to the front door. Kyle followed her. 'Don't bother coming back unless you've got the cash,' he said, kicking the door shut.

As she returned to the camper van, Anna checked that her iPhone's voice recording of the conversation had worked. Then she phoned Jim and told him about Debbie's complete refusal and Heather's conditional willingness to talk to her. She didn't tell him what she'd learnt about the keyring. His first and only instinct, she knew, would be to chase down the lead himself. And despite his warnings, she felt she'd more than earned the right to do that.

'If we pay for information how do we know Heather won't just be telling us what we want to hear?' said Jim.

'I'm positive she recognised some of the photos. And that was before money was mentioned. Look, we've got to move fast if we want Heather to talk. Villiers may already know Brennan's given you the Hopeland case-file. He stopped the victims talking once, and given the chance, he'll do it again.'

The line was silent briefly, then Jim asked, 'Do you have a bank account?'

'Yes.'

'OK, I'll transfer you the money.'

Anna gave Jim her account details and said she'd call again when she'd spoken to Heather. She trawled the internet for information about pagan shops in Manchester. There were two of them – Moonchild and The Mystic Palace. It was almost ten p.m. The shops would be long closed – if they'd ever been open on a Sunday. Even so, she could barely resist the urge to head off in search of them. For most of her life she'd been obsessing about this moment. Now it was here, the prospect of waiting even one night to follow up on the lead was excruciating. She wasn't particularly tired, but she drew the curtains and put down the bed as if that would hurry the passing of the night. She lay reading about the Horned God. He had almost as many names as there were websites dedicated to him. Amongst other names, he was known as the Horned One, Cernunnos, Herne, Bran, the Old One, Karnayna, Atho, Old Horny, Faunus, Actaeon and Dianus. He was the male deity of the Wiccan religion. A wildman of the forests, a hunter, a primal symbol of strength and fertility, of life, death and rebirth. Sometimes he was represented as having the hind legs of a goat or stag with a man's muscular upper body. Other times he had the body of a man and the head of a beast. But always he had a pair of horns or antlers sprouting out of his head.

She Googled 'Paganism and human sacrifice' and found herself wading through a mass of murky material that neither proved nor disproved it was, or had ever been, practised. Some websites talked about historical evidence of pagans ritually killing their own children to ensure prosperity. Others stated that all such claims were nothing more than propaganda used to demonise pagans. As so often in Anna's experience, the truth was simply whatever you chose to believe. In amongst the claims and counter-claims, though, one particular comment stuck in her mind – 'The only evil in paganism is in the heart of the practitioner.' Her thoughts returned to what Heather had said about Spider being evil. Some people doubted the existence of true evil. Not Anna. She'd looked it directly in the eye and knew it for what it was – a monster whose hunger was insatiable. For men like Spider, the truth didn't matter. All that mattered was feeding the monster within.

CHAPTER SIX

Anna was dreaming. In her dream she saw Jessica so vividly it was almost as though she could reach out and touch her. Spider was there too – or at least the upper part of him was. The lower half had been transformed into hairy cloven-hoofed legs. Two twisting horns rose from his head. He was on top of Jessica, rutting mercilessly, his face contorted into a mask uglier than any beast. One of his hands was pressed over her mouth to stifle her screams, the other gripped her throat. Anna wanted to drag him off her sister, pound her fists into his face, push her fingers into his eyes. But she was rooted to the spot, helpless to do anything other than watch. Tears of frustrated fury streamed down her cheeks.

A noise pulled her out of sleep. Her phone was ringing. She groped for it and saw her home number on the screen. It was two o'clock in the morning. Why the hell was her mother ringing at that time? Had there been another silent phone call? Or perhaps Villiers and his pals had fired off a more forceful warning. Her heart pounding, she answered the call. 'What is it, Mum? What's wrong?'

Silence.

'Mum? Are you there?'

Again, silence greeted her words. A silence so loud it seemed to throb out of the phone. Anna's mind raced. Was her mum ill? Was she having a stroke or something? No. If that were the case, she would have dialled 999. Anna suddenly felt certain it wasn't her mum on the other end of the line. A cold feeling rose from her stomach. She fought to keep the fear out of her voice as she said, 'If you hurt my mother I'll kill you.'

She hung up and frantically navigated to Jim's number. 'Come on, answer the fucking phone,' she muttered as the dial tone trilled in her ear.

'Anna, wha—' Jim started to say, his voice croaky with sleep.

'You've got to go to my mum's house,' she broke in. 'Someone's there. They might have hurt her.'

'Slow down. Tell me what happened.'

'I got a silent phone call from my home number.'

'Are you sure it wasn't just a bad line?'

'Yes. We're wasting time. You need to get round there.'

'OK, I'm on my way. I'll call you when I get there.'

The line went dead. Anna dialled her home number and got an engaged tone. Had the phone been left off the hook? Or was the silent caller trying to contact her again? She stared at her phone, rocking anxiously. Her mum was the one thing left in her life that she loved. If anything happened to her... An anguished groan escaped her lips. She hadn't truly believed anyone would try to get at her by hurting her mum. Now she saw how naive she'd been.

****

Swearing at himself for not ignoring Anna and putting a car on Fiona Young's house, Jim jerked on his clothes, grabbed a torch and ran for the door. This was exactly what he'd feared would happen. It was always the weakest who suffered most. People like Fiona Young. People like Margaret. He shook off the bloody images that leapt into his mind. Surely Villiers wasn't desperate enough to hurt Fiona. Not yet. As he drove sharply away from the block of flats, he phoned Reece. 'Are you at home?' he asked when his colleague picked up.

'Uh-huh.'

'I need you to meet me ASAP.' Jim gave Reece Fiona Young's address, adding, 'And make sure you're wearing your stab vest.'

'What's going on, Jim?'

'I'll explain when I see you. Now get your arse moving.'

When Jim arrived at the house, Reece was already there. There were no lights on in the house. The driveway was empty. Jim got out of his car, Taser at the ready, and motioned for Reece to follow him.

Quickly and quietly, Jim approached the front door and tried its handle. The door was locked. He moved around the side of the house. The back gate was open. The back door was open too. The wooden frame was splintered around the lock. They padded through a dark little kitchen into a hallway. Jim shone his torch into the living room. Empty. A cordless phone was on the bottom step of the stairs. Seconds ticked away on its screen, indicating a call was in progress. Leaving it untouched, they climbed the stairs. The bathroom door stood ajar. A glance showed no one was in there. Jim gently opened a door to a bedroom cluttered with books and piles of paper. Guessing it was Anna's room, he moved on to the adjacent door. Beyond the door was a double bed. A figure was snoring softly under the duvet. Relief swept through Jim as he directed his torch at Fiona Young's sleeping face. She suddenly sat up with a gasp, shielding her eyes. 'Who are you?' The question came shrill and tremulous.

'We're police,' said Jim, switching on the landing light and taking out his ID. 'I'm Chief Inspector Jim Monahan. And this is Detective Inspector Reece Geary.'

'What are you doing in my house?'

'Your daughter contacted me. She thought you might be in danger.'

'Why would she think that? And how did you get in here?'

'Perhaps it would be best if you got dressed and we talked downstairs, Mrs Young.'

The two men returned downstairs. Jim picked up the phone with a handkerchief and ended the call. 'Go and knock up the neighbours,' he told Reece.

Jim waited for Fiona Young in the living room. She appeared after a minute or two in her dressing gown and slippers, her eyes puffy with sleep. 'So come on, Chief Inspector, out with it. What's Anna got herself into now?'

'Hasn't she told you?'

'She never tells me anything. She doesn't like to worry me.'

Jim gave Fiona a very abridged rundown of the case Anna was working on. He made no mention of its connection to her daughter's abduction. Mainly because he knew Anna wouldn't want him to. But also because he sensed a brittleness about Fiona that suggested she wouldn't deal with it well if he did. 'Is there anyone you could go and stay with for a few days? A friend or relative?'

'I'm not leaving this house.'

Jim gestured for Fiona to follow him into the kitchen. He pointed at the splintered doorframe. 'Someone broke in here tonight. It was a warning, and one you should take extremely seriously.'

Fiona's face pinched with worry. But she crossed her arms and repeated, 'I'm not leaving this house. I've lived here over forty years. And I'll be damned if I'm going to let anyone drive me out.'

Jim saw the same stubborn resolve in Fiona's eyes that he'd seen in Anna's, and knew he'd be wasting his time trying to change her mind. 'In that case I'm going to put a patrol car outside your house.'

Fiona frowned at the prospect, but made no protest. 'What about my daughter? What are you doing to protect her?'

'There's nothing I can do right now. Besides, I don't think she'd accept protection if I offered it.'

'Knowing my Anna, I'm sure you're right. But still, if anything happens to her I'm going to hold you responsible. I get the impression she wouldn't be involved in this if it wasn't for you.'

Jim nodded as if to say, *Fair enough.* Looking at Fiona's careworn face, he felt a tug of guilt at the way he'd used Anna. Fiona had already suffered so much loss. If she lost Anna too, it didn't bear thinking about what it would do to her.

Shuddering at the night air flowing into the house, she pointed at the back door. 'What are you going to do about that?'

'Have you got a hammer and nails?'

'I don't know. I'll have to look in my husband's...' Fiona paused a breath and corrected herself. 'My late husband's toolbox.' She went into a small pantry. Gingerly, like she was handling something valuable, she took out a battered metal box. Amongst other things, it contained a hammer and a jar of nails and screws.

'I'll nail the door shut for tonight. Tomorrow I'll send someone round to replace it. But before I touch anything, I'm going to have to call in a SOCO—'

'A what?'

'A Scene of Crime Officer. They gather forensic evidence.'

Fiona heaved a sigh. 'Looks like I'm not going to be getting back to bed anytime soon then. Not that I could sleep if I did.' Her gaze returned to the door and she shuddered again. 'How long do you think Anna will be in Manchester for?'

'Not long.' It suddenly occurred to Jim that Anna would be waiting on tenterhooks to hear from him. 'Excuse me a moment.'

He went outside and phoned her. She answered on the first ring and asked anxiously, 'Is she OK?'

'She's fine. Do you want to speak to her?'

'No. Just tell me what happened.'

'Someone broke in the back door.'

'The fuckers!'

'Listen, Anna, after you speak to Heather Shanks tomorrow I want you to return to Sheffield.'

'What about Jamal Jackson?'

'He wasn't taken to any of the houses. So chances are you'll get nothing out of him we don't already know.'

'Yeah, but that doesn't mean I won't learn something that helps me track down Spider.'

'I'm sorry, Anna, but this has gone far enough. I can't risk you getting hurt.'

Anna's voice grew hard with determination. 'And I'm sorry, Jim, but unless you lock me up, you're not going to stop me from seeing this thing through. Besides, the last thing we should be doing is backing off. What we should be doing is showing them that if they fuck with us we'll fuck with them right back.'

'And how do you propose we do that?'

Anna gave a humourless little grunt that suggested she knew exactly how. 'I take it you're going to be keeping a close eye on my mum from now on.'

'Of course. What are you going to do?'

'You'll find out soon enough.'

Anna hung up. Jim stood in thoughtful, frowning silence a moment, before phoning for a SOCO. When he returned inside, Fiona was cradling a mug of tea in the living room. 'Your daughter's an extremely stubborn woman,' he said.

Her lips pulled into a flat smile. 'She's always been the same. Once she makes up her mind to do something, there's no stopping her.'

Jim turned at the sound of footsteps and saw Reece. 'Any luck?'

Reece shook his head. 'I've spoken to both sets of neighbours. Nobody saw or heard anything.'

Jim wasn't surprised. Villiers and his accomplices didn't hire amateurs to do their dirty work. 'Forensics will be here soon. Not that I expect them to find anything.'

'Can I have a word before they get here?' asked Reece.

Jim guessed at once what Reece wanted to have a word about. He followed the big detective into the back garden. 'You've obviously rattled a few cages,' said Reece. 'I take it there have been developments.'

'You take it right.' In a low voice, Jim brought Reece up to speed on everything that had happened since they'd spoken on Saturday.

Reece blew out an astonished breath. 'Jesus. Well no one can say putting the names out there didn't get things moving. Does the DCS know about this Spider's connection to Jessica—'

Jim made a quick shushing motion. 'The only people who know about that are you, me and Anna Young. And that's the way it's going to stay. At least until I find out what Heather has to say to Anna.'

'You're taking a big risk, Jim.'

'I know,' he said heavily. 'But what other choice do I have?'

****

It didn't take Anna long to track down Thomas Villiers' address on the internet, even though his telephone was ex-directory. A small fee bought her access to the most recent electoral roll. Villiers lived in the well-heeled Sheffield suburb of Dore. A Diane Villiers was registered to the same address. His wife, no doubt. The slimy little scumbag probably had kids too. A dog. All that crap. Every trapping of respectability and normality provided another layer of protection between who he appeared to be and who he really was.

Next, Anna looked up Linda Kirby's phone number. Ever since her daughter Grace's murder, Linda had been loudly campaigning for the death penalty to be reinstated. She and her supporters had gathered thousands of signatures and marched to 10 Downing Street to present them to the Prime Minister. She made no bones about it. Her ultimate wish was to look into Freddie Harding's eyes as he drew his last breath. It wasn't going to happen, of course. The death penalty was an issue no right-minded politician would touch. But that hadn't deterred her. Anna had spoken to her once at a rally for signatures outside Sheffield City Hall. She'd told her about Jessica's abduction. Not because she thought Linda would be able to help her, but because it felt good to talk to someone who could even remotely understand how she felt. Linda was a small, timid-looking woman. But she'd spoken with the fervour of a newly converted believer about how prison was too good for men like Freddie Harding, adding conspiratorially, 'Shall I tell you what I really think, Anna? Even a lethal injection's too good for filth like him. If it was up to me, I'd do to him what he did to those poor girls. I'd break his bones one by one, gouge out his eyes, pull out his teeth. And when he was finally dead, I'd string him up by his balls for all to see.'

Anna didn't doubt for a second that Linda had meant what she said. She'd never heard such pure anger as there was in her voice. Her own parents' anger had been leavened with a heartbreaking sadness. There'd been no sadness in Linda's voice, only an all-consuming desire for bloody retribution. Instead of destroying Linda, Grace's murder had remade her in its own brutal image. Anna had spent countless hours wondering what she would do if she ever found Jessica's abductors. Would she seek Old Testament justice? An eye for an eye. Or would she let the law take its course? The answer depended on her mood. Usually she pictured them rotting in prison. But sometimes in the dead of night, she fantasised about hurting them badly and slowly.

Linda picked up the phone and asked, 'Who the bloody hell's this?'

'It's Anna Young. We spoke once about my sister Jessica.'

'Anna Young?' Linda's voice softened. 'Oh yes, I remember. What can I do for you, love?'

'I'm sorry for waking you, but there's something I think you ought to know.' Anna told Linda about Herbert Winstanley's book and how the authorities had been shielding the names in it from public exposure. She went into particular detail about Thomas Villiers – his connections to Grace's murderers; where he worked; where he lived.

'Christ, how could they let him near those kids knowing what they know?' Linda asked incredulously.

'I've been asking myself that since I found out about the book. As far as I can see, it comes down to two things: who he is and who he knows.'

'Well that bastard's going to find out who I am and who I know.'

That same throat-clogging rage was back in Linda's voice. Anna permitted herself a faint smile of satisfaction at the thought that life was about to get very uncomfortable indeed for Villiers. 'Do you have internet access?'

'Yes. I'd never used a computer in my life before Grace was killed. Now I can't get by without one.'

'Search for me and Herbert Winstanley. You'll find the full list of names.'

'Will do. And I'll let you know what I'm going to do about Villiers.' Linda drew in a deep breath – a breath that said she'd been ready for this moment for a long time. 'I'll tell you this right now, Anna. We're going to show all of them we won't take any more. Enough is enough.'

Anna said goodbye, cracked open the curtains and sat watching for the dawn. Tiredness burnt behind her eyes. Not the tiredness of sleep. There was too much adrenalin coursing through her for that. It was the bone-tiredness of years of searching, years of frustration and pain. Linda was right, enough was fucking enough.

CHAPTER SEVEN

Nine a.m. seemed to take forever to arrive. The minute the bank opened, Anna hurried inside and withdrew the money Jim had transferred to her account. She fought her way through the morning traffic back to Heather's maisonette and hammered on its door. Kyle appeared in boxer shorts and the same vest he'd been wearing the previous day. He scowled blearily at Anna. 'What the fuck do you want?'

'What do you think?' Anna patted her coat pocket. 'I've got what we agreed on.'

'You can keep your money. We don't want it.'

Anna frowned. 'But we had a deal. Three thousand for the information.'

Kyle's lips curled up over his stained teeth. 'Fuck your three thousand. I wouldn't give you the shit from my arse for that much.'

Anna saw the gleam in Kyle's eyes and guessed immediately what had happened – someone had come in with a far superior offer. Coupled with the events of the night, it added up to one obvious conclusion – the police department was as leaky as a broken tap. She craned her neck to see past Kyle. 'Heather! It's Anna Young.'

'Keep your voice down. You'll wake Leah. She's not feeling well.'

Ignoring him, Anna continued, 'Don't do this to yourself, Heather. No matter how much they're paying you, it's not worth it.'

Kyle thrust his face close to hers. 'One more word from you and I'm gonna fetch the dog.'

Her nose wrinkling at the stink of his morning breath, Anna held her ground just long enough to let him know she wasn't afraid. Then she walked away.

'And don't come back here, bitch,' he shouted after her.

When she was out of Kyle's sight, Anna phoned Jim and said, 'Someone got to Heather. She's refusing to talk to me.'

'Shit.' Jim's voice was sharp with disappointment. 'And we were so close too. Do you think you can change her mind?'

'I don't know. If I could get her away from that arsehole she lives with, maybe I could talk her around. But that would take time.'

'Might as well give it a shot. What else have you got to do?'

Anna considered telling Jim about the Horned God lead. Lying to him didn't sit easily with her. But now that Heather had been silenced – probably through the same mix of money and intimidation as in '89 – she felt even more protective about the lead. 'Nothing.' She quickly changed the subject. 'Any news on the break-in?'

'There were no prints left behind, and no one saw anything.'

'Did you expect any different?'

'No. These people know what they're doing. They've been getting away with this for a long time.'

'Yeah, well not much longer if I can help it.'

Anna hung up and located Moonchild and The Mystic Palace on Google maps. She fully intended to talk to Heather again, but not until she'd found out where the lead took her. The shops were on opposite sides of the city centre. She started the van and headed for the closest. Moonchild was a tiny place on a backstreet whose faded sign depicted a sickle moon in a starry sky. The gloomy interior was thick with burning incense and cluttered with astrological candles, healing crystals, books on myths and magic, tarot cards, pagan jewellery, Ouija boards and all manner of other mystical tat. A man with long greying hair was sitting behind the counter. A rack of keyrings caught Anna's eye. She rotated it and her stomach gave a squeeze. There it was! The exact same keyring that had fallen out of Spider's pocket. She unhooked it from the rack and ran her fingers over its curved horns and bearded goat-like face. She took out the Gliderol key and attached it to the keyring, before approaching the counter.

'Six quid, please,' said the man.

Anna paid him. 'This is the Horned God, right?'

'That's one of his names. I call him Old Horny myself, obviously because of the horns, but also because, well, he's a horny old bugger.' He pointed to a bookshelf. 'If you're interested, I've got some books about him.'

'Thanks, but no thanks.' Anna withdrew the police sketch. 'What I'm really interested in is if you recognise this man? You might know him as William Keyes or Spider. He has a spider's web tattoo on his chest.'

'A spider's web tattoo, you say.' There was a glimmer of recognition in the man's eyes. As he took a long look at the sketch, the glimmer solidified into certainty. 'Now that's a face I haven't seen in a long time. He used to come in here,' he puffed his cheeks, 'it must be twenty-odd years ago. He didn't call himself either of the names you mentioned, though. He called himself by his pagan name. Clotho Daeja. It means deadly demon. He was a bloody odd character.'

'How do you mean, odd?'

'I mean he wasn't a very nice bloke. He had some, shall we say, extreme views.'

'About human sacrifice?'

A trace of wariness came into the man's expression. 'Let's just say he was the kind of pagan who gives the rest of us a bad name. Why are you so interested in him anyway?'

'He...' Anna searched for the right words, 'stole something from me.'

'Well unless it was something you can't do without, I'd steer well clear of him.'

'When was the last time you saw him?'

'Like I said, twenty something years ago. Maybe in '89 or '90. I had to ban him from the shop. He was pestering the customers, trying to convert them to what he called the real Wicca.'

'What's the real Wicca?'

'There's no such thing. Paganism's what you make it. I told him that and he flipped out. Called me a fake. Threatened to burn this place down. He reckoned he was going to show the world what it means to be a true Wiccan.'

'And you've never heard from him since?'

The man shook his head. 'I never want to hear from him either. Good riddance to bad rubbish, that's what I say.'

Anna thanked him and returned to the camper van. She sat frowning thoughtfully at the keyring for a long moment. There was a faint smile on the bearded face. Almost like a taunt. She took out her iPhone and Googled 'Clotho Daeja'. Nothing of interest came up. She tried again, including the search term 'real

Wicca'. This time she got a list of links to articles with titles such as 'How to become a Wiccan' and 'What is Wicca?'. She repeated her search with slight variations until she found a link that caught her eye. It was entitled 'The True Wiccan'. It took her to a database of UK pagan shops and practices. The entry read 'I am the True Wiccan. I do not sell New Age fakery. I sell the truth. Come and see me if that's what you're looking for.'

The truth. The words stood out as though they'd been written in blood. It was like some sort of mocking echo of her blog's title. There was a phone number under the listing but no address. The number had a Leeds area code. She dialled it. She struggled to stay calm as the dial tone rang. Someone picked up.

'Hello.' It was a man's voice with a broad Yorkshire accent.

Despite herself, Anna's heart was thumping in her mouth as she asked, 'Am I speaking to the True Wiccan?'

'Who?'

'Are you the True Wiccan?'

'Sorry, I think you've got the wrong number.'

Anna told the man the number she'd dialled. 'That's my number,' he confirmed. 'But I've no idea who the True Wiccan is. Maybe they were a previous tenant. You could try speaking to my landlord. Do you want his number?'

'Please.'

The man gave Anna another Leeds number. She dialled it and got an answering service message. 'This is Tony Hulten Lettings.' Once again, the voice had a nasal Yorkshire accent. 'There's no one in the office right now, but if you leave a—'

Anna cut off the message and Googled 'Tony Hulten Lettings'. She found a listing with an address in Harehills, Leeds. Feeling slightly deflated, but relieved that the lead was still tenuously alive, she studied a road map, then threw the camper van into gear.

****

Jim sifted through the statements volunteered by those named in Herbert's book. All of them were as well-rehearsed as a politician's speech. And all of them led to the same place the investigation had been going both before and after its suspension – nowhere. 'Shit,' he muttered for about the tenth time since speaking to Anna. No matter what moves he made, Villiers and Co always seemed to be one ahead, backing him further and further into a corner. A cornered animal was often the most dangerous, but if none of the Hopeland victims talked he might yet prove to be something of a toothless lion. He wasn't simply interested in what the victims had to say. After all, Brennan had already coaxed most of that out of them. It wasn't even getting the names of their abusers that mattered most to him. As Garrett had pointed out, a good solicitor would tear them to shreds in court for withdrawing their statements. No, what he wanted most was a sign that one of them was willing to break the dam of silence. The abuse had been going on for decades. It involved a network of people spread the length and breadth of the country. There had to be dozens more victims like Debbie, Heather and Jamal out there. If they saw that one person had the courage to speak out, perhaps they would come forward. And then one would become two, three, four... Until finally sheer weight of numbers would make it impossible for their accusations to be ignored. But they had to find that one elusive person, otherwise the dam would remain intact.

Reece and Scott Greenwood entered the office. In the light of day, Reece looked if anything even more tired than he had before the weekend. His wired, bloodshot eyes suggested the stress of dealing with Staci's illness was getting on top of him. Scott looked the same as he always did – smart, alert, solid.

'We're kind of at a loose end,' he said.

Jim sighed. 'You and me both. Have you got anything else you could be working on?'

'Plenty.'

'Then go do it.'

'Yes, sir,' said Scott, but he remained where he was, waiting to hear what Jim had to say to Reece.

Jim wafted him out of the room. 'I'll give you a shout if I need you.'

'I take it it's not going well with the Hopeland victims,' Reece said, when they were alone.

'It's that obvious, is it?'

'You look as though you found a turd in your cornflakes.'

A cheerless smile pulled at one corner of Jim's mouth. 'Someone got to Heather Shanks. Anna hasn't spoken to Jamal Jackson, but it's a good bet the pressure's been put on him too.'

Jim's office phone rang. He answered it. 'Hello, this is—'

Linda Kirby's accusing voice cut him off. 'I bloody well trusted you! I would've expected this of Mr Garrett, but not you, Jim. I thought you were different. More fool me.'

Jim guessed at once what had happened. 'You've spoken to Anna Young.'

'That's right and she told me all about how you've been protecting those filthy perverts.'

'I'm just following orders.'

'So were the Nazis when they murdered millions.'

Jim winced at the comparison. Linda was right. Evil thrived on blind obedience. And silence. Two things she herself had been guilty of in the past. But no longer. He'd never seen such a change in a person as had come over Linda since her daughter's death. Gone was the woman who'd mutely stood by whilst her husband physically abused their daughter. In her place was a bold, outspoken woman, relentlessly driven by rage. Not for the first time, Jim felt a sliver of sadness at the thought that it had taken something so tragic to spark Linda's courage.

'How many more children have to be abused, how many more people have to die before you bastards do something?' continued Linda.

'We already are.'

'Oh yeah, you're doing something, alright. Covering up the truth.'

'I promise you, we wouldn't—'

'Save it. I've heard enough empty promises from you lot to last me a lifetime. Well here's a real promise for you. I'm going to do something about Thomas Villiers. I'm going to make him regret the day he was born.'

'Are you threatening him?'

'Too bloody right I am!'

'Listen to me, Linda, Villiers isn't someone you want to butt heads with.'

Linda gave a contemptuous bark. 'Neither am I.'

'Please, you could do more harm than good.'

'How? How could I possibly do more harm than what you've already done? Shame on you.'

With this last retort, the line went dead. 'Linda Kirby?' said Reece.

Jim nodded. 'She gave me an earful about protecting Villiers.'

'She's out of order. You don't deserve that.'

Jim pulled a face as though he wasn't convinced Reece was right.

'Why so gloomy?' asked Reece. 'Surely this is a good thing. If Linda Kirby kicks up a big enough stink, it might get into the news. I thought that's what you wanted.'

'It is. But what I don't want is some kind of vigilante action being taken against Villiers.'

'You must've known there was a chance of that when you put the list out there.'

Jim accepted Reece's words with another heavy sigh. 'I'd better let Garrett know what the score is.'

'What do you want me to do?'

'I don't know. Maybe you could try praying Anna Young comes up with something.'

'I didn't think prayers were your bag.'

'Yeah, well, it's amazing what you'll try when you're desperate.'

'Tell me about it.'

Catching the pained note in Reece's voice, Jim asked, 'How did it go in London?'

Reece's mouth twitched. 'They want to send Staci to South Africa for treatment.'

'Listen, Reece, if you need money—'

Reece cut Jim off with a shake of his head. 'Thanks for the offer, but it won't cost anything. It's an experimental treatment. They'll be using her as a guinea pig.'

'Sounds risky.'

'It is, but it's all we've got.'

'Are you going with her?'

'No. I need to stay here and...' Reece trailed off for a second, his lips twitching again. 'We don't want to take Amelia out of school. We're trying to keep things as normal as possible for her, but it's hard.'

'Does she know what's going on?'

'She knows her mum's ill, but not that she might—' Reece's voice clogged on what could only have been the word 'die'. His broad shoulders lifted as he hauled in a shaky breath.

'When's Staci going?'

'We're waiting to hear. It shouldn't be long.'

'If you need time off to take her to the airport just let me know.'

'Cheers, Jim. You're a good friend.' For an instant, Reece looked like he wanted to say something more. Then, as though fearing he might lose control of his emotions, he turned quickly and headed into the main office.

****

As she drove, Anna's gaze was drawn to the vast, desolate sweeps of moorland that flanked the M62. Moors whose boggy depths concealed so many secrets. She found herself wondering whether Jessica was buried out there somewhere, waiting to be dug up like some archaeological artefact. The thought was as cold and lonely as a peaty grave. She didn't believe in ghosts, but she could imagine the spirits of the wronged wandering those wild expanses. If Jessica was dead, there was only one place she should be – lying next to her dad in Norton Cemetery. She'd be able to rest then. They all would.

An hour or so later, Anna was driving along Harehills Lane past street after street of terraced housing. She pulled over at a row of local shops. Her gaze came to rest on a sign that read 'Tony Hulten Lettings'. She got out of the van, approached a window full of properties up for let and pretended to peruse them. Tony Hulten Lettings was little more than the front room of a terraced house converted into an office with a desk and chairs. A man was reading a newspaper at the desk. Not *the* man she was looking for. This one was late middle aged and overweight with a seedy, unshaven face. He smiled at Anna as she entered the office.

'Can I help you, young lady?' he asked.

'Are you Tony Hulten?'

'That's me, or at least it was last time I looked.'

'I'm looking for a man who used to live in one of your properties. I wondered if you had a forwarding address for him.'

'Which property?'

'I'm not sure, but this is its phone number.' Anna showed Tony the number on her phone. His eyes returned narrowly to hers.

'What's the name of the person you're looking for?'

'I'm not exactly sure about that either. He might have called himself Clotho Daeja. I have a picture of him.'

Anna took out the sketch. Tony gave it a perfunctory glance as though he already knew what he was going to see. And her heart was suddenly going fast again with the knowledge that the True Wiccan and Clotho Daeja *were* the same person.

'That looks like a police drawing,' observed Tony.

'It is.'

'So you're a policewoman.'

Careful to keep her excitement from showing, Anna tapped the sketch. 'I'm just someone who wants to find this man.'

Tony rested back in his chair, folding his arms. 'Even if I had a forwarding address, I can't go giving out that information willy-nilly.'

Anna caught a note in Tony's voice that seemed to suggest he wasn't as inflexible as he appeared to be. 'I'd be willing to pay for it.'

'How much?'

'One hundred.'

'Three hundred.'

Anna didn't have the time or patience to haggle. She peeled off the required amount from the money Jim had transferred to her account.

'Yeah, I remember Mr Daeja,' said Tony. 'He rented a house off me on Cowper Road. Lived there from '91 until... I think it was 2007. He was a funny bloke. And I don't mean funny ha-ha. He never bothered me, but he put the willies up some people round here. He had this way of looking at you if you did something he didn't like. You could tell he was thinking about doing something nasty to you.'

'Did he work?'

'I don't know.'

'Surely he had to provide some sort of proof that he could afford the rent.'

'He had plenty of cash and he always paid his rent three months in advance. That was good enough for me. I was sorry to see him go.'

'Why did he go?'

Tony shrugged. 'He didn't say and I never asked.'

'Did he live alone?'

'As far as I'm aware. Look, all I'm concerned about is the rent. What my tenants get up to in the privacy of their own homes is nothing to do with me.'

'What about a forwarding address?'

'He didn't leave one.'

A rise of irritation came into Anna's voice. 'So that's it, is it? That's all I get for my money.'

'Not quite all. There's one other thing. I happen to know that Mr Daeja used to rent another property a few miles from here. Maybe he still does.'

'A house?'

'No. A lock-up garage.'

Anna's breath caught in her throat. She slid her hand into her pocket and gripped the key. 'Where?'

Tony rooted through a drawer, withdrew a business card and

handed it to Anna. 'Turner Storage Solutions' was printed on the card along with a phone number and two addresses. Tony pointed at one of the addresses. 'That's where the garages are. I've no idea which garage Mr Daeja rented. You could try talking to Donald Turner. The bloke who owns them. I don't think he'll tell you anything though. Donald doesn't like giving out information about his customers. The only reason I know Mr Daeja was one of them is because I recommended Donald to him.'

Even before Tony had finished speaking, Anna was heading out the door. She punched the address into Google and brought up an aerial view of the garages. They were on the south-eastern edge of the city, sandwiched between a housing estate and a thick band of woodland. Twenty minutes or so later she was driving through a relatively affluent-looking area of detached houses and bungalows. A narrow lane enclosed by hedges and shadowed by trees dead-ended at a padlocked wire gate. Two signs on the gate read 'Turner Storage Solutions' and 'Warning! CCTV in use. Trespassers will be prosecuted.' Beyond the gate, three parallel rows of flat-roofed breezeblock garages with blue roller-doors sloped gently towards the woods. Anna sized up the fence. It was topped with razor wire. There was no way she was climbing over it without tearing herself to shreds.

She clambered over a hedge into a grassy field and skirted around the site, searching for a gap in the fence. She hadn't gone far when she came to a place where the wire curled up at the bottom. Lifting it, she crawled through the gap. She made no attempt to avoid the CCTV cameras as she hurried to the garages. Let them prosecute. What did she give a fuck? Quivering with nervous energy, she tried the key in the first garage she came to. It slid easily into the lock, but wouldn't turn. She moved onto the next garage, and the next, and the next... Then the second row of garages, then the third. Her trembling intensified as she checked out the final few garages. Only three to go... two... one. Her tongue flicked dryly over her lips. This had to be it! She inserted the key and twisted. Nothing. She applied more pressure. Still it refused to turn. She hammered her fist against the door, hissing, 'Fuck.'

She closed her eyes, exhaling her disappointment. The lead wasn't dead. Donald Turner probably had other lock-up garages in the city. She would simply have to wheedle their locations out of him. As she turned to leave, her gaze lingered on some bushes that extended from the woods through the fence. She glimpsed something reddish beyond them. Brickwork! Her eyes traced the outline of a sloping roof, so overgrown with ivy and moss that it was difficult to recognise it for what it was at a glance. She started towards the structure, slowly at first, then breaking into a run. As she rounded the bushes, she saw that it was another garage, but standing on its own and obviously far older than the others. All that was visible of it was part of a windowless wall and a heavy-looking, flaky painted wooden door – a door, she noted, that had been fitted with a much newer lock. She inserted the key into it. Even before she twisted it, she knew – just knew in her gut – that it was going to turn.

The click as the lock opened sent an electric jolt through her. She reached for the handle, but hesitated. If Spider's fingerprints were on it, she didn't want to smudge them. She prised her fingers under the door and strained to lift it. The hinges reluctantly whined into motion. It had clearly been some time since it was last opened. After maybe half a metre, wisps of spiders' webs floating from its underside, it ground to a halt. A musty, oily smell tickled her nostrils as she peered inside. Empty. She wasn't surprised. Spider had probably cleared the garage out at the same time he vacated the Cowper Road house. Still, she couldn't help but feel another sharp pang of disappointment.

She slid beneath the door and walked slowly around, squinting through the gloom at the bare walls, the ivy curling under the roof tiles, the dusty concrete floor. She dropped to her haunches at the rear of the garage and ran her fingers along a thin gouge in the floor a couple of centimetres deep and maybe a metre long. Two metres or so to the left was an identical parallel gouge. Something heavy had been dragged along the floor.

She straightened, her gaze roaming the garage again. Had Jessica been brought here? Had she died here? She drew in a deep breath through her nostrils as though trying to detect a familiar scent. Then she headed back outside. She'd followed the lead as far as she could. She saw little point in talking to Donald Turner herself. He almost certainly knew no more about Spider's whereabouts than Tony Hulten. No, it was up to the police now. Surely, between the garage and Cowper Road, their forensics people would turn up something of interest.

She took out her phone to call Jim, but her gaze strayed down the side of the garage to where the fence had been neatly cut from the bottom up to half its height. Beyond it, a faint overgrown path disappeared into the trees. She ducked through the fence and followed the path. Brambles snagged her trousers. She snapped a branch off a tree. The sound echoed like a gunshot through the gloomy tangle of tree trunks. A flock of rooks rose from the treetops, wheeled around several times cawing furiously, then settled back down. There was silence – a deep, watchful silence, as if the wood and its inhabitants were suddenly alert to her presence. She stared uneasily into the trees for a moment. Then she continued on her way, pushing the brambles aside with the branch. The further she went into the woods, the more densely packed the trees became, until the leaf canopy was so thick it almost blotted out the sky. Occasional shafts of sunlight illuminated a carpet of mosses, dead branches and rotting leaves. The air was cool and earthy, like a cave. At any moment, she half expected to catch a glimpse of a horned head. Not that she believed for one second in all that crap about the Horned God. But she could all too easily picture Spider prancing around here in pagan get-up, perhaps imagining himself as sexually potent and uninhibited as the deity he worshipped, instead of the simple pervert he was.

Anna stopped at the edge of a grassy clearing. At its centre was a squat, thick-trunked oak tree, obviously of great age. A scattering of leaves clung to its branches, which twisted outwards as if in some kind of agonised appeal. Its partially exposed roots curled into the earth like clutching fingers. But it wasn't the tree's eerily human appearance that raised goose-flesh on Anna's arms. At roughly head height a circular area of bark had been cut away and a face had been etched into the exposed wood. It had a flat, inexpressive mouth, a broad nose, deep, squinting eyes and a wrinkled forehead out of which protruded a pair of curved, tapering horns. It was simply, even crudely carved. Yet that only gave it a sort of primitive authenticity most of the images of the Horned God she'd viewed online lacked.

She advanced with the stick raised defensively, as if afraid the tree might suddenly come alive and attack her. Dozens of different-coloured frayed and faded ribbons were tied to its branches. Some of them held feathers. Others scraps of fur. A metallic gleam caught Anna's eye. One ribbon was threaded through a tarnished silver ring with an interlacing Celtic design. Her eyebrows pulled together. The ring was small enough to fit a girl's finger. Not far from it a cheap-looking bead necklace encircled a branch. What were they? Offerings? More importantly, who were their owners? In another context their presence would have seemed perfectly innocent. But here they exuded a sinister significance.

The carving drew Anna's gaze again. Without thinking, she stretched out a hand to trace its outline. Its surface was uneven but smooth, and darkened by exposure to the elements. She snatched her hand back as though she'd been burnt, reminding herself sharply that with every touch she could be obscuring vital forensic evidence. She began to circumnavigate the tree, stepping over its gnarled roots. She stumbled and almost fell as her foot disappeared through a mulch of leaves into a hollow at the tree's base. She stooped to clear away the leaves. They'd been piled on top of a layer of woven together sticks. They concealed a circular hole that angled gently downwards underneath the tree. She wondered if it was an animal burrow, but dismissed the idea. It was too large, even for a badger. She directed her phone's flashlight into the hole, palely illuminating a beard of wispy roots dangling from its roof. Brushing them aside with the stick, she spotted what looked like a little bundle of rags about a metre down. She snagged them and carefully drew them to the surface. They unravelled, leaving a trail of old brown bones. Not human bones. They were much too small and delicate. Most likely a bird, she decided, turning a tiny skull over. They'd been wrapped in what looked like a mouldy teacloth. She used a tissue to gather up the bones and return them to the cloth. Then she peered back into the hole.

There was something else down there. Beyond the reach of the stick. Anna lowered herself onto her belly. Her shoulders brushed the sides of the hole as, with the stick and phone extended in front of her, she squirmed into it. She blinked as tendrils of roots tickled her eyes. The earthy smell of the woods was much more intense there. It had a richness, a darkness that was almost primeval. When she was immersed up to her waist, she stopped and stretched the stick out. Its tip snagged another bundle of rags, larger than the first. She tried to draw them towards her, but they seemed to be caught on something. She wriggled further forwards. The hole broadened and steepened. Her entire body was inside it now. She glanced back towards the light, a feeling of claustrophobia rising in her chest. Fighting it down, she released the stick and reached out with her hand. The bundle was maybe twenty centimetres beyond her fingertips. She inched herself towards it. Suddenly, she began to slide. Instinctively, she braced her hands against the walls of the hole, blotting out the phone's flashlight. For a fleeting instant she had the sensation that she was being sucked in and swallowed up by the earth. Then her face butted up against something. She refocused the light on what appeared to be green and purple worm-eaten fabric. A couple of black plastic buttons suggested the fabric had once been an item of clothing. It was wrapped around a hard object. Carefully, she undid the buttons. As the fabric slipped aside, she sucked in a sharp breath. The object was a skull – not an animal skull, a human one.

The empty eye-sockets gaped sightlessly at Anna. Its jaw hung open in a mockery of a grin. Its mottled white-brown surface was fleshless, but wisps of brittle hair clung to it. Long blonde hair. Like Jessica's. Anna's pulse beat in her ears. Was this her? Was the search finally over? The fabric dissolved beneath her fingers as she peeled away more of it, revealing a ribcage with a coin-slot sized hole to the left of the sternum. The bones were bent inwards, clearly the result of a knife being thrust through them. An image came into her mind of Spider looming over Jessica, a knife raised in his hands, his face warped with pleasure. She couldn't imagine, though, the terror Jessica must have felt at that moment – if such a moment had existed. To die in such a way. No one deserved that. Except maybe the fucker who would commit such a crime in the first place.

Tears threatened to rise into Anna's eyes. She didn't let them out. Crying wouldn't help catch Spider. Clutching handfuls of roots, she worked her way backwards. She emerged blinking like a mole into the sunlight. Her gaze flitted uneasily around the clearing as she dialled Jim. When he picked up, she said breathlessly, 'I think I've found her.'

'Found who?' he asked.

She steadied her breathing, then said, 'My sister.'

CHAPTER EIGHT

Jim and Reece stood beside their West Yorkshire Police counterparts watching plastic-suited officers carefully remove the skeleton from the hole. Other officers swarmed around the tree, taking photos, dusting the carving for prints, bagging and tagging the ribbons and items tied in them, combing the undergrowth. When Jim saw the skeleton laid out full length on plastic sheeting, he guessed that Anna was most probably wrong. Jessica Young was four foot eleven at the time of her abduction. The skeleton belonged to someone who'd been a good few inches taller. Unless Spider and Freddie Harding had kept her alive for several years – which was extremely unlikely considering Harding's MO – this wasn't her skeleton. Ruth Magill, the senior pathologist, examined the skeleton, paying close attention to the skull, teeth, ribcage and pelvic area.

'What are we looking at?' asked Jim.

'I'll need to do a more thorough examination to be certain,' said Ruth. 'But from the general lack of wear and tear, the absence of wisdom teeth and the size of the pelvic inlet, I'd say we're looking at an adolescent female. Five foot four or five. Dyed blonde hair with brown roots.'

That final detail confirmed Jim's guess – Jessica Young was a natural blonde.

'Possibly she was something of an alternative type,' continued Ruth.

'Why do you say that?'

Ruth pointed to a scrap of clothing. 'She was wrapped in a tie-dye skirt. I used to wear them myself back when I was in my teenage hippy phase.'

'It makes sense that that kind of girl would be attracted to someone with Spider's far-out beliefs,' observed Reece.

'Cause of death seems fairly obvious. The puncture wound is directly over the heart. Death would have been instantaneous. Of course, it's impossible to say at this stage how long she's been down there. Could be months or years.'

'Any signs of ligatures on the wrists or ankles?' asked Jim.

'No. But any ligatures may well have rotted away with the flesh.'

Jim's gaze moved from the skeleton to the crude face carved into the tree. It stared inscrutably back at him.

'What are you thinking?' asked Reece.

Jim's hand dipped unconsciously into his pocket, then emerged empty. At times like this his fingers always itched for a cigarette. Anna had filled him in over the phone about how she'd found her way to the skeleton. Although he'd given her Freddie Harding's key more in hope than expectation, he wasn't surprised she'd located the door it fitted. Nor was he surprised she'd ignored his plea to keep nothing from him. He was quickly coming to realise that she had an investigative brain to put most of his colleagues to shame. But she was also a loose cannon. He could no more control her than Garrett could control him. 'This is a place of worship, right? And what do worshippers do every Sunday morning?'

'Go to church.'

'So maybe our guy comes here once every full moon, or whatever, to do his thing.'

'In which case we should put some surveillance on this place.'

Jim's mouth curled sceptically. His voice dropped so only Reece could hear. 'I'd agree with you if it wasn't for the fact that Villiers probably already knows what's been found. And if he knows then no doubt Spider or Clotho Daeja, or whatever the hell he's calling himself now, does too.'

'Chief Inspector Monahan.'

Jim turned towards the sound of his name. Garrett was striding towards him, his jaw set in a grim line.

'We need to talk,' said Garrett. His voice was flat and authoritative, but a cold undercurrent of anger was detectable. Without waiting for a reply, the Chief Superintendent headed back the way he'd come. Exchanging a glance with Reece, Jim followed. They passed between the lock-up garages. Forensics officers were going over Spider and Freddie Harding's garage with the proverbial fine-toothed comb. A scene that, Jim knew, would be being repeated again at the Cowper Road house where Spider had lived for sixteen years. If the bastard had left any trace of himself behind – a partial fingerprint, a strand of hair, a flake of skin, anything – forensics would sniff it out like bloodhounds.

Garrett led Jim to the mobile operations lorry. Anna was sitting in the back of it, her clothes and hands still grimy from crawling into the hole. There was a sort of numbness in her eyes, as if she was struggling to process what she'd found. Garrett looked from Jim to Anna, his arms crossed as if awaiting an answer to a question. 'One of you had better start talking,' he said sharply. 'Because none of us is leaving here until I know what the bloody hell's going on.'

'I told you most of it yesterday,' said Jim. 'You didn't believe it then. So why would you now?'

'We didn't have a body yesterday.'

'We had thirty-seven bodies,' Jim threw back, anger sparking in his voice. 'This is just one more to add to the list.'

'You're saying this girl is connected to Edward Forester and Freddie Harding?'

Jim looked uncertainly at Garrett. The Chief Superintendent was a by-the-book careerist. In other words, to use Reece's vernacular, he was an arsehole with a capital A. But there was another side to him. One that, as far as Jim was aware, no one on the force besides himself had seen. Garrett wasn't as inflexible as he seemed. If pushed hard enough, he would bend. As proved by Jim's continued presence in the job. Considering the weight of evidence, surely he would now have no choice but to open up on Villiers with every weapon in their arsenal. And if he refused to do so, then there was one final card Jim could play. He could threaten to reveal the truth about how he'd discovered Edward Forester's grisly secret. Of course, that would not only mean the end of Garrett's career, but Reece's and his own too. 'I'm saying it's all connected. Forester, Harding, Villiers, the Hopeland abuse, Jessica Young's abduction—'

'Hang on,' broke in Garrett, his forehead furrowing. 'Now you're telling me Jessica Young was a victim of Forester and Harding.'

Jim looked at Anna. 'Show him the sketch.'

She brought up the image of her sister's abductor on her iPhone. Garrett squinted at it. 'It's the caretaker from Lance Brennan's Hopeland file.'

Anna shook her head. 'That's the sketch the police made from my description of the man who took Jessica.'

Garrett's eyes grew big in realisation. 'Jesus.'

'There's more,' said Jim. He held his hand out to Anna. 'The key.'

She unhooked the key from the Horned God keyring and handed it to him. He showed it to Garrett. 'Do you recognise this?'

'No. Should I?'

'Yeah, you should. It's a copy of a key we found in Edward Forester's bunker. A key that had Freddie Harding's prints on it.'

Garrett's frown hardened. He thrust a finger at Anna. 'Then why did she have it?'

'Because I gave it to her.'

'So you admit you've been leaking evidence to Miss Young.'

'I admit I'm willing to do whatever it takes to break this case. But then you knew that when you gave me the job, didn't you?'

'That's not why I offered you the job. I offered you it because you're bloody good at what you do.'

A sardonic smile stretched across Jim's lips. 'Come on, let's not kid each other. We both know why I got this job, the same as we both know why you got your promotion.'

Garrett's gaze slid uneasily to Anna, then back to Jim. There was resentment in his eyes – resentment at the knowledge that just as Jim's lie had put the Chief Superintendent's star and crown on his shoulder, so he could take it away too. His voice was low and overly controlled as he said, 'I don't think we should be discussing this in front of Miss Young.'

'Neither do I. I think we should be talking about why Freddie Harding's key opens a garage that was rented by a man who used to work for Thomas Villiers.'

Garrett took the key off Jim. He stared at it thoughtfully, then heaved a sigh. 'What you said the other day was right. I'm getting pressure on this like I've never known before. The powers that be want this case to die away as quickly and quietly as possible.'

'But we're not going to let that happen, are we?' There was an unmistakable note of implied threat in Jim's voice.

'No.' Garrett's knuckles whitened on the key. With a sort of morose resolve, as though he was thinking, *Why is this happening to me?* he said, 'We're going to tear Thomas Villiers' life apart. And all the rest of their lives too. But first we've got to deal with this.' He opened his hand. 'How are you going to explain Miss Young having Freddie Harding's key?'

'I'm not. I was the only one with a copy, so it's obvious where it came from. And I'm willing to take full responsibility when this is over. But until then I need you to keep them off my back.'

Garrett pursed his lips doubtfully. 'I'll do my best. But they're gunning for you. I had a call from the IPCC this morning. They're going to be investigating the leak.'

Jim gave a little snort of derision. 'And what about the fact that I can't make a move without Villiers knowing about it? Are they going to investigate who's leaking information to him?'

With another sigh, Garrett shook his head. His eyes narrowed suddenly. 'I hope you don't think I've been speaking to him.'

'If I thought that we wouldn't be having this conversation.' Jim knew Garrett would be willing to do almost anything to further his career. But he felt sure that *almost anything* didn't stretch to protecting criminals. Garrett had repeatedly said as much himself. And regardless of his misgivings about Garrett's ambitions, he'd never been given any reason to doubt that the Chief Superintendent wasn't as good as his word.

Garrett's expression relaxed, not much, but enough to make it plain that having Jim's trust was important to him.

'That doesn't mean you haven't been unintentionally passing on information to Villiers' source,' pointed out Jim.

'The same applies to you.'

Jim grimaced agreement. 'That's why we need to be especially careful about what we say to whom from now on.'

'What about Miss Young?'

'What about me?' Anna demanded, her eyes flaring to life.

Garrett treated her to a searching look. 'Can we trust you to keep everything you've heard here to yourself?'

'Of course you fucking can. That's my sister out there. Do you really think I'd do anything that might prevent her killer from being—'

'No, it's not,' interrupted Jim.

Anna turned to him sharply. 'What?'

'It's not your sister's body.'

Anna blinked. Her tongue darted over her lower lip. 'Are you sure?' Her voice was tentative, as if she both wanted and didn't want to believe Jim. She'd been searching for Jessica for so many years. So many long, long years. The thought that her sister had been murdered and stuffed into that hole was devastating beyond words. And yet in some corner of her mind she could barely bring herself to acknowledge, she'd felt a sense of relief at the possibility that her search might finally have come to an end.

'Yes. I'm sorry, I should have told you as soon as I came in here.'

Anna's gaze dropped away from Jim. 'So it's not over,' she murmured more to herself than anybody else. She took a steadying breath and lifted her eyes. 'Do you have any idea who it could be?'

'Not yet. If she was reported missing, we might get a hit on the DNA database.'

Garrett's phone rang. Raising a finger for quiet, he put the phone to his ear. Lines of tension worked their way outwards from behind his glasses as he listened to the caller. 'Well keep it under control,' he said exasperatedly. 'He'll be there ASAP.' He hung up and turned to Jim. 'You're needed back in Sheffield. Linda Kirby's turned up at Villiers' house along with a mob of her supporters.'

'Shit, that's all we need. Is he at home?'

'Yes. We've got men with him, but they're worried the crowd will turn violent if they try to get him out. You'd better speak to Linda. Calm things down. Because if anything happens to Villiers I won't be able to protect you.'

Flashing Anna a look, Jim headed for the door. She met his gaze squarely with no apology in her eyes. As far as she was concerned, Villiers deserved whatever was coming to him and more. Garrett followed Jim outside. 'Chief Inspector Monahan… Jim. There was no need to threaten me in there. I'm on your side.'

Jim looked at his Chief Superintendent – the overly pressed uniform, the smooth, pompous face – and it struck him how maybe one time in a thousand someone turned out to be better than you thought they were. 'I know,' he said, then he turned to hurry back to the woods. He found Reece where he'd left him, watching the bones being bagged.

'I've just got off the phone to Scott,' Reece told Jim. 'He's tracked down Donald Turner, the owner of the lock-ups. Do you want to go talk to him?'

'Later. Right now, we need to get back to Sheffield.'

'Why?'

Jim explained the situation as they made their way to their

cars. 'I never thought I'd be saying this, Reece, but we need to make sure no harm comes to Villiers.'

'How did things go with Garrett?'

'He knows everything.'

Reece's eyebrows lifted. 'And you're still walking around with a badge.'

'For now.'

'Maybe he's not such a prick as he seems,' mused Reece.

'Maybe, but even he won't be able to keep me in the job if Linda Kirby gets her hands on Villiers.'

****

Thomas Villiers' house overlooked a hump of moorland that rippled up against the city like a purple-brown wave. It was late afternoon when Jim and Reece arrived there. Normally, the road would have been busy with commuters. But not that day. Police had cordoned off either end of it. Jim flashed his badge at a constable who moved aside some cones to let them through. He heard the crowd before he saw it. Chants of, 'Lies, lies, lies!' filtered through his open window. The crowd was clustered outside Villiers' house – a big, detached place set well back from the road behind a wall and gates. There were maybe three or four hundred people. Many of them were wearing white t-shirts with Grace Kirby's face on the front. Not Grace's face as it had been when she died – worn down and hollowed out by life – but Grace's face as it had been before she fell into Stephen Baxley's clutches – beautiful and smiling, yet touched by a sadness that shone from her blue eyes. Above her face were the words 'NO JUSTICE'. Some of the crowd were carrying placards whose slogans cried out 'WHY ARE THE POLICE PROTECTING CHILD ABUSERS?', 'WE DEMAND ANSWERS', 'NO MORE LIES' and 'ENOUGH IS ENOUGH'.

A line of constables had been drawn up in front of Villiers' gates, separated from the crowd by the width of the pavement. Shouts of, 'Move back!' from the constables competed with the chanting of the crowd. Jim parked a stone's throw from the scene and got out of his car. As he waited for Reece to join him, his gaze searched the crowd for Linda Kirby. He wasn't surprised to spot her at the front, gesticulating angrily in a policeman's face. The policeman had one hand extended out towards her. The other gripped a truncheon. The atmosphere was as explosive as a powder keg dangling over a bonfire.

Jim and Reece approached Linda between the battle lines. 'Fucking pigs!' yelled someone, marking them for what they were in their suits. 'Lying bastards,' came another shout, followed by a glob of phlegm that hit Jim in the face. A policeman stepped forward to apprehend the guilty party, but Jim raised a hand to stay him. Wiping his face, he called to Linda. She jerked towards him, her eyes that had been so timid the first time they'd met now burning with passionate, indignant rage.

'Look!' She thrust an accusatory finger at Jim. 'Here comes one of the chief liars!'

Her words provoked another chorus of insults. A man grabbed Jim's arm. Reece brought a heavy hand down on the assailant's wrist, breaking his hold. Someone flung a coin that bounced off Reece's forehead, opening up a small cut. Again, the constables made as if to charge. Again, Jim raised his hands, yelling, 'Remain where you are. That's an order!' He turned to Linda. 'Can we talk?'

'I'm done talking,' she retorted. 'Now's the time for action.'

'Please, Linda. All I'm asking for is five minutes. Just listen to what I've got to say. And if you don't like what you hear, then do what you need to do. I for one won't stand in your way.'

Linda eyed Jim uncertainly, as if she suspected some trick. Then she said, 'Alright, five minutes, for the sake of everything you did for my Grace.'

They moved away from the crowd. Linda faced Jim, her arms folded, her mouth set hard. 'You have every right to be angry with us,' he began. 'We've let you down in the worst way possible. But as of today that's going to change. No more softly, softly. We're going to pull Villiers' life apart piece by piece until we find out what we need to know.'

'Why?' Linda's voice was sharp with scepticism. 'What's changed since yesterday?'

'New evidence has come to light that could be the break we've been waiting for. I can't say much more right now, except to tell you things are finally moving. But if you do this—' Jim jerked his chin at the crowd. 'If you damage Villiers' property or, worse still, hurt him you could also damage the entire investigation.'

'Why should I believe a single bloody word you say?'

Jim leant in close to Linda. 'Who do you think passed Anna Young the information on Herbert Winstanley's book?'

Her scowl turned thoughtful. 'Anna mentioned a source with police connections. Not a policeman.'

'If you don't believe me, call her and she can tell you herself.'

Linda mulled Jim's words over. The line of her mouth softened. When she next spoke, the harshness was gone from her voice. 'I should have known. I'm sorry, Jim.'

'No need for apologies. Just keep things peaceful here and I swear to you I'll do everything I can to give your Grace and all the other victims the justice they deserve.'

'OK. I'm going to trust you one more time. I'm going to believe that you'll do what you say.'

'Thank you, Linda. Oh, and I don't suppose I need ask you to keep all of this to yourself.'

Linda made a mouth-zipped gesture. They returned to the crowd. As Linda raised her hands and made a calming gesture to her supporters, Jim pressed the intercom on the gate. 'This is DCI Monahan. Let me in.'

There was a buzz and the gates swung inwards. Jim handed Reece a tissue and the big man staunched the bleeding on his forehead as they approached the front door. A constable opened it and directed them into a large, well-furnished living room. Villiers was nursing a tumbler of some spirit by French doors that looked out on a large patio and lawn. Beyond the garden, a field and a strip of trees insulated the house from the edge of the city proper. He was dressed in a polo shirt and chinos. Out of his suit he looked smaller, less imposing. He looked too as if he had a heavy cold. His eyes were bleary and he was dabbing his nostrils with a handkerchief. A gleam as sharp as his beaky nose sprang into his eyes at the sight of Jim. 'Chief Inspector Monahan,' he said with a bitter twist of his lips. 'I'm amazed you dare show your face here.'

'I just wanted to let you know the situation's under control,' said Jim, his tone impersonal.

'Under control?' Villiers gave a snort of disbelief. 'There's a mob out there baying for my blood. I'm a prisoner in my own home. My wife is upstairs in floods of tears. My...' A little catch came into his voice. He swallowed it and continued, 'My children are refusing to speak to me. And it's all your fault. And you expect me to believe a word you say?'

'I've spoken to Linda Kirby—'

'Oh yes, and what did you say to her? That she doesn't need to kill me because you're going to do the job yourself.'

Jim moved closer to Villiers – close enough that he could smell the whisky on his breath. 'I'd be careful what you say, if I were you, Mr Villiers. Slander is a serious matter.'

'Slander, hah! You're damn right it's a serious matter. And I'm going to make sure you pay for what you've done to me. First I'm going to have you out of your job. Then I'm going to take you to court for every penny you've got. And finally I'll see you put behind bars.'

There was a ranting edge to Villiers' voice that Jim hadn't heard before. Some people might have mistaken his anger for strength, but Jim knew it for exactly what it was – weakness. Villiers was wobbling. A few more pushes and he might fall over.

'I don't think so.' Jim's voice was icily calm. 'I think you know what's going to happen now. And from the sounds of it so do your wife and children.'

Villiers whitened with fury. 'Get out of my house!' he yelled. 'Go on. Get out.'

'Goodbye, Mr Villiers. We'll talk again soon.'

'Not if I've got anything to do with it. You're finished, Monahan. Do you hear me? Finished!'

'Oh no. I've barely begun.'

Jim turned his back on Villiers' quivering face and returned outside. The crowd were still chanting, but their voices had lost the threatening edge. 'Well, you've definitely got under his skin,' commented Reece.

'Before I'm done with him I'll be so deep under there the fucker won't be able to see any face but mine when he closes his eyes.'

'We still don't have anything concrete on him.'

'Maybe not, but we've got a chance of finding what we need now. And that's a hell of a lot more than we had two days ago.'

As they made their way back past the crowd, Linda's supporters threw nothing worse than glares at them. Jim's phone rang. 'We've lifted some prints off the garage door,' Scott Greenwood informed him. 'We're running them now.'

The news was promising, but Jim knew better than to get excited. The prints most likely belonged to the owner of the lock-ups. 'And what about Donald Turner? What did he have to say?'

'Nothing much. Mr Daeja rented the lock-up between 1991 and 2007. Mr Turner claims not to have had any contact with him since then. All payments were made in cash. Mr Turner also claims to have no knowledge of what the garage was used for. He says he makes it a rule not to snoop into his customers' business. He describes Mr Daeja at the time of last seeing him as having a goatee beard and long hair in a ponytail. Oh, and by the way, there's no record of the name Clotho Daeja on any of the databases. It appears to be a completely made-up identity. Nor are there any tax records for a company called The True Wiccan.' Scott's voice took on a conspiratorial tone. 'Listen, sir, the DCS told me to warn you not to return to Leeds. There are some heavy-duty characters looking for you here.'

'IPCC?'

'Worse. Special Branch. They've been asking all sorts of questions about you and Anna Young.'

With an unsurprised rumble of his throat, Jim thanked Scott and hung up. He turned to speak to Reece and saw that he was also on the phone. He guessed at once that it was bad news. Reece's face was colourless and furrowed. He got off the phone and hurried past Jim. 'What's happened?' Jim called after him.

'Staci's collapsed,' Reece replied anxiously. 'They've got her at the Northern General.' He ducked into his car. Tyres biting hard, he sped towards the roadblock.

The helplessness Jim had heard in Reece's voice caused a familiar thought to push its way into his world-weary mind. *What does the job matter? What does any of this bullshit matter if you can't protect the ones you love?* It was the same thought that had paralysed him for weeks after Margaret's death. He shook it away with a jerk of his head, reminding himself that this wasn't about the job any more. It was about justice. For a long time he'd thought the two things were mutually dependent. Now he knew otherwise.

He drove to the roadblock. A TV van had turned up. A constable was shaking his head at a journalist. Jim got out of his car and said, 'Let them through.'

'But, sir, my orders are—' the constable began to protest.

'I don't give a monkey's what your orders are, Constable. I'm telling you to let them through.'

'Yes, sir.'

As the constable moved the cones, the journalist made to say something to Jim. But Jim waved him away, saying, 'Speak to Linda Kirby. She'll tell you everything you need to know.'

He looked towards Villiers' house. Another thought came to him *Why not just kill the bastard? It wouldn't be difficult to get away with. Half the city's out for his blood.* Again, he shook his head. *No. That would be too easy on him. Better to take away everything he has and let him kill himself.* That would be true justice.

CHAPTER NINE

As afternoon wore into evening, the crowd gradually lost its voice and began to disperse. Jim had hung around partly to make sure things didn't get out of hand on either side, but mainly because there was little else for him to do. During the hours he'd been there, more TV vans had turned up, along with reporters from local and national newspapers. Linda Kirby had done interview after interview, speaking with fierce eloquence about the abuse her daughter and unknown numbers of others had suffered, and about the powers-that-be's attempts to hush it up. Villiers and his fellow perverts, it seemed, were about to hit the front pages.

Several times, Jim had tried to phone Reece to find out how Staci was doing but only got his answering service. Reece's silence gave him a bad feeling. He recognised that there was something at the centre of his own being – something hard like an impenetrable callus – that allowed him to simply go on no matter what shit life flung at him. He recognised too that Reece wasn't the type who could simply go on. He was the type who, if he lost the thing he loved most, would fall apart and never get himself back together.

When the road was finally empty of demonstrators, Jim got into his car and somewhat reluctantly set off in the direction of his flat. Regardless of Garrett's warning, his instinct was to head back to Leeds and work the case into the small hours. But experience had taught him what happened if he didn't give his body the rest it needed.

He flicked on the indicator but didn't turn onto his road. There was an unfamiliar car outside his flat. A BMW 5 Series – a car commonly used as an unmarked pursuit vehicle. In the softening light, he made out two suited men in the front seats. Who were they? Special Branch seemed the most likely possibility. But they could also be IPCC. Taking a quick mental note of the BMW's reg, he accelerated out of view and pulled over. He phoned Police HQ and ran the reg. It didn't show up on the DVLA database. That decided him – they were Special Branch. He restarted the engine and continued driving away from his road. He had no intention of tangling with Special Branch. At least, not tonight.

He headed into the city centre, got himself a room at the Holiday Inn overlooking the murky waters of the River Don and lay watching the news. He was disappointed to see nothing about the demonstration at Villiers' house. No doubt, some powerful strings were being pulled to supress the story. They wouldn't be able to do so for much longer, though. Not if Garrett was as good as his word. If Villiers was publicly declared a suspect, it would give the story a legitimacy no one would be able to deny.

Jim's phone rang. This time it was Garrett. 'Where are you?' asked the DCS.

'Lying low at the Holiday Inn. There's someone on my house.'

'That doesn't surprise me. You've stirred up a real hornet's nest, Jim. Special Branch have been throwing their weight around. They've taken our Miss Young.'

Jim's heart gave a quick beat. 'Where?'

'I've no idea, but they won't let us talk to her.' Garrett took on a tone of offended authority. 'I told them they're obstructing a murder inquiry, but these people seem to think they can do as they please.'

'Did you check them out?'

'Believe me, they're for real. Only Special Branch officers could be as arrogant as them. They outright accused you of being the source of the leak. They even had the gall to suggest you be suspended from duty.'

'And am I?'

'No, you're bloody well not. I decide how best to deal with my own people, and until such time as they have evidence to back up their allegation you'll remain on duty.'

For the second time that day, Jim had the strange sensation of feeling something like a nagging affection for Garrett. The DCS was going way out on a limb by backing him. It was one thing being loyal to your people. It was another entirely to refuse to discipline someone whose culpability was plain for all to see. That merely made it look as though you'd lost control of the officers under your command.

A note of warning replaced Garrett's indignation as he continued, 'But I'm telling you this, we need to move fast because I get the distinct feeling it won't be long before the decision is taken out of my hands.'

'Any luck with the prints?'

'That's the second reason I'm calling. We got a hit. And I'm guessing you won't be surprised to hear they belong to a man who's supposedly been dead for twenty-six years.'

Garrett was right. Jim wasn't surprised in the slightest. Spider was seemingly an expert at assuming dead or fictional identities. If the prints had belonged to someone alive and easily traceable, Jim would have doubted their worth. The fact that their maker was supposedly dead fitted the pattern perfectly, giving him a gut feeling that rather than leading them down another blind alley, the prints had revealed Spider's true identity. 'When you say "supposedly", I take it you mean there's a chance this man's alive.'

'You take it right. I'm sending you a mugshot of him.'

There was a ping as the photo arrived. The instant Jim opened it he knew his instincts were on the mark. The man was little more than a boy, perhaps eighteen or nineteen. He had the same short dark hair, the same slightly flattened nose, and the same chubby cheeks as the sketches of Jessica Young's abductor and Spider. The only thing that was vaguely different was his eyes. In the sketches they were dead, like a doll's eyes. But in the photo they had a kind of sly directness, like a fox. 'It's our man.'

'His name's Gavin Walsh and he was a thoroughly unpleasant piece of work. Gavin had just turned nineteen when he went missing in July '87 a few weeks after being cleared of the rape of a fourteen-year-old girl. The girl's name was Jody McLean. Gavin's father, Ronald, worked for Jody's father, Kevin.'

'Kevin McLean. Why does that name seem familiar to me?'

'Kevin McLean was a prominent Birmingham gangster with suspected connections to Irish organised crime groups.'

'That's right. He was jailed back in the eighties for murdering a policeman, wasn't he?'

'He shot a constable during a routine traffic stop. The attack was completely unprovoked. He received a life sentence and died in jail in 2003.'

'So is Walsh's father a criminal too?'

'No. He's got no record. Along with his criminal enterprises, Kevin Mclean owned several legitimate businesses in Birmingham.

Ronald Walsh was his accountant. Apparently the two men were good friends. That is, until Jody accused Gavin of raping her. Gavin was a keen birdwatcher who spent his weekends pursuing his hobby in the countryside around Birmingham. One Saturday he took Jody with him and it was during this daytrip that he supposedly raped her. Jody didn't report the assault right away. It came out several weeks later when she broke down and told a teacher who then called the police. Gavin was interviewed but denied the accusation. A full investigation was carried out, but it was decided there wasn't enough evidence to charge Gavin and the case was dropped. Two days later he went missing. His bloodstained clothes were found in woods a couple of miles from his house. Suspicion immediately fell on Jody McLean's older brothers, Patrick and Kieran, who'd publicly sworn revenge. However, no body was ever found. So no convictions were brought against the brothers. Despite the absence of a body, Ronald Walsh and his wife, Sharon, fought to have their son declared dead. Which he eventually was in 1997.'

'Are they still alive?'

'Yes. According to the DVLA database, they live in Nottingham now.'

Garrett gave Jim the address. Jim glanced at his watch. It was half eight. He could be at the Walshes' house in an hour. He ached with the need for a hot bath and bed, but there was no time for that now. He reached for his jacket. 'Any news on the skeleton?'

'The DNA testing is being fast-tracked. We should have the results in a day or two.'

'I'm heading to Nottingham. I'll call you when I've spoken to the Walshes.'

As Jim rushed down to his car, he phoned Anna and got her answering service. 'This is Detective Chief Inspector Jim

Monahan,' he said in a businesslike voice. If Anna was still in Special Branch's custody, there was a good chance they were monitoring her phone. Any attempt at subterfuge would only serve to highlight his guilt. Better to be open. After all, he had a legitimate reason for contacting her. 'I urgently need to speak to you. Could you please return my call as soon as you get this message.'

Next, Jim phoned Harry Dutton, a trusted old contact in the Met. 'Special Branch are talking to someone involved in a case of mine. I'm trying to find out where they've got her. Her name's Anna Young.'

'I'll ask around and get back to you,' said Harry.

Jim was speeding along the southbound carriageway of the M1 when his phone rang. Harry's voice came tensely down the line. 'Jesus Christ, Jim, who the fuck is this Anna Young? I almost got my ear bitten off for asking about her. On second thoughts, don't tell me. I think it's better if I don't know. Special Branch have got her in Watford. That's all I could find out.'

It reassured Jim somewhat to know the officers who'd taken Anna were at least who they'd claimed to be. Crooked or not, they surely wouldn't dare harm her physically. Psychologically was another matter. These people knew every trick in the book when it came to wearing down and scaring detainees into spilling their guts. Anna had proved herself as tough as they come, but everyone had their weaknesses. Anna's was her mother. They'd already threatened to take away Fiona's house. No doubt they had plenty of other threats of a similar nature up their sleeves. He was half tempted to bypass Nottingham and go in search of Anna. But he knew that even if he found her, he wouldn't be allowed to see her. He'd just have to hope that, like his tired body, she could hold out.

Forty or so minutes later, he pulled up outside a modest detached house on a quiet, leafy suburban street. There was a Volvo in the driveway. Lights glowed behind curtains in the downstairs windows. The very image of normality.

Ideally, he would have liked to find out more about the house's occupants before talking to them. Who exactly were the Walshes? How had Ronald Walsh come to work for a known criminal? What had their relationship with their son been like? He would have liked to get a look at their phone records too. Perhaps even run surveillance on them for a few days. But there was nothing ideal about this situation.

He knocked on the door of one of the Walshes' neighbours. A woman answered. 'Sorry to disturb you,' he said, showing her his ID, 'but I need to ask you, and anyone else who lives here, a couple of questions.' The woman called her husband to the door. Jim showed them the mugshot of the nineteen-year-old Gavin Walsh. 'Have you ever seen this man at the Walshes' house or anywhere else on this street?' They both replied no. 'Try to imagine him older with a goatee beard and a ponytail. Ring any bells?' Again, the same response.

'What's this about?' asked the husband.

'Nothing for you to worry about. Thanks for your time.'

Jim worked his way up and down the street, knocking on every door, asking the same questions, getting the same replies. He wasn't surprised. Gavin Walsh was an extremely cautious man. He'd proved that time and again over the years with his disappearing acts.

Finally, Jim knocked at the Walshes' house. An exterior light came on and the front door was opened by a man whom Jim guessed to be somewhere in his late sixties. Like Gavin, he had intensely dark eyes. But otherwise there was little resemblance. His face was longer and thinner, his nose was sharper, and he was bald except for a frizz of grey hair at the sides of his head.

'Are you Ronald Walsh?'

'Yes. And who are you?'

Noting the Brummie accent, Jim produced his ID. 'If I may, I'd like to ask you a few questions.'

Lines gathered around Ronald's eyes. 'About what?'

'Your son.'

The lines spread and deepened, like cracks in a dry stream bed. Ronald stepped outside, pulling the door to behind him. 'My son is dead.'

'As I understand it his body was never found.'

'My son is dead,' repeated Ronald, as if stating an undisputable fact. 'If you want to know where his body is, I suggest you speak to the McLeans.'

Jim gave a thoughtful wag of his head. 'You know, Mr Walsh, that's something that strikes me as odd. If the McLeans were careful enough to hide your son's body where no one would ever find it, why would they leave behind his bloodstained clothes?'

'I'll tell you why. Because they had to let everyone know what they'd done. It was about not losing face.' Ronald's lips curled with hate. 'That's what everything's about with people like them. That and money.'

There was no arguing with that. Jim changed tack. 'Is your wife in, Mr Walsh?'

'Yes, but I don't want you talking to her. She's not a well woman.'

'I'm sorry to hear that, but I won't take up much of her time.'

Ronald shook his head vehemently. 'I won't have you upsetting her for no good reason.'

'I assure you, Mr Walsh, I wouldn't be here if it wasn't for a good reason.'

Still shaking his head, Ronald turned to head back into his house. Jim caught hold of his arm in a firm, but not so firm as to be painful grip. 'Aren't you even interested what that reason is?'

'My son is dead,' Ronald said once again, like the words were some kind of all-answering mantra. 'That's all I need to know.'

'But what if—'

'Are you not listening to me?' Ronald broke in, his voice a sharp rasp. 'There is no "what if". Now please leave us alone.'

As Ronald made to close the door, Jim braced a hand against it. 'We could have this conversation down the station, if you want to play it that way.'

Ronald looked at Jim as if to say, *Do you take me for a fool?* 'I know my rights, Chief Inspector Monahan. I don't have to go anywhere with you unless you're charging me with something. Now remove your hand from my door.'

Jim reluctantly did so, and before he could say anything else, Ronald shut the door in his face. Jim returned to his car, phoned Garrett and relayed his conversation with Ronald. 'Sounds to me like Mr Walsh is hiding something,' said the DCS.

A wrinkle of uncertainty appeared between Jim's eyes. 'Usually when people are hiding something they play it cooler. I'd be inclined to think Mr Walsh was genuine, except for one thing. You said the Walshes fought to have their son declared dead. And when I spoke to Mr Walsh tonight he refused to even entertain the thought that his son might be alive. I just can't get my head round that.'

'Maybe he knew exactly what his son was capable of, and so was relieved when it seemed he'd been murdered.'

'You've got a son of your own. If he turned out to be a rapist, even a killer, would you want him dead?'

Garrett considered this briefly, then conceded, 'No. I might want myself dead, but not him.'

Jim eyed the Walshes' house curiously. A light had come on in the upstairs main bedroom window. 'I'm going to stay on the Walshes tonight and see what I can see. It might be worth having a look at their phone records too.'

'I'll put DI Greenwood on it. Now I'd better get back to work. It's going to be a busy day tomorrow. I have an appointment with Judge Lawson in the morning. I've got a lot to do if I'm going to convince him to issue a search and seizure for Villiers' house.'

'Let's hope no one's got to Lawson before us.'

A slight rise of indignation came into Garrett's voice. 'Lawson's a good man.'

'You would have said the same about Charles Knight a year ago.'

Garrett sighed. 'Regardless, we have to follow proper procedure or whatever evidence we gather will be worthless. You know that as well as I do. We can't keep telling lies to cover our tracks.'

Jim grunted begrudging agreement. Garrett was right. A good lawyer like Miles Burnham would have the case thrown out long before trial if procedure wasn't followed to the letter. 'I don't think we'll find much of interest at Villiers' house anyway. He's much too careful for that.'

'Well, if nothing else, it'll let him know we mean business now.'

'True, but what we really need to do is start talking to the children at the Craig Thorpe Youth Trust home and former residents of Hopeland.'

'We will do, believe me. But we've got to move carefully. This is an extremely sensitive case. There's too much at stake and too many innocent people who could get hurt if we don't do things properly.'

Jim prickled with irritation at this reminder that Garrett's overly conservative side was never far from the surface. 'And what about the other names in Herbert's book?'

'We'll get to them too. And their families, friends and colleagues. But for now I think we should concentrate on Villiers. Like you said the other day, he's the weak link. Break him and we break the case open.'

There was no arguing with Garrett's logic. Still, it burnt Jim to think of Villiers' accomplices remaining at least partly in the shadows. He knew it would most likely only be for a few more days, but even that was too long. The sooner they were officially outed as suspects, the sooner their power would begin to bleed away. He wanted to read their names in every newspaper, see their faces on every TV channel. So that even if they managed to avoid prosecution, their reputations would be indelibly stained by being hauled through the court of public opinion. 'Good luck with Lawson.'

'Thanks, Jim. And you try to get some rest. Remember, you need to take care of that heart of yours.'

As Jim hung up, his gaze was drawn to the downstairs window of the Walshes' house. The curtains twitched. Someone – no doubt Ronald Walsh – was furtively watching him. He started up the engine and pulled around the corner. He glanced at the clock. He'd give it half an hour, then he'd find a spot from where he could inconspicuously watch the house. As he waited, he tried Anna's and Reece's phones again. Still no answer from either. He exhaled heavily. It was going to be a long night.

CHAPTER TEN

Jim was jerked out of a fitful doze by the sound of a car door closing. He lifted a hand to wipe away the fog of sleep, for an instant not knowing where he was. He'd been dreaming about Margaret, about a future that could never be. The dream had taunted him with images of them being together in some warm, sunny place. It was a dream he'd had many times before, and he always woke from it with a choking sob. Sometimes he couldn't bear the thought of sleep because of it, other times he closed his eyes in the hope that it would come again.

The morning sun was streaming palely through the windscreen. It was twenty past eight. Between bushes that partially screened him from view, he focused blinkingly on the Walshes' house. The front door was open. Ronald was in the driver's seat of the Volvo. A woman, who from her appearance surely had to be Sharon Walsh, emerged from the house. She was mid-sixties, short and solidly built. Her broad, round face bore a striking resemblance to Gavin that was accentuated by short, too dark to be natural hair. Her movements were purposeful, as though she was in a rush. She didn't appear to be ill. But then her husband might not have meant that she was physically ill. Jim could easily imagine how the murder of her son might have affected her mentally. The best part of thirty years had passed since then. But as he'd pointed out to Garrett, there were some wounds time could never heal.

The Volvo reversed out of the driveway and accelerated away. Jim was about to follow it when he saw something that stopped him cold. A girl stepped from the house, waving at the receding car. She was about Sharon Walsh's height, but slimmer. A satchel was slung over her shoulder. She was dressed in a knee-length black skirt, a white shirt and a navy-blue school blazer. She looked to be about fourteen or fifteen. Surely too young to be Ronald and Sharon's daughter. It wasn't her age, though, that truly sparked his curiosity.

She set off walking in Jim's direction. He made a show of fiddling with the car radio as she passed. She didn't give him a glance. She had earphones on and was singing along silently to whatever she was listening to. Jim could see nothing in her bland teenage face that suggested Ronald had told her about his visit. He glanced uncertainly in the direction of the Volvo, then got out of his car and began to tail the girl.

She made her way to a bus stop crowded with other schoolchildren and workers heading into the city centre. As she waited for a bus, she chatted to several girls. Jim phoned Scott Greenwood. 'How's it going with the phone records?'

'I'm still working on getting a subpoena.'

'I need you to do something else. There's a girl living with the Walshes. Find out everything you can about her. And I mean everything. Who her biological parents are. Where she was born. When her birth was registered.'

'Will do. Have you spoken to Reece? He's not come into the office.'

A bus pulled in and the girl got on board. Quickly explaining the situation with Staci, Jim followed the girl onto the bus. She took a seat with her friends. He sat several seats back from her. Over the chugging of the engine, he caught snippets of her conversation. Just usual teenage girl talk – who was wearing what, who was going out with whom. Five stops later, the bus emptied of schoolchildren at the gates of a large comp. Jim disembarked too. As he watched the girl head into the school, his phone rang. When he saw the caller's number, he eagerly put the phone to his ear. But his voice was carefully professional as he said, 'This is DCI Jim Monahan. Who am I speaking to?'

'Red fucking Riding Hood, who do you think?'

Jim felt a rise of relief at the familiar abrasive voice. 'Anna, are you OK?'

'Yeah, I'm fine. Knackered but fine. Those Special Branch pricks kept me up all night, hammering me with questions and threats.'

'What sort of threats?'

'Just the usual crap. How they're going to stop my benefits and have me and Mum kicked out of our house. How if anything happens to anyone on the list they're going to prosecute me for inciting a crime. I told them I hope they get the chance.' The bravado suddenly left Anna in a sigh. 'They're going to do it, you know. They're going to take away our house. Eviction proceedings have already begun. They showed me the papers. I honestly don't know if Mum could survive without that house. It's her last remaining connection to Jessica and Dad.'

'No it's not. You are.'

'You don't understand.'

'Yes I do.' Jim thought of the house he'd shared with Margaret, of the reluctance he'd felt to sell it, and the relief that had rushed over him when he finally worked up the courage to do so. True, the house had been a connection, but it had also been a burden, weighing on him so heavily he couldn't move.

Anna sighed again. 'Anyway, it doesn't matter because I'm not going to give them what they want.'

Jim didn't need to ask what they wanted. He already knew the answer. They wanted to do to him what they'd done to Lance Brennan. 'I'm in Nottingham. You need to get yourself here. There's something, or rather someone, I think you should see.'

'Who?'

'I'd rather not say over the phone.'

'Why? Do you think Special Branch are listening in?'

'Maybe, but that's...' Jim paused as if searching for a way to explain something inexplicable. 'When you get here you'll understand.'

'OK, but it's going to take me some time. I'm in Watford and my van's still in Leeds. I'll have to pick it up, then head back down to you.'

Jim arranged to meet Anna in a pub he'd spotted not far from the Walshes' house. He caught a return bus back to his car. Ronald and Sharon were still out. There was nothing else to be done for the moment. He drove to a nearby café and ordered breakfast. His phone rang again. It was Reece. Bracing himself for the worst, he answered the call.

'How is she?'

'Not good, Jim.' Reece sounded exhausted. 'Her liver's just about ready to pack in. It looks like she's going to need a transplant.'

'Fucking hell. Is there nothing they can do?'

'They're already doing everything they can and it's making no difference. She needs to get to South Africa or—' Emotion choked Reece.

Jim winced at the anguish in his friend's voice. 'Any word on when that's going to happen?'

'No, but she's going to be too ill to travel if it doesn't happen soon.' Reece drew a breath and collected himself. 'What about you? How's the investigation going?'

'Forget the investigation. You just concentrate on looking after Staci and Amelia.'

The choke came back into Reece's voice at the mention of Staci's daughter. 'I keep thinking how do I tell Amelia if her mum dies? I mean, for Christ's sake, how do you tell an eight-year-old something like that?'

His question was almost a plea. Jim made no reply. Experience had taught him that there was no easy way to break that kind of news.

With another long breath, Reece returned the conversation to the investigation. 'Have forensics ID'd the skeleton?'

'No, but I told you to forget about all that. Believe me, Reece, work is the last thing you should be thinking about right now.'

'You're right, Jim. It's just...' Reece trailed off as if he didn't have the energy to explain.

'It's OK.' Reece didn't need to explain himself. Jim understood it was easier for him to focus on work rather than what was happening in his personal life. He'd been there himself. 'And don't worry about Garrett. I'll let him know what's going on.'

'Thanks, Jim. You've done so much for me this past year. I'm sorry for letting you down.'

'Don't talk daft. You're not letting anyone down.' Jim's voice assumed a gentle pretence of authority. 'Now get back to that girl of yours. That's an order.'

'Yes, sir,' Reece replied, his tone briefly lightening. The heaviness returned as he added, 'I'll call you as soon as I know what's happening with South Africa.'

Jim resumed his breakfast of decaf tea and muesli. With each tasteless mouthful, he thought of Margaret, of how much she would have approved. It made his lips curl in self-contempt to remember how, after she walked out on him, he used to take a childish pleasure in doing things he knew she would disapprove of. How could he have wasted so much energy on such self-destructive behaviour? How could he have been so blind to what was truly important? Well, he wasn't blind any more. He saw the truth with a stinging clarity. He was an idiot, a fool, good for nothing except everything that was bad about life. That was why he was so proficient at chasing down criminals.

After breakfast, he returned to the Walshes' house. At mid-morning they reappeared and unloaded shopping bags from their Volvo. Then Ronald set to mowing the front lawn, whilst Sharon polished the insides of the house's windows. It was a perfectly normal domestic scene. And yet something about it made Jim's forehead crease faintly. It seemed to him that the Walshes performed their tasks with a kind of exaggerated enthusiasm, like actors in a show.

It was early afternoon when Scott Greenwood phoned back. 'The girl's name is Emily Walsh,' he told Jim. 'She's fifteen. I've been on to the General Register's Office. According to her birth certificate, Ronald and Sharon are her biological parents.'

'They're a bit old, don't you think?'

'Maybe they had IVF.'

'Maybe,' Jim echoed, unconvinced. 'Where and when was Emily born?'

'The Maternity Unit at Queen's Medical Centre, Nottingham, on the twenty-eighth of May 1998.'

'And I take it all the documents were in order.'

'According to the guy I spoke to. Do you want his name and number?'

'No. What about the phone records?'

'Sorry, Jim, no dice. We're going to need more than Gavin Walsh's fingerprints to convince Judge Lawson to cough up a subpoena. He did approve the search and seizure warrant for Villiers' house, though.'

'That's something, I suppose.' Jim drew a certain grim satisfaction from the thought of Villiers' house being turned upside down, his personal documents and computers being seized. And who knew, maybe something of interest would be found.

He got off the phone and returned his attention to the Walshes' house. There was no sign of activity. The show – if that's what it had been – was over for now. He looked up Queen's Medical Centre. It was three or four miles away on the west side of the city. He punched the address into the satnav and set off.

The hospital was a multi-storey, block-like building. He followed the signs for Maternity and showed the nurse at reception his ID. 'I want to confirm whether or not the information I have about someone born here is correct.'

'Do you have the mother's name and her child's date of birth?'

He told the nurse what she needed to know and she disappeared into an office at the rear of reception. She reappeared shortly with a printout. 'Sharon Walsh gave birth to a girl in this unit via natural delivery at three twenty a.m. on the date you gave.'

'Does it say who delivered her?'

'Midwife Janet Shaw.'

'Would it be possible for me to speak to her?'

'Janet's not on duty. I can give you her home phone number.'

'That'd be great.'

Jim entered Janet Shaw's number into his phone. He thanked the nurse, headed outside and hit dial. No one picked up. He left an answerphone message, saying who he was and asking

Mrs Shaw to call him. He returned to his car and the Walshes' house. As he parked up, he glimpsed a figure in an upstairs window. Sharon Walsh. She was staring between the bushes directly at him. He returned her gaze and she quickly retreated from view. Their eyes had only met for an instant, but it was enough to give him the distinct feeling that she knew who and what he was. He rubbed his unshaven jaw, frowning. So the great show her husband had made about not upsetting her had been just that – a show. Which begged the question: why had Ronald been so adamant about him not talking to Sharon? The answer seemed plain. It wasn't Sharon that Ronald didn't want him to talk to. It was Emily. They probably hadn't told her about the murky side of her family's past.

Jim's phone rang. Janet Shaw's number flashed up. He put the phone to his ear. 'Thanks for calling me back, Mrs Shaw.'

'What can I do for you, Chief Inspector?' she replied.

Jim explained what he was trying to find out. 'Do you remember delivering Sharon Walsh's baby?'

'If the hospital birth records say I did, then I did.'

'That's not what I'm asking. I want to know if you specifically remember doing so.'

'You've got to be kidding me. I've been a midwife for thirty-odd years. Do you know how many thousands of babies I've delivered?'

'I thought you'd say something like that, but this is extremely important. I really need you to try and think back.'

Janet sighed. 'I'll try.'

Jim described Sharon and Ronald. Janet was silent a moment, then she said. 'Sorry, I'd like to be of help but nothing's coming to me. Look, why don't I call round my colleagues, see if any of them remembers this woman? I doubt they will, but it's worth a try. I'll get back in contact if I find anything out.'

Jim thanked her and hung up. If his suspicions about the Walshes were correct, there was a chance she was lying to him. But he didn't think it was much of a chance. Experience told him that the vast majority of people – average people, not clever bastards like Villiers – would avoid the police like the plague if they had anything to hide.

He glanced at the dashboard clock. It was nearly three. The schools would be kicking out soon. He started the engine and turned out of the street. If Sharon had made him, there was little point in sitting on the house. As he drove, a text message beeped on his phone. It was from Anna and read 'I'm at the pub.'

When Jim pulled into the pub car park, Anna was sitting in the open doors of her camper van, smoking a cigarette and sipping a pint of cider. There were dark smudges under her eyes. Her short blonde hair lay flat and greasy on her head. She gave Jim a weary but undefeated smile as he lowered his window and said, 'Get in.'

Anna locked up her van, then, still clutching her pint, ducked into the car. Jim gestured at her drink. 'You don't need that.'

'Bollocks I don't after what I've just been through. I tell you, train travel in this country is no joke.'

Jim couldn't help a small smile at her dry humour. By the time they arrived at the school, Anna had drained her glass and children were streaming out of the gates. Jim scanned the ranks of faces. Laughing faces, serious faces, faces as yet unmarked by the dirt of life. His gaze came to rest on one such face. Emily was chatting to a boy who looked to be the same age as her. Her cheeks were slightly flushed, like apples ready to be picked. Her expression was open and unguarded with the merest hint of shyness. There was nothing of the closed wariness, the deadness he'd seen behind the eyes of abuse victims. It made him ache inside to think how her face would change if his suspicions proved correct.

He pointed at her. 'There.'

Anna's eyes followed the line of his finger. 'What am I supposed to be lookin—' she started to say. Her voice broke off with a harsh click, like something snapping shut. She squeezed her eyelids together and opened them, as if she didn't trust what she was seeing. Her fingers were white on the pint glass.

'What do you think?' asked Jim. Not that he needed to. Her reaction said everything.

Anna made an inarticulate sound in her throat. Suddenly, the glass broke in her hand. Blinking like someone jarred out of trance, she looked at her palm. Blood was welling from a shallow cut.

Jim handed her a wad of tissue. 'Here. Press that to it.'

She did so bemusedly. Her gaze returned to Emily. 'I feel like I'm fifteen years old again and I'm waiting for Jessica at the school gates to walk home with her.' Her voice was quiet and distant. She shook her head and returned to the present. 'Who is she?'

'Her name's Emily Walsh. She's fifteen years old and supposedly the only living child of Ronald and Sharon Walsh.'

'What do you mean, "supposedly the only living child"?'

'The Walshes had a son. Gavin. You know him better as Spider.'

As Jim filled Anna in on Gavin Walsh's short life and its seemingly violent end, her eyes followed Emily as if afraid of losing sight of her. Waving goodbye to the boy, Emily approached a group of girls at a bus stop. The girls were laughing and making kissy faces at her. It was only gentle teasing, but still Anna had a sudden almost overwhelming urge to jump out of the car and yell at them to leave Jessica alone. No, not Jessica. Emily. The girl's name was Emily. *Leave Emily alone, you little bitches!* 'You realise what this means, don't you?' she said, trembling with barely contained emotion. 'If Emily's fifteen, she was born in 1998. Jessica was taken in February 1993. So Spider—' She paused to correct herself. 'Gavin Walsh must have kept her alive for at least five years. And if he kept her alive for that long, maybe she's still alive.'

All Jim's years on the job suggested such a thing was out of the question. And yet there was no denying the logic of Anna's words. The possibility hinged on one as yet unknown factor. 'That's assuming Emily really is your sister's daughter.'

'Of course she fucking is!' Anna retorted with total conviction. 'Look at her. Look at her hair, her eyes, her build. She's all Jessica.'

'Not according to her birth certificate or the records of Queen's Medical Centre.'

'Then they're fakes. Just like William Keyes and Clotho Daeja are fakes. You said Ronald Walsh worked for a Birmingham gangster. He must have all sorts of contacts who know how to fake identities. He obviously helped his son to disappear back in '87. And that's another thing. Ronald and Sharon must be far too old by now to have such a young daughter.'

'I think you're right. The problem is proving it.'

'Where's the problem? All we have to do is get a sample of Emily's DNA and match it to my sister's.'

'We need a court order for a DNA test. And we're not going to get a court order based on Emily looking like Jessica.'

'Fuck a court order. I'll get a sample myself.'

'How?'

'I don't know. Maybe I'll break into her bedroom, steal her hairbrush.'

'I can't let you do that. We need to do this by the book and make sure any evidence we gather is admissible in court.'

Anna looked at Jim incredulously. 'You didn't seem to mind bending the rules when you came to me for help.'

'That was then. I was desperate. The investigation was dead. Things are moving now. A search warrant was granted today for Villiers' house.'

'How does that help me? How does it help Jessica?'

'If we can nail Villiers, he might give up his accomplices.'

'But that's going to take time. Time my sister doesn't have. Don't you see? Gavin Walsh probably already knows you're onto his parents. If he thinks you're getting too close to him, he could kill Jessica.'

'Would he, though? If you're right, Gavin's kept your sister alive for twenty years. He's fed her, clothed her. You don't do that unless you have some sort of deep attachment to someone. And don't forget, Gavin left the Cowper Road house in 2007, possibly because he feared discovery. According to your theory, he must have moved Jessica with him. If he did it once, what's to stop him doing it again? Look, all I want is for you to hold off for a few days. We might get a hit on the skeleton's DNA that leads to something. Or we might find something that proves Emily Walsh's birth records were falsified.'

Anna stared at her bleeding hand, her face screwed up with uncertainty. 'Do you think Emily knows the truth?'

'Would you trust a child with a secret like that?'

The uncertainty left Anna's face. She reached suddenly for the door handle. 'Where are you going?' asked Jim.

'I'm gonna talk to her.'

Jim caught hold of Anna's arm. 'That's not a good idea.'

Anna looked at him with eyes as raw as the cut on her palm. 'Why the fuck did you bring me here if you were just going to ask me to do nothing?'

'Because you have a right to know what the score is.'

Anna stabbed a finger in Emily's direction. 'So does she. What if she's in danger? What if Gavin Walsh turned out like he did because his parents abused him? And what if they're doing the same to Emily?'

'I don't think that's the case.'

'How can you know that?'

'I can't,' admitted Jim. 'All I can go on is what I see. And I don't see any pain in her eyes.'

Anna gave a dismissive hiss. 'Some kids are better at hiding pain than others,' she said with the conviction of experience. 'We need to get her away from them.'

'We don't have any right.'

'She's my niece. I have every right.'

'What if she won't listen to you?'

A caustic gleam came into Anna's eyes. 'Maybe I'll kidnap her.'

Jim frowned at her. Was she being serious? He couldn't tell. 'Don't even joke—' he started to say, but broke off as Anna jerked her arm free. A bus had pulled up at the bus stop. She jumped out the car and, prompting a chorus of horns, sprinted across two lanes of traffic towards it. He made to follow her, but a van blocked his way. As he dodged around it, he saw Anna boarding the bus. The doors hissed shut and the bus accelerated away. Swearing under his breath, he darted back to his car and set off in pursuit.

CHAPTER ELEVEN

Emily made her way to the back of the bus and sat down between her friends. 'Are you coming to the shops?' asked one of them.

Emily shook her head. 'I promised my parents I'd go straight home today.'

'Aw, go on, Emily. Tell them the bus broke down or something.'

Emily hesitated to reply. Normally she would have given in to her friends, but her parents had been so serious and insistent. Not only had they made her promise to come straight home, they'd also made her promise not to talk to any strangers along the way. 'Why would I talk to any strangers?' she'd asked. She'd got no answer other than a repeated insistence that she made the promises they wanted to hear. Her dad had even threatened to keep her home if she didn't do so. His expression had been both pleading and angry. Another question had come to her lips. 'What's going on?'

To which her dad had exploded, 'Fucking hell, for once will you just do as I say without asking questions!'

She'd never heard him swear like that before. It had weirded her out. Even scared her a little. Tears had started into her eyes. Her dad had stroked her hair then and said gently, 'I'm sorry for shouting, Emily. It's just that I'm worried about you. You're growing up so fast. Too fast. Sometimes I look at you and wonder where my little girl's gone.'

It had seemed obvious to Emily from his words what they were worried about. Boys. There was a lad at school she'd been seeing on and off for some time. She'd written about him in her diary. Had they sneaked a look at it? The possibility had been irritating her all day. But she was in two minds over whether to confront them about it. She didn't want to unnecessarily open a can of worms. They were a lot older than her friends' parents. And their views matched their age. They'd made it abundantly clear that they didn't approve of teenage romance.

As Emily mulled over what to do, both in regards to the shops and her parents, she noticed a woman looking at her. The woman had dashed onto the bus at the last second. There were no seats left, so she was standing in the aisle, facing the back of the bus. She was wiry-thin with short blonde hair that looked as though it needed a wash and grey eyes – eyes that were fixed on Emily with an intensity that made her uncomfortable. Emily dropped her eyes briefly, then looked up. The woman was still watching her.

'That woman's staring at you,' said one of Emily's friends.

'Do you know her?' asked another.

Emily pouted in thought. Now that her friends mentioned it, there was something vaguely familiar about the woman's face, but she couldn't place what it was. Maybe she'd seen her somewhere before. 'I don't think so.'

'Well, she's looking at you like she knows you.'

'Maybe she fancies you.'

Emily's friends laughed. Blinking, she lowered her gaze again. Her thoughts returned to her parents. Maybe she'd been wrong. Maybe it was this woman who was somehow worrying them. The bus pulled in at a stop. Several people disembarked. The woman took one of the vacated seats and sat staring out the window. Emily's friends resumed trying to convince her to go to the shops. She shook her head. She had a sudden urge to get home and make sure her parents were OK.

When the bus reached Emily's stop, she somewhat uneasily said goodbye to her friends. It was only a short walk to her house, but she didn't particularly feel like making it alone. She noted with relief that the woman showed no sign of standing to get off. As she passed her, she flicked her a look. She'd thought the woman was in her twenties, but up close she looked older. There were lines under her eyes and where her bony cheeks pinched in to meet her mouth. Her eyes rose to Emily's. Emily was struck once again by the recognition that seemed to gleam in them. But even more unsettling was the need she saw. It was as if the woman was barely restraining herself from grabbing hold of her. Emily flinched from her gaze and hurried to the exit. As the bus continued on its way, her friends knocked on the window to catch her attention and pointed animatedly at something behind her.

'Emily.'

The voice was female with a broad Yorkshire accent. She threw a glance over her shoulder and her heart quickened. The woman had followed her off the bus. And she knew her name! She felt certain then that this woman was the cause of her parents' strange behaviour. But who was she? And what did she want? She was half tempted to fire off the questions, but then she noticed something that made her heart beat even faster. In one hand the woman was clutching what appeared to be a bloodstained tissue. Whose blood was it? Her own or someone else's? A vision suddenly came to Emily of her parents laid on the living-room floor covered in blood. She broke into a half-run.

'Emily,' the woman called again. 'Wait. I need to talk to you.'

Emily ignored her, hoping she would go away. She heard an onrushing of footsteps. A hand encircled her upper arm. 'Let go!' she yelled. 'Or I'll scream.'

The woman released her. 'I'm not going to hurt you. Please, I swear I only want to help you.' There was a desperate need to be believed in her voice.

Emily turned to face the woman, curiosity partially overcoming her anxiety. 'Why would I need your help?'

'My name's Anna Young.'

'Yeah, so? Am I supposed to know who you are?'

Anna shook her head. 'We don't have much time.' She pulled out a phone and showed it to Emily. Its screen displayed a drawing of a man with a round face, dark-brown eyes and hair. 'Do you recognise him?'

Emily's eyebrows tightened. She'd seen photos of her mum from when she was young, and the drawing instantly reminded her of them. The thought came to her. Was this woman a cop? She didn't look like one. But then again, what did a cop look like? She'd never had any contact with the police. Nor to her knowledge had her parents. Were they in trouble with them? She found it almost impossible to believe. They were so strait-laced. So boringly honest. And yet, thinking back on it, her dad's reaction to her questions seemed to suggest just that. She warily shook her head. If her parents were in some kind of trouble, she wasn't about to help the police get them.

'His name's Gavin Walsh,' continued Anna.

'Gavin Walsh? You mean like he's related to me?'

'He's your brother.'

Her face puckering incredulously, Emily shook her head. 'I'm an only child.'

'You're wrong. Gavin Walsh was born in Birmingham in 1968 and was supposedly murdered there in 1987.'

'Murdered?' Emily took a step backwards, unnerved by the word.

'By the brothers of a girl he raped. Only he wasn't murdered. He fled Birmingham and assumed a new identity.'

Emily shook her head again, more vehemently. 'You've made a mistake or you're lying.'

Sympathy softened Anna's voice. 'I'm sorry, Emily, I realise how difficult this must—' She broke off at the sound of a car pulling in sharply alongside them. Urgency replaced the sympathy. 'Listen to me, Emily. You're in danger.'

Emily's eyes darted past Anna. A man in a crumpled grey suit was getting out of the car. He was heavily built with deep-set brown eyes and a salt-and-pepper moustache. He didn't look happy. She took several more quick backwards steps. What the fuck was this? Were they going to force her into the car?

'Please, Emily,' continued Anna. 'Your parents aren't what they seem.'

'What do you mean?' Emily's voice was trembling, close to tears.

'They're not who—'

'Anna!' shouted the man. 'That's enough.'

Emily turned to run, but Anna sprang forward to grab her again. 'You can't go back to them.' Her eyes were bulging. 'I won't let you.'

'You're crazy! I'll call the police!'

Emily tried to wrench her arm free. This time Anna didn't let go. She jerked her chin at the man. 'He is the police. If you don't believe me, ask him about your so-called parents and—'

'I said, that's enough,' he interrupted again, catching hold of Anna's hand and prising it off Emily.

The instant she was free, Emily ran for home. Her satchel came open and a book fell out. She didn't stop to pick it up. She didn't look back until the house came into sight. The woman – what had she said her name was? Anna Young. Anna and the supposed policeman were nowhere to be seen. Breathing hard, Emily shoved her key into the front door. Slamming doors behind herself, she ran upstairs and fell face first onto her bed. Her mind was whirling like an out-of-control fairground ride. Anna's parting shot still seemed to echo in her ears. *Ask him about your so-called parents.* Had she been suggesting that they weren't really her parents? And what about all the other things she'd said? Was it possible they were true? Or was she just some madwoman?

She stiffened at a gentle knock on her bedroom door. An equally gentle voice asked, 'Emily, are you OK?'

Emily opened her mouth to say no, but something – some shadow of doubt – made her say, 'Yes.'

The door opened and Sharon Walsh poked her head into the room. 'You don't sound it.'

The sight of her mum's soft, concerned face rammed home to Emily the craziness of Anna's words. Her parents had never raised a hand to her. Her mum was a born-again Christian. Violence went against everything she believed in. *How can I be in danger from them?* Emily asked herself. Again, she made to speak, intending to tell her mum what had happened. And again, doubt stayed her tongue as she thought about how her dad had behaved that morning. His anger had been so out of character. Something was obviously bothering him. Surely it wasn't a coincidence that this Anna Young had shown up the same day. A thought occurred to her: maybe Anna had something to do with the girl who was supposedly raped. Maybe she even was the girl. 'I'm fine. I just wanted to go to the shops with my friends. That's all.'

Sharon's concern turned into a sigh of weary relief. 'There'll be plenty of other days for you to go shopping. Are you coming downstairs?'

Emily shook her head. 'I've got some homework to do.'

'I'll give you a shout when tea's ready.'

Sharon looked at her daughter a moment longer, as if wondering whether to say something else, before closing the door. Emily listened for her mum's footsteps on the stairs, then she propped a chair against the door handle – something she always did when she didn't want anyone walking in on her. She flopped back onto the bed, closed her eyes and immediately opened them again. There were so many conflicting thoughts and emotions battling for space inside her. Her head felt ready to pop. She had to know whether Anna was telling the truth. She retrieved a laptop and flipped it open.

****

'Get the hell off me!' spat Anna, struggling against Jim's grip.

'Not until you calm down.'

'Fuck you. I am calm.'

'Yeah, like a hurricane.' Jim twisted Anna's arm up behind her back and thrust her towards his car. 'Do you want me to put the cuffs on you? Because I will do if you make me.'

'I'd like to see you fucking try.'

With practised ease Jim pushed Anna's head down and into the car. He followed her onto the back seat. She glared at him like a cornered animal. 'Why did you stop me?'

'You know why. Just what did you hope to achieve by that

little performance? Did you really think Emily would listen to you?'

'She was listening until you showed up.'

'Bullshit. The poor girl was terrified.'

'Better that than let those people hurt her.'

'Why would Ronald and Sharon hurt her? They've raised her as their own child.'

Anna scowled. 'Yeah, and who knows what their idea of raising a child is.'

Jim heaved a sigh. Anna was right. Child abuse was cyclical. Victims often – although far from always – grew up to be victimisers. 'Look, the best thing – the only thing – we can do for Emily right now is find proof that she's not Ronald and Sharon's daughter.'

'And how the fuck are we going to do that without taking her DNA?'

As if in answer, Jim's phone rang. It was Janet Shaw. Had she found out something that proved Emily Walsh's birth record was falsified? If she had it would almost be enough to make him believe in fate or providence or whatever you wanted to call it. 'Something strange,' said Janet. 'I've been ringing around my colleagues. None of them remember Sharon Walsh either. But that's not the strange thing. I always keep a diary. So I dug out my diary from 1998. And guess what. At the time of Emily Walsh's birth I was on holiday in Turkey.'

'Are you sure of that?'

'One hundred per cent. I'm looking at the entry and exit stamps in my old passport right now. I was there with my husband from the twenty-sixth of May until the ninth of June. So you see I couldn't possibly have delivered Emily Walsh.'

Jim snapped his fingers triumphantly. 'Thank you, Mrs Shaw. Myself or one of my colleagues will be in contact with you again shortly. In the meantime, please don't mention this to anyone else.' He relayed the conversation to Anna. 'You see,' he said. 'Somewhere in the web of lies, there's always something, some small detail that eventually catches up with the bastards.'

'But is that enough to get a warrant for DNA testing?'

'It's enough to start working on getting one. So are you going to back off from Emily Walsh?'

Anna nodded, although not very convincingly. Jim wrinkled his forehead at her. 'Maybe you should go back to Sheffield.'

'No fucking way am I taking my eyes off the Walshes. You'd have to drag me away from here kicking and screaming. Look, I give you my word I'm not going to do anything for now except watch them. But you'd better come up with that warrant fast.'

Jim got on the phone to Garrett and explained the situation. 'Let me get this straight,' the Chief Superintendent said doubtfully, 'you think Emily Walsh is Jessica Young's daughter.'

'I don't think it, I know it. And if you saw the girl you would too.'

'If you're right, it would mean...' Garrett's breath filled the line. 'Christ, I don't even want to think about what it would mean. OK, we're going to need to put more evidence together. Go back to the hospital, make sure this isn't some computer mistake. Speak to everyone you can who worked there in '98. And when you're done with that, start speaking to the Walshes' neighbours and relatives, see if any of them remember Sharon Walsh being pregnant. I'll put a request in to the NHS information centre for her health records. And I'll have DI Greenwood get on to social services in case Emily Walsh has ever come onto their radar.'

'How's the search and seizure going?'

'There's nothing to tell. We haven't turned up anything incriminating yet. And here's some more bad news. Miles

Burnham has managed to get a court injunction preventing the media from publishing Villiers' name.'

Jim's mouth drew into a tight line. The news disappointed but didn't surprise him.

'There is one bit of good news,' went on Garrett. 'The Craig Thorpe Youth Trust has suspended Villiers pending the outcome of our investigation.'

Jim made a dubious noise. The operative words were 'suspended' and 'pending'. If the investigation went south, no doubt Villiers would walk straight back into his job or another like it. He got off the phone and said to Anna, 'I need to head over to Queen's Medical Centre. Are you coming?'

Anna shook her head. 'I told you I'm not taking my eyes off the Walshes.'

Jim eyed her uncertainly. 'Can I trust you?'

'Relax, I won't go kicking their door down or anything like that.'

'And contact me at once if—'

'I will,' Anna cut in impatiently. It made her uneasy having Emily out of her sight. At the very least she wanted to put her eyes on the Walshes' house. 'Now come on, let's get fucking moving.'

Jim drove her back to the camper van. He gave her the Walshes' address and a lingering glance that said, *Don't let me down*, before accelerating away. Anna headed to the house and parked a few doors down. Her lips curled. It was a nice-looking place. And, no doubt, Ronald and Sharon Walsh were nice-looking people. Nice like shiny apples, rotten at the core.

The curtains were drawn in one of the upstairs windows. She wondered if it was Emily's bedroom window. She thought about Emily. Her straight blonde hair, her blue eyes, her delicate features. And she thought about Jessica, superimposing the images. They fitted together perfectly. Like two halves of a puzzle. She wondered what Jessica looked like now. What would twenty years of being kept prisoner have done to her? She slipped into the old fantasy of finding her, rescuing her, taking her home to their mum. But this time she imagined Emily with them. She imagined them all together. Something broken but whole. A real family.

****

Emily Googled 'Anna Young' and got thousands of hits. The top one was for a blog called 'The Truth'. She clicked it and an 'Error 404 Page Not Found' appeared. She tried several of the others. Each led to the same reblogged article by Anna about some sort of paedophile ring. Many bloggers praised Anna for her bravery in pursuit of the truth. But there were also anonymous commenters who accused her of being a liar and a fantasist. Emily took it all in with a growing tightness in her abdomen. What did any of this have to do with her and her family? Surely nothing. The thought was reinforced by the fact that she could find no mention of 'Gavin Walsh'. She Googled the name along with 'Murder, 1987'. It turned up no relevant results. She tried again substituting 'Rape' for 'Murder'. Still nothing. She brought up a list of Birmingham newspapers and clicked the top hit. She navigated to the 'contact me' page and scrolled through a list of editors and reporters, wondering who would be best to contact. She stopped on 'Crime: Lindsey Allen'. She punched the reporter's number into her mobile phone. A woman with a Brummie accent came on the line. 'This is Lindsey Allen, *Birmingham Evening Post*.'

'My name's Emily Walsh,' Emily began nervously. 'I... er... I'm trying to find out about a crime that happened in Birmingham.'

'A crime we ran a story about?'

'I don't know. That's why I'm calling.'

'Have you searched the online version of the newspaper?'

'Yes. I couldn't find anything. The crime happened in 1987.'

'Ah, well, the online archives only go back a year. For something that long ago you'd have to search through the microfilm archives. They're kept on file here and at the Birmingham Central Library.'

'But I don't live in Birmingham. Could you look for me?'

'I'm sorry, but I—'

'Please, Miss Allen,' broke in Emily, a note of desperation in her tremulous teenage voice. 'I really need your help. I think someone might be trying to hurt my family. And it's got something to do with this thing that supposedly happened in 1987.'

'How old are you, Emily?' asked Lindsey, suddenly sounding interested.

'Fifteen.'

'Well, Emily, if someone's threatening your family you should call the police.'

'She's not actually made any threats. She's just saying these... these horrible things.'

'What things?'

'She says there was this man, Gavin Walsh. And that he raped someone and was murdered because of it, only he wasn't really murdered.'

'Who's Gavin Walsh? A relative?'

Emily hesitated to reply. What if Anna Young wasn't a liar and a fantasist? Emily didn't want some reporter getting hold of the story and putting it in a newspaper. 'I don't know.'

'Well, what about the person who's been saying these things, do you know who she is?'

'I... er... no,' Emily lied, not very convincingly. Her parents had always drummed it into her how important it was to tell the truth.

Lindsey was silent a moment, then she said, 'OK, Emily, I'll take a look for you.'

'Oh, thank you, Miss Allen,' Emily exclaimed gratefully. 'How long will it take?'

'I should be able to get back to you some time tomorrow. Is there anything else you can tell me about Gavin Walsh?'

'No. I'm sorry.'

'That's OK. It should be enough to go on. Do you want me to contact you on the same number you're calling from?'

Emily replied yes and thanked the reporter again. From downstairs her mum called to her, 'Tea's ready.'

'I've got to go.' Emily cut off the call. She deleted her browser history, then made her way to the kitchen. Her parents were already at the table. Her dad treated her to a searching look as she sat down. Avoiding his eyes, she began picking at her food.

'Aren't you forgetting something?' Sharon gently chastised.

'Oh, sorry, Mum.'

'Don't apologise to me.' Sharon rolled her eyes at the ceiling. 'Apologise to Him.'

Emily looked up. 'Sorry.'

Sharon folded her hands together and closed her eyes. As her husband and Emily did likewise, she began, 'Bless us O Lord and for these thy gifts which we are about to receive, may the Lord make us truly thankful. Amen.'

'Thank you, Emily,' Ronald said, reaching to give her forearm a squeeze. She thought he meant for humouring her mum – he knew she didn't share her mum's faith – but he continued, 'Thank you for coming straight home. Your mum and I were just saying how lucky we are to have a daughter like you. So many teenagers don't listen to their parents these days.'

Emily blinked guiltily. It suddenly felt like a massive betrayal having contacted Lindsey Allen. Her entire life her parents had lavished her with as much attention and love as any child could want. And how had she repaid them? By doubting them at the words of a stranger, that's how.

'Your mum and I have got an optician's appointment first thing in the morning,' said Ronald. 'Do you need anything from town?'

Emily shook her head. 'I'm sorry, Dad.'

'What for?'

She gave an awkward little shrug. 'You and Mum are so... I mean you do so much for me. I sometimes feel like I don't deserve it.'

Sharon took Emily's other wrist. 'You're the best daughter we could ever have, Emily. And nothing you do will ever change the way we feel about you.'

That was too much for Emily. She stood up. 'I'm not really hungry. Can I go to my room?'

'Are you OK, love?' asked Ronald, his eyes concerned but also curious once more. 'Is there anything you want to tell us?'

Emily shook her head, her lips compressed.

Ronald motioned to the door. 'Go on then.'

Resisting the urge to break into a run, Emily left the kitchen. She threw herself onto her bed, tears welling in her eyes. She'd almost blurted it all out – her encounter with Anna, the phone call to the reporter. But something still stopped her from doing so. She couldn't bear the thought of the hurt she knew her parents would feel. That was part of it, but not the main part. Even their loving words hadn't been able to extract the splinter of doubt lodged in her brain. And she hated herself because of it.

CHAPTER TWELVE

Anna's eyes blinked open at a soft knock on the van's side door. She lifted her head and looked at the dashboard clock: 11:35 p.m. 'Shit,' she muttered. She must have fallen asleep without realising it. Cautiously, she peered between the curtains drawn across the windows. Seeing Jim's grizzled face, she opened the door.

He climbed into the van, thumbing over his shoulder at the Walshes' unlit house. 'Looks like they're asleep.'

'I was too,' Anna admitted.

He placed a plastic bag on the table and removed two polystyrene cups and several silver-foil trays from it. 'Coffee and Chinese takeaway. I got you chicken. Everyone likes chicken, right?'

'Thanks. I haven't eaten since this morning.' Anna peeled the top off a tray. The smell of spicy food made her realise how hungry she was.

As they ate, Jim said, 'I've had an interesting evening. I've spoken to several midwives and doctors who worked at Queen's Medical Centre back in '98. Not a single one remembers

Sharon Walsh. Neither does the hospital have any record of her having antenatal care. Which seems especially strange when you consider Sharon would've been fifty-one at the time of Emily's birth. Surely a woman of that age would've been keen to have every test and scan available to make sure her baby was healthy. And here's another curious little fact for you.' Jim pointed at the house. 'Sharon and Ronald moved in there around the same time Emily was born. Before that they lived in Keyworth. A village to the south-east of Nottingham.'

'I suppose the sudden appearance of a baby in a small community like that would've caused awkward questions to be asked.'

'That's exactly what I thought. I'm heading there in the morning to speak to their former neighbours. And after I'm done with that, I've got to go to Leicester to speak to the parents of Alison Sullivan.'

'Who's she?'

'She's the girl you found under the tree. We got a DNA hit.' Jim flipped open his notepad. 'She went missing on the second of June 2007. A fortnight or so before Mr Daeja moved out of Cowper Road. She was sixteen years old. According to her parents, she was going through an alternative stage. They were concerned because she'd recently got into paganism and the occult. On the morning of her disappearance, Alison left the house, supposedly to go to college. Instead she went to Leicester train station, where she was caught on CCTV boarding a train to Leeds. She was also recorded at Leeds station and in a nearby shopping precinct where she met a man.'

'You mean Gavin Walsh was captured on camera!'

Jim nodded. 'Don't get too excited. There's not much to see.' He brought up a grainy colour CCTV still on his phone. It showed a girl with long blonde hair wearing a green and purple tie-dye skirt and a knee-length blue leather jacket. She was sitting on a bench next to a slightly paunchy man in faded black jeans and a t-shirt. A wide-brimmed bushman-style hat concealed his face except for a long goatee beard. 'This image was shown on the national news. It must have panicked Gavin into leaving Cowper Road.'

Anna studied the image closely. It was difficult to make out Alison Sullivan's expression. But Anna thought she detected a hint of a smile. Her mind returned to the online listing that had, no doubt, lured Alison to Leeds: *I am The True Wiccan. I do not sell New Age fakery. I sell the truth. Come and see me if that's what you're looking for.*

Gavin had offered the truth, but all he'd had to give was pain. Maybe, Anna reflected bitterly, that *was* the truth. In all her years of searching she'd never found anything to prove differently. 'Do Alison's parents know she's dead?'

'No,' Jim said heavily. 'Not yet.'

Catching his meaning, Anna gave a little shake of her head. 'It's a dirty job but someone's got to do it, eh?' For years after Jessica's abduction, every knock on the front door had left her cold with panic at the thought that it was a policeman come with the news she dreaded most. Sighing, she pushed up her glasses and rubbed her eyes.

'You look done in. Why don't you get some more sleep? I'll take first watch and wake you in a few hours.'

'I don't feel like sleeping. Besides, you need your rest more than me. It's you who's got the dodgy ticker.'

Anna took out a sleeping bag and pillow for Jim. He curled up on the sofa and was soon snoring deeply. She watched the house, wondering if Emily was awake too and contemplating her own truth, her own pain. The dark hours dragged by. Anna chain-smoked to keep herself awake. Once Jim stirred in his sleep and muttered something. She thought she made out a name. *Margaret.* She looked at him with something approaching sympathy. She'd heard what had been done to his wife by Freddie Harding. They'd both had someone they loved snatched away from them. But there wasn't even the slimmest of chances that his 'someone' was coming back. Except in his dreams. *So let him sleep,* she thought. *Let him dream.*

Night gradually gave way to a steel-blue dawn. The earliest risers amongst the street's residents emerged from their houses and headed off to work. At the sound of a passing car, Jim sat up blinking in the pale light. 'Why didn't you wake me?'

'I told you, I didn't feel like sleeping.'

Jim rubbed his bladder area. 'I need to find a toilet or a bush. My prostate isn't what it used to be.'

'That's a little more information than I need.'

Smiling faintly, Jim pulled on his shoes and clambered out of the van. Anna set a kettle boiling on a camping stove. When Jim returned, she handed him a mug of tea. He sipped it and examined his face in a mirror. 'Christ, I look about ninety.'

'I don't know about that,' said Anna. 'Get rid of the tash and you wouldn't look too bad for an old geezer.'

Jim stroked his moustache. 'I've had this for twenty-odd years.'

'All the more reason to get rid.'

Jim took an electric razor from his pocket and plugged it into the cigarette lighter with an adaptor. After shaving his cheeks and throat, he hovered uncertainly over his moustache. Why had he grown it? He couldn't remember. It was just something that, over the years, had become a part of who he was. But who was he? He'd lost sight of that a long time even before Margaret walked out on him. All he knew was that things were changing and he had to change with them or he was as good as dead. He pressed the razor against his moustache. When it was gone, he studied himself in the mirror again. A face that was both the same yet strikingly different stared back. It gave him a strangely disconnected feeling. He reached up to touch his upper lip, and was almost surprised to see the man in the mirror do likewise.

'That's knocked about five years off you,' said Anna. 'Now all you need to do is sort your hair and clothes out.'

A crooked smile tugged at Jim's mouth again. 'One step at a time.'

After heating up the remnants of the previous night's meal for breakfast, Jim said, 'Right, I'd better head over to Keyworth and see if I can catch the Walshes' former neighbours before they go to work.' He gave Anna a meaningful look.

'Jesus, do we have to go through this every time you leave? Yes, I'll call if anything happens.'

As Jim exited the van, Anna's gaze returned to the house. The downstairs curtains were open. She glimpsed a man who fitted Jim's description of Ronald Walsh moving around in his dressing-gown. At a quarter to nine, Ronald and a woman Anna presumed to be Sharon left the house, both casually but smartly dressed, a picture of middle-class respectability. Sharon got into the Volvo. Ronald stood staring at the camper van, before quickly following her into the car as Emily appeared in her school uniform. Anna felt a tightening of her heart at the sight of her. In the clear morning light, with her hair slightly damp and bang straight, Emily looked, if possible, even more like Jessica. She was a touch pale and puffy around the eyes, as though she hadn't got much sleep. Had she lain awake all night agonising over what she'd been told? wondered Anna. Or had she confronted her parents about Gavin? And if so, what had they told her? Not the truth, that was for sure.

Their whole life was a lie. The truth was as alien to them as lying was to Anna.

It was all Anna could do to resist the urge to jump out of the van and drag Emily away from Ronald and Sharon, drag her all the way back to where she belonged – Sheffield. Anna tailed the Volvo to the school. Emily kissed her parents, then left the car. They waited until she was well inside the gates before pulling away. Anna didn't follow them. She was more interested in making sure no harm came to Emily. That was the important – perhaps the *most* important – thing. The realisation hit Anna with a jolt. She'd never thought anything would ever rival her desire to find Jessica. Emily was a link to the past, but she was also a bridge to the future – a future Anna had never considered even in her wildest imaginings; a future she was fiercely determined to have.

The school bell rang. Anna watched Emily file inside the building with her fellow pupils, then she reached to take her glasses off. She'd slept maybe two hours out of the last forty-eight. Now seemed like the best time to catch up on some much needed shut-eye. But first she had to have a cigarette. She lit one and rested her head back. Noticing a figure emerge from the school, she quickly replaced her glasses. It was Emily! She was walking fast, almost running. Her face wasn't just a little pale now. It was as white as a hangover with… with what? Shock? Excitement? The thought came to Anna: *She's found out something that backs up my words. Either that or she's about to try and do so.* As Emily darted across the road and flagged down a bus, a second thought occurred to Anna, one that quickened her pulse. *Maybe she's not merely going to try and find the truth, maybe she's going to try and see it, even speak to it.*

****

Emily was heading to her form room for registration when her phone rang. She snatched it out. It was the call she'd been expecting, wanting and dreading. 'All phones must be switched off on school premises,' shouted a teacher.

Dodging into the girls' toilets, Emily put the phone to her ear. 'Hello, Miss Allen.'

'Hi, Emily. Please call me Lindsey.'

'Did you find anything out, Lindsey?' Emily asked with a nervous swallow.

'Yes I did. I found several articles about Gavin Walsh dating to 1987. In June of that year he was accused of rape by a fourteen-year-old girl named Jody McLean. But he was never charged. Not long afterwards Gavin went missing. His bloodstained clothes were found not far from where he lived with his parents, Ronald and Sharon. Police suspected Jody's brothers, Patrick and Kieran, had murdered Gavin. But they couldn't find a body. I've spoken to a colleague who worked here at the time. Apparently there was some speculation as to whether Gavin had faked his death, but the police didn't take it seriously. You see the McLeans were – well, still are – a notorious crime family here in Birmingham. If they wanted Gavin dead, then he was as good as dead. What's your email address? I'll send you the articles.'

Emily made no reply. Her head was reeling. She felt sick and sweaty. She didn't know what to think. She didn't want to think. But the reporter's words kept coming back at her. They turned everything she believed to be true into a lie. They snatched away the supports of her identity. Questions hammered at her brain. *Why didn't my parents tell me about Gavin? Who is he exactly? Who am I?*

Assuming Gavin was alive, what she'd just learnt had to some extent answered the first of those questions. Her parents had kept his existence a secret to protect him from the McLeans. She couldn't help but feel, though, that there was more to it than that. If she was such a good daughter, why hadn't they trusted her? Surely she had a right to know she had a brother. If that's what he was. Anna Young's words pushed their way into her mind again. *Your parents aren't what they seem. Your so-called parents...*

'Are you there?' asked Lindsey.

'Yes.' Emily told the reporter her email address, her voice a monotone of shock.

'Yesterday you seemed to suggest that this person who's threatening your family believes Gavin Walsh is still alive. Can you tell me why that is?'

'I... I'm sorry, I can't talk any more right now.'

Emily hung up and stared dazedly at the floor for a moment. Shoving the phone into her pocket, she hurried from the toilets. As she headed for the school's entrance, a teacher called after her. She didn't give them a glance. She didn't care if she got into trouble. Nothing mattered any more. Nothing, that is, except answering the questions.

When she reached the gates a bus was pulling up. She dashed across the road and boarded it. She didn't sit down. The questions wouldn't allow it. Her phone beeped as an email came through from Lindsey Allen. 'Here are the articles,' read the reporter's message. 'Call me anytime if you want to talk more.' She opened an attachment and was confronted by the headline 'Police Search For The Body Of Suspected Murder Victim' and a grainy photo of a young man. Once again, the resemblance to her parents, especially her mum, was unmistakable.

She got off the bus at her stop and ran home. Barely pausing to close the front door, she headed up to her parents' bedroom. She began rifling through the bedside tables, flinging their contents – socks, underwear, her mum's sleeping pills – carelessly onto the carpet. She pulled out the drawers, checking to see if anything was hidden behind them. The dressing table and its contents received the same treatment. One of the drawers contained a locked wooden jewellery box. She searched without success for the key. She pushed a nail file into the lock and twisted it. Again, without success. Finally, she hurled the box at the floor. It popped open, scattering jewellery across the carpet. Inside was a removable tray divided into several compartments. She lifted it out, revealing more jewellery. She turned her attention to the wardrobe. Out came the clothes, the spare blankets, the suitcases. All of it dumped in a heap. She wasn't even sure what she was looking for. All she knew was that she had to look.

She left the wreckage of the bedroom, went into her dad's study and booted up the computer. She'd never touched it before. It was strictly for his accountancy work, although these days he was all but retired. A password prompt appeared and she typed in 'Ronald'. 'The user name or password is incorrect' flashed up. She tried her mum's name, her own name, combinations of all their names. Each time the same message. She frowned thoughtfully at the screen, then typed 'Gavin'. The password was accepted. She logged on to her dad's email account. Her gaze skimmed over the inbox. There hadn't been much activity recently. There were messages from clients mixed in amongst the usual junk mail. She looked in the 'Sent' folder. Again, there was nothing of interest. Next she opened the 'Deleted Items' folder. It was empty. She clicked 'Recover Deleted Items'. Two messages appeared. The first read 'A policeman came here tonight asking about you. What's going on?' Her dad had sent the message at ten twenty-five p.m. two days ago to someone called 'The Wicca Man'. Five minutes later he'd received the reply, 'It's nothing for you to be concerned about. Just carry on like normal.'

Surely 'The Wicca Man' was Gavin. Who else could it be? She clicked the 'New Email' icon and typed The Wicca Man's email address followed by the message 'We need to meet.' Her finger hovered over the mouse. Was this what she wanted? What if there *was* some even deeper, darker secret behind her parents' silence? Her life was pretty good. Did she really want to risk ruining it? She thrust the doubts aside. It was too late to back out now. It had been the moment she'd contacted Lindsey Allen. She hit 'Send' and chewed her lips as she waited for a reply. Barely a minute passed before one came. It read simply, 'Why?'

She thought for a moment, before typing 'Emily knows about you. The policeman told her. I think its time you and her met.'

This time The Wicca Man took a while longer to respond. 'So do I but it's too dangerous.'

Her fingers trembling with nervous excitement, Emily replied, 'No its not. The policeman hasnt been back.'

Another minute or so passed, then: 'I'll meet you at the usual place in two hours.'

Emily's face knotted. Where was the usual place? Her mind raced for a response that would coax the answer out of The Wicca Man without raising his suspicions. She couldn't think of one. All she could come up with was: 'I dont want to take Emily there. Lets meet at sherwood forest visitor centre.' She squeezed her eyes half shut, asking herself, *Why did you suggest that place?* It had just kind of popped into her head. Her dad loved the Robin Hood legend and he'd taken her there dozens of times throughout her childhood.

One minute passed… three minutes… five… *He's not going to reply*, she thought. But then an email landed in the inbox. It read, 'OK.'

Emily hauled in a shaky breath. In a couple of hours she would have all the answers she wanted, and maybe more than she wanted. She looked up bus times. There was a bus from the city centre shortly after ten o'clock that arrived at the visitor centre an hour or so later. She glanced at a clock. It was almost half nine. She needed to get a move on if she was going to catch the bus. She quickly deleted all her emails and the replies and shut the computer down. She hurried from the study, pausing at the door of her parents' bedroom. It looked as though it had been hit by a hurricane. Her parents would know something was up the instant they saw it. They might even contact Gavin to warn him. Still, there was no time to tidy it up. She would just have to hope she got to Gavin before they returned home.

She changed into jeans and a sweatshirt and darted downstairs. She paused again by the front door. It passed through her mind to get a knife from the kitchen. What if Gavin was dangerous? She might need something to defend herself with. She dismissed the thought. The reporter had said Gavin was only accused of rape. He was never charged. That meant he was innocent, didn't it? And besides, they were family. Surely he wouldn't hurt his own family. She locked the door behind herself and started running.

CHAPTER THIRTEEN

Where the hell's she going now? wondered Anna as she watched Emily sprint away from the house. She obviously wasn't returning to school, seeing as she'd changed out of her uniform. Anna waited until Emily turned the corner at the end of the street, then she started up the van and accelerated after her. Emily caught another bus. Anna tailed it into the city centre, where Emily disembarked at a cavernous bus station. Anna parked up and furtively followed her on foot. Peering around a concrete pillar, she watched her buy a ticket and run for a bus that was already pulling away. Emily hammered on the doors and the driver opened them for her.

Anna noted the bus's destination. Ollerton – a small town an hour or so to the north of Nottingham. She stayed out of sight as the bus passed, then darted back to the van. As she set off after the bus, she phoned Jim. 'Where are you?'

'In Leicester, not far from Alison Sullivan's parents' house. I managed to speak to a couple of the Walshes' former neighbours earlier. And guess what?'

'They didn't remember Sharon being pregnant.'

'Got it in one. Where are you? It sounds like you're driving.'

'I am and I think maybe you should get back here.' Anna filled Jim in on what had happened that morning.

'I'm on my way.' His words were accompanied by the sound of a car turning sharply. 'Don't hang up. I want to hear exactly what's going on at your end.'

The bus headed along Mansfield Road, leaving behind the city centre, passing ranks of suburban housing that finally gave way to flat fields of wheat, barley and oilseed rape. Anna relayed a running commentary to Jim on when and where the bus stopped and who got off and on. It turned onto Ollerton Road and made its way north through a countryside dotted with pockets of woodland that gradually melded into an unbroken forest. The trees crept closer and closer to the road, until their leaves dappled Anna's windscreen with shadows. A sign announced that she was entering Sherwood Forest. As she peered into the gloom of the trees, she found herself wondering whether somewhere amongst them there was another tree like the one in Leeds. Was that where Emily was heading?

She uneasily told Jim where she was and asked, 'How far away are you?' There was no reply. She glanced at her phone. The reception bar was non-existent. 'Fuck.' She hissed the word through her teeth, glaring at the trees as if they were out to get her.

A single reception bar returned as the car emerged from the trees at the edge of Edwinstowe, a village of white cottages and red-brick houses that the forest encircled like a protecting hand. She dialled Jim again. His voice crackled brokenly over the line. 'Whe... a...'

'I'm in Edwinstowe,' said Anna.

'I ca... you.'

Did he mean he couldn't hear? 'Edwinstowe,' Anna shouted. 'What about you?'

Jim said something, but it was too faint to make out.

'Say again.'

The bus slowed at a crossroads in the centre of the village. A snippet of Jim's voice came through. 'I... Calvert...'

'Are you saying you're at Calverton?' asked Anna. Calverton was a village north-east of Nottingham. If Jim was there, he was still a good half an hour behind the bus. The bus accelerated and Anna did likewise. The line broke up completely again. As they passed out of the village and back into the forest, the reception bar dropped to zero and a 'No Service' message flashed up.

A mile or so beyond the village, the bus turned into the large, tree-shaded car park of Sherwood Forest Nature Reserve. The car park was empty except for a couple of cars. Anna didn't dare follow the bus into it for fear of being spotted. She pulled over at the edge of the road where the car park was visible through a thin screen of trees. The bus stopped at a little wooden shelter. When it continued on its way, Anna saw that Emily had got off. The girl was standing with her back to the road, turning her head from side to side as though looking for something, or more likely someone. Anna could think of only one person who that someone could be.

Emily set off walking into the forest. Anna dialled Jim again, more in hope than expectation. The line rang three times, then went dead. She lost sight of Emily amongst the trees. She jumped out of the van, scurried across the car park and pressed herself flat against a tree. Peeking around it, she saw Emily heading along a path signposted 'Visitor Centre'. She took a quick photo of the sign and sent it to Jim. Maybe it would get through. Maybe not. Either way, Jim would see her van parked on the road and know she was somewhere in the vicinity. Staying off the path, moving from tree to tree, she continued following Emily.

* * * *

As Emily walked, her gaze roamed amongst the trees. In the hazy sunlight there was a soft, almost dreamlike quality to the forest that drew her mind back to the many hours she'd spent there as a young child. There was a play park nearby, but she'd preferred to play amongst the slender birches and thick oaks, climbing, hiding, pretending to be an outlaw. It was only since discovering an interest in boys that she'd grown her hair and started wearing makeup. Not so long ago she'd been a tomboy with grubby hands and grazed knees. She'd especially liked to play inside the hollow trees, of which there were plenty in the forest. There was one in particular – a huge gnarled oak – that had been her favourite. Its trunk had snapped about four metres from the ground, allowing the sun entrance to its interior.

Her pace slowed as she entered a clearing that contained a small assortment of one-storeyed, mossy-roofed buildings painted various shades of green to blend in with their surroundings. Nothing had changed since her previous visit. The buildings were centred around a life-size model of Robin Hood and Little John fighting with staves. She brought up the photo of Gavin on her phone. It had been taken twenty-six years ago. *Will I be able to recognise him?* she wondered. *Will he recognise me? Has he ever even seen me?*

Other than herself and an old couple walking a dog, the clearing was deserted. She peered through the window of a café. A man was eating a sandwich at one of the tables. He had grey hair and glasses. Surely he was too old to be Gavin. She looked at the time on her phone. It was only twenty-five past eleven. Maybe Gavin wasn't here yet. She wandered around the dusty exhibits, glancing without interest at scenes from the Robin Hood legend that had once fired her imagination. Ten minutes dragged by. A few people came and went. None of them looked remotely like Gavin. Her brow pinched thoughtfully. Maybe he'd decided it was too risky to come after all.

She sat on a bench for a few minutes, then walked to the far end of the clearing where a sign directed visitors to the Major Oak – an immense hollow tree that Robin Hood and his men had supposedly sheltered within. Perhaps Gavin was there. She started along the path. Her gaze was drawn to a tree a short distance away to her right – the broken old oak that had been her childhood favourite. Something had caught her eye. A flicker of movement? A little cautiously, she approached the tree and looked behind it. Nothing. She squinted into the flaring crack at the base of the trunk. A hand suddenly emerged from it. She made to cry out, but before she could do so the hand smothered her mouth. A second hand grabbed her arm and yanked her inside the tree. As she struggled to break free in the wood-smelling gloom, a soft but distinctly male voice said, 'It's me. Gavin.'

The hands released Emily. Her heart hammering, she pressed back against the tree trunk. She found herself looking into a face that was different yet unmistakably the same as the one from the *Birmingham Evening Post* article. Much of it was masked by a thick black beard that – like her mum's hair – was several shades too dark to be natural. Equally black hair was pulled back into a receding ponytail. The face was weather-beaten, cut through with deep lines that flared from the corners of the eyes – eyes as dark as the tree's bark. Their stockily built owner was dressed in a brown wax jacket and camouflaged trousers that almost made him seem part of the tree. As Emily took him in, he did the same to her. He smiled. Not a warm smile, but not a threatening one either. More a kind of calculated show of friendliness.

'Hello, Emily. Where's Dad?'

'He's back at the visitor centre,' lied Emily, suddenly wishing he was. Even though the tree's interior was carved with dozens of names, she'd always thought of it as a secret place. A safe place. But Gavin's proximity within its close confines made her feel deeply vulnerable.

His smile broadened. 'No he's not. It was you who sent those emails.'

Emily made no reply. She glanced at the crack in the trunk as though she was thinking of making a run for it.

'It's OK,' said Gavin, reading her apprehension. 'I'm not angry. I'm glad you sent them.'

She tentatively met his gaze. 'How did you know?'

'A couple of reasons.' Gavin ticked them off on thick, callused fingers. 'Firstly, Dad's a stickler for proper grammar. He'd never miss an apostrophe. Secondly, the forest *is* the usual place where we meet. How do you think I knew about this tree? When you were little I used to watch you play here.' His eyes flickered with a sudden intensity. 'And do you know what I'd think? I'd think to myself that you were the most beautiful child I'd ever seen. You're even more beautiful now.'

Not knowing what to make of the compliment or the way Gavin was looking at her, Emily blinked awkwardly. 'So we've met before?'

'No. I used to watch you from a distance.' A little twist of bitterness came into Gavin's smile. 'And when Dad stopped bringing you with him I couldn't even do that.'

'Why did he stop bringing me?'

'He said it was because you didn't want to come here any more. But that wasn't it, was it?'

Emily gave a little shrug. 'I never stopped enjoying coming here. I'm not really bothered about all the Robin Hood stuff, but the forest—'

'Yes, the forest!' Gavin cut in eagerly. 'You feel it, don't you?' He closed his eyes, inhaling deeply. 'You feel the power of this place.'

'I… I don't know. I just like it here.' Emily stiffened as Gavin reached out and put his hand on her arm again.

'That's because you're like I was. You hear the trees speaking to you, but you don't understand what they're saying. I can teach you to understand. I can open your ears and your eyes. I can show you the truth. That's what you came here for, isn't it?'

Emily hesitated to answer. There was a different kind of light in Gavin's eyes now. Emily occasionally went – or rather allowed herself to be dragged – along to the Evangelical Church her mum attended. Gavin had the same look in his eyes as the minister there did when he was preaching. She'd never felt comfortable around such faith. She just didn't *feel* it. For a long time she'd wondered if that made her a bad person. She'd even had nightmares about going to hell. One night, she'd tearfully confided in her dad and he'd replied gently, *If you're a bad person then I must be too, because I don't feel it either.* After that, she'd had no more nightmares.

'Well,' continued Gavin, a hint of impatience in his voice, 'isn't it?'

'Yes, I want to know the truth, but not about trees and all that stuff. I want to know about you and me.'

'It's all part of the same thing, Emily. It's all one whole.' Gavin braced his hands against the walls of the tree as though trying to hold them back. 'The tree, the forest, you, me. You can't know one thing without knowing the other.'

'Are you some kind of druid?'

Gavin laughed and wrinkled his nose, as though the idea both amused and disgusted him. 'Druids are a made-up concept. I'm a child of Cernunnos, the Horned God. And his only law is that there is no law. Can you imagine that, Emily? A world in which there's no right, no wrong. Just the freedom to be and do anything you want. I can show you that world. I can—' He broke off at the sound of voices outside and peered through the crack. Two women passed by, one of them pushing a pram. His voice dropped to a whisper. 'We've stayed here too long. Come on.'

'Where are we going?'

'Somewhere we can talk alone.'

'We are alone.'

'I mean properly alone. There are too many people around here. Too many eyes and ears.'

Gavin swiftly slid through the crack and headed into the trees. Emily followed more slowly. Did she want to be truly alone with him? She wasn't sure she did. But what if she didn't go with him? Would she ever get the answers she was so desperate for? He glanced back at her. His eyes flitted nervously beyond her. Then he continued on his way. She stared after him. *You've come this far*, she told herself. *There's no point backing out now.* Taking a deep breath, she hurried to catch him up. And as she did so, his words went round in her head. *A world in which there's no right, no wrong.* Part of her wondered what such a world would be like. Another part never wanted to find out.

****

Anna took a photo of the 'Major Oak' sign and sent it to Jim. She blinked as though her eyes were playing tricks on her. One second Emily had been standing by a tree. The next she was gone. Poof! Like magic. Her eyes scoured the surrounding trees. Nothing. What the hell was going on here? She resisted an urge to dart forward and try to find out. What if Emily suspected she was being followed? She might have dived into the bracken that carpeted the forest floor and be waiting to see if her suspicion proved true. Anna reminded herself too that someone else might be lying in wait, watching both for Emily and anyone following her.

She dropped to her knees and worked her way around to the right of the tree, keeping a distance of fifty or so metres between herself and it. She stopped moving when she saw the crack that allowed entrance to the tree's hollow interior. Was Emily in there with Gavin? At that distance it was impossible to tell. Her mind returned once again to the tree in Leeds. An image came to her of Emily with a knife protruding from her chest. It was all she could do to stop herself from crawling close enough to get a look inside the tree. *Be patient*, she told herself. *If either of them is in there, you'll find out soon enough.* She lay on her belly, peering between bracken fronds, her fingers curled around a thick dead branch. Several minutes edged by. More doubts crowded in on her. What if Emily had somehow managed to slip away with Gavin? The longer she lay there the less chance she had of catching them up. Her eyes were drawn to the path by movement, then darted back to the tree as a face appeared at the crack. For a second she had the crazy impression that she was seeing a living carving of the Horned God. She half expected a pair of curved horns to sprout into view. Then she saw past the illusion, saw the face that had haunted her for twenty years.

Her first instinct was to charge at Gavin and pummel his ugly bastard face with the branch. Just keep on pummelling and pummelling until it was nothing more than battered flesh and broken bone. But if she did that she would never find Jessica. Rigid with hatred, she watched Gavin slither into full view. Emily emerged behind him. As he slunk off into the undergrowth, she stared after him, her eyes not quite afraid, but wary, like a deer uncertain whether to give flight or stay. She decided upon the latter.

Anna's hand tightened on the stick, and not only because Gavin was heading almost directly towards her. As Emily had started after Gavin, a sly smile had spread under his beard. Anna pressed herself as flat as possible, hardly breathing. Gavin was less than twenty metres away now, slightly off to her right. She placed her palm against the ground, ready if necessary to spring up swinging. She would have to get in a good first hit if she was to have any chance of overpowering Gavin. He wasn't much taller than her, but his shoulders were twice as broad.

'Do you live near here?' asked Emily.

Gavin made no reply. He veered away from Anna's hiding place, turning onto what looked like an animal path. Anna forced herself to wait until Gavin and Emily were a good couple of hundred metres away. She hurriedly pushed herself upright and took a photo of the hollow tree and the animal path, before pursuing them. The sun was out, casting lines of light and shadow across the forest floor. Anna kept to the shadows as much as possible, taking photos every few hundred metres and sending them to Jim like a trail of crumbs for him to follow. She was constantly on the verge of losing sight of Gavin and Emily, but she dared not draw any closer. Other than birdsong and the sighing of the wind amongst the leaves, the forest was silent, and every sound she made seemed abnormally amplified in her ears. Several times she dropped to her haunches or dodged behind a tree, fearing she'd done something to give herself away.

After maybe half a mile, they came to a broad grassy track. A battered blue Land Rover with a mouldy white roof was parked at the side of the track. A tarp-covered trailer was attached to the back of it. One edge of the tarp had come loose and billowed gently in the breeze, exposing cut logs. Anna made to take a photo, but Gavin glanced over his shoulder. She ducked down, heart hammering. He wasn't looking at her though. He was looking at Emily. He said something inaudible, then climbed into the driver's seat. Anna's mind raced. She couldn't follow a vehicle on foot. From the direction of the track, she guessed it branched off the road she was parked on. But by the time she could get back to the camper van and find the track again, Gavin and Emily would be long gone. What the fuck was she to do? Suddenly she knew. On her knees and elbows, she crept closer to the Land Rover. Emily was standing by the passenger door, as if uncertain whether she wanted to get in.

'How far is it?' Anna faintly heard her ask. She couldn't make out Gavin's reply, but Emily got into the vehicle. The engine growled into life. This was it. It was now or never. Anna darted forwards and dived under the tarp. Splinters of wood speared her palms. She barely noticed. Adrenalin filling her veins, the pungent scent of freshly cut wood filling her nostrils, she waited to find out if she'd been seen. The Land Rover accelerated along the track, heading deeper into the forest. Relief rushed through her. She'd got away with it! For now.

As the trailer rattled over the track, Anna poked her phone out from under the tarp and took more photos. For two or three miles the track cut straight as a ruled line into the heart of the forest. The trees changed from haphazard birch and oak to rigid rows of pines that let little light through their branches. The

Land Rover turned left and descended gently for half a mile or so before making a right, then another right and a sharp left. Then it juddered to a halt, but the engine remained on. There was the sound of a gate scraping open. The Land Rover pulled forward a short distance. Through a tear in the tarp, Anna glimpsed Gavin closing and padlocking a wooden farm gate with a hand-painted 'PRIVATE' sign nailed to it. When Gavin returned to the car, Anna photographed the gate. After half a minute more, the vehicle stopped again and the engine was cut. The doors opened and closed. Anna craned her neck to try and get a glimpse of what was going on. But all she could see were the pointed tips of pines swaying against the cloudless sky.

Footsteps moved away from the Land Rover. Her straining ears caught what sounded like a key turning in a lock. There was the dull thud of a door being closed. She waited a minute or two to make sure her ears weren't misleading her. Then, cautious as a rabbit leaving the safety of a burrow, she slid from beneath the tarp and ducked down behind the trailer. The Land Rover was parked at the end of a rutted track, its edges overgrown with brambles and nettles. Behind her and to her right, pines marched in two rows that formed a right angle at the gate. To her left was a grassy field, enclosed by barbed wire and thick hedgerows, and dotted with vehicles in various states of disrepair. There was another Land Rover, its axles resting on bricks, the guts of its engine scattered over the ground. And there were two vans – a newish-looking red Ford Escort, and an ancient Transit, so eaten up with rust that its white paintwork was barely visible. She felt a clutching sensation around her throat. Was it the same van Gavin had thrown Jessica into the back of?

The smell of woodsmoke tickled Anna's nostrils. To the right of the Transit was a bare patch of scorched earth with a metal barrel-like structure about one and a half metres tall at its centre. Smoke seeped from the edges of a lid that sloped to a central point like a Chinese peasant's hat. A charcoal kiln. That explained the trailer of logs. Beyond the Land Rover was a small, grey, two-storey cottage with a slate roof, grimy windows and a door that had been daubed with a crude rainbow of paint. A couple of rotten-looking dead rabbits were hanging from a hook on the door. Anna spotted some movement in a downstairs window. She jerked back behind the trailer as Gavin's weathered face appeared at the glass. Shit! Had he seen her? Long moments passed. Nothing happened. She released a slow but shaky breath and considered her next move. Should she wait for back-up or should she move in closer to the spider's lair?

CHAPTER FOURTEEN

'I've just passed Calverton,' Jim said loudly into his phone, then the line died again. Where had Anna said she was? All he'd been able to make out was, *I'm... Ed...* He tried calling her back, but got an answering service. He expelled a sharp breath of frustration. He knew the bus's final destination was Ollerton, but he didn't know the exact route it took to get there. Reluctantly, he pulled over and brought up the bus timetable on his phone. He was glad he'd done so when he saw that the bus took a minor detour through Edwinstowe and Sherwood Forest before arriving at Ollerton. It took the bus fifty-two minutes to get from Nottingham to Edwinstowe. Almost exactly the same amount of time had passed since Anna had first called him that morning. So that had to be where she was. His phone rang. He answered it quickly, expecting it to be Anna.

Garrett's voice came over the line. 'Good news, Jim. I managed to get hold of Sharon Walsh's health records. She was diagnosed with endometriosis in 1996. She's infertile. Emily can't be her daughter.'

Instead of replying, Jim accelerated hard back into the road.

'Hello? Are you there?' asked Garrett.

'Yes,' Jim said flatly, concentrating on overtaking a car.

'I thought you'd sound more pleased. This should be enough to get a warrant for DNA.'

'I am pleased, but something's going down here.' Jim quickly filled Garrett in on the situation.

'That sounds promising. Very promising. Do you want me to send over a helicopter?'

'No. If Emily is meeting Gavin, that'll only send him scurrying back to whatever hole he's been hiding in. We need to keep a low profile.'

'OK, but I'm going to contact the local police and put them on alert.'

'You can't do that. We can't afford to risk Villiers getting wind of this.'

Garrett was silent a moment, then he said, 'You're playing a dangerous game, Jim.'

'Yeah, well it's the only game I've got left.'

Jim cut off the call and focused all his attention on the road. The bus took just under half an hour to travel from Farnsfield, which was a few miles north of him, to Edwinstowe. He figured he could cover the same ground in maybe two-thirds of the time. First the fields on his left, then those on his right gave way to trees. He passed through them into Edwinstowe. He scanned the quiet streets for Anna's camper van. Beyond the village the trees closed in again. He spotted the van near the entrance to a car park. Spurred on by an ever-increasing sense of urgency, he pulled in behind it and jumped out of the car. Surely there was only one reason for Emily to get off the bus here – to meet someone away from prying eyes.

He peered into the van. As expected, it was empty. He ran across the car park to the bus shelter, his gaze scouring the trees.

At the far side of the car park was a path. To the left it led back towards Edwinstowe. To the right it wound gently through the trees to the visitor centre. It didn't seem likely that Emily would have headed back to the village. He followed the sign for the visitor centre. Moving more cautiously now, he checked out the café and exhibits. Anna and Emily were nowhere to be seen. Emily must have headed further into the forest, he reasoned. Assuming, of course, she'd come this way at all. He approached a man painting one of the buildings and flashed his ID. 'Have you seen a girl pass by here? She's fifteen years old, blonde, slim, about five three.'

'No, sorry,' replied the man.

Jim asked the same question in the café. 'Yes, I think I've seen her,' answered the woman behind the counter. 'She poked her head in here about half an hour or so ago. She looked like she was looking for someone.'

'Did you see where she went?'

The woman shook her head. Jim thanked her and returned outside. If Emily had stuck to the path, there were only two ways she could have gone – either back to the car park or towards the Major Oak. He headed for the Major Oak. Numerous smaller paths branched off the main one into the trees. After about ten minutes' walk, the path broadened into a clearing with the Major Oak – a squat, fat tree, its broad-spreading branches supported by metal struts – at one side and a picnic area at the other. Two women were sitting at a table, one of them feeding a baby. Jim described Anna and Emily to them. They hadn't seen either. He looked about himself uncertainly. Beyond the clearing the path looped back towards the visitor centre. It seemed more likely to him that Emily would have headed deeper into the forest.

His phone vibrated as a message came through. It was from Anna. He opened it. A photo of the sign to the visitor centre appeared. It had been sent at 11:21. Forty-six minutes ago. Another message arrived. A photo of the sign for the Major Oak sent fifteen minutes after the first. Anna was obviously pointing him in the direction of Emily. He tried phoning her. No answer. There seemed little point in continuing blindly along the path. Better to wait and see if Anna sent more photos. He hunkered down against a tree at the edge of the clearing. A couple of minutes passed. A third photo arrived. It was of a broken old oak tree. The edge of one of the visitor centre buildings was visible in the top left of the photo.

As Jim ran back along the path, more photos landed in his inbox. They showed a faint path leading through the trees. The broken tree wasn't difficult to locate. He glanced inside its hollow trunk and studied the ground around it. There were no signs of footprints. But then the ground was dry and blanketed with dead leaves. About fifty metres from the tree he came across a clump of bracken with several flattened fronds. The position matched the angle from which the photo of the tree had been taken. His eyes continued roaming the ground and found what they were looking for – the faint path. He set off along it.

The deeper into the forest he got, the denser the undergrowth became. Several times it threatened to swallow the path, forcing him to pause until he spotted some point of reference from one of the photos. After about a quarter of an hour he came to a grassy track. At its nearest edge there were tyre marks in the soft turf. He frowned. Had Emily got into a vehicle with someone? If so, how had Anna followed them? He judged the main road to be somewhere away to his right. The tyre tracks led in the opposite direction, petering out after several metres. Yet another photo arrived on his phone. He wasn't surprised to see an image of the track. It was blurry as though it had been taken whilst in motion. A dark line slanted across the top of it.

Looking to his right, he picked out several trees that appeared in the photo. Had it been taken facing backwards in a vehicle? Maybe the line was the rim of a window.

It had been sent at 12:06. Jim swore through his teeth. He was still twenty-five minutes behind Anna. If she and Emily were in a vehicle, they could be miles away by now. In which case, there was no point him continuing the pursuit on foot. He turned to head back to the main road along the track. He'd only taken a couple of steps when his phone rang. It was Reece. He hesitated to answer the call. But the thought came to him, *What if something's happened to Staci? What if she's died?* After Margaret's murder, Reece had been there for him day and night. If not for him, he might well have done something stupid like thrown himself off a cliff. He had to at least make sure his friend wasn't on the verge of some similarly distraught act. He put the phone to his ear and, trying to keep the dread out of his voice, asked, 'How's things?'

'I'm on my way home from East Midlands Airport,' replied Reece. 'Staci's on a flight to Cape Town.' The uneven breathing of someone struggling to hold it together filled the line. 'I'm wondering if I'll ever see her again.'

Jim wished he could reassure Reece that he would. But he knew it was better to say nothing at all than give empty reassurances. 'Yeah, you must be. But listen, Reece, I can't talk right now. I think I might be on to something big. I may even be close to finding Spider.'

'No shit. Where are you?'

'Sherwood Forest.'

'I'm not far from there. I'm just coming up to junction twenty-eight on the M1. I can be at the forest in twenty-five minutes. Half an hour tops.'

'Are you sure you're up to it?'

'Course I fucking am. Besides, what else am I going to do? Go home and cry into a mug of tea?'

A faint smile passed over Jim's lips. If he had to tackle Gavin, it certainly wouldn't do any harm to have the big man backing him up. 'OK. Head to the visitor centre car park. I probably won't be there. I'm trying to catch up with Anna. She's tailing Emily Walsh.'

'Who's Emily Walsh?'

'There's no time to explain now. Call me when you get to the car park.'

Jim pocketed his phone and started jogging in the direction of the main road. The track arched gently away from where he was parked, but he wanted to be certain of where it met the road. As he ran, photos continued to come in. Assuming the perspective was skewed by Anna taking them facing backwards, one appeared to show a left turn in the track, another a right, then a second right, then a left. As before, a dark line cut off the upper portion of the photos. That decided Jim. Anna had either managed to sneak in, or been captured and forced into, the back of whatever vehicle Emily was in. As she seemed to have her hands free, the former struck him as more likely. She surely wouldn't have been able to avoid discovery in a car. Perhaps the vehicle was a van of some sort. Creases gathered on his brow. Perhaps it was a van similar to the one that had been used to abduct Jessica Young.

Then came a photo of a padlocked farm gate. A padlock meant private land, and private land could mean a house. The photo had been sent at 12:21. Less than five minutes ago. Which meant Emily might have been taken to a house or some other property within roughly fifteen minutes' drive of where he was standing. He dialled Anna again. This time she picked up! He opened his mouth to ask, *Where are you?* But before he could do so her voice came down the line in an intense whisper. 'I've found *him*. I'm at the fucker's house.'

By *him* Anna could only mean one person – Gavin! 'Is Emily with him?'

'Yes.'

'I'm on the forest track close to the main road. How far away are you?'

'Maybe four or five—' The line broke up briefly, then Anna's voice came back through. '—you take a left, then, after about half a mile, a right, then a quick right...'

Again, Anna's voice faded out of hearing. 'Stay right where you are,' said Jim. 'Do not try to apprehend Gavin yourself. Do you hear?'

There was no reply. The line went dead. Jim quickened his pace, suppressing his rising excitement, reminding himself that a spider wasn't caught until it was caught.

****

Emily's step faltered as she neared the cottage's front door. Her nose wrinkled at the two dead rabbits dangling against its garishly colourful surface. The sickly scent of rot they gave off suggested they'd been there for some time. As did the maggots infesting their grey-brown fur. 'What are they there for?' she asked, revulsion thickening her voice.

'To keep away unwanted visitors,' said Gavin, opening the door.

Emily glanced around herself. Unwanted visitors? She couldn't imagine Gavin got any visitors at all. There wasn't another house in sight. She followed him into a gloomy, low-ceilinged hallway with a stone-flagged floor, dirty-white walls and a flight of carpetless stairs. To her right was a closed door.

At the far end of the hallway a table with what looked like a thick butcher's chopping board on it was visible through an open door. A musky smell of incense hung in the air. Gavin locked the front door, then hung his jacket on a peg. Underneath it he was wearing a faded baggy black t-shirt tucked into the waistband of his camouflaged trousers. A long, wooden-handled knife was holstered on his waist. Noticing Emily looking at it, he patted the handle. 'This is my skinning knife. I catch and kill all the meat I eat myself. When you eat an animal, you absorb some of its spirit too. If you only eat domestic meat, then you'll be tame and domestic. If you only eat wild meat, you'll become like the animals of the forest – wild and healthy, and most importantly, free.'

Gavin moved through the closed door into a narrow living room that ran the length of the house. Light filtered through small, dusty windows at either end of the room. To the left of the door was a threadbare sofa facing a stone fireplace heaped with the remnants of a fire. A scorched kettle hung above the ashes. The hearth was stacked high with chopped logs, some of which had toppled onto a goatskin rug. To one side of the fireplace were some rough home-made shelves piled with books. On the wall above it there was a carving of a bearded face with staring eyes, pointed ears and curving horns. The walls were littered with dozens of similar carvings. In some the man appeared to have leaves sprouting from his face. In others the face wasn't that of a man at all, but looked more like a goat or a stag. One particular carving caught Emily's eyes. It depicted a figure with cloven hooves and shaggy hairy legs attached to a muscular torso and horned head. The man – if that's what it was – was sitting cross-legged and in his arms he held a naked, long-haired girl. The girl's breasts were small. Her body and limbs were slender. She dangled limply in the man's arms. The man looked not at the girl, but straight back at Emily. There was nothing lewd in his expression, just a kind of remorseless blankness.

'The carvings are a hobby of mine,' said Gavin. 'Do you like them?'

No, they give me the creeps, thought Emily. But she didn't say it for fear of offending Gavin. Instead she gave a non-committal shrug.

'You know who he is, don't you?' continued Gavin.

Recalling what he'd said at the hollow tree, Emily replied, 'The Horned God.'

Gavin nodded. 'He is the Lord of Nature. He gives us everything and all he asks in return is that we honour him.' His voice sharpened with contempt. 'Unlike the false gods of the Christians and Muslims, he does not ask us to kneel. He asks us to indulge in every pleasure we desire. For our bodies are his bodies. And so our pleasure is his pleasure.'

Emily shifted uneasily as the thought came to her, *What if your only pleasure is hurting others? What then?* Again, she couldn't bring herself to speak her mind. Not because she was worried about offending Gavin this time, but because she was afraid what answer he would give. Besides, she hadn't come here to talk about this shit. She'd come here to find out who she was. 'Anna Young said something about our parents not being what they seem. What did she mean?'

Gavin stared at her, stroking his beard thoughtfully. 'Perhaps it would be best if I begin by explaining why Dad stopped bringing you to the forest. Like you said, it wasn't because you stopped wanting to come. It was because he thought it was too dangerous.'

'Because of the McLeans?'

Gavin's eyes grew heavy-lidded. He looked at Emily for another moment, as if savouring some thought. 'No, not because of the McLeans. Because of—'

Breaking off, he reached into a trouser pocket and withdrew a vibrating phone. He put it to his ear, but said nothing. Deep furrows formed on his tanned forehead. Shoving the phone back into his pocket, he wheeled around to peer out the front window.

'Who was that?' Emily asked as Gavin bobbed his head as though trying to get a look at something.

'Stay here,' he retorted, turning to head for the door.

Emily followed him into the hallway. 'What's going on?'

Gavin hastened towards the rear of the house, pausing only to shoot her a backwards glance. His voice came in a growl of warning. 'I said fucking well stay here!'

She flinched to a halt, the uncertainty that had been in her eyes since meeting Gavin tipping towards outright fear. His words of a moment earlier returned to her. *No, not because of the McLeans. Because of—* And suddenly she knew what he'd been about to say. *Because of me.* He was the reason their dad had stopped bringing her to the forest. He was the one who made it dangerous. What was he? she wondered. Some kind of pervert who couldn't – or wouldn't – control his urges? More to the point, did she really want to hang around and find out? Her gaze returned to the carving of the Horned God and the girl. It answered the question for her – no. Sure, she was desperate to find out the truth of who she was. But she wasn't so desperate as to risk ending up like that.

She turned to the front door. Gavin hadn't left the key in it. She would have to follow him out the back way. As she padded along the hallway, she wondered about the phone call. Had he gone outside to meet the caller? Another possibility occurred to her. Perhaps the call had been a warning of some kind. Maybe someone was at the house who shouldn't be there. Anna Young's face flashed into her mind. Had she somehow followed them?

She put a hand over her nose as she entered the kitchen. There was a strong animal smell. Rows of pheasants, wood pigeons and rabbits hung from ceiling beams. The chopping board was deeply scored with knife marks and stained rusty brown. A chair was pushed up to the table with a labelless bottle of some homebrew in front of it. There was a greasy cooker with a pan of watery brown liquid on its hob. In a chipped farmhouse sink next to the back door, there were several aluminium trays containing what looked suspiciously like the leftovers of a takeaway chicken curry. It appeared Gavin was something of a bullshitter.

The door was closed. Emily tried the handle. To her relief, the door creaked open. She poked her head outside. At the back of the house there was a small, windowless barn with a corrugated roof. Beyond the barn a long garden stretched towards a tall hedge. Someone had made an attempt to cultivate the garden. There were four rectangular earthen beds with rows of canes. But the beds were clogged with weeds and the surrounding grass was overgrown, except for a circular area around a sapling tree. A path had been cut through the grass to the tree, whose slender branches were decorated with dozens of fluttering coloured ribbons.

Gavin was nowhere to be seen. Her eyes searched vainly for a gate or a gap in the hedge. Unless he was in the barn, Gavin must have headed around the front of the house. She was going to have to go that way too. She cautiously peered around the corner of the house closest to the forest. Halfway along the side there was a gap in the hedge filled with coils of barbed wire. Maybe the coils could be pulled aside and she could slip away into the trees. As she started towards the wire, she spotted Gavin emerging from another gap in the hedge adjacent to the Land Rover. He was moving slowly like a predator poised to strike. She gave a sharp little intake of breath. In his right hand he was gripping the skinning knife.

CHAPTER FIFTEEN

Anna tried phoning Jim back. Nothing. She returned her attention to the house, peeking one eye around the trailer. Gavin was no longer at the window. The thought of Emily alone in there with him gave her a horrible feeling in her stomach. Surely even he wouldn't hurt his own daughter. Would he? Her mind returned to Jessica, the Hopeland children's home, the corpse under the tree. And she knew that the answer was *Yes he would.* There were no depths that irredeemable filth wouldn't sink to in order to satisfy his twisted needs. From where she was she couldn't see anything through the little window. She needed to get closer. She needed to make sure Gavin wasn't putting his slimy hands on Emily. She started to glance around for a way to approach the house unseen, but stopped herself. Jim had told her to stay put. She knew he was right. If she moved from behind the trailer, she risked being seen. And if she was seen, the possible consequences for herself, Emily, and maybe even Jessica, didn't bear thinking about. The best thing she could do was wait for Jim to find his way to her.

Anna looked at the time on her phone. It was 12:27. Jim was at the grassy track, which meant he was roughly fifteen minutes away from her. *Fifteen minutes' drive*, she corrected herself. If he was on foot – which he almost certainly was – he would have to return to the main road to pick up his car. In which case it would take him more like thirty or even forty minutes to get to her. She drew in a steadying breath. Whether it took him fifteen or forty minutes, it would be the longest wait of her life.

'Gavin!'

Emily's shrill voice sliced through the silence of the forest. The cry had come from the right-hand side of the house. Her heart accelerating crazily, Anna jerked to look in that direction. What she saw set her blood pumping even faster. Gavin was stalking towards her, a long knife glinting in his hand. There was no time to run away. She sprang upright and grabbed a log from the trailer. Gavin thrust the blade at her stomach. She blocked it with the log. The blade glanced off it, slicing into her fingers. She felt nothing but a slight cold sting. Then Gavin was pulling the blade back for a second strike. This time she was ready. Jessica's abduction had prompted her to learn self-defence. She knew the best defence against a knife attack was evasion and counterstrike. As the knife flashed towards her, she sidestepped it and brought the log down against Gavin's hand. The strike had just enough height and force behind it to knock the knife out of his grip. With a low grunt of pain, he drove his elbow into her face. The blow caught her on the cheekbone, snapping her head sideways and dislodging her glasses.

Tears sprang into Anna's eyes. Through them she blurrily saw Gavin stooping to retrieve the knife. She thrust her knee into his midriff. He caught hold of her leg. She tried to wrench it free, and suddenly they were both falling. She landed on her side with

Gavin across her legs. He scrambled to get fully on top of her. As she'd been taught to do, she elevated her knees. For a second, her wiry muscles quivering with the effort, she managed to lift him into the air. But he was too heavy, too powerful. His weight flattened her out, pinning her to the ground. He reached to grab her throat. *Always protect your throat!* That had been one of her self-defence instructor's mantras. If a stronger opponent got their hands on your throat, nothing you did would stop them from squeezing the life out of you. She tucked her chin tightly to her chest, preventing him from getting a proper grip. Simultaneously, she grabbed Gavin's wrists and pushed them towards each other. One of his thumbs came within range of her teeth. She bit down on it with all her strength. Yelping like a wounded dog, he wrenched his thumb out of her mouth. The instant he did so, she bucked her hips and twisted from under him. She didn't try to separate from him, though. Instead she swung a leg over him and straddled his waist.

Now it was her turn! She'd waited for and dreamt about this moment for most of her life. With a kind of calm frenzy, she clasped Gavin's head and dug her thumbs into his eyes. He jerked his face to the side, and she ducked down to clamp her teeth onto his ear. The salty, metallic taste of blood flooded her mouth. Screaming again, he tried to throw her off. But she was on him like a limpet, biting, tearing, gouging. He pummelled his fists into her arms and ribs, blows heavy enough to shake her whole body. She knew she couldn't withstand many of them. She knew too that even with her training, he would most probably eventually overpower her. But she felt no fear. Just an incredible, almost euphoric, sense of release.

'Stop it! Stop it!'

Emily's voice rang out again, much closer now. Anna didn't stop. She couldn't. It was as if a dam had burst inside her and nothing could hold the flood back. Emily grabbed her arm and pulled her sideways. Realising Gavin would end up back on top of her unless she did otherwise, Anna rolled away from him and scrambled to her feet. He did likewise. Both of them were breathing hard. Gavin's hair had come loose from its ponytail and hung in a scraggly mess around his shoulders. Sweat glistened on his forehead. Blood streamed from his torn left ear and deep scratches on his cheeks. There was blood smeared over Anna's face too – both her own and Gavin's. Her right eye was rapidly swelling shut. Her other eye frantically searched the ground. She spotted what she was looking for in Emily's hand. Gavin did too.

'Give me the knife,' he panted, extending a hand.

'Don't do it,' exclaimed Anna. 'He'll kill us both.'

'Liar! You're the one who came here to kill me.'

'I came here to find Jessica.'

Emily's eyes were saucers of uncertainty. The knife trembled in her hand like an icicle about to drop. 'Who's Jessica?'

'She's my sister. This fucker abducted her.'

'More lies!' spat Gavin. 'You people have ruined my life with your false accusations.'

Anna could have almost laughed. *Me? Ruined your fucking life?* she felt like screaming back at him, but he wasn't worth the breath it would take. 'Why do you think he was kept secret from you, Emily? He's a rapist, a murderer.'

'Shut your stinking mouth, bitch.' Gavin edged towards Emily.

She took a faltering backward step. 'Don't come any closer.'

Gavin's voice dropped to a demanding hiss. 'We're blood, Emily. No matter what, always be loyal to your blood.'

'You're my blood too, Emily,' Anna countered.

Confusion twisted at Emily's features. 'What... what do you mean?'

'My sister, Jessica, is your mum.'

'Don't listen to her,' Gavin yelled over Anna. 'She's trying to mess with your head.'

Her eyes glazing with tears, Emily murmured, 'If she's my mum, who's my dad?'

Anna eyed Gavin meaningfully. Emily looked at him too. Her mouth worked in mute realisation as she thought of her mum and dad, of how old they were. The doubts had always been there, she realised, like niggling whispers at the back of her mind. Now they yelled at her in unison, *Too old. They've always seemed too old to be my parents!* Gavin wasn't too old. Tears spilled down her freckled cheeks. As though she couldn't bear the sight of him, she closed her eyes. It was only for a second, but it was enough. Gavin and Anna both went for the knife. Gavin was fractionally faster. He grabbed the knife by the blade and wrenched it from Emily's hand. As he righted the knife, Anna caught hold of his wrist. 'Run, Emily!' she shouted. She didn't look to see if Emily heeded her words. She kept her eyes fixed on the knife. She tried to twist and lock Gavin's arm, but her hands were slick with blood from two bone-deep cuts on her knuckles. Feeling her grip slipping, she let go and sprang away. He lunged at her stomach. She sucked it in and dodged aside again. Her back came up against the trailer. She knew then that she was in trouble. *Never get caught with your back against anything.* That was one of the fundamentals of self-defence. If your ability to move was limited, so was your ability to defend yourself.

Gavin made another thrust, going for her face this time. She jerked her head back and the blade whistled by within a millimetre of her eyes. She didn't attempt a counterstrike. The most important thing was to get into open space, put some distance between herself and the blade. As she twisted away from the trailer, she caught sight of Emily. The teenager appeared to be rooted to the ground like one of the encircling trees. Anna opened her mouth to shout *Run!* again, but her voice was cut off by the breath that suddenly whooshed through her teeth. It felt as though she'd been punched hard in the back. From the look of horror on Emily's face, though, she knew she hadn't been hit with merely a fist. A dull but incredibly intense pressure filling the right side of her chest, she staggered to one knee. She tried to get back up, but her legs didn't seem to want to obey her mind. She slumped forward, bracing her hands against the ground, wheezing like an asthmatic. The pressure was rapidly building to a throbbing crescendo. Something yanked at her back, almost lifting her off the ground. She cried out hoarsely as an electric jolt of pain lanced through her. Then Gavin was standing over her with the bloodstained knife poised for a downward strike. *This is it*, her brain screamed at her. *This is where I die.* The fear was almost as overwhelming as the pain. But she'd be fucking damned if she was going to let Gavin see that. She glared defiantly up at him and in return he gave a slight nod, as if to say, *Good game.*

'No!' The word burst out of Emily as she flung herself between Anna and Gavin.

'Move,' he demanded.

She shook her head frantically, trembling arms outspread.

'Do...' rasped Anna, fighting for the air to speak, 'as he... says.' She didn't want to die. But even more than that she wanted Emily to live.

'No,' Emily said again. 'Please, Gavin. Please don't kill her.'

'What do you care what I do to her?' scowled Gavin. 'She's nothing to you.' His darkly inscrutable eyes stared into Emily's pleading blue ones for a breathless moment. His tongue flickered thoughtfully between his lips. When his voice next came, it was as soft as a snake's hiss. 'I have to leave this place. Will you come with me?'

'Where?'

'Wherever I go.'

Now it was Anna's turn to say, 'No!' She forced the word out with all the savage strength of her hatred for Gavin.

Emily looked at her with eyes that said, *What choice do I have?* Her gaze returned to Gavin and she nodded.

He sheathed his knife. That same sly smile Anna had seen in the forest played over his lips. Only now he didn't hide it from Emily. He reached to cup a hand against her cheek. A moan of helpless rage escaped Anna at the sight. Her fingers dug into the turf as though it was Gavin's flesh. He moved forward and, for a second, it seemed he was going to embrace or even kiss Emily. She stiffened as though in anticipation of this. But instead, he stepped around her and stooped to hook his hands under Anna's armpits. She feebly tried to push him away, but only succeeded in collapsing onto her face.

He spoke sharply into her ear. 'This is your lucky day, bitch.' Shooting Emily a glance, he added, 'Get her legs. Quickly! We haven't got much time.'

Emily took hold of Anna's feet.

'Not her feet. Wrap your arms behind her knees,' said Gavin, speaking with the authority of someone who knew what they were doing when it came to carrying a body.

Anna's breath gurgled as they lifted her off the ground. With every passing minute, it was getting harder to breathe. The throbbing had become a burning. It was like someone was holding a lighted match to her skin. Gavin backed down the side of the house. Emily stumbled and her grip slipped. A choking cough wracked Anna as her backside hit the ground. She gritted her teeth with the effort to cling on to consciousness.

'I'm sorry! I'm sorry!' said Emily, struggling to regain her grip. She looked fearfully at Anna's face. 'There's blood coming out of her mouth.'

'She's probably got a punctured lung,' said Gavin.

'Is she going to die?'

'Maybe, maybe not. It depends how long it takes for her to get medical attention.'

'We have to call an ambulance.'

Gavin treated Emily to an *Are you serious?* look. 'There are people on their way here.'

'What people?'

'It doesn't matter what people. The point is, if she's lucky they'll find her in time. If not...'

'But—'

'No buts. That's the best deal she's going to get.'

When they reached the barn, Gavin none too gently set down his end of Anna. She coughed again and more blood-streaked saliva frothed from her mouth. Emily stooped to wipe it off with her sleeve. Gavin batted her hand away. 'You don't know where she's been,' he snapped. 'Do you want to catch AIDS? You're no good—' He broke off as though he'd been about to say more than he wanted to.

He unlocked a padlock and opened the barn door. The smell of tree sap and charcoal wafted out. Hooking his hands back under Anna's armpits, he dragged her inside. He flicked a switch and a bare light bulb flickered into life, illuminating what looked to be a partially complete sculpture of a body curled up fetally amidst gnarled womb-like tree roots. In one corner was a jumble of rusty garden tools. Logs and plastic sacks of charcoal were stacked against the walls to either side of a battered old chest freezer. Even in her agony, Anna noted a couple of telling modifications to the freezer: a padlock had been fitted to its lid; a metal pipe about six inches long and of equal diameter protruded from its front. Her mind flashed back to the Leeds garage, the parallel gouges on its floor. The freezer was the right width to have made the gouges. She thought too of the girl under the tree. Alison Sullivan. Had she been kept prisoner in the freezer? Had Jessica too? The freezer looked old enough.

'Where's Jessica?' she managed to wheeze.

Gavin made no reply. But his eyes said, *You'll never know.* He rifled through Anna's pockets, pulled out her phone and turned to leave. His gaze lingered on the sculpture. Gently, almost reverently, he ran his fingers over its surface. A pained little spasm contorting his face, he jerked his hand away and hurried from the barn. Emily hesitated to follow him. She stared at Anna with a mix of uncertainty, anxiety and apology.

'Come on,' demanded Gavin. 'We've got to go.'

I'm sorry, Emily mouthed at Anna. The door creaked shut, sealing Anna in a darkness split by arrows of light that pierced cracks in the roof. The padlock snapped into place with metallic finality. Fighting pain and weakness, Anna struggled into a sitting position. She knew there wasn't a second to waste. Her breathing was growing shallower and more rapid. And although her skin burnt where the knife had gone in, deep inside she felt icy cold. Her teeth were chattering and her limbs were shaking. At self-defence class she'd also learnt first aid. She knew that she was going into shock. She knew too, when she peeled off her t-shirt and felt for the wound, that Gavin had been right – the blade had punctured her lung. About two inches below her right shoulder blade and just in from her spine was a clean-edged wound, the lips of which sucked together as she inhaled. Air was flooding into her chest cavity. If she didn't patch the hole, the build-up of pressure around her lung would soon cause it to collapse and she would die.

As fast as she could, she crawled to the sacks of charcoal and tore at one of them. The plastic was strong. She didn't have the strength to rip it. She moved to the garden tools and groped amongst them until she found what she needed – a set of shears. The blades were rusty, but sharp enough to cut away a piece of plastic. With one hand, she pressed the plastic to the wound. With the other, she wadded her t-shirt against the plastic. Then she leant back firmly against the freezer. She felt her breathing ease as the pressure within her lung was restored. She knew it was only a temporary fix, though. She was still bleeding internally. Her lung was filling with blood, gradually drowning her from the inside out. Her gaze fixed on the chink of light at the bottom of the door. The wood looked rotten. She reckoned she could use the garden tools to prise her way through it. But if she moved, she took the pressure off the wound. And if she did that, she would be unconscious in minutes.

Pressure. That was the most important thing. She had to keep the pressure on the wound, keep the air flowing in and out of her pain-wracked body. In, out, in out... From somewhere off in the distance she heard an engine. *Jim!* she thought, but instantly knew she was wrong. It had only been ten minutes or so since they'd spoken on the phone. Not enough time for him to get here, even if he'd been in a vehicle. Besides, he surely wouldn't have announced his arrival. More likely it was Gavin and Emily leaving in the Land Rover, or perhaps the red van. The engine faded away, seemingly confirming her suspicion.

She closed her eyes and fought to find some calm within herself. Faces flashed across her mind. Her mother's, Jessica's, Emily's. All of them running together like spilled paint. Her head began to nod towards her chest. She snapped her eyes open, feeling to make sure the plastic patch hadn't come loose. *Pressure*, she told herself sharply. *Breathe in... Breathe out... Pressure, pressure, always pressure...*

CHAPTER SIXTEEN

As Gavin locked the barn door, Emily wiped her eyes with a trembling hand and stared at him – the scruffy beard, the long thinning hair, the blood streaming from his torn ear, the dark, devious eyes. Was he really her father? Had he really abducted Anna's sister? The questions hardly seemed to matter right then. What mattered was getting away from him. Her tearful gaze moved to the trees. An urge to make a run for it clutched her. She broke free of it with a twitch of her head. If she ran, Gavin would kill Anna. She had to stay with him until they were well away from this place and hope she got a chance to give him the slip or maybe phone for help. As though he was listening to her thoughts, Gavin held a hand out to her. 'Give me your phone.'

She hesitated to do so.

'Give me your phone,' he repeated, and this time there was an edge in his voice that made her obey. He brought out Anna's phone as well and placed both on the ground and picked up a large stone. Shards of plastic went flying as he pulverised them. He took hold of Emily's arm and guided her back into the house. Pushing her ahead of him, he hurried upstairs to a gloomy bedroom that smelt of incense and sweat. The room was crowded with yet more sculptures. One depicted the Horned God rutting between the legs of a girlishly slender figure. In another he was thrusting against an identical figure from behind. The victim, or offering, or whatever she was supposed to be, had long, straight hair, big eyes, round cheeks and pouty lips. Suddenly it struck Emily that she might have been looking at sculptures based on herself. But she knew it couldn't be her. Her dad – or, if Anna was to be believed, her granddad – had stopped taking her to Sherwood Forest when she was ten. The figure looked more like that of a teenager balancing on the cusp between childhood and adulthood. Could it be Jessica Young? she wondered. Was she looking at her mother?

Gavin pointed to an unmade bed. 'Sit.' As Emily eyed him apprehensively, he added in a softer tone, 'I'm not going to hurt you. I'd never hurt you, Emily.'

His expression was sincere, his voice soothingly convincing, so much so that she found herself almost believing him. Almost. She lowered herself onto the edge of the mattress. He took a rucksack out of a cupboard. 'I always keep a bag packed,' he explained, grabbing a laptop from the floorboards and stuffing it into the rucksack. He slung the bag over his shoulder, before getting hold of Emily again and pulling her downstairs so quickly she almost lost her footing. 'I have to be ready to run at any time of day or night because of her,' he jerked his bearded chin towards the back of the house, 'and because of the McLeans.'

They ran out of the front door to the red Ford Escort van. Gavin pushed Emily into the passenger seat, before darting around to the driver's side. He chucked the rucksack into the back and started the engine. The wheels chewed up the grass as he accelerated towards the gate. 'Can you imagine what it's like to live like that, Emily?' he continued with a note of self-pity in his voice. 'To be persecuted and hunted simply because you choose not be what society says you must be? That's another truth you'll come to know. What society doesn't understand, it fears. And what it fears, it destroys.'

The van jolted to a halt at the gate. Gavin jumped out and opened it. His head swivelled from side to side. Seeing that the lane was clear, he ducked back into the van and pressed hard on the accelerator again. They rattled along with the forest on their left and fields of rapeseed blossom on their right. 'Where are we going?' asked Emily.

'First we're going to get rid of this van. After that...' Gavin smiled. 'Well, the world's our oyster. Where would you like to go?'

Home, thought Emily. But it struck her with a sharp pang of despair that she didn't know where home was any more. 'I don't know,' she murmured.

'How about the Philippines? I've always fancied living somewhere hot.'

Emily shot a look at him. Was he joking? She couldn't tell. Although he was smiling, there was no humour in his eyes. She had no intention of staying with him a moment longer than was necessary, but that didn't stop her from playing along. 'I haven't got a passport.'

Gavin made a dismissive motion. 'A passport is nothing. All you need is belief. Believe in Cernunnos and he will believe in you. Then anything's possible.'

Is he crazy? wondered Emily. *Surely he doesn't truly believe that crap.*

After about half a mile, the trees gave way to fields bordering a farmyard. The lane ended at a busy main road. Gavin scanned it, his gaze lingering briefly on a parked car. Then he made a right turn, heading for the outskirts of what looked to be a village or small town. They passed a sign that read 'Warsop'. Emily had heard of the place, but never been there before. The road was lined by the usual mix of modest detached and semi-detached houses. People were out walking their dogs, pushing pushchairs, cutting hedges. It seemed somehow incredible to Emily that life simply went on as normal all around when her world was imploding.

Gavin braked at a red light, beyond which a group of workmen were repairing the road. *This is my chance*, thought Emily. Her hand darted towards the door handle.

Suddenly, Gavin's hand was on her wrist. His fingers dug in hard enough to make her wince. 'Don't.' His voice was ominously toneless.

'You're hurting me!' Emily retorted, the pain giving her courage. 'You said you'd never hurt me.'

'And you said you'd come with me.'

'Why would I go to the Philippines with you? I don't even know who you are.'

'I'm your father.'

For an instant, Emily couldn't find her breath. *I'm your father*. The words seemed to echo in her head. Anna had implied as much. But still, hearing him say it hit her like a punch to the chest. The lights changed. Gavin accelerated past the workmen. The chance was gone. 'So Anna was telling the truth.'

'Yes and no. Jessica's your mother, but I didn't abduct her.' Gavin's voice took on a distant quality. 'We were in love. But her parents tried to keep us apart. You see, I was nineteen and she was your age. I pleaded with her parents, but they wouldn't listen. They threatened to go to the police, have me brought up on statutory rape charges. So we did the only thing we could do. We ran away together. The police searched everywhere for us, but I knew how to stay hidden from them. I'd already spent a year on the run from the McLeans.'

Emily scrutinised Gavin's face, as if searching for visible signs of a lie. Was this more bullshit? Or was it the truth he'd promised? He glanced across at her with a kind of pleading in his eyes. 'Have you ever been in love?'

'There's a boy at school,' Emily began a little awkwardly.

'Is he the same age as you?'

'No. He's in the year above.'

'And you love him?'

'I don't know. Sometimes I think I do, but...' Emily's voice faded into uncertainty.

'You don't love him,' stated Gavin. 'When you love someone, you don't have to think about it. You just know it. And nobody can stop you feeling what you feel. Not your parents. Not society. They tell you you're doing wrong. But there's no wrong or right in love. True love isn't about boundaries like age. It's about breaking free and living your own life, not the life others want you to live. Don't you wish you could live like that?'

'I suppose so.'

'Of course you do!' That evangelical gleam was back in Gavin's eyes. 'Come with me, Emily. Live free. Live for yourself!'

'But what about—'

'What about what?' Gavin broke in, his voice rising impatiently.

'What about school?'

Gavin snorted. 'Fuck school. The best thing you could ever do for yourself is unlearn everything you've learnt there.'

'And Mum and Dad? What about them?'

'You mean Grandma and Granddad,' corrected Gavin.

'They're well-meaning, but they're fools. They can teach you nothing but how to lead a small life. I can show you how to live your dreams and desires.'

Emily's gaze dropped away from Gavin. Her heart was palpitating, and not simply because she was scared. His words charged through her like a high-voltage current. The idea of them was thrilling. But at the same time she saw their hollowness. How could Gavin speak of love in one breath and living only for yourself in the next? Surely the two things didn't go together. And if he loved Jessica so much then why wasn't she here with them?

'Besides,' continued Gavin, 'even if you want to, you can't go back to your grandparents. Not if Anna Young lives. She knows you're not their daughter, and she'll do everything she can to prove it. She'll have you taken away from them, put in care. And believe me, that's the last place on earth you want to be. You're soft and pure, Emily. The kids in those places are hard and tainted. You wouldn't last five minutes with them.'

Those words didn't ring hollow. There was a weight to them that dragged Emily's head down. Here, finally, was the truth. The life she'd known was over. There was no going back. Gavin might be a liar, he might be a rapist, he might be evil or insane or both. Or he might be what he claimed to be – a victim of circumstance and society. But whatever he was or wasn't, he *was* her dad. Maybe he really could teach her something nobody else could teach, give her something nobody else could give. There was only one way to find out – by staying with him. But if she was even going to consider doing that, there was a question she had to have answered first. 'Where's my real mum?'

Gavin's beard twitched. Blinking as though holding back tears, he turned onto a narrow, hedged lane. One silent minute passed. Two. The lane wound its way through some trees.

Gavin pulled over in front of a spiked metal security fence that enclosed a brick garage. He cut the engine, drew a shuddering breath. 'She was killed.'

Emily felt a sharp sting in her heart. 'How?'

'By you.'

The pain turned to bemusement. 'What do you mean? How could I have killed her?'

'By being born. We couldn't risk going to hospital for the birth. So I read everything I could about how to deliver a baby. But it wasn't enough. Jessica was in labour for three days and you just wouldn't come out. She was exhausted, feverish. I begged her to go to hospital but she refused. She knew they'd take you away from us. Finally your head appeared, then your body and you were...' Gavin sought the right word. 'Perfect. I tied off the umbilical cord and cut it. I thought everything was OK, but then came the blood. More blood than I'd ever seen. I tried to stop it, but...' His voice threatened to break. He closed his eyes, a solitary tear descending his cheek. Emily hesitantly reached to touch his arm, but drew her hand back. His grief looked genuine enough. Even so, she wasn't ready for the intimacy of sympathy. Not yet.

'Jessica died right there in front of me,' murmured Gavin. 'I was heartbroken. I wanted to die too. I was in no fit state to look after you. So I gave you to Mum and Dad. They'd always wanted a daughter. I knew they'd give you the love I couldn't.'

'But why couldn't you love me?'

'I wanted to, Emily. More than anything. That's why I used to come and watch you play. The problem was every time I saw you, I saw Jessica too.' Gavin's eyes moved like hands over Emily's face. Something squirmed inside her as he went on, 'I saw her in your mouth, your cheeks, your hair. But most of all I saw her in your eyes. The way they glittered like...' Again, he paused to find the right words, 'like swimming pools full of diamonds.'

The description was so cheesily over the top that Emily found herself thinking once more, *Is he for real?*

'And then this feeling would hit me.' Emily flinched as Gavin unsheathed his hunting knife. 'Like all I wanted was to take this out and open up my wrists. I thought time would make things easier. But it didn't. Every year you grew to look more like Jessica and every year the feeling got stronger. Dad knows me better than anyone. I didn't need to say anything. He saw how it was. So he made up some excuse to keep you away from me.'

'So it wasn't too dangerous for me to see you. It was too dangerous for you to see me.'

Gavin nodded sadly.

'Then why do you want to be with me now?'

'When Dad told me the police had come around asking questions, I knew Anna Young had to be behind it. And I knew it was only a matter of time before they worked out who you really were. I realised the time had come for you to learn the truth. And for us to be together, like a father and daughter should be. We have a connection nothing can break, Emily.' Gavin moved his hand rapidly back and forth between them. 'Don't you feel it? Don't you feel that connection?'

Emily didn't know what she felt. So much had happened in such a short space of time that she barely knew which way was up and which was down any more. Gavin was willing to do anything to avoid capture. That was one thing she was certain of. She couldn't get the image of him plunging the knife into Anna out of her mind. There had been such a look in his eyes as he'd done it – a look like she'd never seen before, or ever wanted to see again.

'I'm not going to apologise for giving you up,' said Gavin. 'That would make me as hypocritical as the society I've rejected. But I do want to make up for lost time. So I'm asking for a chance – a chance to be a father to you, a chance to call you my own.'

Asking? Emily eyed the bloodstained knife in Gavin's hand. Was he really asking? Did she really have a choice? Would he sink the knife into her back if she tried to leave him? As these questions crossed her mind, it occurred to her that Gavin still hadn't answered her original question. 'You haven't told me where my mum is.'

'I gave her to him.' Gavin pointed to the ignition where a keyring of a red, goat-faced man with horns dangled. 'And in return he gave me the strength to go on.'

'What do you mean, you gave her to him?'

He glanced tensely at a passing car. 'There's no more time for talking. What's it going to be, Emily?'

As Gavin spoke, Emily noticed a tightening of his knuckles on the knife. A tremor passed through the blade. A tremor passed through her too. Suddenly she knew. He *wasn't* asking. He lived only for himself. Took whatever he wanted. And right now he wanted her. But she didn't want him. He made her skin crawl with the longing to be anywhere but with him. She knew too that she couldn't let him see how she felt. She had to bury her revulsion deep. 'OK,' she said, and forced herself to add, 'Dad.'

'Dad.' Gavin echoed the word as if it had a flavour he was uncertain of and added one of his own, 'Daughter.' He slid the knife back into its sheath. 'Wait here.'

He got out of the van, unlocked a gate and approached the garage. Softly but quickly, Emily opened the passenger door. She winced at the squeaking of ill-oiled hinges. Gavin glanced towards her. For the space of a breath their eyes met. Then she was sprinting along the lane. She didn't look to see if he was giving chase, she just pumped her arms and legs as hard as she could. Her heart lurched when, after fifteen or twenty seconds, the van's engine flared into life. He was coming! Her eyes desperately searched for a gap in the hedge. She spotted a closed farm gate on her right about a hundred metres away. If she could just make it there she reckoned she'd have a good chance of getting away. She was young and fit. Gavin was old – or at least in his forties – and overweight. Surely she could outrun him.

Eighty metres to go. Fifty. Twenty. *Go on, go on*, her mind urged, *you're going to make it!* Beyond the hedge was a grassy field with houses lining its far side. Houses meant people, and people meant help. As she veered towards the gate, she glimpsed the van out of the corner of her eye and knew she was wrong. She *wasn't* going to make it. The van was almost on her. She tried to dive out of its way, but Gavin flung open the driver's side door. It clipped her with stunning force, sending a bolt of pain through her left hip, spinning her into the gate. She rebounded onto the ground, tears clouding her vision. Clutching at the gate, she groggily fought to haul herself upright. 'Help!' she cried, although there was no one to hear her except Gavin.

Her voice was muffled by a hand covering her mouth. An arm encircled her waist and lifted her off her feet. 'I didn't want it to be this way,' said Gavin, carrying Emily to the van. She struggled to break free, but the blow had knocked most of the strength out of her. He dumped her onto the passenger seat and climbed in beside her.

'Liar!' she spat at him, her voice quivering between anger and fear.

'Nothing is true,' Gavin stated with flat certainty. '*That* is the only truth.'

Keeping an iron grip on Emily with one hand, he drove to the garage and pulled inside it. He shoved Emily out of the van and she saw that the garage sheltered a white motorhome.

He dragged Emily through a door into the motorhome's living area, which was kitted out with a right-angled sofa, an electric heater and a television on a wall bracket. To the left was a small kitchen with a cooker, fridge, cupboards and drawers. Beyond that a ladder led up to a bed perched over the driver's and passenger's seats.

Gavin forced Emily down onto the sofa. From an overhead cupboard he took out a roll of duct tape and two pairs of plastic zip-lock handcuffs. Emily's head was clearer now. There was a dead, throbbing sensation in her hip and leg, and her right wrist felt badly sprained from being bent back by the gate. With or without the injuries, she knew she had no chance of fighting off Gavin. Even so, she instinctively tried to push him away.

'Please, Emily,' he said. 'Don't make this any harder than it needs to be.'

'Help!' she screamed again as he flipped her onto her stomach and twisted her arms up behind her. The plastic cuffs bit into her wrists as he drew them tight. He pulled off her pumps and did the same to her ankles, then rolled her back over. She thrashed her head from side to side as he straddled her and strapped a leather gag with what looked like a red snooker ball at its centre across her mouth. The gag smelt like old spit. After several more minutes of futile struggle, she subsided into helpless, smothered sobs.

Gavin looked down at her with a kind of mock sadness in his eyes. He stroked her hair back from her forehead, wiped away her tears. 'Don't cry, my daughter, my love.' He bent close and breathed hotly into her ear, 'My bride.'

CHAPTER SEVENTEEN

When Jim reached the end of the track, he found that it was barred from the main road by a horizontal metal pole padlocked between low wooden posts. Breathing hard, a dull, squeezing sensation in his chest, he hopped over the pole and ran to his car. He glanced at the dashboard clock. It had been twelve minutes since he spoke to Reece. His colleague was still a quarter of an hour or more away. There was no time to wait for him. He floored the accelerator and swerved sharply off the road into the barrier. There was a metallic crunch as it burst inwards. Then he was juddering full-tilt along the corridor of trees, eyes peeled for turns in the track that matched Anna's photos.

After about a mile and a half, he passed a right turn. Shortly after that he came to a crossroads, beyond which the forest abruptly changed from birch and oak to pine. Another half a mile or so brought him to a T junction. A glance at Anna's photo told him this was the turn he wanted. As with the first photo of the track, certain identifying features – a broken branch, potholes, the position of shadows – supported his deduction that she'd been facing backwards when she took it. The track descended to a curving right-hand bend, then another right. If he'd judged it correctly, somewhere up ahead was a sharp left, then a farm gate. Less than a minute later he found what he was looking for. Maybe twenty metres beyond the turn was a gate situated on the angle of another leftwards bend. A sign read 'PRIVATE'. As he'd suspected might be the case, a couple of hundred metres beyond it was a house – a rundown place surrounded by an equally unkempt, junk-filled garden. A rusty white Transit van made him think of Jessica Young.

Jim frowned. It was undoubtedly the same gate as in the final photo Anna had sent. But unlike in the photo, the gate was open and the padlock dangled, unlocked, from the end of a chain. Had Gavin left the house? And if he had, why hadn't he locked the gate behind himself? Had he been in a hurry?

A Land Rover hooked up to a tarp-covered trailer was parked in the dirt driveway. He guessed Anna must have hitched a secret ride in the trailer. His frown intensified. The house's front door was open too. A cautious man like Gavin surely wouldn't have left his door open. Not even out here in the middle of nowhere. What the hell was going on?

His gaze combed the garden for Anna. She was nowhere to be seen. He tried phoning her. The call went straight to voicemail. *Something's wrong*, his gut shouted. *Why would she have turned her phone off?* He took the Taser out of the glove compartment and approached the house, skirting through the trees outside the hedge. He paused briefly to peer through a gap in the hedge adjacent to the Land Rover. There was nothing new to be seen. The house's windows were too small and dirty for him to get a good look inside them at that distance. He continued along the hedge until he came to a second gap that faced the house's windowless side wall. To the rear of the house was a barn. He stood motionless for a few seconds, watching and listening. There was no Anna. No noise. Nothing.

He pulled aside a coil of barbed wire and slid through the hedge. Taser at the ready, he darted to the wall and crept along it. A glint drew his eyes to the ground. Scattered over the path outside the barn were the shattered pieces of two mobile phones. Was one of those phones Anna's? Had Gavin discovered her presence? And if so, what had he done to her? His mind racing over these questions, he peered around the rear of the house. The back door was wide open too. Unlike the barn door. That was bolted and padlocked.

He sneaked a look through the kitchen window. Empty. He moved to the barn, pressed an eye to a thin gap between the door and frame. It was too dark to see anything, but he caught a faint sound like someone fighting for air. 'Anna,' he hissed.

'Jim,' came the low, wheezy reply. The instant he heard Anna's voice, it seemed obvious what had happened – Gavin had locked her in the barn and fled, most likely taking Emily with him. It was obvious too that Gavin hadn't simply imprisoned Anna. She sounded as though she scarcely had sufficient breath to speak.

The time for creeping around was over. Jim snatched up a stone and smashed it into the bolt until it broke loose from the frame. He yanked the door open. Sunlight streamed into the barn, and into Anna's blinking face. He knew it was bad as soon as he saw her. Her cheeks were bluish grey. Bright-red blood was smeared around her mouth. He was already pulling out his phone as he rushed towards her.

'Where are you hurt?'

'Back,' Anna gasped. 'He stabbed me.'

A quick look at the scrap of plastic suctioned to Anna's upper back told Jim it could prove fatal to move her. The knife had punctured a lung. If the plastic came loose, inrushing air would collapse the lung. He turned his attention to his phone, praying for a signal. There was a weak one. He punched in a number. 'Dispatch, this is DCI Jim Monahan. I have a medical emergency. A woman with a serious knife wound to her back.'

'What's your location?'

Jim gave the dispatcher directions. The line was silent a moment, then the dispatcher came back on. 'An air ambulance and ground units are on the way.'

Jim repeated this to Anna. Gasping for breath, she said, 'Gavin's gone... I heard an engine. He took Emily with him.'

'How long ago?'

'Not sure. Maybe twenty minutes.'

Jim clenched his teeth in frustration. They could be fifty or more miles away by now. 'Do you know what he's driving? There's a Land Rover and a white van in front of the house.'

'Red Escort van...' Anna slurred, her glazed eyes rolling back in their sockets, her head lolling sideways.

Jim caught hold of her. 'No, no, keep looking at me, Anna,' he urged. Her eyes came back down and focused on his. 'That's it. Good girl. Do you know the van's reg?'

'No.'

'Does Gavin still have long hair and a goatee beard?'

'Yes, but he's got a full beard now.' Anna searched for oxygen and continued, 'He was wearing camo trousers and a black t-shirt.' She managed a small crooked smile. 'I gave the fucker a lovebite on the left ear. Nearly tore it off.'

'What about Emily?'

'Black jeans. Hooded grey sweatshirt.'

Jim got back on the phone to the dispatcher. 'The suspect fled the scene some twenty minutes ago in a red Escort van, registration unknown. He has a girl with him, possibly against her will.' He gave Gavin and Emily's particulars, adding, 'Gavin Walsh is to be considered armed and extremely dangerous. I need you to inform DCS John Garrett of the situation immediately.'

Jim hung up and gently took hold of Anna's hand. It was cold and sweaty. Sweat lathered her face too from the effort of breathing. He knew it was touch and go whether she would live. And the thought of it filled him with a queasy sense that he was sliding back towards the pit he'd fallen into after Margaret's murder. Still, his cop's brain couldn't help but fire questions at him. Uppermost amongst them was: had Gavin spotted Anna by chance or had he been warned of her presence? 'What happened?'

'I think he saw me.'

That seemed to suggest the former was the case.

'He came at me from behind,' Anna went on raggedly.

'Why didn't he finish you off?'

'Emily stopped him by—' Anna choked off into an agonised gurgle.

Jim held her steady. 'Save your breath now, Anna. Help will be here soon.' His phone rang. It was Reece. He put it to his ear.

'I'm at the visitor centre car park,' Reece told him.

Jim quickly relayed the situation to him.

'Fucking hell,' exclaimed Reece. 'How bad is she?'

Looking Anna in the eyes, Jim said with a sureness he didn't feel, 'It's pretty bad. But she's a tough girl. She'll make it.'

'What do you want me to do?'

'Head over here. Someone's going to have to coordinate a search of the property.' Jim eyed the metal tube protruding from the padlocked freezer Anna was propped against. 'I've a feeling we're going to find some interesting things.'

'I'm on my way.'

Jim got off the phone and checked the padlock. Instead of a keyhole, it had a three digit combination set to 333. It came open with a tug. He flipped up the freezer lid. 'Empty,' he replied to Anna's enquiring look. There were several dark, crusty smears on the underside of the lid. Dry blood? What he saw next seemed to confirm it was – two pink-painted broken fingernails. He thought with a cold twist of his stomach about what it would be like to be imprisoned in the coffinlike freezer sobbing, screaming and clawing in pure blind terror.

He heard the faint whoop-whoop of a helicopter. 'I'll be back in a minute,' he said to Anna. 'You just hold on. Do you hear me?'

She gave a slight nod. Jim headed outside. The red and yellow air ambulance was approaching from the south. He waved his arms at it. The noise rose to a deafening level. The helicopter hovered over the house momentarily, before descending into the back garden. The hurricane blast of its rotor blades flattened the grass and a sapling tree. Covering his ears, Jim waited for it to set down then ran towards it. Four paramedics in luminous jackets and red jumpsuits climbed out to meet him. 'She's in the barn,' he told them.

Grabbing a stretcher and medical bags, the paramedics followed Jim to Anna. 'How long ago was she stabbed?' asked one of them.

'Maybe half an hour,' said Jim.

'And how long was the knife?'

'I don't know.'

'What's her name?'

'Anna.'

'Anna, can you hear me?' asked the paramedic.

'Yes,' she wheezed.

'We're going to examine you. Try to stay as still as possible.'

The paramedics gently manoeuvred Anna forwards, cut off her bra and removed the improvised dressing. Blood immediately bubbled from the wound. 'Tension pneumothorax,' said one of the paramedics. Another peeled open a circular plastic chest seal and applied it to the wound. As Anna inhaled, a whoopee cushion-like valve sucked shut, preventing air from entering. As she exhaled the valve opened.

'Internal bleeding may be causing your lung to compress,' a paramedic calmly informed her, placing an oxygen mask over her face. 'We need to insert a chest drain. I'm going to give you some morphine for the pain first.'

The paramedic inserted a syringe needle beneath Anna's right armpit level with her nipple and depressed the plunger, mercifully dousing the fire of pain. He swabbed the same area with iodine, before making a scalpel incision. Anna groaned as a plastic tube was pushed into the incision. It felt as though a thick rope was being forced through the eye of a needle. 'I need you to take a couple of deep breaths,' said the paramedic. 'This will force out the air and blood trapped in your lung and expand it back to normal size.'

As, with great effort, Anna did so, blood drained into the chest tube. Jim's phone rang again. This time it was Garrett.

'Take that outside please,' said a paramedic.

Jim hurried from the barn. 'What's the situation?' the DCS asked.

'The paramedics are working on Anna.'

'Will she live?'

'I don't know.'

'Jesus Christ, Jim. This is exactly the kind of thing I was afraid might happen.'

This wouldn't be happening if I hadn't been put in a position where I felt compelled to leak information, Jim wanted to retort. But there was no time for recriminations or guilt. Gavin was out there somewhere with Emily. And God only knew what plans he had for her. 'Who's in charge locally of the search for Gavin?'

'DI Tim Atkins of the East Midlands Special Operations Unit. He's assured me they're putting every available—'

'Hang on,' interrupted Jim. 'They're moving Anna.'

The paramedics emerged from the barn with Anna on a stretcher. Jim was relieved to see that she was still conscious. Quickly and steadily, they carried her to the helicopter. Jim followed them. 'Is she going to be OK?'

'We need to move fast,' came the telling reply.

The paramedics lifted Anna into the back of the helicopter and secured her stretcher. 'I'm coming with you,' said Jim, climbing in beside her.

She shook her head weakly and spoke through the oxygen mask. 'Find Gavin. Don't let him hurt Emily.'

'Do you want me to contact your mother?'

Another shake of the head. 'I—' A groan cut off her words, then she managed to continue, 'I don't want to worry her.'

Jim passed a paramedic his card. 'Keep me updated.'

He retreated towards the cottage. The sapling was bent flat once more as the helicopter's rotor blades gathered speed. Jim noticed now that, like the Leeds tree, its branches were festooned with ribbons. Suddenly its roots tore loose and it tumbled across the lawn, taking a rectangle of turf with it. He watched the helicopter ascend into the clear blue sky and head south. His gaze dropped back to the garden. Something caught his eye where the tree had been uprooted. It looked like a stick poking up through the earth. But as he approached it, he saw it wasn't a stick. It was a bone. And it clearly hadn't been buried all that long. There were still tatters of dirty brown flesh clinging to it.

'Jim, are you still there?' Garrett's voice came from the phone.

Jim returned it to his ear. 'I've found a bone. It looks like a humerus.'

Garrett echoed the name in Jim's mind. 'Jessica Young.'

Jim turned towards the sound of approaching sirens. Blue lights were flashing in the lane. 'The ground units are here.'

Wondering if he wanted Garrett to be right, he hung up and made his way to the front garden. At least if it was Jessica, Anna would finally have closure, if such a thing was ever truly possible. And assuming, of course, that she survived. He heaved a long sigh.

Several marked and unmarked vehicles pulled through the gate. Reece's car was amongst them. Jim held up his ID and announced his name and rank. A middle-aged detective approached him and extended his hand. 'DI Tim Atkins of—'

'I know who you are,' cut in Jim. 'We need a pathologist here. There's a body in the back garden. I haven't been inside the house. I don't think there's anyone in there, but your men should proceed with caution. And once you've secured the house, there's a freezer in the barn that you're going to want to check out.'

Reece hurried across to the two men. He was wearing jeans and a shirt. There were sleepless bruises and anxious creases around his eyes. 'How's Anna?'

'She's alive. They've airlifted her to hospital.'

Reece blew out a breath of relief. 'Thank Christ. So she's going to be OK?'

Jim answered with a tense twitch of his shoulders. 'This is DI Reece Geary,' he told DI Atkins. 'He's going to stay here and help with the search.'

'Where are you going?' asked Reece.

'To speak to Ronald and Sharon Walsh. Maybe they'll be more forthcoming now that Gavin's got Emily with him.'

'Why would they be?'

'Because unless I'm very much mistaken, they really love her.'

CHAPTER EIGHTEEN

Bride. The word kept drumming in Emily's head as she watched Gavin apply a dressing to his injured ear. He was insane. He had to be. Why else would he want to marry his own daughter? When he was done with his ear, he set to work on buzzing off his hair and beard with clippers. Clean-shaven and bald, he looked more like his younger self, yet at the same time older. His cheeks retained some chubbiness, but the marks of a life on the run had etched deep grooves into them. He stripped off his clothes, exposing a lacy green spider's web tattoo that spread outwards like a target from the centre of his hairless chest. Noticing her looking at his tattoo, he said, 'Do you like it? Shall I tell you what it means? Life is a web that holds us all, Emily. What you've got to decide is, are you a spider or a fly? I know which one I am. What about you?'

I'm whatever you're not! Emily retorted in her head.

Panic squeezed her stomach as Gavin approached her. *He's going to rape me!* her mind screamed. She fought the urge to close her eyes. She wouldn't fight him. That would only get her hurt, maybe even killed. But she would look him in the eyes. She would make sure he saw her disgust, her loathing.

A muted sob of relief shook her as Gavin took some clothes out of an overhead cupboard. He pulled on a pair of beige trousers and a red-checked shirt. Tipping what appeared to be a bundle of blonde hair from a bag, he moved to stand in front of a mirror. He placed the wig on his head and carefully arranged it so that the mop of hair overlapped his ears, concealing the bandage. He turned to Emily. 'How do I look?'

Like the fucking freak you are, she thought. The wig contrasted oddly with Gavin's dark eyes, giving him a camp look that Emily would have found comical if she hadn't been so terrified. He approached her again and stooped to kiss her forehead. A repulsively tender kiss. He smelt her skin and sighed. 'I haven't felt this way since I met your mother. The instant I saw Jessica I knew we were meant to be together. And it was the same with you today.'

Gavin lifted Emily off the sofa and laid her on the floor. He flicked a couple of latches and upturned the sofa's cushions, revealing a hollow space. He picked her up again and lowered her into the hollow. He retrieved a pillow from the bed and placed it under her head. 'We don't want you to be uncomfortable, do we? Now you just lie still and be quiet, like a good girl.' He replaced the cushions, sealing her in darkness.

She listened to his footsteps moving away. The motorhome's engine came alive. She squirmed against her bonds, but it was no good. The plastic cuffs were on too tight. She felt the motorhome move forwards a short distance. There came the muffled sound of the garage doors and gate being shut. Then the vehicle was moving again. But where was he taking her? Did he really mean to spirit her out of the country? And if he did, what was he going to do with her once they got to the Philippines? Would he force her to live as his wife? Force her to have his children? She suddenly felt like something was constricting her chest. Her head spun as though she was about to pass out. The blackness seemed to be getting deeper, sucking her in like a whirlpool. A familiar voice reached her faintly through it. At first she thought she'd imagined it. But then it came again. She latched on to it, used it to drag herself back from the brink of oblivion.

'Where are you, Gavin?' asked her dad. *No, not my dad, my granddad,* some distant, cruelly coherent part of her mind reminded her once again. She ignored it. It didn't matter what he was. All that mattered was that he was there and he surely wouldn't let Gavin hurt her. She banged her knees against the underside of the wooden base the sofa cushions rested on. Even as she did so, the same part of her mind told her it was futile. How could her granddad be there if he didn't know where Gavin was? The answer was obvious. He wasn't there. He was on the other end of a phone line and Gavin had him on loudspeaker. Moreover, the speaker was turned up high, like Gavin wanted her to hear what was being said.

'It doesn't matter where I am,' replied Gavin. 'There's no need to worry about me. I'm fine. Emily's fine. We're both fine.'

'What do you mean, Emily's fine?' There was a sudden tightness in Ronald Walsh's voice.

'I've got her with me. I'm going to be looking after her from now on.'

'She... she's with you?' stammered Ronald. Emily had never heard him stammer before.

There was a sound like an impatient huff of breath. Then Gavin replied, 'That's what I just said, didn't I?'

'Can I speak to her?'

'Not right now. She's busy.'

'Doing what?'

Another huff. 'It doesn't matter what she's doing. What matters is that the time has finally come for me to be a father to her.'

'A father?'

'Christ, is there an echo on the line? Yes, a father. I thought you'd be pleased.' There was an almost childishly petulant challenge in Gavin's tone.

'Oh I am pleased, Gavin.' Ronald's mollifying, hollow voice suggested just the opposite. 'But are you sure this is what you want?'

'Of course I'm sure. Why else would I be doing this?'

'What exactly is it that you're doing?'

'We're going away. A long, long way away. You probably won't see either of us again.'

'Now hang on, Gavin. Let's think this through a minute. You can't just take Emily away like this. She has a life here in Nottingham.'

'Life!' Gavin loaded the word with contempt. 'Go to school, go to university, get a job, get married, have kids. You call *that* a life? I'll give her a real life. I'll show her things she could never have imagined. I'll—'

Another voice came on the line and interrupted Gavin. 'We've done everything you ever asked of us, Gavin,' said Sharon Walsh, trembling on the edge of tears. 'We've never asked anything in return except this one thing. Don't take Emily away from us.'

Gavin sighed and in an overly patient voice, as though explaining something to a well-meaning idiot, he said, 'Emily is my daughter. Mine, not yours. How can I take something away from you that never belonged to you in the first place?'

The tremors turned into sobs. Emily winced at the sound. Her grandmother was a liar and a hypocrite and she hated her for it. And yet she hated, too, to hear her in such pain. 'Please, Gavin,' wept Sharon, 'I'm begging you not to do this.'

'Put Dad back on.'

'Please, Gavin, please, please—'

'Put him on or I'll hang up!'

There was a brief silence, punctuated by the half-stifled sound of Sharon sobbing. Then Ronald came back on the line, his voice tense but controlled. 'Your mother only wants what's best for both you and Emily.'

'She's never understood what's best for me. Neither of you have. And as for Emily, if I don't know what's best for her no one does.'

'But are you sure she won't be a burden to you?'

'Loneliness is the heaviest burden. Now that we're together, neither of us will ever have to be lonely again.'

Ronald exhaled a long, exhausted breath that said, *You win.* 'What do you want us to do?'

'I don't want you to do anything. Just carry on as normal.'

'OK, Gavin. When will we hear from you again?'

'I don't know. Probably not for a long time.'

'What if there's an emergency and we need to contact you?'

'This number will work for as long as it takes us to get out of the country. After that...' Gavin tailed off meaningfully.

'We...' Emotion briefly threatened to get the better of Ronald. He cleared his throat and continued, 'We love you very much, son. You and Emily both. Please make sure she knows that.'

'Uh-huh, will do,' Gavin said disinterestedly. 'Got to go now, Dad. Byeee.' He shouted back to Emily, 'Did you hear that? The old fart says he loves you.'

Tears streamed down Emily's cheeks in the darkness. She wanted to look her grandparents in the face and scream at them, *How can you let him do this to me if you love me?* Her ears pricked at the sound of approaching sirens. Was it the police looking for them? She kicked her feet against the side of the motorhome, hoping and, irrespective of her lack of faith, praying that someone heard. The sirens built to a piercing wail, then faded into the distance. She squeezed her eyes shut. She felt utterly forsaken and, despite what Gavin had said, crushingly alone.

'I told you to lie quietly,' said Gavin. 'Do as Daddy says, my love. Don't make me come back there.'

There was a slight thickening in his voice, a little rise of anticipation, almost as if he hoped she would disobey him. A shudder passed through her, then she lay like a dead body.

After a short time, Gavin spoke again, but not to Emily. There was no petulance in his voice now. It was measured and businesslike. 'Have you heard what's happened?'

A man's voice came through the loudspeaker, and this one was unfamiliar. 'Of course we've heard.' The accent was pure public school, the tone effortlessly superior.

'I need your help.'

'Don't you think we've helped you enough?'

'I think you should consider what the consequences might be if I'm caught.'

There was a slight pause, then, 'What do you want?'

'I want out of this country. I've always fancied visiting the Philippines.'

'Good choice. I think that can be arranged.'

'I'm going to need two passports – one for myself and one for my daughter – and enough cash for us to live off comfortably for the foreseeable future.'

A note of surprise entered the man's voice. 'You seriously intend to take your daughter with you?'

'I'm not leaving the country without her.'

'And she's willing to go?'

'She will be by the time we leave. You know how persuasive I can be.'

Nothing you say or do will make me want to come with you, thought Emily. But there was an unshakable confidence in Gavin's voice that drove a nail of doubt into her mind. Did he possess some special power from his god that could make her do as he wished? She scowled at herself for even contemplating the idea. The only power he had was that of violence and lies.

'The arrangements will take a day or two,' said the man. 'Do you think you can stay off the radar until then?'

'Shouldn't be too difficult. Oh, and keep this in mind: if anything unpleasant should happen to me, if I should be run over or shot in the back of the head, then information will be sent to the police about where to find certain photos and videos.'

There was another silence, longer than the first, as if the man was chewing on the unpleasant taste of Gavin's words. Then, his tone no longer quite so supercilious, he said, 'I'll be in touch.'

Putting on a mock posh accent, Gavin said to Emily, 'He'll be in touch.' He laughed as if he'd made a joke. But it was no joke. 'I told you, my love, believe in Cernunnos and he will make anything possible.'

Again, doubt pierced Emily's mind. What if he was right? What if... What if... And suddenly the spinning sensation was back and she felt as if there was nothing beneath her and nothing above or around her. She was alone and falling.

CHAPTER NINETEEN

Jim drove to Nottingham like a man possessed. No word came through about the whereabouts of Gavin. He wasn't surprised. A man like him would have been ready for this contingency. He would have planned an escape route and, considering he'd risked leaving Anna behind with breath still in her body, almost certainly kept a switch vehicle somewhere nearby. No word came about Anna either. That was good. The longer it took the hospital to get in touch, the greater the chance she'd be alive when they did.

Ronald Walsh's Volvo was parked in the driveway. Jim blocked it in with his own car. It hardly seemed likely the Walshes would attempt to run. But you never knew. He hammered on the front door. 'Police! Open up now!'

Ronald came to the door. Jim scoured his face for any indication that he knew what had gone down. Ronald looked tired but composed. His dark eyes returned Jim's gaze steadily. 'What do you want?'

He was as inscrutable as Jim had expected. But what about his wife? Maybe her nerves weren't so steely. 'I want to speak to your wife.'

'I told you before, my wife's ill.'

'I don't give a shit. Get her here now or I'm coming in.'

'You have no right.'

In reply, Jim thrust out an arm, swept Ronald to one side and stepped past him into the hallway.

'That's assault,' Ronald thundered. 'I'll have you brought up on charges.'

Ignoring him, Jim strode into the living room. Sharon wasn't there. His gaze lingered on a recent-looking school photo of Emily on the mantelpiece. The sky-blue eyes, the soft spray of freckles, the full lips. It was the same face that had driven Gavin to abduct Jessica Young. Had it now incited him to do the same to his own daughter? Jim knew it was a strong possibility. Almost a certainty. For a man like Gavin there were no boundaries, no taboos. There was only what he wanted and how he could get it. 'Sharon Walsh,' he called out. 'This is DCI Jim Monahan. I need to talk to you about your son.'

Ronald started to reel out his standard response. 'Our son is dea—'

He was silenced as Jim added revealingly, 'And about your granddaughter.'

A stifled sob came from the back of the house. Jim shoved open a door. Sharon was sitting at the kitchen table, a tissue clutched to her mouth. The instant he saw her he knew Gavin had been in touch. It was written in the tears spilling from her eyes. She flinched as he stepped towards her and demanded, 'Where are they?'

'Leave my wife alone and get out of our house.' Ronald grabbed Jim's arm to wrench him around.

With a rapid, expert movement, Jim caught hold of Ronald's hand, twisted his arm and bent his wrist forward, forcing his face down onto the table. Ronald yelped in pain. Sharon jumped to her feet, eyes darting around as though looking for a way out or maybe something to defend her husband with.

'Sit down!' ordered Jim. To Ronald, he added, 'And you, stop struggling or I'll put you in cuffs.'

'Do as he says,' groaned Ronald. Shoulders quaking with the effort to control her sobs, Sharon dropped back onto the chair.

'I'm going to release you, Mr Walsh,' said Jim. 'I want you to go and sit next to your wife. Is that clear?'

'Crystal.'

Jim let go of Ronald. Grimacing and rubbing his wrist, Ronald moved to sit down. 'Are you alright, Ron?' Sharon asked.

He gave a terse nod, glaring at Jim across the table. 'I'm going to have your job for this.'

'Yeah, well, you'll have to get in line for that particular honour,' Jim replied to the familiar threat. He plucked up the phone from the kitchen worktop and dialled 1471. The last call was from a local number the previous afternoon. He pressed 3 to return it. A woman picked up and said, 'Vision Express, Victoria Shopping Centre. How can I help?'

Jim hung up, unsurprised the call had nothing to do with Gavin. He would have been amazed if Gavin had been foolish enough to contact his parents' landline, let alone not withhold his number. No doubt there was a mobile phone secreted somewhere or perhaps nestling on the bottom of the nearby River Trent. He turned his probing gaze on Sharon. 'Where's Emily?'

Ronald answered for her. 'At school.'

'I didn't ask you. I asked her. Where's Emily?'

'At school,' Sharon said tremulously.

'Are you sure of that?'

'Yes. We dropped her off there this morning.'

'Did you see her go into the school?'

'No but... Has something happened to her?'

'You tell me.'

'I...' Sharon looked to her husband for help.

'Stop playing games with us,' said Ronald.

'I'm not the one playing games here, Mr Walsh. All I want is to know where your son and granddaughter are?'

'Our son, or rather his grave, is in a cemetery in Birmingham. We don't have a granddaughter.'

Jim leant forward and stabbed the table with his finger. 'Enough of the bullshit. It's cards on the table time. Your son is with your granddaughter.' Ronald opened his mouth to speak, but before he could Jim continued, 'Don't bother denying it. I know everything. I know Gavin's alive. I know he's spent the past twenty-six years living under assumed identities, abusing, raping, abducting and murdering children whenever he's had the chance.'

'No!' cried Sharon, shaking her head in fervent denial.

'Yes,' Jim fired back. 'And I know Gavin conceived a daughter with one of his victims. A daughter you've raised as your own.'

'Where's your proof?' asked Ronald. His voice was still steady, but the skin around his eyes was twitching.

'Your wife was diagnosed with endometriosis in '96, Mr Walsh. She's infertile.'

'That proves nothing.'

'Maybe not, but it's enough to get a warrant for DNA testing. What do you think will happen when those tests show Emily is the daughter of your son and Jessica Young? You'll both be arrested for aiding and abetting a crime.'

'Who's Jessica Young?'

'You know full well who she is. Just as I know you don't care about being arrested. What you care about is your son and granddaughter.'

Ronald's eyes dropped away from Jim as if in confirmation of his words. Jim's tone softened a notch. 'And I understand why you feel you have to protect your son no matter what. But here's the thing, by protecting Gavin you condemn Emily.'

Sharon shook her head again, clasping her hands over her ears. Jim moved close behind her and said loud enough that she couldn't block it out, 'You blame yourself, don't you? I can see that. You wonder whether this would be happening if you hadn't turned a blind eye to your husband working for a criminal.'

'I tried my best to bring Gavin up right,' Sharon said in a tearful whisper. 'But nothing I did made any—'

She flinched into silence as Ronald snapped, 'Shut up, Sharon.'

Firing him a warning glance, Jim continued speaking to Sharon. 'Nothing you did made any difference. You could only watch helplessly as the little boy you loved grew into a monster. And when he committed his first rape, you told yourself he was innocent. But deep down you knew the truth. You knew he was guilty, didn't you?'

A nod, barely perceptible, but there. Sharon winced as Ronald's fingers closed tightly around her wrist. In turn, Jim placed a hand firmly on his shoulder. 'Don't make me restrain you again, Mr Walsh.'

Ronald drew his hand back. 'My wife and I have nothing more to say to you,' he stated, pointedly looking away from Jim. 'If you have evidence to back up your accusations, then arrest us. Otherwise, leave us alone.'

Jim was half tempted to call Ronald's bluff, slap the cuffs on the Walshes and read them their rights. But without DNA evidence of Emily's true parentage, it would be an empty gesture.

And there was no guarantee that sufficient quality DNA would be recovered from the house to prove parentage. 'Is that true, Mrs Walsh? Do you want me to leave?'

Sharon hesitated a second, her face a mass of tear-streaked creases. Then she nodded again, more noticeably this time. Jim's gaze travelled the kitchen, coming to rest on a crucifix hanging on the wall. He moved back around the table so that he was facing Sharon and Ronald. 'You can't save Gavin. He's lost. But you can save Emily. All you need to do is tell me where they are.'

No response. No eye contact.

'Look inside yourselves,' persisted Jim. 'Look at what God would want you to do.'

Sharon made a tortured little sound in her throat. Ronald curled an arm around her shoulders, held her tight and steady.

Jim wheeled suddenly and left the room. He picked up the photo of Emily from the mantelpiece, returned to the kitchen and placed it on the table. Sharon turned her head away from it. 'Look at her,' Jim said angrily. 'You know what Gavin's going to do to her, don't you? He's going to rape her over and over again, like he did her mother. And when he's bored with her, maybe a month, maybe five years from now, he's going to kill her and bury her in some nameless hole. And you'll have to live with the knowledge that you could have stopped him. And when you die and the day of your judgement comes, you'll have to face God with that—'

'Get out of my fucking house!' broke in Ronald, springing to his feet, his face clenched with rage.

Jim's voice dropped back to a calm tone. 'I'm not going anywhere, Mr Walsh. None of us are. So you might as well sit down.'

'You can't hold us here like this.'

Jim leant towards him, resting his hands on the table. *Can't I?* said his eyes. *Try me.* Ronald blinked and reluctantly sank onto his seat.

Jim took out his phone and dialled Garrett. 'I'm with the Walshes,' he told him, holding Ronald's gaze. 'How's that DNA warrant coming along?'

'We should have it within the hour.'

'Could you arrange for a forensics team to be at the house when it's granted?'

'Will do, Jim. Any news on Anna Young?'

His eyes moved to Sharon, watching for her reaction as he replied, 'I still haven't heard from the hospital.'

She lifted her tear-swimming eyes to his.

'What about the Walshes?' asked Garrett. 'I don't suppose you've been able to get anything out of them?'

'Not yet. But I get the sense that Mrs Walsh is a good woman. She knows the right thing to do.'

As Jim lowered the phone, Sharon asked, 'Has someone been hurt?'

'Didn't your beloved son tell you? He stabbed Anna Young.'

'That's impossible. Our son is dead,' Ronald countered with obstinate vehemence.

Keeping his gaze on Sharon, Jim said, 'There's a good chance she'll die. If she does, that'll make, what, three people we know of that Gavin's killed.' He counted the names off on his fingers. 'There's Alison Sullivan. She was sixteen when he stabbed her through the heart and stuffed her body in a hole under a tree in Leeds. Then there's Jessica Young. She was only thirteen when he snatched her off the street near her home in Sheffield. Mind you, strictly speaking, I don't suppose we can include her on the list yet. I mean, we don't know for sure that the skeleton we found at Gavin's house today is hers.'

As Jim spoke, Sharon lowered her head and clasped her hands together in front of her face. Her lips moved in whispered prayer, 'Forgive me my sins, O Lord. Forgive those sins which I know, and the sins which I know not...'

'Then there's Dave Ward,' continued Jim. 'He was one of the children from the Hopeland children's home in Manchester that Gavin and others raped. Dave was going to testify against his abusers. That is, until he was conveniently found dead with a heroin needle in his arm. I guess you could say Gavin killed him too.'

Sharon's voice faltered, then rose in quavering appeal. 'Forgive them, O Lord. Forgive them all of Thy great goodness—'

Ronald silenced her with a slam of his fist against the table. 'I have a right to contact a solicitor.'

'And when forensics show up you'll be allowed to exercise that right,' said Jim. 'Until then you can just sit there and fucking chew on it.'

Jim lowered himself onto a chair opposite the Walshes. He crossed his arms, his gaze alternating between them. Ronald returned his stare with the seething anger of a man who wasn't used to being ordered around. Sharon still appeared to be praying. Her hands were clasped together so tightly the knuckles showed white and red. Jim knew that if he could get her away from her husband there was a chance she would break down and open up to him. He also knew there was no way Ronald would let that happen unless he was physically forced to. And Jim wasn't ready to cross that line. Not yet.

Ten minutes crawled silently by. Twenty. 'How long are you going to make us sit here?' asked Ronald.

'As long as it takes.'

'Can I at least make myself a drink?'

Jim retrieved a glass from the drainer, filled it with water and set it down in front of Ronald. 'Thank you,' Ronald said drily.

More minutes dragged by. Jim's phone rang. It was a Nottingham number he didn't recognise. Steeling himself for the worst, he answered it. 'This is Dr Marian Pierce of Queen's Medical Centre,' came the voice on the other end of the line. 'I'm phoning about Anna Young.'

'How's she doing, Doctor?'

'To be honest, things weren't looking too good until just a short time ago. But she seems to have turned a corner now. It looks like she's going to survive.'

On the inside, Jim felt a surge of relief. On the outside, he kept his face poker-straight. 'Thanks for letting me know.'

He hung up, sagging as though a great weight had been laid across his shoulders. Sharon looked at him anxiously. 'Anna Young died a few minutes ago,' he said.

His words wrenched a loud sob from her. Ronald tried to put his arm around her again, but she pushed him away, crying out, 'Oh God! Oh God!'

As though he didn't know what else to do, her husband proffered her the glass of water. 'Here, Sharon, drink this and calm down.' It was more of a plea than a demand.

She slapped the glass out of his hand. 'I don't want to calm down.' She reached haltingly for the school photo as though she didn't dare or, perhaps more accurately, didn't deserve to touch it. 'I want my Emily. I want my beautiful little girl back.'

'You can have her back,' said Jim. 'All you've got to do is tell me where Gavin is.'

'Liar,' exploded Ronald. 'No matter what happens, you'll never let her come back to us.'

'So you admit she's not your daughter.'

'I admit nothing, you bastard.' Eyes shining wildly, Ronald sprang to his feet. He wrenched open a cutlery drawer and reached for a knife.

'Ronald!' Sharon screamed in horror.

Ronald hesitated. *Go on, take it*, thought Jim, his fingers curling around the grip of the Taser in his pocket. *Give me an excuse to get you out of the way.*

There was a knock at the front door. Ronald flinched as if he'd been snapped out of a dream. He slowly turned and sat back down. 'I'm sorry, Sharon.' He avoided her eyes, his voice trembling with barely restrained anguish.

The knock came again. Jim went to the door. It was the forensics team and a couple of detectives. He showed them his ID. 'I was told you'd want to serve this,' said one, handing Jim the warrant.

'Wait here a moment.'

Jim returned to the kitchen. He swore inwardly when he saw the Walshes. They were holding hands now and their faces were set into grim lines. As though in the brief moment he'd been out of the room, they'd found a renewed sense of togetherness, a fresh well of resolve. He placed the warrant on the table. 'This gives us the legal authority to collect DNA samples from your property and you. One last chance. Help me and I'll help you. If Emily survives this, I promise I'll make sure she knows you did the right thing in the end.'

Stony silence. They looked through him as though he wasn't there. He sighed and called a forensics officer into the kitchen. 'Do Mrs Walsh first,' he said.

'Open your mouth, please,' the officer instructed Sharon, taking a long cotton wool bud from a clear plastic tube. He ran the bud around the inside of her mouth and reinserted it into the tube. Then he plucked several hairs from her head with tweezers, checked to make sure the roots were attached and dropped them into a tube.

As the officer turned to Ronald, Jim said to Sharon, 'Would you come with me and show me Emily's bedroom.'

'She's not going anywhere without me,' said Ronald, his grip tightening on her hand.

When the swabs were done, the Walshes led Jim and the forensics team upstairs to a typical teenage girl's bedroom. The walls were papered with band posters, the dressing-table cluttered with cosmetics, the bed crowded with teddy bears and dolls. As the forensics officers set to work searching for usable hair samples, Jim nosed around the other rooms.

'There's no need for you to go in there,' said Ronald as Jim reached for a door handle. Jim ignored him. The door led into a bedroom that looked as if it had been done over by a burglar. Clothes, blankets and jewellery were strewn across the carpet.

'What happened here?' Jim asked. Two possibilities occurred to him. Either Sharon had lost the plot after talking to Gavin and started flinging stuff around. Or Emily had made the mess earlier in the day searching for information about Gavin. If the latter were the case, she'd obviously found what she was looking for. If the former, then maybe Ronald had been too caught up in dealing with his wife to dispose of evidence. Either way it was worth requesting a full search warrant.

Ronald closed the door without replying. There were two more doors on the landing. One led to a bathroom, the other to a study. A forensics officer was bagging the toothbrushes. Jim's gaze travelled the study. Shelves of books, a small filing cabinet, a desk with a computer screen, keyboard and printer, but no sign of a hard drive. There was a tangle of unplugged wires and a dusty rectangular outline on the carpet under the desk. Jim mentally shelved the search warrant request. Clearly Ronald hadn't had his hands too full. Jim treated him to a knowing glance. His composure fully regained, Ronald didn't blink.

Jim returned to the kitchen, followed closely by Ronald and Sharon. 'I'm going to need this,' he said, removing the photo of Emily from its frame.

'Well you can't have—' Ronald started to say, but Sharon broke in.

'Take it. I've got more copies if you need them too.'

Jim nodded and Sharon retrieved an envelope containing several photos of varying sizes from the living room.

'We're done,' a forensics officer called from the hallway.

'You think we're on different sides,' Jim said to Sharon. 'But we're not.' He held her gaze a moment longer, willing her to tell him what he wanted to know. But she stood stiffly, lips pressed tightly together.

He placed his card on the table and said, 'Thanks for the photos.' Then he turned to head out of the front door. He gave the spare photos to one of the detectives. 'This is Emily Walsh. The girl we believe is with Gavin Walsh.'

'I'll make sure these are circulated,' promised the detective.

****

Frustration gnawed at Jim as he drove back to Sherwood Forest. He searched his mind vainly for something else he might have said or done to make Sharon Walsh crack. He felt sure she'd come close to giving up Gavin. But close meant nothing in this game. Over four hours had slipped by since Gavin went on the run. He could be in London by now. Or even on a boat out of the country. He certainly had powerful enough contacts to arrange such a thing. 'Fuck,' Jim said through clenched teeth, driving the heel of his hand into the dashboard. He drew a deep breath and exhaled his anger, reminding himself that things could be worse. Much worse. Anna could be dead.

He flashed his ID to a constable at the end of the lane leading to Gavin's cottage. The constable drew back a cordon of tape. Jim left his car at the old farm gate and made his way somewhat wearily past a long line of police vehicles to the back garden. A forensics tent had been erected over the exposed bone. Excavated soil was piled on a tarp outside it. Officers were criss-crossing the garden and the woods beyond with German shepherds trained to sniff out decomposing corpses. More officers were visible sifting meticulously through the kitchen, bagging and tagging anything of interest.

Reece emerged from the house. 'Jim, how did it go?'

He indicated it hadn't gone well with a shake of his head. 'There is one bit of good news. It looks like Anna's going to pull through.'

Reece puffed his cheeks. 'Thank fuck.'

'What's the score with the bone?'

'It was attached to the skeleton of an adolescent female. The pathologist estimates she's been in the ground roughly two or three months.'

'So it's not Jessica Young.' Jim's eyes faded away from Reece as he wondered how Anna would feel to know yet again that her search wasn't over.

'There was a puncture wound to the left of the sternum.'

'Sounds familiar. Any idea who she is?'

'We're checking recent missing person reports. So far there are seven possibilities.'

'Show me.' There was little chance that identifying the dead girl would lead them to Gavin, but it was better than sitting around waiting to see if the units involved in the manhunt struck lucky.

Reece led Jim to the incident command vehicle and handed him a sheaf of printouts. There were four white girls, two Asian and one black. They ranged in age from thirteen to eighteen. Four had gone missing from London, one from Birmingham, one from Cardiff and one from Manchester. Most would be runaways from poor and unstable homes. Girls born with little or no future, ripe for exploitation by predators like Gavin. 'These all went missing between February and April of this year,' said Reece.

'We need to go back much further than that. He keeps them alive, holds them prisoner.' Jim pointed towards the barn. 'That's what the modified freezer's about. Like with Edward Forester, it's not the killing he gets off on. It's the sex, the control.' His phone rang. It was a mobile number he didn't recognise. He answered the call. 'This is DCI—'

A woman's whispered voice, so choked with emotion as to be barely coherent, cut him off, 'I've tried… tried to make him a good person… Oh God how I've tried…'

Jim's heart was suddenly beating fast. He hurried from the incident command unit, glancing around to make sure there was no one to overhear him as he replied, 'I know, Mrs Walsh, I know you've tried.'

'How could this happen? How? Is it something I've done?' Sharon's voice rose in tormented incomprehension. Then quickly dropped back down low, as though she too was afraid of being overheard. 'Or is it something else, something he was born with? Is there a demon inside him making him do these things?'

'Maybe.' Jim didn't believe in demons – at least not in the supernatural sense. If there was a demon inside Gavin, it was of his own making. But he didn't want to say anything that would put a barrier between himself and Sharon.

'I've begged and begged him to come to my church and let us exorcise him. But he just laughs in my face. I…' Tears clogged her voice. She sucked them back. 'God forgive me, I wish he'd never been born.'

For a moment, Sharon's tearful breathing was the only sound on the line. Jim waited for her to continue. He knew this wasn't the time to try and force anything from her. It was the time to let her make her choice. Suddenly, as if she had to get the words out fast or they wouldn't get out at all, she reeled off a number at him. He jotted it down.

'Is this Gavin's mobile number?'

Another pause, then a strangled, 'Yes.'

'You've made the right choice, Mrs Walsh.'

'Have I?' Sharon's tone was thick with a loathing that seemed more directed at herself than Jim. 'Please save your condescension, Mr Monahan. Just get Emily away from him before they leave the country.'

'What makes you think Gavin intends to leave the country?'

'Because he said he does.'

'And did he also say where they're going?'

'No. I'll be praying for you.'

The line went dead. Jim didn't need prayers when he had GPS. He phoned his contact in the Met. Considering Special Branch's involvement, he'd rather not have risked it but he had no choice if he wanted to track Gavin's phone without alerting Garrett. And he knew Garrett wouldn't let him play things the way he wanted to. Not after what had happened to Anna. 'I need a big favour, Harry. No questions asked.'

'No can do, Jim. I'm still in the shit bin after the last one I did you.'

'There's a young girl's life at stake. If you don't help me, she's as good as dead.'

'Oh you bastard,' grumbled Harry. 'That's a low blow.'

'I'll beg too, if it saves her life.'

Harry heaved a breath down the line. 'I'm almost tempted to take you up on that offer. But first tell me what you need.'

'I need you to track my suspect's mobile phone.'

'I can't do that without a court order.'

'C'mon, Harry. We both know the Met has its ways of getting around little complications like court orders.'

There was a moment's silence, then Harry said, 'Give me the number and I'll see what I can do. No promises.'

As Jim waited for Harry to get back to him, Reece approached him and asked, 'Who was that? What's going on?'

Holding up a hand, Jim moved away from Reece. After what seemed more like hours than the minutes that had actually passed, Harry phoned and told him what he so desperately wanted to hear. 'The phone's stationary, close to the A169, about six miles north-east of Pickering and half a mile east of the turn-off for Lockton.'

Jim rolled his eyes skywards as though offering up thanks. 'I owe you big time, Harry.'

'No kidding you do. I'll let you know if the position changes.'

Jim brought up a map of North Yorkshire on his phone. Lockton was a village on the edge of the moors. The area was isolated and not far from the east coast. A good place to lie low whilst waiting for a private boat or plane out of the country to be arranged. A mile or so east of the village and the A169 was a belt of woodland that ran roughly parallel to the road. 'More fucking woods,' muttered Jim.

He hurried towards his car, motioning for Reece to follow. He punched the destination into the satnav. The journey was a little over a hundred miles, roughly two and a quarter hours' drive if you observed the speed limits. Which he had no intention of doing. 'Lockton. That's in North Yorkshire, isn't it?' said Reece. 'What's in Lockton?'

Without answering, Jim twisted the ignition key.

'Whoa,' said Reece as Jim turned the car around. 'I can't just leave the crime scene.'

'This is more important.'

'You've got a line on Gavin, haven't you?'

'That was his mother who phoned me in the command unit. She gave me his mobile number. GPS indicates he's hiding out near Lockton.'

Reece's eyebrows lifted high. 'Shit, his own mum rolled on him. What does she want in return?'

'She wants her granddaughter not to be raped and murdered.'

Reece nodded as if to say, *Understandable.* 'So I take it we're doing this alone.'

'No back-up, no chance of anyone leaking the surprise.'

'Garrett's not going to be happy.'

Jim smiled grimly. 'He never is.'

Reece's forehead creased suddenly. 'Hey, I just noticed.' He tapped his upper lip. 'Where's the tash?'

CHAPTER TWENTY

There was the metallic snap of latches being undone. The cushions were lifted. Light streamed into Emily's blinking eyes. Through a blur of tears, she saw Gavin stooping towards her. He'd taken off the wig. Her heart kicked against her ribcage. He was holding the skinning knife! He slid it between her numb ankles and cut off the plastic cuffs. Then he lifted her into a sitting position. He didn't cut the cuffs off her wrists. 'Wriggle your toes,' he said, removing the gag.

Emily did so, slowly at first, gradually regaining normal movement as the blood tingled through her feet.

'Are you thirsty?' asked Gavin.

Emily nodded. He put a bottle of water to her lips and she drank deeply.

'Hungry?'

Another nod. Adrift in the darkness, she'd come to a decision. She would play along with Gavin's insanity. Try to gain his trust. Wait for him to let down his guard. And when he did, she would make another run for it. Her legs trembled as he helped her to stand. He replaced the sofa cushions and indicated for her to sit. She obeyed and he smiled at her. It wasn't a pleasant smile. The beard had disguised the meanness of his small, thick-lipped mouth. He took a tray of long-stemmed mushrooms and a lump of what looked like some sort of red meat out of the fridge. As he sliced the meat, Emily's gaze flitted furtively past him. Outside the windows on both sides of the motorhome, rows of tall pines shivered in the wind. Creases gathered thoughtfully between her eyebrows. Were they back in Sherwood Forest? Surely they couldn't be. Imprisoned beneath the sofa, she'd struggled to hold onto a sense of time. Even so, she guessed they'd been on the road several hours before arriving where they were. It occurred to her that Gavin could have driven around in circles to disorientate her. But she doubted he would have risked doing so. He might be crazy, but he wasn't stupid.

'Is extra-bloody OK?' asked Gavin. Emily's eyes jerked to him. The fear in them receded a fraction as he went on, 'Cook a steak too long and you kill its flavour and nutrients.'

She nodded again.

He frowned slightly. 'You're allowed to speak.'

'Yes,' Emily said, her voice flat.

Gavin's shrewd smile returned. 'You know, you may look like your mum, but I think inside you're more like me.'

I'm nothing like you! Emily caught the words on her lips, not only because she wanted to stay on Gavin's good side – if such a thing existed – but because she suddenly found herself wondering whether they were true. What if he was right? What if he'd passed something of his insanity on to her, like a hereditary disease? The idea of it was almost as frightening as her predicament.

'I was the quiet type too when I was your age,' he continued. 'I was like a closed book. Lord Cernunnos taught me how to open up and let the world and all its pleasures in. His is the voice that can never be tamed. The voice of the wild things.' He closed his eyes. 'Listen to the forest, Emily. Can you hear it? It's telling you to be yourself. To live without guilt, shame and remorse.' He ran one hand down over his face and chest, stopping just short of his groin. He looked at her, his eyes faintly glassy. 'I can see in your face that you don't hear it. But don't worry, my love. You will soon. And then we two shall be as one.'

Emily felt tears rising in her again. She held them back with everything she had.

Gavin speared the steaks and laid them in a frying pan with the mushrooms. The aroma of frying meat filled the motorhome. It was a smell Emily normally liked. But right then it made her stomach churn. After a few seconds, Gavin transferred the contents of the pan to a plate on a fold-down table. He sliced off a corner of steak. Blood seeped from the almost raw meat. He lifted a fork towards her mouth. 'Open wide, my love.'

She forced herself to do as he said. The meat had a strong gamy flavour. It was as tender as any she'd eaten. As she attempted to swallow it, her throat contracted with the urge to vomit. Clamping her teeth together, she somehow managed to push it down her gullet. 'Now for a mushroom,' said Gavin.

'If you take off the handcuffs, I'll feed myself,' said Emily.

Gavin cocked his head as though considering her offer. 'I'd like nothing more than to remove the cuffs, but look what happened last time I trusted you.'

'Please, Gavin, I promise I'll behave.'

He blew a little laugh through his nose. 'Who said I want you to behave?' Emily held back a shudder as he slid his callused hand along her jaw. 'I want to see the real you, the wild, untamed you.' He resumed feeding her, adding, 'And another thing, don't call me Gavin. I rejected that false name when I shed the bonds of society. My true name is Clotho Daeja. We'll have to find your true name too. To know your true name is to know your true self. And to know your true self is to know what is divine.'

I thought nothing was true, Emily resisted the urge to sneer at him.

To her relief, he ate the second steak and half the mushrooms. 'Do you smoke?' he asked, seating himself cross-legged on the floor at her feet and rolling a cigarette.

Emily shook her head. 'I tried it once, but I didn't like it.'

'That's good. Smoking pollutes the body. I only smoke on special occasions these days. And what could be a more special occasion than this?' He lit his cigarette and peered up at Emily like a disciple waiting for some revelation. 'Tell me about yourself.'

'What do you want to know?'

'Everything.'

Emily was silent a moment, then began awkwardly, 'I like hanging out with my friends, listening to music, going to the movies—'

'No you don't,' broke in Gavin. 'You just think you like those things because society has conditioned you to fit in, to be a consumer. I want you to look inside yourself and tell me what you *really* like.'

Emily's forehead puckered. *What do I really like?* she wondered. She'd never given it much consideration. She'd always just gone along with what her friends did. 'I... I kind of like silence. And I like the night-time. My friends are afraid of the dark, but I'm not.'

Gavin nodded as though he approved. 'Tell me, if you were a wild animal, what would you be?'

Emily's eyes dropped in thought, then she said, 'I'd be a bird.'

'A bird flying free through the silence of the forest night.' Gavin clicked his fingers. 'Adaryn Purae. The pure bird. That's your true name.'

'Adaryn Purae,' murmured Emily. It sounded like something from a fantasy novel.

'Say it loud,' said Gavin. 'Let the Lord of the Forest hear your voice.'

She repeated the name. Gavin closed his eyes, breathing in deeply as though he was inhaling her voice. 'Again, again.'

He began to sway in time to the name. And, almost unconsciously, Emily found herself swaying too. A warm woozy sensation was sliding over her. She felt like she'd swallowed dust and there was a bitter taste in the back of her throat. Gavin's eyes snapped open and she saw that his pupils were huge and black. 'I feel funny,' she said.

Gavin burst out laughing. His laughter climbed to a hysterical pitch as Emily continued, 'I think I'm getting ill.'

'You're not getting ill,' he said, between gasps. 'You're getting well. The magic's starting to work.'

Emily closed her eyes and when she opened them it was as though she was seeing Gavin through the wrong end of binoculars. He looked like a wizened laughing gnome. *What's wrong with me?* she wondered. *Have I been drugged?*

The gnome hopped to its feet and approached her. She shrank away as it reached for her with hands that appeared massively oversized in comparison to its arms. 'Lie down, Adaryn,' it said, manoeuvring her onto her side. 'Sleep.'

She closed her eyes again. Lights were flashing behind them as though she'd looked into the sun for too long. 'I can't sleep.'

'Shh. The Horned One is coming. He will be here soon. You must sleep and be ready for him.'

Emily shook her head weakly. The lights were making her brain pound. And there was a buzzing in her ears like she'd stuck her head into a beehive. The sound travelled through her, vibrating along her bones all the way to the tips of her toes. She could no longer feel the sofa beneath her. But she wasn't falling like before. She was floating. No, not floating. Flying. She was a bird flying higher and higher into the sky. Far below – so far it was little more than a dark shape – was the motorhome. And all around, like a limitless ocean, was a forest.

'I can't sleep,' she said again, opening her eyes. The gnome was gone. So was Gavin. She sat up with a gasp, her gaze darting around the motorhome. She was alone! *Am I hallucinating?* she wondered. *Or is this real?* She instinctively bit her lip. Pain. Pain was real. This was her chance! She stood up and, swaying precariously, tried to take a step. Her feet seemed impossibly heavy. She felt sweat pricking out on her face with the effort of moving them. There was the sound of a toilet flushing. A door adjacent to the kitchen area opened and Gavin stepped into view. He'd stripped down to baggy white underpants, over which his large, solid-looking stomach bulged like a sack of grain. The spider's web tattoo seemed to thrum with a faintly irradiated light. He was holding a pen and a notepad.

'I thought you were sleeping,' he said, frowning knowingly at Emily.

'I'm thirsty.'

Gavin retrieved the water from the fridge and put it to Emily's lips. She gulped it down and exhaled with relief because it was like a cool hand caressing her throat. As he guided her back to the sofa, she asked, 'What are you writing?'

'Our wedding vows.'

Now it was Emily's turn to laugh – a horrified laugh that wouldn't stop no matter how hard she tried to stifle it.

'That's it,' grinned Gavin. 'Let it out. Let it all out, Adaryn.'

Upon hearing the name, her laughter grew even louder. She doubled over, gasping for breath, tears streaming down her cheeks. *Gavin's a bad dream*, she thought. *And I'm going to wake up any minute now. Please let me wake up. Please…* But she didn't wake up. She twisted away from him, pressing her face into the sofa. The laughter finally died away, but not the tears. They continued to seep into the cushions. Images danced behind her eyes – her friends, her on-off boyfriend, her school. People and things she would never see anywhere but in her mind again. Gavin wasn't the dream. They were.

'I know you're in pain,' said Gavin. 'That's because the old you is dying. But don't be afraid. Soon the new you will be born.'

Shut up! Emily screamed in her mind. *Shut up! Shut up!*

After a while – she couldn't have said how long a while, time seemed to be doing strange things – she glanced surreptitiously at Gavin. He was hunched over his notepad at the table, his tongue poking out in a look of idiot concentration. Her nose wrinkled. At that moment she didn't fear him. She merely loathed him with an intensity she'd never experienced before. She wanted to cut off his stupid tongue. As though she was looking at herself from outside her own body, a vision appeared of her doing it with his hunting knife. Then she saw herself plunging the knife into him over and over again, a maniacal grin twisting at her mouth. *Oh my God*, she thought in horror, *I am like him!*

She rolled back towards the cushions, trying to make her mind a blank space. But more images kept coming at her – fragmented memories from her entire life. Sometimes they flashed before her eyes as if she was on the brink of death. Other times someone seemed to have hit a slow motion button. She felt strangely disconnected from the memories, as though they belonged to someone else. They began to blur and flow into each other, like colours in a child's painting. Nothing made sense any more. Nothing was true. The world was dissolving into one big brown mass of shit. It made her want to puke. Nausea pushed irresistibly from her stomach into her throat. Lurching upright, she vomited a sludge of half-digested food onto the floor. Not the floor of the caravan. This floor was grassy and strewn with daisies. Her gaze jerked around. She was in a small clearing, encircled by oak and pine trees. She was no longer wearing her jeans and sweatshirt, but a long green dress with flared sleeves and a jagged hem. And her hands were free! Her bewildered elation at the realisation was tempered by the thought, *This isn't real. I'm tripping.*

The feeling of unreality was reinforced by the music drifting into the clearing. It was the sound of a flute playing a slow, haunting melody. Emily scrabbled backwards on her hands as a figure, naked except for a leather belt strung with multicoloured ribbons, emerged from the trees. The figure had a red face and black-ringed eyes. Curling horns sprouted from its head. For a terrifying instant, she thought she was seeing the Horned God sprung to life. Then she noticed the spider's web tattoo. It was Gavin!

In time to the music, Gavin pranced around the clearing, thrusting his hips in Emily's direction. She watched as though mesmerised as the music and his grotesque dance gathered pace, gradually building to a shrill, frantic climax. The music stopped suddenly and Gavin dropped to his knees in front of Emily, bowing his face to the ground. 'You are my goddess,' he said breathlessly, 'and I am your god. Today we become as one.' He grabbed her hand, took a ribbon from his belt and wrapped his right wrist tightly to her left with it. He raised their bound hands to the sky. 'O Horned One! We call upon you. O Dark One! We call upon you. O Lord of Life and Death! We call upon you. O, Cernunnos! Come to this sacred grove. Come to us who await your blessing. Come! Come! Join with us in the binding of our life forces.'

The clearing was silent a moment. Then a deep male voice boomed from amongst the trees. Emily stiffened. Was it a trick? Was someone else in the woods with them? Or was she going mad? Perhaps that's what Gavin wanted. To drive her crazy. To break her and remake her in his own image. 'Hear ye the words of he whose names are beyond count and comprehension,' proclaimed the voice. 'I am the fire that burns wildest, the flame that rages in the hearts of the free. I am death and rebirth, the night and the sun. Mine is the voice all must heed. And I bless this union with all earthly pleasures.'

'Thank you, O Great Father!' Gavin called back.

Emily shook her head violently. 'This isn't happening, this isn't happening.'

The voice spoke over her. 'Look deep into each other's eyes now. Come together and let your vows be the entwining of your limbs and the intermingling of your sacred seed.'

Gavin turned to Emily. The paint on his face was streaked with sweat. Red dribbles ran down his chest and belly towards his penis, which poked like a third horn through the ribbons at his waist. 'Yes, my Lord,' he said thickly.

'No!' screamed Emily. 'No! No!'

CHAPTER TWENTY-ONE

Jim drove fast, but the journey seemed to go by excruciatingly slowly. They passed the outskirts of Doncaster, Leeds and York, barely speaking except when Jim's phone rang. It was Garrett. He switched the phone off. He didn't want to have to lie about where he was and what he was doing. 'Turn yours off too,' he said to Reece.

'What if Staci calls?'

'Turn it off,' Jim said with slow emphasis.

Reece reluctantly did so. 'When she gets back from South Africa, I'm quitting the force. I don't care about the job any more. All I care about is being with her.'

Jim said nothing. Reece glanced across at him. 'Well aren't you going to try and convince me out of it?'

Jim shook his head. 'I'd do the same thing if—' *If Margaret was alive.* That's what he'd been about to say. But even after all these months it was still too painful for him to speak her name.

They passed through the quiet little market town of Pickering. The road undulated gently between drystone walls and hedgerows that enclosed grassy fields and pockets of woodland. The sun was softening in a big blue sky. 'Where the fuck is this place?' muttered Jim. Moments later he spotted a lane branching off the left-hand side of the main road. 'Lockton ¼' read a sign. To the right of it was an open farm gate. A dirt track led alongside a hedgerow towards a line of trees.

'That's got to be it,' said Reece.

Jim turned onto the track. He drove slowly, keeping the engine revs low. At the far side of the field, the track dipped out of sight of the road and passed through another farm gate. This one was closed. A sign on it read 'Private Woodland'. He stopped the car and scanned the woods. There was no red van or any other vehicle to be seen. He quietly got out and opened the boot. He lifted out a stab vest and a metal truncheon and proffered them to Reece.

'What about you?' whispered Reece.

Jim removed the Taser from his jacket. His eyes brooked no argument. Reece strapped on the vest, extended the truncheon and nodded to indicate he was ready. They warily approached the gate. A bundle of chain and a padlock lay at the foot of one of the posts. Reece stooped to inspect it. 'Cut,' he mouthed silently.

They opened the gate a little and slid through it. The trees instantly closed in, overshadowing the track. Jim pointed and Reece slunk into the shadows to the left. Jim stole along the track's opposite edge. After three hundred metres or so, natural woodland of oak and other indigenous trees gave way to densely planted pines. Jim stopped abruptly and pointed again. Reece nodded to indicate he could see the motorhome parked in a space between the trees on his side of the track.

They moved from tree to tree towards the vehicle. The curtains in the back of it were closed. There was no one in the front. Jim noted down its reg, then darted across the track and peered through the windscreen. A curtain had been drawn behind the driver's and passenger's seats. He moved around to the back door where Reece was waiting. They stood listening. Not a sound, except for birdsong. Jim motioned to the door handle, and as Reece reached for it, he raised the Taser into firing position. Reece's hand hesitated. He looked over his shoulder, mouthing, 'Do you hear that?'

From somewhere amongst the trees, carried on the breeze, came the faintly audible sound of music. Jim pointed. 'It's coming from over there.'

'Sounds like a flute.'

They exchanged a meaningful glance. During their research into the Horned God, they'd both come across images of the pagan deity playing a flute. They headed into the trees. The music grew louder and faster, echoing through the woods, bouncing off the tree trunks, making it difficult to pinpoint exactly where it was coming from. Suddenly it stopped. They stopped too. Then came a man's voice, which, with its Brummie accent, surely belonged to Gavin. They moved towards it. A second voice rang out in reply, so close that both detectives dodged for the cover of an oak tree. They exchanged another glance. Did Gavin have an accomplice with him? Jim sneaked a look around the tree and got his answer. On the ground a short distance away was a portable CD player from whose speakers boomed the second voice.

'Bless this union with all earthly pleasures,' whispered Reece. 'What the fuck does that mean?'

It was sickeningly obvious to Jim what it meant. Taser at the ready, he advanced past the CD player. Gavin replied to the supposed voice of the Horned God, his own voice thickened by lust. A distinctly female scream tore through the woods. Jim broke into a run. A bizarre sight greeted him as he emerged into a sun-splashed clearing. A stocky man wearing a two-horned skull cap and a skirt of ribbons was lying on top of Emily. The man had Emily's wrists pinned and was prising her legs apart with his knees. He was so intent on what he was doing that he didn't hear Jim's approach. Jim took aim and fired. The Taser wires shot out and its hooks embedded themselves in the man's back. There was a crackle of electricity and he cried out convulsively. Emily squirmed from beneath him. She fought to disentangle something from both their wrists. Then she scrambled to her feet, panting, sobbing.

'Police!' Jim made a sweeping motion. 'Move away from him.'

Emily looked at him as though she doubted he was real. The man tried to push himself upright. Another jolt of electricity flipped him onto his back, teeth clamped together, arms bent and rigid. His face was painted red and beardless, but his eyes were unmistakable. 'It's our man!' Jim called to Reece. He pointed to the scabbard on Gavin's belt. 'Get his kni—' He was cut short by the breath rushing between his lips as someone slammed into him from behind, sending him sprawling. He released the Taser and tried to scramble to his feet. A knee drove into the small of his back. Powerful hands twisted his arms up behind him. As he fought to force enough air into his lungs to shout a warning to Reece, he felt the bite of steel handcuffs on his wrists.

'What... what...' stammered Emily, her eyes bewildered saucers.

'Stay where you are,' ordered Jim's assailant. 'You're safe. No one's going to hurt you.'

Jim's mouth gaped wordlessly. The sound of the voice left him even more breathless than the blow to his back had. It was Reece!

Gavin climbed to his feet, reaching around to yank out the Taser prongs. He stared nervously at Reece. 'Are you one of *us*?'

'No,' Reece stated coldly. He gave a jerk of his chin. 'Get the fuck out of here.'

Gavin glanced at Emily.

'Don't look at her,' snapped Reece.

'She's mine.'

'Not any more. Now go on, move your fat arse.'

Gavin darted his tongue uncertainly across his lips. With a sudden movement, he drew his knife and sprang at Emily. Reece sprang forward too. He was faster than the older man whose central nervous system was still reeling from being zapped by hundreds of volts. As Gavin reached to curl his arm around Emily's throat, Reece hit it with the truncheon. Gavin gave a yelp, but didn't drop the knife. He lunged at Reece's midriff. The blade deflected off the stab vest. Reece whipped the truncheon down again, catching Gavin a heavy blow on the skull cap. There was a crack of breaking bone and one of the horns shattered. Gavin's legs wobbled. He dropped to one knee and thrust the knife upwards. Reece grunted as the blade sank into his inner right thigh. He staggered backwards, catching hold of Emily and dragging her with him.

Gavin straightened groggily, still clutching the bloodied knife. Reece pushed Emily behind himself and raised the truncheon. *Fucking try it*, his eyes said to Gavin.

Gavin's tongue flicked across his lips again. He gave Emily a look of pained longing. 'We will be together, my love.' He paused as if for dramatic effect, before adding, 'By the horns of Cernunnos, I swear it!'

He retreated to the edge of the clearing, turned and ran.

When the sound of Gavin's footfalls had faded into the distance, Reece turned to Emily. 'Are you OK?'

She looked at him as though he was speaking a foreign language. He swayed suddenly then regained his balance. He felt his injured thigh and looked at his hand. His fingers were soaked with blood. He unbuttoned his jeans and gingerly slid them down. Blood jetted from the red slit of the wound. 'Oh shit,' he said, vainly trying to stem the bleeding with his hand.

'Uncuff me,' Jim said urgently. 'We need to get a tourniquet on that leg.'

Reece stripped off his shirt and tied the sleeves around his leg a couple of inches above the wound. Blood spurted fitfully from it as, with his jeans around his ankles, he staggered towards the trees.

'Don't be foolish, Reece,' continued Jim as his partner stooped to search the ground. 'Let me help you.'

Reece picked up a stick, slid it under the knotted sleeves and began to twist. The blood slowed to a steady stream, then a trickle. Suddenly, the knot came loose. He tried to retie it, but his fingers were fumbling and clumsy as though numbed by cold. He swayed again, fell back heavily against a tree and slumped to the ground.

'Emily!' Jim shouted. She stared at Reece blankly, showing no sign of having heard. 'His femoral artery's been cut. If you don't do as I say he'll be dead in minutes.'

Blinking as though coming back to herself from some far-off place, she turned to him. 'You need to retie the knot and twist the stick in it,' he continued. 'Quickly now.'

As Emily knelt by Reece, Jim rolled onto his side and used his elbow to push himself to his knees. He rose to his feet, hurried to peer over Emily's shoulder and saw that she'd managed to stop the worst of the bleeding. 'Well done, Emily,' he said, dropping to his haunches. 'Now keep one hand on the tourniquet and put the other in my right jacket pocket. There's a bunch of keys in there. Take it out.' Emily did so and Jim added, 'You see the small black key. Use it to unlock the handcuffs.'

There was a click and the cuffs fell open. From the direction of the track came the sound of an engine starting up. Jim quickly removed his mobile phone from his jacket. Then he took the jacket off, bundled it up and pressed it against Reece's thigh. Reece groaned and looked at him with glassy, fluttering eyes. 'I had to do it, Jim,' The words came in a thin whisper. 'Staci was dying and there was nothing I could do. They contacted me, offered to pay for her treatment.'

'Who's "they"?'

Reece gave a weak shake of his head. 'They'll let her die if I tell you. I'm sorry, Jim.'

'It's OK, Reece. It doesn't matter now.' The engine noise was fading into the distance. Jim looked hopefully at his mobile phone. There was no service. He turned to Emily. 'I've got to find some reception and call for help. You need to stay here and keep the pressure on the wound. Do you understand?'

Emily's eyes were frightened, but she nodded.

In what seemed to Jim like an eerie half-echo of Anna's parting words, Reece said, 'Don't tell Staci what I did.'

Jim looked at his partner with sad, soft eyes. He felt no anger towards him. How could he? Staci was Reece's love, his reason for living. He'd only done what he had to do, what anyone would have done in the same situation. 'I'll be back soon. You just hold on.'

Jim sprinted through the woods. When he reached the track, he checked his phone. The reception bar had jumped up a couple of notches. He dialled and put the phone to his ear. 'This is DCI Jim Monahan, I have an officer down in need of urgent medical assistance,' he breathlessly told the dispatcher. For the second time that day he was informed that an air ambulance was on its way. He gave a description of Gavin and his vehicle, before heading back into the trees.

'Help!' he heard Emily crying out. 'Help!'

Ignoring the familiar constricting sensation in his chest, Jim put on an extra burst of speed. When he reached the clearing, Reece's eyes were closed, his head was sagging to one side and there was a telltale bluish tinge to his lips. Jim felt for a pulse. He couldn't find one. 'How long's he been like this?'

'I... I'm not sure,' Emily stammered. 'Maybe a minute. He seemed OK, but then he just kind of closed his eyes. Is he breathing?'

In answer, Jim manoeuvred Reece flat onto his back. He checked the inside of Reece's mouth was clear. Lacing his fingers together, he placed the heel of his hand on Reece's chest and pressed down hard. After thirty compressions, he tilted Reece's head, pinched his nose and breathed twice into his mouth, watching to make sure his chest inflated. Then he resumed the compressions. Over and over, he continued the cycle. Thirty compressions, two breaths, thirty compressions, two breaths... Reece showed no sign of responding. Sweat glistened on Jim's face. His breathing was ragged. His heart felt ready to burst.

'You're going to have to take over,' he gasped at Emily. He took hold of the tourniquet and improvised bandage.

Emily began the compressions, looking at Jim as if to say, *Am I doing this right?*

'Harder,' he said. 'Keep a steady rate... Now two breaths... That's it, you're doing good. Keep going.'

Jim's eyes anxiously swept the sky. Twilight was seeping in; the ghost of a moon was visible. There was no sign of the air ambulance. And when it arrived, the paramedics were going to need guiding to Reece. Jim unlaced his shoes. With one lace, he secured the torsion stick to Reece's leg so that the tourniquet couldn't loosen. With the other, he bound his jacket over the wound. 'Take a rest,' he said to Emily.

They were exchanging places for the fifth time when they heard the whoomp-whoomp of rotor blades. 'I have to fetch the paramedics,' said Jim.

Emily opened her mouth to say something. But before she could, Jim added, 'Save your breath for him.'

He kicked off his laceless shoes and, on legs that felt like rubber tubes, ran back into the trees. He'd rather have remained with Reece, but in her obviously drugged state Emily might easily become disorientated in the woods. Besides, although he desperately refused to admit it to himself, he knew in his overstrained heart that it wouldn't make any difference who stayed or went. The paramedics were too late.

CHAPTER TWENTY-TWO

A crushing sense of déjà vu weighed on Jim as he sat in the hospital corridor with his head resting in his bloodstained hands. Oh Christ. Dead. Reece was dead. The paramedics had confirmed it at the scene. Margaret was dead. Amy was dead. Everyone he loved or got close to died. It was like he was cursed. He wanted to run out of there and keep running until he found some place where he was absolutely and truly alone, where no one could hurt him and he could hurt no one. But the same feelings that made him want to run, pinned him in place. His fingers dug into his pounding skull as he thought of all the faces, all the grief. If he left now it would all have been for nothing. And anyhow, if he was cursed there was no point running. The only way he knew to break a curse was by destroying those who'd cast it. His mind began to grimly reel off the list of names he felt he'd lived with his entire life – Sebastian Dawson-Cromer, Rupert Hartwell, Andrew Templeton, William Howell, Thomas fucking Villiers—

'DCI Monahan.'

Jim jerked his head up and found himself looking at a female doctor. 'How is she?'

'There are no signs of rape. Apart from some cuts and bruises, she should be fine when the effects of the hallucinogen she's ingested wear off in a few hours. Right now, though, she's not making much sense. She keeps going on about a horned man.'

'If you'd seen what she's seen that would make perfect sense.'

'She's refusing to give us any information about her next of kin. Have you contacted her family?'

'No, and neither should you. Will you please take me to her?' Dizziness swirled through Jim as he stood up. He put a hand out to steady himself on the wall.

'Are you OK?'

'I'm fine.'

'You don't look it. Your colour's way off. Before I take you to Emily, I'd like to check your blood pressure.'

Reluctantly, Jim followed the doctor into a curtained cubicle. He perched on a trolley bed as she took his blood pressure. She listened to his heart with a stethoscope and asked him to take several deep breaths. 'You're showing signs of arrhythmia and your blood pressure is high. Do you have any history of heart problems?'

'I had a heart attack last year,' Jim admitted. 'But that's all sorted now. I'm just stressed, that's all.'

'Maybe, but if I were you I'd err on the side of caution. My advice is, go home and rest and if your symptoms worsen—'

'Thanks for your concern, Doctor,' interrupted Jim. 'But I really need to speak to Emily right away.'

'OK. Have it your own way, but don't say I didn't warn you.'

The doctor led Jim to a cubicle where Emily was lying on a bed with a nurse watching over her. The green dress had been replaced by a hospital gown. She looked at Jim with eyes that were still glassy and dilated. Eyes blank with shock and despair.

His heart constricted in a different way as he thought of the carefree girl he'd watched laughing with her friends only a day ago. That girl was dead too now.

The doctor pointed to a plastic bag containing the dress. 'I thought you might need it for evidence.'

Jim nodded his thanks. As the doctor and nurse left the cubicle, Emily asked, 'Have you caught Gavin?'

'Not yet,' said Jim. Seeing fear flash over her face, he added reassuringly, 'But we will. We found him once and we'll find him again. It's only a matter of time.'

'How *did* you find us?'

'We tracked Gavin's phone.'

'Well, can't you track it again?'

'We're trying, but it seems to be switched off.'

Emily's eyes faded away from Jim. 'He could be anywhere,' she murmured, twitching as though a cold hand had touched her. 'He could even be in this hospital.'

'Wherever he is, he won't get near you again. There'll be a police guard on you day and night until we catch him.'

'But what if the guard is one of *them,* like that other policeman?' She used the word *them* as though she was referring to some invisible, omnipresent group of beings.

'They won't be. I'll make sure of that.'

Emily looked at Jim with the desperate desire to believe what he was saying. 'Gavin thinks he's got magic powers or something. He said anything's possible so long as you believe in the Horned God. Do you think he's crazy?'

'I don't know, but I know he doesn't have magic powers. He's just a man. A warped, pathetic man.'

Her features contracted. 'He's my dad.'

Jim said nothing. What could you say in the face of such merciless truth?

Emily's eyes drifted again. She hugged her arms across herself, lips moving as if in silent prayer. Jim waited for her to come back to herself, then said, 'I know it's difficult right now, Emily, but I need you to focus and tell me everything that's happened to you since this morning.'

Emily squeezed her eyes shut with the effort of putting her scrambled thoughts into order. She began with the phone call from Lindsey Allen. Jim took notes as she described how she'd arranged to meet Gavin, the journey to the forest, the hollow tree, the things he'd said about the Horned God, about living in a world where there was no right or wrong. Her voice faltered when she came to the fight between him and Anna. Tears swelled into her eyes. 'I had his knife in my hand. I could have saved Anna.'

'You did save her,' said Jim. 'She survived.'

The tears spilled over. She wept softly with relief for a few seconds, before wiping her eyes and saying more to herself than Jim, 'I have an aunt.'

'And another grandma.' The DNA test results weren't in yet, but Jim had no doubt they would back up his words. And he saw how badly Emily needed something – some glimmer of future hope – to hold on to. 'A grandma who I'm sure will be desperate to meet you. But that's for another time. Right now we need to concentrate on the task before us.'

Emily continued her story. Jim noted that her voice was perhaps a fraction stronger. Her face hardened into a scowl as she recounted Gavin's conversation with Ronald and Sharon. 'How could they lie to me my whole life like that? They're as bad as Gavin.'

Remembering his promise to Sharon, Jim said, 'It was your grandma who gave us Gavin's phone number, without which we wouldn't have found you.'

Emily digested this information for a moment, before giving a sharp shake of her head, as if to say, *That's not enough.* Jim didn't try to convince her otherwise. He understood why Ronald and Sharon had chosen Gavin over the law. Nonetheless, they'd made their choices and they had to live with them, just as he lived with his. His own mind began to drift, returning once again to Amy, to Margaret. Emily yanked him back into the moment as she said, 'Later, Gavin spoke on the phone to a man.'

'How much later?'

'Not long. Maybe ten minutes.'

'Did the man give a name?'

'No.'

'What was his voice like?'

'It was posh English.'

Posh English. That described the vast majority of the men in Herbert Winstanley's black book. 'Do you think you'd recognise it if you heard it again?'

Emily shrugged. 'The man said he'd get us out of the country. Gavin wanted to go to the Philippines.'

'No extradition treaty,' Jim remarked. 'What else did he say?'

'That it would take a day or two to arrange.'

Jim glanced at his watch. It had been roughly two hours since Gavin escaped. Taking into account when the phone call had been made, that meant they had a possible window of forty or so hours to catch him. Then he would be gone, free to continue his depravity in a country beyond their reach.

'But he won't go without me,' continued Emily, her gaze dropping to a red welt where Gavin had bound her wrist to his.

Jim was inclined to agree. He'd seen the longing in Gavin's eyes as he looked at Emily, he'd heard the want in his voice. 'Was anything mentioned about how you would travel to the Philippines?'

'No. That was pretty much the end of the phone call, except for one more thing Gavin said.'

Something in Emily's voice made Jim look up from his notepad. 'Which was?'

'He said that if anything bad happened to him, if he was shot or something like that, information would be sent to the police about some photos and videos.'

Jim's forehead squeezed into a dark, brooding expression. So Gavin had incriminating evidence that he was using to blackmail those he'd helped acquire victims for. And all it would take for the authorities to get their hands on that evidence was for someone to give the sociopathic little scumbag the justice he deserved. Jim gave an internal shake of his head. No, he couldn't allow himself to think like that. He'd been down that path before and it had nearly destroyed him. He motioned for Emily to go on with her story.

Rapidly, as though purging the words from her mind, she described what had happened after Gavin released her from inside the sofa. 'He must be insane,' she said. 'Why else would he want to marry his own daughter?'

'He doesn't see you as his daughter. At least not in a way you or I would understand. To him you're just an object. All this crap about the Horned God, that's simply his way of justifying what he does. Believe me, Emily, I've met more of his kind than I ever want to remember. People like him are incapable of love or guilt or telling the truth. They're hollow inside. Empty.'

Emily touched her chest tentatively, almost as though she was afraid of what it might contain. 'What makes them like that?'

'I wish I knew,' sighed Jim, turning to open the cubicle's curtain.

'Where are you going?' Emily asked anxiously.

Again, a feeling of déjà vu pressed down on Jim. A sense that he'd been here before and would be here again. Like he was a character in a play, doomed to repeat the same mistakes over and over. 'I'm not going anywhere,' he assured her. 'I just need to let the doctor know we're finished talking.'

'We're transferring Emily to a private room on a ward,' the doctor informed Jim. 'We'll keep her in overnight just to be on the safe side.'

Jim followed as a porter wheeled Emily's bed through antiseptic-smelling corridors to a lift. Once she was safely installed in the room, Jim said, 'Try to get some sleep. I'll be right outside.'

After washing the blood off his hands at a sink, he settled down heavily on a chair and scrolled through his contact numbers until he found Staci. What time was it in South Africa? he wondered. What did it matter what fucking time it was? The kind of news he had for her was no respecter of time. His finger hovered over the number. An image of Staci as she'd looked the last time he saw her came into his mind – she'd looked as if a breath of wind might blow her over. And now he was about to unleash a hurricane on her.

Footsteps attracted his attention. He looked up to see Garrett approaching. The DCS peered through the observation window at Emily, before pulling up a chair next to Jim. A moment of silence passed, like a mark of respect. Then Garrett said, 'I'm sorry, Jim. I know how close you were to Reece. He was a...' A slight hesitation made Garrett's voice ring insincere, 'a good detective.'

'No he wasn't,' said Jim. 'But he was a good husband.'

'Have you spoken to his wife?'

'No.'

'Do you want me to do it?'

Jim shook his head.

'Do you think she knew what Reece was doing for her?'

'No. And she won't find out from me either. Bad enough that her husband's dead. But to know that it's because of her illness...' Jim tailed off meaningfully. He doubted Staci would survive knowing that. Not in her current condition. She had to find out at some point, of course. There would be no burial with honours for Reece. No posthumous bravery awards. But the longer they could keep it from her the better.

'As far as Anna Young's concerned, I can't stress how important it is that you don't talk to her about Reece.'

'So it's back to damage control, is it?' Jim said, with a sardonic twitch of his lips. 'Protect the department's reputation at all costs.'

'Someone has to do it or the people will lose faith in us,' Garrett stated unapologetically. 'And we can't allow that to happen.'

Why not? Jim felt like retorting. *Why protect a system that's rotten to the core? Perhaps it's time to tear the whole thing down and build something new.* He kept his thoughts to himself. He knew he'd be wasting them on Garrett. Besides, he didn't have the energy for such a debate. Gesturing towards Emily's room, Garrett made to speak. Anticipating what he was going to ask, Jim handed him his notepad. He closed his eyes and rested his head back against the wall as Garrett read his notes.

'"A world where there's no right or wrong",' quoted Garrett. 'Gavin Walsh sounds like a classic sociopath.'

'Through and through,' agreed Jim.

Garrett tapped the notepad as he read about Gavin's phone conversation with the anonymous man. 'This looks promising. We've already put in a request for his call records.'

'We should also have Emily listen to recordings of all the men from Herbert's book. See if she recognises any of their voices.'

'I was just having that same thought.' Garrett's eyes widened behind his glasses. 'What's this about photos and videos? If this is true, it might be the key to... well, everything. Someone must be holding this evidence for Gavin. Surely the most likely candidates are his parents? If we can get them to give it up—'

'They won't do that,' broke in Jim.

'How do you know? Sharon Walsh already gave up her son to us.'

'In order to save her granddaughter.'

'We have evidence that they've falsified birth documents and withheld information about criminal activity.'

'That won't be enough leverage.'

'Then we'll dangle the possibility of a reunion with Emily in front of them.'

'They're not stupid. They know that's not going to happen.'

'It could do. Right now they're still her legal guardians.'

Jim frowned at Garrett. The Chief Superintendent raised his hands in reassurance. 'It could happen, but it's not going to. The DNA results will be in tomorrow and then we should have definitive proof that they're not Emily's parents.'

A constable entered the ward and approached them. Jim eyed him narrowly. 'What's this?'

'Emily's guard for the night.'

'That won't be necessary. I'll stay with her.'

'A policeman's been killed, Jim. You need to come in and give a statement.'

'And I will do when I'm sure Emily's safe.'

Garrett leant in close, his voice dropping. 'Look, I understand your trust has been shaken. I feel the same way. But even if you stay, you can't watch her twenty-four hours a day. You've got to sleep. So at some point – from the looks of you, some point in the near future – you're going to have to trust someone.'

Jim knew Garrett was right. He was dangerously close to exhaustion. He'd be no good to anyone if he had another heart attack. Still, he wasn't about to leave Emily in the hands of someone he didn't know. Even if had known the constable, he would have wanted to vet his background for weaknesses that could be exploited by Villiers and his accomplices. He'd liked Reece. More than liked. He'd thought of him almost as the son he'd never had. His feelings had blinded him. He wasn't going to make that mistake again. He folded his arms, wearing a weary but immovable expression. Garrett gave a small nod as though he'd expected as much. He motioned for the constable to leave. 'Good luck speaking to Reece's wife,' he said, standing to leave himself.

Jim's gaze returned to his phone. He ran a hand over his face, pulling the corners of his eyes down. It wasn't luck he needed. It was the strength to do what he must. His head turned towards the sound of a low, haunted wail from Emily's room. He rose to look through the observation window. Emily was pushing at the air as though fending off an attacker. Her eyeballs were moving rapidly beneath their closed lids. She was having a nightmare. Jim thought about waking her, but he knew it would do no good. The nightmare would only return.

Heaving a sigh, he dialled Staci.

CHAPTER TWENTY-THREE

Jim pulled up outside the house. It was a reassuringly anonymous little semi on the northern edge of Nottingham. The opposite side of the city to the Walshes' house. Emily stared at it, unmoving, a shadow of anxiety in her eyes. She hadn't wanted to return to the city, but for now she had no other option. Her school was there, her friends were there, her life was there. Jim watched her watching the house. At first, he'd questioned the sense of placing her with a foster family in Nottingham, arguing instead for a safe house in Sheffield. But the more he thought about it, the more he came to realise this was the best thing for her. She'd already suffered so much upheaval. As the victim counsellor who'd assessed her had said, she needed familiarity, a reference point to anchor her back to the everyday world.

'You'll be perfectly safe here, Emily. Your foster carers are both retired police officers.' Jim pointed to an unmarked car with two men in it. 'And you see them. They're plain-clothes constables. They'll be keeping a close eye on you.' He'd handpicked the constables and two others who were to relieve them at night. None of them had any previous connection to the investigation, so there was no reason they should have been got to. All had spotless service records and no history of financial problems.

The anxiety didn't leave Emily's eyes, but she got out of the car. Jim retrieved a plastic bag from the back seat. He gently ushered her ahead of him to the house. They were met at the door by a smiling late-middle-aged couple and a suited social worker. He handed over the bag. 'There's a toothbrush and a few other things in there, but she's going to need some new clothes.'

'We'll make sure Emily has everything she needs, Chief Inspector,' the social worker assured him.

Jim turned to Emily. He managed a smile. It wasn't easy. Not when he was so raw with the memory of the previous night's conversation with Staci. It would take a long time for the sound of her sobbing, broken voice to fade from his mind. 'How did it happen?' she'd distraughtly demanded to know. *Reece was killed by a suspect we were pursuing*, was all Jim had told her. Which was true and yet concealed the real, unbearable truth. The only scrap of comfort he'd taken from the conversation was that Staci wasn't alone. Reece had lied about Amelia not going with her, no doubt to justify his need to stay in the country and keep tabs on the investigation. Jim was glad he had. Amelia was her mother's reason to fight and survive.

'I'm sorry I couldn't help you,' said Emily.

On the way to Nottingham, Jim had stopped in at Sheffield Police HQ and played Emily interview recordings of the men from Herbert's book. She hadn't recognised any of their voices.

'You have helped us, Emily. Without you we wouldn't have found Gavin. Now you've got my number. Call me anytime. I'll be in touch if there are any developments in our search.'

'Thank you, Mr Monahan.'

Jim accepted the thanks with a nod. 'Take care, Emily. Hopefully we'll speak again very soon.'

He returned to his car, feeling her gaze follow him. He accelerated away without looking back. He knew that if he saw her sad, scared eyes it would only make it all the more difficult to leave her there. He headed towards Sheffield, his flat and bed. The afternoon promised to be a long stretch of interviews – both with and by him – and writing up reports, but first he needed a couple of hours' sleep.

His phone rang. Garrett's name flashed up. No doubt he was calling to pile another disappointment on what had so far been a day of them. First had come the news that the only calls on Gavin's phone records were between him and a mobile number that had been traced to his parent's house. Gavin had obviously used a different phone to contact whoever was arranging to spirit him out of the country. Then came the discovery of the motorhome at an isolated farm on the North Yorkshire Moors, twenty or so miles north of Pickering. A farmhand found the vehicle concealed in a barn. The farmer – an elderly widower – was missing. So was his Land Rover. The general theory was that Gavin had taken the farmer hostage in case he got cornered and needed a bargaining chip. Jim didn't rate the chances of the farmer being seen alive again. Gavin would only hold onto him and the Land Rover long enough for his contact to set up a switch vehicle. At which point he would dispose of them both.

The final double dollop of shit on the cake was Reece's phone records and finances. Phone records showed a series of calls both received from and made to a mobile number. One of the calls had been received shortly before the break-in at Fiona Young's house. Jim had found himself wondering whether Reece was responsible for that particular attempt to intimidate Anna. He'd remembered how Reece had already been at the house when he arrived. Something else had occurred to him too. It wasn't until after the break-in that he'd told Reece Anna was talking to the Hopeland victims, which suggested there was at least one more leak in the department. Or rather departments, seeing as Garrett had made enquiries about the Hopeland case-file to people at Greater Manchester Police and Special Branch. And those people had contacted other people, who'd contacted others, and so on, making it all but impossible to pin down any leaks. With depressing inevitability, Reece had made another call directly after learning Anna was tailing Emily. The number was for an unregistered pay-as-you-go phone. Attempts to trace it had been unsuccessful. Reece's finances had similarly proved to be a dead end. His bank account was clean. Whatever money he'd been promised had obviously been paid directly to the South African private medical company treating Staci. The company had so far refused to give any details about where the payment came from.

Jim put the phone to his ear. 'Some good news at last,' said Garrett. 'The DNA result came in. Emily is Jessica Young's daughter. Scott Greenwood's bringing in Ronald and Sharon as we speak.'

'Are we going to charge them?'

'That depends on how forthcoming they are.'

'Threats won't move them.'

'We'll see about that. I'm on my way back from North Yorkshire. I'll see you at headquarters.'

With a shake of his head, Jim hung up. If Gavin's parents were holding on to information about the photos and videos, there was no way they would give it up to avoid being charged. Not when those photos and videos were probably the only thing keeping Gavin alive. Sharon may have wished her son was never born, but there was a big difference between that and pronouncing a death sentence on him.

Jim phoned Queen's Medical Centre and asked to be put through to the ward Anna was on. A nurse answered and he asked how Anna was doing. 'I couldn't say why, but she's really picked up since this morning,' said the nurse.

Jim knew why. Early that morning he'd instructed a constable to contact Anna and let her know Emily was safe.

'Would you like to speak to her?' asked the nurse.

'No.' His reluctance to speak to Anna had nothing to do with Garrett and everything to do with Amy, Margaret and Reece. Enough good people were dead. This was where it ended. It was time to put some distance between Anna and himself. 'Could you give her a message? Tell her the DNA result came back and she was right.'

As Jim hung up once again, a hollow sense of loneliness settled over him. He didn't try to push the feeling away. Loneliness he could accept. But if someone else he cared for died... The mere thought of it was almost too much to bear.

He was relieved to find Special Branch were no longer sitting outside his flat. No doubt they'd been put on the back foot by the events of the past two days. He ate a quick cold meal and flopped onto the bed. Tears slid from beneath his closed eyes. But even his grief couldn't keep him from sleep for long. He sank into a mercifully dreamless darkness. It seemed only seconds later when he was awakened by his mobile phone. Looking groggily at its screen, he saw a number he didn't recognise. He answered the call. 'Hello.'

'Mr Monahan.'

The voice cleared the fug of sleep from his mind. 'Emily. What is it? Where are you?' He could hear traffic in the background.

'I'm in a phone box. I'm not sure where. I snuck out the back of the house.'

'You need to return there at once.'

'I don't want to. I don't trust those people.'

'Why?'

'I...' Emily's hesitation told Jim why. It wasn't her foster carers she didn't trust. It was everyone, excluding perhaps himself and Anna. Her heartbreakingly hopeful next words confirmed his thoughts. 'Couldn't I come and stay with you, Mr Monahan? Just for a few days.'

'I'm sorry, Emily, that's not possible.'

'You can't force me to go back to that house.' There was a hitch of tears in her voice.

'I'm not going to, I promise you,' Jim said gently. 'Will you do something for me? Look around. Can you see a street name?'

There was a slight pause, then, 'Yes. Thackeray's Lane.'

'Are there any shops or cafés close by?'

'There's a café.'

'What's it called?'

Emily told Jim and he added, 'Right, I'm on my way to you. Wait for me in the café.'

'OK.'

Jim heard the click of the phone being put down. He phoned one of the constables who were supposed to be watching Emily. 'We were just about to call you,' the constable said nervously. 'Sorry, sir, but the Walsh girl has gone missing.'

'I know. She's contacted me.' Jim told the constable where Emily was. 'Head over there but keep your distance. Don't let her see you.'

'Yes, sir.'

Jim hauled on his clothes and headed for his car. As he drove back to Nottingham, he kept thinking and trying not to think about what he'd like to do to Gavin Walsh, Thomas Villiers and all the other destroyers of innocence and trust. How easy it would be to wrap his hands around their throats and choke the sickness from them.

He pulled over outside the café. Emily was nursing a Coke in the window. His gaze travelled the street intently. There were plenty of parked vehicles. All of which were empty except for that of the plain-clothes constables. Some people were gathered at a bus top. Gavin wasn't amongst them. Flashing the constables a 'stay where you are' gesture, he approached Emily and sat down opposite her. She avoided his gaze. Neither of them spoke for a moment. Then, still not looking at him, Emily said very quietly, 'I keep thinking about how it would solve all our problems if someone killed Gavin.'

Jim suddenly felt ashamed for his earlier thoughts. 'No it wouldn't.'

She raised her clear young eyes to his jaded ones. 'But—'

'Don't,' Jim broke in. 'Don't say it. Don't think it. Believe me, Emily, you don't want those thoughts in your head.'

Emily blinked back to the floor, a knot between her eyes. Jim stood up. 'Come on,' he said more lightly. 'We're leaving.'

'Where are we going?'

'You'll find out soon enough.' Seeing the suspicion in Emily's face, Jim added, 'Don't worry, I won't break my promise.'

They made their way to Jim's car. As he accelerated away from the kerb, he noted the constables doing likewise in his rear-view mirror. Emily sat nervously in her seat as they skirted southwards around the city centre. They pulled into the car park of a sprawling multi-storey building with a sign that read 'QUEEN'S MEDICAL CENTRE' above its main entrance. Looking at him in realisation, she said, 'Anna?'

Jim nodded and got out of the car. Emily followed him, her movements less hesitant, a different kind of nervousness in her eyes. They caught a lift up to the ward Anna was on.

Jim asked a nurse where they could find her and she directed them to a single room. The door to the room was closed. Jim stole a look through its observation window. Anna was in bed. She appeared to be asleep. She was pale, but faint spots of colour showed on her cheekbones. Jim was glad to see she was breathing without the aid of an oxygen mask. Her mother was sitting in an armchair at her side, one hand resting on Anna's wrist. Someone had obviously seen fit to contact her despite Anna's wishes. She was staring at a magazine, but her eyes didn't seem to be seeing the pages. There was a distant look in them.

'Who's that with Anna?' asked Emily.

'Your grandma. Her name's Fiona.' Jim pointed to a seating area by the ward's entrance. 'I'll wait for you there.'

'Aren't you coming in with me?'

Jim shook his head. Even if he'd wanted to speak to Anna, this moment wasn't for him to share in. 'Just do me one favour. Anna's going to ask you what happened with Gavin. Don't tell her. At least, not yet.'

****

Emily studied her grandmother through the window, searching for something familiar. She found it in the deep blue of her eyes and the slight flare of her upper lip. She took a breath and opened the door. Her grandmother turned to look at her. Emily heard the faint, sharp intake of her breath. The magazine slipped to the floor.

Putting a hand to her chest as though she had a pain there, Fiona rose slowly from the chair. 'Anna told me about you.' Her voice was an awed murmur. 'She told me how much you look like Jessica. But I didn't... I...'

Like someone sleepwalking, she approached Emily. She stretched out a trembling hand to touch her face, as if to reassure herself she wasn't seeing things. Then she drew Emily to her and hugged her. Emily squeezed her eyes shut, her shoulders suddenly quaking with tears. 'Shh,' soothed Fiona. 'It's OK.'

Gradually, Emily's tears subsided. Keeping her hands on Emily's shoulders, Fiona pulled back to look at her face. Although she was smiling, there were tears in her eyes too. 'My granddaughter,' she said. 'My beautiful granddaughter Emily.'

A movement from the bed drew Emily's gaze. Anna's eyes were open. She was watching her mother and niece. She pushed herself higher on the pillow, smiling through a wince. 'Hi.'

Fiona turned to her and stated the obvious. 'Emily's come to see you.' There was still a kind of disbelief in her voice.

'Are you alright?' asked Emily.

Anna nodded. 'Because of you. Gavin would've killed me if you hadn't stopped him.'

'I thought he had killed you.'

With an air of semi-serious bravado, Anna replied, 'Nah, I'm tougher than I look.' She gestured towards the wound on her back. 'It'll take more than that to finish me off.'

'Tough has nothing to do with it,' Fiona put in disapprovingly. 'You're lucky to be here.' Her frown dissolved as she ushered Emily to the chair. 'Sit down, love. You must be exhausted after what you've been through.'

Fiona stood looking at Emily as though she couldn't take her eyes off her. Emily blinked away from her gaze. 'I'm sorry,' said Fiona, seeing her unease. 'I shouldn't stare at you like this. It's just... Here, let me show you something.' She took a photo out of her handbag and passed it to Emily. It was of a bright-eyed young girl with a freckled, smiling face framed by long blonde hair. Emily swallowed hard. It gave her a strange, almost eerie feeling to look at the photo, as if she was seeing herself in a subtly distorted mirror.

'That's Jessica,' Fiona told her, once again stating the obvious. A slight catch came into her voice. 'She was the sweetest little girl. She would have made a wonderful mum.'

'She still might,' said Anna.

Fiona made an unconvinced sound in her throat. Emily thought of what Gavin had told her about Jessica dying in childbirth. She wondered whether she should tell them. But then she recalled what DCI Monahan had said about Gavin. Men like him were incapable of telling the truth. As impossible as it seemed, maybe Anna was right. The thought was a hopeful torture. She couldn't bear to look at the photo any more. She made to give it back to her grandmother. Fiona shook her head. 'You keep it, love. I've got plenty of others.'

Emily slid the photo into her pocket, careful not to bend it. 'Thanks..., Grandma.'

Fiona smiled. 'I never thought I'd hear anyone call me that.' She looked at Anna. 'And how does it feel to be an auntie?'

Anna reached to give Emily's hand a squeeze. 'It feels nice. Like we're a proper family again.'

A proper family again. The words were like a warm breeze blowing through Emily, melting the loneliness that had chilled her heart since finding out about the betrayal by the *people* – she couldn't bear to call them Grandma and Granddad, even in her mind – who'd pretended to be her parents and concealed who and what her real father was. To her surprise, she found herself smiling too. It was a smile with sadness lurking close behind, but a smile nonetheless. It disappeared when Anna said, 'So come on, tell me what happened after Gavin left me to die.'

Emily lowered her eyes again, compressing her lips into a tense line. It wasn't an act. Going through that story with the police had been like reliving a nightmare. The thought of repeating it made her hands sweat.

'Anna,' Fiona said in a tone of tender reproach. 'Can't you see the poor girl's been through enough already without having to rehash it all? She's unharmed and here with us. That's all that matters.'

Anna shot her mum an incredulous look. 'How can you say that when Gavin Walsh is still out there?'

'Because there's nothing we can do about that.'

Anna opened her mouth as if to argue further, but glancing at Emily's troubled face, she shut it again without saying anything. A silent moment passed. Stooping to catch Emily's eyes, Fiona asked, 'Where are you staying, love?'

'With foster carers.'

'Are they nice?'

Emily shrugged. 'They seem OK.'

'Did they bring you here?'

'No. Mr Monahan did.'

'Oh he did, did he?' said Anna. 'And where's Mr Monahan now?'

'Waiting in the corridor.'

Anna greeted this news with a bemused shake of her head, but a warning glance from Fiona stopped her from saying anything more.

'I should go,' said Emily, but she didn't move from the seat.

Fiona and Anna exchanged another glance, as though Emily's words reminded them of something they'd been discussing. Fiona gave a quick nod as if to say, *Go on.* 'Before you go, Mum and I have something we want to ask you, Emily,' said Anna. 'Would you like to come and live with us in Sheffield? Don't—'

'Yes,' Emily answered before Anna could finish.

'I was going to say don't feel like you have to give us an answer straight away,' Anna said with a little laugh, taken aback by the speed of Emily's response. 'There's no pressure. Take your time. Think it over.'

'I have thought it over. My answer's yes.'

'Well, OK. That's sorted then.' Looking at her mum again, Anna saw something in her dark-ringed eyes that hadn't been there in more years than she wanted to remember: happiness, a barely contained joy at the thought of Emily coming to live with them. It was like finding a glowing ember in a long-dead fire. It made her feel – if only briefly – as though anything was possible.

'Can I come and live with you today?' Emily asked her grandmother.

'I'd like nothing more, love, but I don't think they'd let you.' Fiona added to Anna, 'Would they?'

'No, I'm afraid they wouldn't. First, Emily has to be legally declared your grandchild, and you her guardian. And that's going to take a little time.' Seeing Emily's wince of disappointment, Anna continued, 'I'll make it happen as fast as possible, Emily. I promise. But in the meantime you're going to have to stay with your foster carers. Do you think you can do that?'

Emily gave a half-hearted nod.

'And if you need us, you always know where we are,' said Fiona. She took both her daughter and granddaughter's hand in hers. For a moment they formed a circle – a perfect circle of renewed hope. Then Emily stood up and embraced her grandmother once more. Fiona kissed her cheek and reluctantly let her go.

Emily paused by the door, looking back at Anna and Fiona as though she feared she might never see them again.

'Be strong, Emily,' said Anna. 'It won't be long.'

Emily nodded again, more determinedly, and left the room.

* * * *

Jim saw what he'd hoped to see in Emily's eyes – a fresh gleam of resilience. Her voice low but steady, she said, 'Take me back to my foster carers.'

As they drove, Emily sat calmly, not resigned, but accepting. 'Promise me, no more sneaking out of the house,' said Jim.

'I promise.' A frown wormed its way across Emily's face. 'I can't imagine what it must be like for Anna and my grandma not knowing what happened to Jessica.'

'It's like being lost in a maze with no way out,' sighed Jim.

'So you don't think they'll ever find out?'

'Not unless we get lucky.'

'I do.' There was a certainty in Emily's voice that caused Jim to glance at her. Her pale, delicate jaw was clenched. Her eyes were fixed on some unseen object. And he knew there was no point trying to tell her that even if Gavin was caught he undoubtedly wouldn't give up one of the last things he had control over. She was already in that same maze, wandering in the same endless circles. He heaved another sigh.

The plain-clothes must have phoned ahead, because Emily's foster carers were waiting at the door for her. 'I'm sorry,' she said to them. They smiled with understanding. Emily gave Jim a look of thanks, then went into the house.

The return drive to Sheffield seemed to go on for a long time. Jim headed for the city centre and Police HQ. His phone rang. The display showed a mobile number he didn't recognise. He put the receiver to his ear and a familiar, abrasive voice came down the line. 'I know what you're doing, Jim,' said Anna. 'I know you're only trying to protect me. But as I've said fuck knows how many times before, you don't need to. I'm a big girl. I make my own decisions and live with the—'

Jim cut off the call. The phone rang again. The same number flashed up. He knew Anna wouldn't stop calling until he spoke to her. Never give up, never move on. That was her code. Her purpose. For her there could be no peace until Jessica was found. So for him there could be no peace either. He was willing to put up with that so long as he didn't find himself in another hospital washing someone else's blood off his hands.

With as much enthusiasm as a condemned man going to the gallows, he got out of the car and made his way into Police HQ.

CHAPTER TWENTY-FOUR

Jim stared at the blown-up map of the UK as if trying to decipher a riddle. Dozens of coloured pins indicated where active leads were being pursued. Dozens more empty pinholes indicated where other leads had led to nothing. For almost a fortnight now hundreds of officers, sniffer dogs, vehicles, helicopters and even boats had been involved in one of the largest manhunts the country had ever witnessed. Gavin's description had been circulated to all ports of exit from the country. And a digital mock-up of his middle-aged face had been distributed to the media, leading to a slew of tip-offs and possible sightings. The missing farmer and his Land Rover had been discovered after four days at an isolated spot in the Lake District. The farmer had been bound and stabbed to death. But that was where the trail began and ended. Gavin seemed to have pulled off another of his great disappearing acts.

Garrett's eyes alternated nervously between Jim and Chief Constable Hunt. The Chief Constable had a deceptive face. When he smiled, his bushy white eyebrows and twinkling eyes made him look like a benevolent grandfather. At such times, it was easy to be misled into thinking he was a soft touch. But in the blink of an eye that twinkle could transform into a glare. When that happened – and it had happened the instant the IPCC officers left – his subordinates knew to keep their mouths shut and weather the storm.

'This is an extremely delicate situation,' Chief Constable Hunt said in his brusque Yorkshire voice, pacing about Jim's office as though the floor offended him. 'If we're not careful, all the work we've done to restore the good name of this department will be wiped out.'

Jim tore his eyes from the map. 'I don't agree.' His words induced Garrett to give a little wince.

The Chief Constable treated Jim to a look like a thunderclap. 'Thomas Villiers is bringing civil proceedings against this department that could cost us hundreds of thousands, if not millions of pounds.' He thrust a finger at Jim. 'You've destroyed that man. He's lost his reputation, his job and his family because of your accusations.'

'Not my accusations,' Jim stated bluntly. 'The accusations of the children he helped abuse.'

Chief Constable Hunt shoved his words aside with a backhand swipe. 'Perhaps you haven't been keeping up with recent events, DCI Monahan, but none of the supposed victims are talking.' He pounded his fist into the palm of his hand for emphasis. 'Not a single bloody one! Add to that the fact that the search and seizure turned up no incriminating evidence and we're left looking like we've victimised an innocent man.'

Jim snorted contemptuously. 'He's guilty and everyone knows it.'

'This isn't about what people know, or rather think they know,' retorted the Chief Constable, a vein of anger swelling on his forehead. 'This is about what can or can't be proven in a court of fucking law!'

Jim shook his head. 'That's what I'm saying. This isn't simply about the law. It's about perception. If we back off from Villiers, we'll be perceived as weak and corrupt. Then no one will ever trust us enough to speak out against him.'

Chief Constable Hunt glanced sidelong at Garrett as if to say, *Can you believe this bloke?* 'OK, DCI Monahan, let me tell you how I *perceive* things to be. You leaked information about an investigation you were leading. The IPCC are ready to bring disciplinary proceedings against you. They believe you should be dismissed for gross misconduct. And I'm inclined to agree with them. However, there is a way out of this mess. A way you can save yourself and this department a lot of trouble and money.' The Chief Constable paused a breath to let his words sink in before continuing, 'Thomas Villiers has said he's willing to drop the civil case and withdraw his complaint if you make a full public apology for harassing him.'

Jim's eyes narrowed with disgust but not surprise. 'What? And you think that's a good idea?'

'Not only do I think it's a good idea, I also want you to make it clear that Mr Villiers is completely innocent of all the accusations.'

Jim turned to Garrett. 'And what about you? You're willing to play along with this, are you?'

Garrett made a helpless, apologetic gesture. 'What else can we do, Jim?'

'I'll tell you what else we can fucking do.' Jim jerked his chin at the mocked-up image of Gavin. 'We can catch that bastard.'

Chief Constable Hunt gave a doubtful huff. 'Face it, DCI Monahan. Gavin Walsh is long gone. He's most probably lying on a beach somewhere right now laughing at us all.'

'I don't think so. Not without Emily Walsh.'

'We've scoured the length and breadth of the country for him. I fail to see how he could have evaded capture, unless he has the ability to vanish into thin air at will.'

'Maybe he has,' Jim muttered drily, recalling what Emily had said about Gavin claiming to possess magic powers.

'What was that?'

'Nothing.'

The Chief Constable made an impatient noise. 'So what's it going to be, DCI Monahan? Will you issue the apology?'

'I'd rather tear my own tongue out, sir.' Jim's voice was strangely calm. Like the eye of a storm.

'Then as of this moment you're off the investigation – an investigation which, need I remind you, had been suspended because of your actions until the revelations about Gavin Walsh came to light.'

You say that almost as though you wish it had stayed that way, Jim thought disdainfully, resisting an urge to pull out his police ID and fling it in the Chief Constable's face. However much he wanted to quit, he knew he couldn't. Not whilst Villiers and all the rest of them were still breathing free air. He was off the case, but that didn't stop him working it. And to do that effectively he needed access to police files and data. He needed to hold on to the bitter end. He rose from his chair and approached the board of names. Stephen Baxley, Laurie Boyce, Charles Knight... Forty-four names. A web of depravity. A maze with no way out. His calm dissolved. The storm took control. He tore the board off the wall and hurled it past the Chief Constable's goggle-eyed face. It ricocheted off the desk, forcing Garrett to dodge aside.

'You're out of your bloody mind,' exclaimed the Chief Constable. 'You might as well hand in your badge right now, because your time is just about up.'

'You'd like that, wouldn't you? You and all the other cronies and arse-lickers.'

Chief Constable Hunt's jaw muscles worked like he was chewing something unpalatable. He spoke in a voice of quiet rage. 'I suggest you make yourself scarce, DCI Monahan, before one of us does something we'll both regret.'

Jim unblinkingly returned the Chief Constable's stare. He'd been around far too long to be intimidated by his angry Yorkshireman act. His eyes moved to Garrett. The DCS struggled to meet them. 'If saving this department means apologising to Villiers, then this department isn't worth saving,' said Jim. Then he turned and left.

A full public apology. The words swirled around his head like debris caught in a whirlwind. They made him want to pound his fists into something. He drove out of the city centre, not thinking where he was going, but unconsciously heading south. He soon reached the edge of the city. The patchwork hump of the moors loomed in front of him. He turned towards Thomas Villiers' house and parked across the road from it. Someone had spray-painted in red letters on the garden wall 'BURN IN HELL CHILD RAPIST'. The gates were closed, the driveway empty, the curtains drawn. Villiers was no doubt keeping his head down in some distant place where no one was likely to recognise him. A Mercedes rolled up to the gates and he saw that he was wrong. It was Villiers! The electronic gates swung open. Villiers pulled into the driveway. Jim accelerated sharply after him, blocking the Mercedes in. He got out of his car. Villiers stayed in his. Jim eyeballed him through the glass. There was no arrogance left in Villiers' eyes. Only anxiety and exhaustion. He looked a shadow of the man Jim had interviewed three weeks or so ago. But that wasn't enough for Jim. He pressed a hand against the window. A hand that itched to get at Villiers.

To punch and punch him until blood and truth flowed from his bastard mouth.

Cringing away from the violence he saw in Jim's eyes, Villiers snatched out a phone. 'I'm calling the police.'

Slowly, as though he was struggling against some unseen force, Jim drew his hand away from the window. He pointed at Villiers as if to say, *I'm coming for you*. Then he returned to his car. As he drove away, he hauled in a breath, knowing how dangerously close he'd come to losing control. And knowing too that Villiers had got the message loud and clear. There would be no apology. Not now. Not ever.

His phone rang. He frowned at it a moment before answering the call. 'What do you want?' His tone was none too friendly.

'To apologise,' said Garrett. 'I told the Chief Constable you wouldn't go through with it, but he refused to listen.'

You should have told him the whole idea's fucking shameful, Jim felt like retorting. He knew it would achieve nothing though. In recent weeks Garrett had proved himself to be more than just the careerist Jim had thought he was. But going directly against the Chief Constable was a line the DCS wouldn't cross.

'Try to see things from his perspective,' continued Garrett. 'It's his duty to protect the reputation of—'

'If this is another attempt to try and convince me to go grovelling to Villiers, you know what you can go do,' Jim cut in.

'Like I said, I know that's never going to happen. I just wanted to tell you I think you're right. Apologising to Thomas Villiers would be a betrayal of everything we stand for. I also thought you should know...' There was a slight hesitation, as though Garrett was unsure if he should say what was in his mind. Then he went on, 'As of today, we're no longer keeping tabs on Emily Walsh. The Chief Constable's convinced Gavin has fled the country.'

Jim's eyebrows knitted. Maybe the Chief Constable was right, but he couldn't bring himself to believe it. Gavin had sworn by his god that Emily and he would be together. And his god – not Cernunnos, but his true god: the god of self-gratification – would not be denied. No doubt word that Emily was unguarded was already leaking out, trickling its insidious way towards Gavin's ears.

'Thanks for letting me know,' said Jim. Without waiting for a reply, he hung up and plotted Emily's address into the satnav.

CHAPTER TWENTY-FIVE

The dream was the same every night. There was nothing cryptic
about it. Emily was running frantically through some dark
place. Running and running, but getting nowhere. Something
was chasing her. She couldn't see what, but she could hear
its breathing. Heavy breathing, like an obscene caller. Her
own breathing was ragged. Her limbs felt impossibly heavy,
weighed down by exhaustion and fear. A voice boomed out
from behind her. 'We will be together!' The words hit her
with physical force, knocking her off balance. Letting out a
strangled cry, she fell to the ground. Powerful hands flipped
her onto her back. She found herself staring up into a face
that glowed with a red iridescence. It wasn't Gavin's face. It
was a goat-like face with slanted eyes and pointed ears. Horns
twisted out of the goat-man's head. His torso was that of a
muscular man, but his legs were woolly with matted brown
hair, through which protruded a grotesquely oversized penis.
She tried to cry out again. No sound would come. She tried
to struggle. Her limbs refused to obey. She was paralysed.
Helpless.

She felt her legs being prised apart. She felt a searing pain as the monster forced his way inside her. Then, suddenly, her eyes were open and her hands were flailing at the empty air above her bed. Mouth agape, tears streaming down her cheeks, she pressed her knees together and clasped her hands over her crotch. Gradually the nightmare's tendrils withdrew into the black hole from which they'd slithered, but the fear refused to let go.

Emily flinched at the sound of a dog barking somewhere outside the house. She slid from beneath the duvet, padded to a window and parted the curtains a finger's breadth. Nothing moved in the orange glow of the streetlamps. Her gaze skimmed over the vehicles parked along the kerb. They all appeared to be unoccupied. But then again it was difficult to be sure. Another bark. Another flinch. She ground her teeth against the sob of resentment that rose in her throat. Was this how it was going to be from now on? Sleepless nights. Anxious days. Afraid to be alone. Constantly looking over her shoulder.

The police had tried to reassure her. 'We don't believe you're in any danger,' the officer who'd come to the house earlier that day had said. 'Which is why we no longer feel it's necessary to keep watch on you.' According to the officer, the manhunt's failure proved Gavin had almost certainly fled the country. But the officer hadn't been in the woods *that* night. He hadn't seen the look in Gavin's eyes.

Heaving a sigh, Emily returned to her bed. But she didn't close her eyes. She lay staring at the light seeping through the curtains, wondering if it would ever again be possible for her to sleep and live without fear.

* * * *

Emily sat biting her lip irritably in the passenger seat of her foster carer's car. With her grandparents no longer in custody, she accepted that being ferried to school was still a required precaution. Although even if she'd been allowed to make her own way, she doubted whether she could bring herself to step out the front door alone.

The car pulled up outside school. Her eyes scoured the street. Then she thanked her carer for the lift and, ignoring the calls of her friends, hurried into school alongside the teacher who'd been assigned to escort her from and to the gates.

In form class, the teacher reading the register had to repeat Emily's name several times before she responded. It was the same in her other classes and the session she had with the school counsellor. Her eyes were lost in some place beyond the reach of her teachers', the counsellor's, even her friends' voices. At first her friends had asked her about what happened. Their questions were met with pained silence. How could they understand what she'd been through or what she was feeling, when she barely understood it herself? One thought preoccupied her. One question that grew angrier every time she asked herself it. *Why should I have to live like this?*

At lunch break, when her friends went to a nearby parade of shops, she ate in an empty classroom. Every noise from the corridor drew an uneasy glance from her. She didn't want to be alone. But neither could she bring herself to go outside. Not even into the playground. She felt caught, frozen in the headlights of her fear. Face twisted with hate, she threw most of her lunch away. *Why the fuck should I have to live like this?*

At home time, as she was escorted to her foster carer's waiting car, a boy approached her. 'Hi, Emily,' he said.

'Hi, Leo,' she replied, barely giving him a glance, quickening her pace.

'Wait up, I want to ask you something. I'm having a party at my house tonight. Will you come?'

Emily grimaced as if the question pained her. She wanted to say yes, but how could she? It wasn't only about being afraid. Parties were for normal people. And she wasn't normal any more. She'd heard people whispering. She'd changed. She was weird. And they were right. She had changed. It wasn't simply that she'd become distrustful and withdrawn. It was something deeper than that, more permanent. It was as if a door had been blasted open in her mind. A door to some place where everything seemed more distant yet sharper, unreal yet too real, like her nightmares. Sometimes she felt as if she still hadn't come down from the mushrooms. Sometimes she wondered if she would ever really come down.

'Everyone's going to be there,' persisted Leo.

She shook her head and broke into a run. When she got to the car, she couldn't bring herself to even say hello to her carer. She had the feeling that if she opened her mouth she would start screaming and crying and wouldn't be able to stop.

Back at the house, she went straight up to her bedroom and crawled under the duvet fully clothed. She scrolled through her phone's contacts list to 'Grandma Fiona' and pressed dial. Her grandmother picked up after a single ring, as though she'd been expecting the call. 'Hello, Emily, love.'

Just the sound of her grandmother's voice soothed away some of the torment. Not nearly all of it, but enough so that she could speak. 'Hi, Grandma.'

'You sound tired.'

'I don't want to be here. I want to be there with you.' The words were true – the thought of moving in with her grandma was pretty much the only thing that had kept Emily going the past fortnight – but they weren't what she truly wanted to say. She feared that if she said what she really wanted to, if she bared what was inside her, then Grandma Fiona wouldn't want her to come live in Sheffield.

'And you will be very soon. Anna tells me everything should be sorted in the next few days. A week at the most.'

'A week,' murmured Emily. Thinking of a week was like thinking of forever. It made her head reel.

A shout came from downstairs. 'Tea's ready, Emily.'

'I've got to go, Grandma.'

'OK. Speak soon. Bye, love.'

'Bye.'

Emily went to the top of the stairs and said, 'I'm not hungry. I've got a headache. I think I'm just going to go to bed.'

'I'll make you up a plate in case you change your mind,' came the reply.

Emily lay staring out the window, forehead wrinkled. She was too tired to read, too tired to listen to music, too tired for anything besides sleep. But she didn't want to sleep, especially not tonight of all nights. As the daylight faded, biting her lips to keep herself awake, she set the alarm on her mobile phone in case sleep ambushed her. *A week.* She wondered if she could survive that long without sleep. And what if she did? Would the dreams stop once she was in Sheffield? Why should they? Gavin would still be out there, as invisible and all-encompassing a presence as the god he worshipped. She cringed as if from an unwanted touch. She felt like crying but didn't have the energy for it. Her eyes were so heavy, so fucking heavy...

... Darkness. She was running, falling. The goat-man, the fear, the pain. Then her phone was beeping, her eyes were snapping open and she was clutching the duvet to her chest, gasping, sobbing. Fighting to control her breathing, she stared at her phone although she knew the time – half ten. Leo's party would be in full swing. Again came the question, *Why should I have to live like this?* Again her forehead wrinkled as if she was hesitating at some thought. But the wrinkles fled as an answer rang out like a challenge in her mind. *I shouldn't. I won't!*

Emily rose from bed and changed into jeans and a hoodie. She brushed her hair and applied thick black eyeliner, then peered out the window. Other than a blonde in a miniskirt and heels, the street was empty. She switched off the light, quietly left the room and closed the door behind her. The sound of the television filtered up from the living room. On soft feet, she descended the stairs and reached for the front door handle. Her hand hesitated, vibrating like a fly caught in a web. The murmur of voices spurred her to action. She slid out into the night. The air was warm, but its touch made her shiver as she hurried away from the house.

****

'Where the hell's she going?' Jim murmured to himself, following Emily with binoculars. He'd been watching the house and surrounding streets since the previous evening. The house was situated on a quiet road that ran along the bottom of a shallow valley. Its rear garden backed onto that of an identical house. Parallel streets of houses and flats rose steeply in front of it. He'd found a spot several streets away where the house was visible from the flat roof of a three-storey block of flats. He'd checked the roof out cautiously before setting up camp, aware that Gavin might be lurking thereabouts for the same reason as him. There was no sign that anyone had recently been there.

He was too far away, he knew, to react quickly should Gavin attempt to snatch Emily from the house. But he was willing to take that risk so as to remain undetected himself. Besides, even with the plain-clothes officers no longer stationed outside the house, he doubted Gavin would attempt such a thing. The man was too clever, too patient. In the past, he'd spent months grooming victims for himself or others. With Emily, circumstances had forced him to move too quickly. But now he had time to watch and wait for his moment.

Jim had expected that moment to most likely arrive when Emily plucked up the courage to make her own way to school. But he hadn't expected this. This was simply begging for trouble. He found himself caught between watching her through the binoculars or tailing her. He knew the route she took to school. But he didn't have a clue where she was going now. If he lost sight of her, he might not be able to find her again.

Emily paused outside the entrance to a park at the end of the road. She glanced around herself as if looking for someone. Even at that distance, Jim could see the nervousness in her movements. 'What's she playing at?' he wondered out loud. As she headed into the park, the ever-present grooves on his forehead deepened. The park was a large expanse of unlit, mostly pathless grass dotted with wooded clumps and enclosed by a thick hedge. Walking through it alone at night wasn't merely naiveté. It was madness. And yet her movements were deliberate, calculated. Her expression too had suggested she knew exactly what she was doing. It was almost as though she was putting herself out there as bait. He suddenly found himself wondering whether this was part of some police operation to lure Gavin into revealing himself. He scoured the bushes and trees, half expecting to see snipers lurking amongst them. But there were none. He dismissed the idea. Surely Garrett would have told him if such an operation was under way.

He jerked the binoculars back towards the park's entrance. A woman was standing where Emily had been a moment ago – a long-haired, buxom blonde in a pink jacket, miniskirt and heels. Maybe ten minutes earlier, he'd seen the same woman heading in the opposite direction past Emily's foster carers' house. Her heels were so high that she'd walked with a peculiar bandy-legged hobble. Her hair hung in thick curtains, so that all he'd glimpsed of her face was the point of her nose and her chin. She had her back to him now. And he was struck by how broad her shoulders were. How manly...

Jim's heart was suddenly thumping like an out of control piston. 'Shit,' he hissed as the blonde started into the park.

Still clutching the binoculars, he sprinted for the stairwell. He jumped into his car and accelerated hard in the direction of the park. Moments later, he slowed the car softly at its entrance. He peered through the binoculars again. The blonde was maybe a hundred metres away, tottering awkwardly across the grass. Roughly the same distance further on, Emily was visible by the glow of the moon and the city as a vague black shape. Snatching out the Taser, Jim left his car. He angled towards a clump of trees to the right of the blonde. Once he was in amongst them, he quickened his pace, trying to overtake her and get a proper look at her face. But the trees ended before he could do so. A short distance away there was another small thicket. He lost sight of Emily as, ascending a gentle slope, she passed behind it. The blonde made her way up the slope too. He forced himself to wait until she was far enough away that he could follow without being noticed.

He skirted around the upper edge of the thicket, attempting again to get ahead of the blonde. Emily hadn't emerged into view, suggesting she was walking parallel to the slope in line with the trees. Either that or she'd stopped for some reason. His pulse and feet moved faster at the thought of what that reason might be. When he reached the far end of the thicket, he pressed himself against a tree. Twenty metres or so beyond the trees a fragmentary hedgerow split the park in two. Emily was standing in a gap in the hedge, facing away from him. She had her back to the blonde too. The blonde was moving slowly, warily. Her hand slid into her jacket and withdrew something. And suddenly Jim didn't need to see her face to know who she really was. The blade glinting in the moonlight told him everything.

He tensed his muscles to move and take the blonde down, but before he could do so two men emerged from the hedge. Jim's first thought was that he'd been right, there was a covert operation under way. But then he saw the steel baseball bat one of the men was carrying. Baseball bats were hardly police issue weapons. Neither did the men look like police. One was built like a bull, with a bald pear-drop head and a close-trimmed salt-and-pepper beard. The other was also bald, but slimmer and clean-shaven with a hard-bitten, broken-nosed face. They were both wearing black leather jackets and blue jeans. Heavy gold rings glimmered on their fingers. And they were smiling. Not friendly smiles.

'Well hello, darling,' the bull of a man said to the blonde in a broad Brummie twang, slapping the bat into his meaty palm.

His broken-nosed companion gave a sandpaper laugh. 'My, my, look at you. What a pretty sight you make.' He had an identical accent.

The blonde retreated several rapid steps and stumbled on the high heels. The hair fell away from a face almost unrecognisably daubed with crimson lipstick, blusher, mascara and electric-blue eyeshadow. But there was no disguising the eyes. Jim would have recognised Gavin Walsh's eyes in a room full of nothing but eyes.

Gavin scrambled to regain his balance, jerking up the knife. 'Who are you? What do you want?' he demanded to know, putting on a high-pitched female voice.

This time both men laughed. 'Don't tell me you don't recognise us,' said the bull, an expression of mock hurt on his big, grinning face. He pointed to his stomach, then his head. 'I know we've got a bit more down there and a lot less up there, but compared to you I'd say we're looking pretty fucking good.'

The broken-nosed man jerked his thumb at Emily. 'Why don't you ask your daughter what we want? She's the one who contacted us.'

As if on dramatic cue, Emily wheeled towards Gavin. There was no fear in her eyes. Only hate. 'I want you dead!'

'How fucked up is that? Your own daughter wants you dead. And luckily Patrick and me are more than happy to oblige her.'

The realisation hit Jim as to who the men were. The bull was Patrick McLean and the other was Kieran. They were the older brothers of Jody McLean, the girl Gavin had been accused of raping in '87. They'd been wrongly suspected of murdering him back then. Now they had their chance to do the job for real.

Gavin suddenly kicked off his high heels at the brothers and half turned to run. Kieran whipped out a handgun. 'Stay where the fuck you are. And drop the blade.'

Gavin stared at the gun a moment, his tongue darting over his crimson lips. Reluctantly, he let the knife fall from his hand. Kieran gestured for him to step away from it. Then Patrick stooped to pick it up. His eyes moved from the glimmering blade to Gavin, hooded with menace. He was no longer smiling. 'Is this the knife you held to our sister's throat as you forced your dick inside her?'

Gavin raised his hands, palms outwards. 'I don't know what you're talking about,' he said, still clinging futilely to his put-on voice.

There was a whistle of air as Patrick swung the baseball bat. It connected flush on the side of Gavin's head with a hollow metallic thud, knocking him off his feet. He rolled several times down the slope, coming to a stop on his back, arms extended upwards to ward off any further blows. Blood ran from beneath his dishevelled wig. Patrick loomed over him, facing away from Jim now. 'Say that again!' he exploded. 'Go on, fucking say it and I'll open your skull like a coconut.'

'No,' Emily put in anxiously. 'You can't kill him yet. You promised me you'd find out where she is first.'

Who's 'she'? wondered Jim. He knew the answer even as he asked himself the question. There was only one person *she* could be – Jessica Young.

'We're just gonna tenderise him a little bit,' Kieran assured her. 'Get him ready for the real fun.' He gestured towards the park's entrance. 'I don't think you want to hang around and see what happens next.'

Emily was silent a moment. Jim could see her hands clenching and unclenching at her sides. 'Yes,' she said, almost whispering, 'I do.'

Kieran gave a shrug as if to say, *Suit yourself.* He followed it with a nod towards his brother. Patrick swung the bat again. 'Hel—' Gavin started to cry out, but the word turned into a gasped oomph as the bat slammed into his abdomen. He tried to roll out of reach, but another expertly aimed whack curled him up into a winded ball.

With each successive bone-crunching blow that rained down

on Gavin, Jim saw the solution to the case moving closer. He saw himself obtaining the photos and videos. He saw himself putting the cuffs on Villiers. But he saw too the look on Emily's face. Although her expression was grimly set, her big blue eyes glistened wetly in the moonlight. She flinched every time the bat hit home. She was dying, he knew. Part of her – the innocent, loving, trusting part – was being beaten to death just as surely as Gavin.

With a trembling effort, Gavin sat up, one hand extended towards Emily. 'I love you,' he mouthed breathlessly through bloody teeth.

'I hate you,' she spat back.

Hate. The word seemed to echo in Jim's head. If Gavin died this way, Emily would never be free from hate. It would poison her whole life. No matter what, he couldn't allow that to happen.

He advanced rapidly towards Kieran and fired the Taser, aiming for his exposed neck. As the prongs bit home, the shock caused Kieran's finger to twitch on the trigger. A shot rang out as he crumpled to the grass. Patrick whirled around, wide-eyed. Jim bent to wrench the gun from Kieran's grasp and took aim at Patrick. 'Drop the bat!'

'Who the fuck are you?'

Emily answered before Jim could do so, her voice shaking with surprise. 'He's the policeman I told you about.'

Jim kept his steely gaze fixed on Patrick. 'Drop it.'

The big man lowered the bat, but kept hold of it. He jerked his face towards Gavin. 'That cunt raped my sister.'

'That doesn't give you the right to beat him to death.'

'Bollocks it doesn't.' Patrick flicked his eyes at Emily. 'What about her? If you stop us, she'll never find out what he did to her mum.'

Jim retreated a few steps so that both Patrick and Emily were in his line of vision. Gavin was groaning and struggling to get to his feet. 'Stay down,' ordered Jim. 'Lie flat on your face with your hands clasped behind your head.'

'But, officer, I'm not who they—' Gavin began in his almost comical mock-female voice.

'Do it!' broke in Jim. 'Or I swear to Christ I'll take great pleasure in putting a bullet in you.'

Gavin cringed back to the ground. Jim glanced at Emily. 'Is this really what you want? Can you live the rest of your life with his blood on your hands? Because if you can I'll walk away right now.'

Emily's forehead twitched. Her lips trembled as if to speak, but nothing came. With a shudder, she remembered something Gavin had said to her in the motorhome. *Life is a web that holds us all, Emily. What you've got to decide is, are you a spider or a fly? I know which one I am. What about you?* She recalled too the retort that had rung out like a warning shot in her mind. *I'm whatever you're not!*

Her gaze fell away from Jim and she shook her head.

Relief surged through him. He'd meant what he said. He knew the only way to save the part of her she'd come so close to destroying was to give her the choice. His gaze returned to Patrick. 'You can either go home or to prison. It's up to you. If you want to go home, toss the bat and the knife.'

Suspicion narrowed Patrick's eyes. 'You're not going to arrest us?'

'If I arrest you, I'll have to arrest Emily. And I don't want to do that.'

Patrick eyeballed Jim a moment longer. With a 'fair enough' shrug, he tossed aside the bat and reached to retrieve the knife from his jacket.

'Slowly,' warned Jim.

Patrick drew the knife out by its blade and sent it the same way as the bat.

'Help your brother up.'

Kieran groaned as Patrick pulled the Taser barbs out of his neck and lifted him to his feet.

'Now get out of here,' continued Jim. 'And don't let me see you again tonight. Because if I do I'm not even going to try to arrest you, I'm just going to start shooting. Am I making myself understood?'

The brothers nodded. Kieran shot Gavin a savage glare. 'Don't think you'll be safe in prison, motherfucker, because you won't be.'

Returning his stare, Gavin pursed the fat red slugs of his lips and made a kissy sound. For a second, Kieran looked as if he might lose control and spring at Gavin's throat, but Patrick caught hold of his arm and drew him towards the hedge.

'Walk where I can see you,' said Jim as the brothers passed back through the gap. He watched until they faded from sight. Then he moved quickly to kneel on Gavin and handcuff him. He turned to Emily. She still couldn't bring herself to meet his gaze. Gently, he put his hand under her chin and lifted it.

'I'm sorry,' she said, tears spilling down her cheeks.

'There's no need to be. Go home and don't ever speak about this to anyone.'

'I don't have a home.'

'Yes you do.'

Her eyes slid past Jim to Gavin.

'You don't need to worry about him any more,' said Jim. 'He won't ever be able to hurt you again.'

With a sudden, trembling breath, she wrenched her gaze from Gavin. She looked at Jim for a brief instant as though there was something else she wanted to say. Then she turned and ran towards the park's entrance.

'I love you, Adaryn,' Gavin called after her. 'Nothing can keep us apart. Not prison. Not socie—' The air whistled from his lungs as Jim pressed a knee into his back again. 'You're hurting me,' he wheezed.

'That's the idea,' said Jim, scanning his surrounds. The park was deserted but for themselves. Or at least what he could see of it was. The McLean brothers had chosen the spot for the ambush well. The trees, hedge and slope concealed them from view on three sides. 'Don't move and keep your gob shut.'

Jim collected up the baseball bat, knife, high heels, Taser and its spent wire. He stuffed everything but the bat into his pockets. Then he hauled Gavin to his feet. 'I can't breathe properly,' grimaced Gavin. 'I think some of my ribs are broken.'

'I told you to keep your gob shut.' Jim none too gently guided him towards the park's entrance, listening and watching for police, aware that someone might have heard the gunshot.

'I need a doctor. I know my rights, you have to take me to—'

Gavin's words turned into a groan as Jim jabbed the baseball bat into his ribs. He doubled over, but Jim grabbed the scruff of his neck and dragged him onwards. When his breathing allowed him to speak, Gavin muttered, 'I'll have you for brutality.'

'That wasn't brutality.' Another jab. Harder this time. Gavin's mouth gaped in mute agony. 'And neither was that. But keep talking and you'll find out what is.'

The remainder of the walk to the car passed in silence, with Gavin darting malignant glances at Jim. Putting one hand on top of Gavin's wig, Jim shoved him into the front passenger seat. 'Remember what I've got in here,' he warned, patting the pocket with the gun in it. He uncuffed one of Gavin's wrists, fed the bracelet through the hand hold above his head and recuffed him. Shooting looks around himself, he hurried to get behind the steering wheel. He headed for the outskirts of Nottingham, driving fast but not conspicuously so.

'You're taking me to Sheffield, aren't you?' said Gavin. 'I know all about you, Chief Inspector Monahan.'

'You know nothing about me,' growled Jim.

'I know that my good friend, Freddie Harding, killed your wife.'

Jim's voice tightened a fraction. 'She wasn't my wife.'

'Maybe not, but you loved her. She's not gone, you know. She's been reborn. Life, death and rebirth are the eternal cycle. You can be with her again. I can show you how. All you have to do is open your heart to Cernunnos and he will—'

Jim drove his elbow into Gavin's jaw, bouncing his head off the window. 'You're a slow learner, Gavin.'

Gavin's head lolled, a thread of bloody spittle dangling from his lips. His eyes rolled back into focus and hoarse laughter grated from his throat. 'Freddie phoned me from prison one time. Do you know what he told me about your wife? He told me she begged for her life, said she'd do anything if he let her live. Suck his cock. Anything.'

Jim slammed on the brakes. He glared at Gavin, his nostrils flaring with barely restrained rage. Gavin returned his gaze, smirking. 'I'm not afraid of you, Chief Inspector. My eyes are open. I see the truth of you. You're a coward.'

Jim blinked away from the taunting eyes. He stared out the window, not seeing the street, but seeing Margaret's dead face. 'You may well be right,' he murmured and resumed driving.

'I know I'm right,' goaded Gavin. 'You're a coward and a liar. You lie to everyone, yourself most of all. That's why your wife is dead. And that's why you couldn't see Detective Geary's betrayal.'

'Go on, keep talking.'

Gavin laughed again. 'First you try to silence me, now you want me to talk. You're even more confused than you look. I pity you. You don't know what you want. You don't know anything. You think you've saved Emily, but you've condemned her. I could have shown her a world without boundaries, without guilt and hypocrisy.'

'Like you showed Alison Sullivan and that girl we found at your cottage. Like you showed Jessica Young.'

'Every time you open your mouth, ignorance flows from it like a river from a tunnel. I could never show Jessica anything. She was my Goddess.'

'*Was* your Goddess?'

'Was, is, will be always and forever more. We were different parts of the same being. We brought balance to each other. Alison and that other girl were confused. But not like you. They were aware of their confusion and came to me for help.'

'And you helped them by killing them.'

'I returned them to the womb of nature so that they could be reborn. I gave them new life.'

Jim gave Gavin a narrow glance.

'You look at me as though you're trying to work out whether I'm insane,' said Gavin. 'But the truth is I'm the only one here who sees things as they really are. To deny yourself what you want, that is the one true crime.'

'I'm not sure your victims would agree with you.'

'There's no such thing as a victim. No innocents, no guilty. No good, no evil. There is only truth and non-truth.'

'Truth and non-truth,' Jim repeated quietly. 'So what's the truth about Jessica Young?'

'I've already told you, but your ears are as closed as your

eyes. If we had more time, maybe I could help you open yourself up to my words. But we'll be in Sheffield soon.'

'I never said we were going to Sheffield.'

Small cracks of surprise broke the surface of Gavin's makeup. 'So where are we going?'

'You'll see.'

Jim's reply silenced Gavin. They headed north on the M1 for a few miles, before turning east into a countryside of dark lanes and silent villages. The landscape became hillier, more isolated. Rolling expanses of moorland rose and fell on either side of the road. 'I used to love it out here when I was a child,' said Jim. 'I don't any more. People like you ruined places like this for me. You turn everything that's beautiful into something ugly.' He pointed towards a hump of heather. 'About ten years ago a dog-walker found a body over there. A young woman. She'd been beaten to death and buried in a shallow grave. Turned out her husband had done it. They'd only been married a month. He never said why he killed her.'

Gavin grinned. 'I see right through you, Chief Inspector. I know what you're trying to do and it won't work.'

The car climbed to the crest of a steep rise, beyond which the road dropped away even more precipitously towards a deep valley. Jim pulled into a small, deserted car park concealed from the road by bushes and a grassy mound. He got out of the car, retrieved a torch, a bottle of water and a plastic bag from the boot. Then he unlocked the handcuffs and pointed the gun at Gavin. 'Get out.'

Rubbing the circulation back into his wrists, Gavin said with mock casualness, 'It's a beautiful night.'

'Start walking.' Jim gestured towards a wooden gate. 'That way.'

Gavin's grin remained in place, but a shadow of uncertainty

flickered in his eyes. 'OK, Chief Inspector. I'll play along with your little game. But we both know where this is going.'

With Gavin walking a couple of paces ahead, they passed through the gate. Jim was careful not to touch it or step in the patch of mud on its far side. The torch threw light on a boulder-strewn path running along the top of a broken, moon-washed crag. Beyond the crag, houses were strung out like fairy lights along the base of the valley. The air was heavy with the scent of peat. Gavin breathed it deep into his lungs. 'Do you smell that? That's *his* smell.'

'No. That's just the smell of what you are – dirt.'

'We're all dirt, Chief Inspector.'

Jim heaved a breath. 'I've heard about as much of your bullshit as I can take. Stop here. Turn to face me.' He shone the torch in Gavin's eyes. 'Get on your knees.'

'I don't kneel for anyone except my God and Goddess.'

'Jessica Young wasn't your goddess. She was a thirteen-year-old girl you abducted, raped and almost certainly murdered. I was toying with the idea of trying to make you tell me where she is. But really I always knew I'd be wasting my time. You'll never tell me. That's the only power you've got left. So I suppose the secret will die with you.'

Jim levelled the gun at Gavin's chest. Gavin didn't flinch. He lifted his eyes to the sky, spreading his arms as if to receive a benediction. Ten seconds passed. Twenty. Smiling scornfully, Gavin met Jim's gaze again. 'You see, Chief Inspector, I know you better than you know yourself. You didn't kill Freddie and you won't kill me.'

Jim's finger tightened on the trigger. There was a faint click. In that instant of realising his mistake, Gavin's mask fell away and his fear was laid bare. There was no time for him to cry out. The muzzle flashed, the crack of the bullet exploded the silence, followed almost simultaneously by the bursting pop of Gavin's fake breasts. He staggered backwards a step and stood swaying, a look of dumb animal disbelief on his face. Then he crumpled to the ground. Dead.

Jim stared down at Gavin for a moment, his face as expressionless as a stone. Then, pulling on forensic gloves, he stooped to strip him naked. As he put the clothes and wig in the plastic bag, blood welled from the black hole in Gavin's chest, obscuring the spider's web tattoo. He poured water over Gavin's face and wiped away the makeup with a wad of tissue. Then he headed back to the car.

He drove over the moors into Sheffield, his mind a blank space, like an unwritten page. He passed through the sleeping suburbs into the city centre, mechanically shifting gears. His ears were ringing. The night-time sounds of the city seemed distant, muffled. He stopped on a bridge adjacent to a foaming weir. He tossed the gun and baseball bat into the river. He drove on until he came to another stretch of water. This time he got rid of the knife. No flicker of emotion showed on his face as it sank from view.

Next he pulled into an all-night garage, bought some matches and lighter fluid, and hoovered and pressure-washed his car. He carefully cleaned the area of the front passenger seat with a cloth and spray cleaner. Then he drove to a patch of wasteland well away from any houses, squirted lighter fluid over Gavin's wig, clothes and high heels and set them alight. He made sure they were burnt beyond recognition before leaving.

As he headed for his flat, it occurred to him that there was one more thing he needed to do. He stopped at a row of shops with several big bins awaiting collection outside them. He untied a bin bag and put the handcuffs in it. By tomorrow morning they would be buried in a landfill and, no doubt, some unlucky hiker or climber would have stumbled across the body whose wrists the handcuffs had bruised.

Upon arriving at his flat, Jim sat staring at it as though there was something in there he didn't want to face up to. Finally, taking a breath, he made his way into its empty silence. He stripped in the hallway and bagged his clothes for later disposal. When he switched on his bedroom light and saw the photograph of Margaret, something seemed to pop in his ears and the world rushed back in at him. He suddenly began to shake. As though his legs could no longer support him, he dropped onto the bed. He clasped the photo to his chest, his face twisted in anguish. He remained like that for the rest of the long night.

CHAPTER TWENTY-SIX

The call Jim was expecting came before it was fully light. He dragged himself out of bed and answered it. 'You were right,' said Garrett. 'Gavin hadn't left the country. He was found early this morning in the Peak District.'

'Alive or dead?' asked Jim, not bothering to try and sound anything but what he was – physically and emotionally drained.

'Dead. A single gunshot wound to the chest.'

'Who found him?'

'A farmer out tending his sheep. The nearest house is half a mile from the scene.'

'Isolated spot. No witnesses. Sounds like an execution. Do you want me to head over there?'

'No. You're off the case, remember? In fact, the Chief Constable thinks it would be best if you took a few days off work altogether.'

'You mean I'm suspended.'

'No, not suspended. Think of it as an enforced holiday.'

Jim held back the bitter laughter rising in his throat. What use did he have for a holiday, enforced or otherwise? 'You should send someone to pick up Ronald and Sharon Walsh. They could be in danger.'

'I already have done. Ronald Walsh is being escorted here as we speak to identify the body.'

'What about Sharon?'

'Hospital. She collapsed when she heard about Gavin.'

Jim absorbed the news with mixed emotions. Sharon Walsh had lost her only child. In a different but equally permanent way, she'd lost her granddaughter too. It was difficult not to feel a trace of sympathy for her. But that sympathy quickly hardened into anger when he thought about Jessica Young and Alison Sullivan and all of Gavin's other victims.

A sheepish note came into Garrett's voice. 'Before I go, Jim, I... Well, I need to ask you where you've been for the past day and a half.'

'Watching Emily Walsh.' There was no point lying about it. Someone was bound to have seen him in the area where Emily was living. Besides, Garrett knew full well where he'd been.

'Did you see anything of interest?'

'No.'

There was a slight but telling pause. Then Garrett said, 'OK, Jim. I'll let you know if there are any further developments.'

Jim hung up, frowning. What had that pause been about? Did Garrett know something? He dismissed the possibility. There was just no way. Not unless Emily or the McLean brothers had blabbed. And that was hardly likely. His gaze moved to the bin liner of clothes. His stomach felt hollow, but breakfast could wait. He quickly dressed, snatched up the black bag and headed for his car. He drove with one eye on the rear-view mirror, watching for signs he was being tailed. A couple of miles from his flat he dumped the bag in a pub's bin.

He didn't return to the flat. He couldn't stand the thought of being there with only his thoughts for company. He found a busy café and tried to satiate the hollowness with an artery-clogging fry-up. But it wasn't a void food could fill.

He continued driving aimlessly around the city, watching people like they were part of a world he'd left behind. He found himself at the spot where Jessica Young had been abducted. Surely now the last place she would ever be seen alive. He got out of the car and stood with his eyes closed as though listening for some sort of sign. There was a lull in the traffic. The murmur of flowing water became audible. His eyes popped open as something Gavin had said came back to him. 'Like a river from a tunnel,' he murmured, turning to peer over the quarry-stone wall that ran alongside the pavement. Beyond some bushes, the narrow channel of the River Sheath flowed towards the city centre. A few metres to the right of where he was standing it disappeared into an arched brick tunnel beneath a small industrial yard. The tunnel, Jim knew, carried the river under the city centre to where it merged with the Don. More words came back to him. His own: *Truth and non-truth. So what's the truth about Jessica Young?* Then Gavin's: *I've already told you, but your ears are as closed as your eyes.*

Jim clambered over the wall, scrambled down to the water's edge and stared into its muddy depths. There was, of course, nothing to be seen. But he knew with the certainty of a man who'd spent most of his life fighting to see through darkness that Jessica Young was down there somewhere. Gavin would have taken great pleasure in knowing that she was so close yet so far from her family.

His face furrowed in thought. The question was: how the hell could he direct Anna or his colleagues to Jessica without revealing his guilt for Gavin's murder? He could send an anonymous letter, but that would make it obvious the murderer wasn't on the side of Villiers and his accomplices. He could plant some evidence. But what kind of evidence? A photo of the river? A map of Sheffield with X marking the spot? Again, too obvious. An idea came to him. It was possibly a bit too subtle. But Anna had proved herself extremely adept at picking up on subtle clues. He drove into the city centre, found a shop that sold what he wanted, then returned to the river.

When he'd finished what needed to be done, he headed for his flat. A familiar Volvo was parked in the street. He pulled up facing it. Ronald Walsh stared back at him from behind the Volvo's steering wheel, his face colourless and immobile. With a sudden marionette-like movement, Ronald got out of the car. Jim reached for his extendable baton and did likewise, his own movements wary. 'Stop there,' he said, when Ronald was a couple of metres away. Ronald's eyes were glassy and bloodshot. Even at that distance, Jim could smell the sour stink of his breath.

'My son is dead,' Ronald said, as he had done so many times before. But this time his voice was slurred with alcohol and grief. 'Do you have any children?'

'No.'

'You're lucky.' Ronald's eyes grimaced away from Jim. 'All they bring is worry and pain.'

'Why are you here?' asked Jim. He thought – but barely dared allow himself to hope – he knew the answer to that question.

'I'm not blind. I know what Gavin was. I know he got what he deserved. But no parent should ever have to bury their own child.'

Jim's expression remained granite-hard. 'At least you *can* bury your child.'

Ronald's thin old face twitched. Lips trembling as though he was speaking to himself, he put a hand in his pocket. Jim tensed to move, but Ronald withdrew an envelope, not a weapon. 'Gavin said that if anything ever happened to him I was to give this to someone who could be trusted to make sure the truth came out.'

Jim reached to take the envelope, but Ronald didn't let go of it. His eyes met Jim's again, burning with a kind of bleary, despairing hate. 'I'm going to find who killed my son and I'm going to kill them.'

Jim gave a little nod as if to say, *You do what you feel you have to do.*

Ronald released the envelope and, lowering his eyes, turned to shuffle to his car. 'I wouldn't go home if I were you,' cautioned Jim. 'There could be dangerous people looking for you.'

'Let them look,' Ronald fired back dismissively. 'I've got some looking of my own to do.'

And so it goes on, thought Jim as he watched Ronald drive away. *On and on...*

He opened the envelope. Inside it was a key with a keyring attached to it. On the keyring was written '40', 'Big Blue's Self-Storage' and a Stockport address. There was a squeal of tyres. Spinning on his heel, he saw a familiar black BMW speeding towards him. He made to duck back into his car. The BMW screeched to a stop and two suited men leapt out of it. One was middle-aged, maybe in his forties. Thinning blonde hair. A heavy-set face and body. The other was equally well-built, but younger and dark-haired.

As Jim jerked his door shut, the older man caught hold of it. 'We want to talk to you,' he said, his tone businesslike.

'Who the fuck's "we"?' Jim demanded to know.

'You know who we are. Now put down the truncheon and get out of the car.'

'Not until I see some ID.'

The man drew his jacket open just enough for Jim to see the handgun holstered against his ribs. Jim stared at him as if weighing up his options. 'Don't do anything foolish,' warned the man. 'There's no need for anyone to get hurt here.'

Slowly, Jim put the extendable baton and the 'Big Blue's Self-Storage' key on the passenger seat.

'Not the key,' said the man. 'Bring that with you.' He retreated several steps as Jim got out of the car. 'Now place it on the roof and step away from the car.'

Jim closed his hand tightly around the key. He knew it was pointless. What could he do against two armed men? But even so he was damned if he was going to give up the key without a fight. Not after everything he'd been through to get it.

'You've got five seconds to do as I say,' the man continued in a calmly threatening voice. 'Then I'm going to take the key from you.' He began to count. 'One... two... three...'

'What are you going to do, shoot an unarmed man in the street?' said Jim.

'I should do for all the aggravation you've caused us. But police killing police is bad for everyone.'

Jim's lips curled with disdain. 'You're not police. You're fucking scum.'

The man took the insult without a flicker. He made a quick, discreet signal to his colleague. The younger man snatched out a Taser and fired. Jim tried to dodge aside, but the man's aim was too good. The barbs snaked out to bite into him. Then it was like an explosion had gone off in his chest. Somehow managing to keep hold of the key, he dropped to the ground with the burnt metallic taste of electricity filling his mouth. The crackling of the Taser stopped, but the pain in his chest continued. He couldn't seem to catch his breath. The older of the men loomed over him, reaching to try and prise away the key. Jim threw a futile rubbery punch. The man easily blocked it and returned a far harder one of his own, bouncing Jim's head off the Tarmac. Blood immediately gushed from Jim's nose. Straightening, the man stamped once, twice, three times on Jim's hand, forcing him to finally let go of the key. The man scooped it up and dodged away as Jim made a weak grab for his ankle. 'You're one stubborn bastard, Monahan,' he said in a tone somewhere between irritation and admiration.

'Fuck you,' Jim rasped.

The man gave him an ironic little salute and returned to the BMW. As the car raced away, Jim worked himself into a sitting position. His breathing coming a little easier, he yanked out the Taser prongs with his uninjured hand. The other rested in his lap, two of its fingers bent at unnatural angles. To have come so close only to have it end this way. It made him feel like he was the butt of some sick joke that everyone was in on except him. He would have cried out in frustration if he'd had sufficient air in his lungs.

The BMW jammed on its brakes at the end of the street as an unmarked car pulled in front of it. A second car angled in behind it, boxing it in. Armed police piled out of the cars, semi-automatic weapons aimed at the BMW. 'Put your hands on the dashboard and don't fucking move!' shouted the AFOs, wrenching open the BMW's doors. They hauled out its occupants, threw them to the ground and cuffed them.

Another car pulled into view. An AFO handed something through its driver's window. Then it accelerated towards Jim. As Garrett got out of it, a grimly bloody smile formed on Jim's lips. 'It seems the joke's on them for once, eh?'

Garrett looked at him as though wondering what he was going on about. With a slight grimace, Jim found himself thinking,

Reece would have got what I meant. Scott Greenwood's voice crackled through the car's radio, relaying the whereabouts of Ronald Walsh. Ronald was drinking from a bottle and driving erratically. Garrett spoke into the receiver. 'Get him off the road before he hurts someone.' Then he held up the key to Jim. 'Is this what I think it is?'

'Yes.'

'Are you up to finding what it fits?'

Jim extended his hand, palm up. 'What do you think?'

Garrett placed the key in Jim's palm. Grunting with the effort, Jim rose to his feet. 'I'll drive,' said Garrett. 'It looks like you've got a couple of broken fingers. If it was anyone but you I'd suggest we stop by the hospital.'

Reflecting that Garrett had begun to read him a bit too well for comfort, Jim dropped heavily into the passenger seat. As they passed the cuffed men, Garrett said, 'If those bastards think they can get away with coming to *my* city and assaulting one of *my* officers, they're going to find out they're very wrong.'

Jim made a low murmur of approval at the new-found steel he heard in Garrett's voice. He rested his head back, wadding tissue against his nostrils. As they made their way out of the city, he noticed Garrett casting him occasional sidelong glances. He knew exactly what topic Garrett was working his way up to broaching. 'Any more thoughts on Gavin Walsh's mur—' the DCS started to say.

'Do you mind if we don't talk,' cut in Jim. 'I just want to close my eyes.'

Garrett shot him a searching look, but didn't press the matter. Jim kept his eyes closed until they arrived at Big Blue's Self-Storage an hour or so later. They got out of the car in a large wire-fenced yard crammed with shipping-style containers. Jim stood staring at the door of container 40, his heart thumping, his hands sweaty-cold. With a movement that was at once eager and hesitant, he unlocked the padlock and pulled the door open. The container echoed emptily as they stepped inside. Jim directed his torch towards its rear. It revealed three cardboard boxes. Garrett pulled on latex gloves and opened the boxes. Two were full of video tapes labelled with names and dates. 'Maurice Chaput 1/7/88', 'Rupert Hartwell 22/2/89', 'Corinne Waterman 3/5/91', 'Thomas Villiers 27/11/88', 'Stephen Baxley 13/3/98'. And so it went on, every name in Herbert Winstanley's black book, and more. Gavin had clearly continued procuring victims for his fellow perverts long after he stopped working at Hopeland. The third box contained photos. Hundreds of them. Photos of men, women and children in grand living rooms and bedrooms. Photos of flesh forced on flesh, innocence stolen, lives obliterated.

'Jesus,' murmured Garrett, his voice as hollow as the container.

Jim looked at the images until he could look no more. He left the container and drew in several deep breaths as if to clean his lungs of some noxious stench. He had everything he needed to take all the bastards down. But he didn't feel triumphant. He felt sick.

CHAPTER TWENTY-SEVEN

The clock read 5:35 a.m. Soft light slanted through the window of Jim's living room. The street outside was peaceful. Most people were still sleeping, but not Jim. And not the teams of armed police who in twenty-five minutes' time would batter down the doors of fifty-four houses and flats across the country. Twenty-five minutes and every living name from Herbert's black book plus sixteen others who'd been identified from the videos and photos – and whose number included two high-ranking officers from the Manchester Met and three from Special Branch – would find themselves in handcuffs. Hopefully.

Jim's phone rang. He snatched it up with his uninjured hand. The fingers of his other hand were splinted and taped together. 'What is it? What's happened?'

'Nothing yet,' replied Garrett. 'We're en route to Villiers' house. I wondered if you wanted to come along and make the arrest.'

'The Chief Constable won't be happy.'

'Yes, well you know what the Chief Constable can go and do.'

Jim smiled thinly at the out-of-character remark. 'I'll meet you there.'

There wasn't much time, but there was something he had to do before he left. He dialled Lance Brennan. When the ex-detective picked up, Jim said, 'It's happening today. Right now. They're all going down.'

There was a silence that seemed to stretch back through twenty-odd years of failure and frustration, then in a voice heavy with emotion Lance said the only thing there was to say: 'Thank you.'

Jim drove through the waking city to Dore. Roadblocks were being set up a hundred metres to either side of Villiers' house. Half a dozen tense-faced AFOs were gathered alongside a van, awaiting the signal to move in.

'Just in time,' said Garrett, glancing at his watch. 'Three minutes.'

Jim eyed the house. The curtains were closed. So were the tall gates at the end of the driveway. 'How are we going to get through the gates?'

'We got the code from the company that installed them.' Garrett slid a curious look at Jim. 'You know, I keep thinking about Gavin Walsh.' He pointed at a printout of all the targets being hit that morning. 'I just can't understand why they'd kill him when they knew what he had on them.'

Jim kept his face carefully expressionless. 'Maybe they thought he was bluffing.'

'Maybe, but why take the risk?'

'Gavin wouldn't leave the country. He was bound to be caught sooner or later. I suppose they decided he was better off dead than in our hands.'

Garrett puckered his lips, unconvinced. 'Another odd thing. Traces of makeup were found on Gavin's face. Why do you think that is?'

'He was probably in disguise. Look, Gavin had multiple

broken bones and bruises. Whoever killed him most likely tried to torture him into revealing where the videos and photos were. Maybe he gave them false information.'

'Why would he do that when the videos and photos were the only thing keeping him alive? And why didn't they kill his parents at the same time?'

They were good questions. Ones to which Jim didn't have ready answers. To his relief, one of the AFOs held up a finger to signal it was time to move. Along with several other detectives, Jim and Garrett followed as the AFOs advanced swiftly towards the house. The lead man punched a code into a keypad and the gates swung open. The AFOs ran to the front door. Three blows from a battering ram buckled the lock and the AFOs charged into the house, shouting repeatedly, 'Police! On the floor and don't move!'

Half the officers secured the ground floor, semi-automatic rifles pressed against their shoulders. The rest thundered upstairs. The living room was empty. So too was the kitchen. The work surfaces were strewn with unwashed pots, but the table was clear except for an envelope propped against a glass in its centre. 'Diane' – Villiers' wife's name – was written on it. Guessing at once what it contained, Jim tore it open. 'Dear Diane,' began the letter. 'There are no words to apologise for the pain I've caused. Please try to understand, I did what I did for our family. To try and give us a better future.'

Jim broke off reading as a shout came from upstairs. 'He's up here. We need a paramedic team.'

He tossed the letter aside. He wasn't interested in Villiers' pathetic attempts to justify his actions. He'd done what he did for himself. No one else.

Jim rushed upstairs. An AFO directed him into a large bathroom. The first thing he saw was the blood. The bath seemed to be full of it. Villiers was lying naked on his back with his arms folded across his chest. Blood flowed in thick dark streams from his wrists into the steaming water. He looked dead. But then his glazed eyes focused on Jim and his pale lips moved in a barely audible whisper. 'You win.'

'No,' replied Jim, his voice flat and suddenly weary. 'We've both lost.'

He left the bathroom and headed for the front door. Garrett followed him outside. 'Do you think he'll live?'

'It'd be better for his family if he doesn't.'

'Maybe you're right,' mused Garrett, looking at Jim with that same intentness as before. 'Maybe it'd be better, too, if we never find out who killed Gavin.'

Jim held Garrett's gaze, wondering if he meant what he said or was clumsily trying to manoeuvre him into saying something incriminating. Garrett suspected he was the killer, that was obvious. But Jim could also see he didn't really believe it. The same thing that had put certainty into Gavin's mind, put doubt into Garrett's – Jim had held back from killing Freddie Harding, so why would he kill Gavin? The thousands of criminal interviews Jim had conducted had taught him how to best deal with such doubts. Without replying, he turned to walk away.

'Where are you going?' asked Garrett.

'I don't know.'

'Well wherever it is, make sure you come back.' There was no sharpness of accusation in Garrett's voice. Only concern.

Jim paused. He gave a little nod. Then he continued walking.

CHAPTER TWENTY-EIGHT

'Here we are,' said Anna, pulling into the driveway of the little semi-detached house where she'd lived all her life and would continue to do so for the foreseeable future – the threats of eviction had died with Gavin. She slid open the camper van's side door and picked up a holdall, wincing as the stitches in her back pulled tight.

Emily hurried around from the passenger door. 'I'll carry that.'

They both turned at the sound of the front door opening. Fiona emerged from the house. She was smiling, but her eyes were nervous. 'I wasn't expecting you for a while yet.' She carefully embraced Anna. Then, more tightly, Emily. Her gaze moved back and forth between them. Tears welled into her eyes.

'Don't start crying again, Mum,' said Anna.

'I'm sorry. I can't help it.' Fiona took Emily's hand and drew her into the house. 'Would you like a cup of tea, love?'

'No thanks.'

'What about something to eat? You must be hungry.'

'Stop fussing her,' Anna gently reproached. She smiled at Emily. 'Do you want to see your bedroom?'

Emily nodded. She followed Anna and Fiona upstairs to a room that smelt of fresh paint. There was a single bed with a white duvet, and a pine bedside table, dressing table, chair and wardrobe. Everything looked new. Fiona pointed to the pastel-yellow walls. 'You can change the colour if you don't like it.'

Not seeming to hear, Emily put her bag down. 'Was this my mum's room?'

'Yes,' said Fiona, exchanging a tense glance with Anna.

Emily's gaze moved slowly around the room, coming to rest on a framed photo of her mother. 'It's nice.' Her voice was quiet, subdued.

A look of relief passed over Fiona's face.

'Tell you what, why don't we leave you alone for a while?' suggested Anna. She ushered her mum from the room, adding, 'We'll be downstairs when you want us.'

'Anna,' said Emily. Both Anna and Fiona turned to her. Emily hesitated to say what was on her mind. Catching the hint, Anna nudged her mum to leave. Somewhat reluctantly, Fiona did so. Emily glanced at the photo again. 'Will you show me where *it* happened?'

'You mean where Jessica was abducted?'

'Yes.'

Anna didn't need to ask why Emily wanted to go there. It was the same reason she herself went back time after time. It was the only place now where she really felt connected to her sister. 'OK, but don't say anything to your grandma. It'll only upset her.'

Emily nodded as if to say, *I know.* 'She still loves Jessica very much, doesn't she?'

'We both do.'

They returned downstairs. Fiona was in the kitchen. 'We're going out,' Anna called to her.

'Where?'

'For a walk. We'll be back soon.'

As they descended the steeply sloping street, Anna couldn't help but keep glancing at Emily. She was suddenly struck by an eerie sensation that she'd stepped back in time twenty years to that fateful Sunday afternoon. She looked towards Bramall Lane, half expecting to hear the roar of the crowd. The sight of the empty red stands dispelled the feeling. She let out a little sigh. They crossed the bridge that spanned the River Sheath, heading along Queens Road in the direction of the city centre. They passed the big box of a building that had once housed the ice rink, but which had since been converted into a casino.

Anna stopped at an anonymous stretch of pavement. 'We were right here when...' She swallowed a tightness in her throat. 'When *it* happened.'

They stood silent for a moment, like mourners at a funeral. 'Are you glad Gavin's dead?' Emily asked in an almost reverently hushed voice.

Clashing emotions pulled Anna's features in different directions. 'Yes and no. Yes, because he'll never again be able to hurt anyone. No, because my last real hope of finding Jessica died with him.'

Emily blinked away from Anna as if to hide something in her eyes. Her forehead contracted. 'Look.' She pointed towards the wall that bordered the pavement. Anna followed the line of her finger. Her forehead mirrored Emily's. Several branches overhanging the wall were strung with ribbons – multicoloured ribbons like those that had decorated the trees Gavin had buried two of his victims beneath.

The ribbons were bright, not faded by time and exposure. Anna cautiously approached the wall, trying to recall how long it was since she'd last visited this spot. Maybe a month. She couldn't be exactly sure. So much had happened since then. But however long it was, she was certain the ribbons hadn't been there. She peered over the wall. More ribbons were tied to neighbouring trees and bushes, forming a fluttering line that led down the bank.

'Wait here,' she said. Gritting her teeth at the pain in her back, she shunted herself over the wall and followed the ribbons. The final one was tied to the end of a branch that trailed in the water.

Anna dropped to her knees and lowered her face until it was almost touching the water. Only her reflection stared back, featureless as a shadow, revealing nothing of her anguished realisation. Tears fell from her eyes. Sweeping them away with her hand, she straightened and clambered back over the wall.

'Did you see anything?' asked Emily.

'No.' Anna laid a hand on her shoulder. 'Come on, let's go home.'